## LITTLE DID SHE KNOW, THIS WAS ONLY THE BEGINNING OF HER PROBLEMS. . . .

She was alone on a Friday night, alone and depressed. She felt detached from the rest of the world, but comforted herself with the thought that millions of others must be just like her. At least she had lucked out with the movie. Her feet were propped up on an ottoman, and she was surrounded by the tools of the true couch potato—snack food and the remote control. "And I'm even talking out loud to myself," she muttered, and opened her mouth for another handful of popcorn. "I'd give anything for the sound of another voice."

*"Then get up and get out of this house!"*

Julia's hand was frozen at her lips. She nearly choked on the popcorn. She stared at the television. That deep, husky feminine voice had come out of the TV! A voice, a woman's voice, had called out to her! She had seen this movie at least five times, and *NEVER* had she heard any character utter those words.

It was as if the television were talking to her.

Julia waited until her heartbeat returned to normal.

Grabbing the remote control, she flicked the set into silence. "I'm having a nervous breakdown. I'm talking to myself, and the TV is answering me." This was a sign, a frightening sign, that she simply had to start a life of her own.

If she didn't know better, she might think the house was haunted . . .

# CONSTANCE O'DAY-FLANNERY

## The
# *Gift*

**ZEBRA BOOKS**
**KENSINGTON PUBLISHING CORP.**

ZEBRA BOOKS are published by

Kensington Publishing Corp.
850 Third Avenue
New York, NY 10022

First Printing: August, 1994

Printed in the United States of America

*To Vernon . . . for loving the pilgrim soul in me.*

## Acknowledgments and Thanks

Leslie Esdaile, my good friend, whose assistance was invaluable.

Gil Medina, who gave me insight into the mindset of Corporate America.

Christine and Irving Laidlaw, my sister and brother-in-law, who allowed me to use their home in France.

Adele Leone, Jay Acton, Denise Little and Walter Zacharius, for their help and support.

And, my "buds"—Kristen Flannery, Bridget Conaway and Jim Hahn. Thanks for keeping me laughing. I miss you all.

# *Prologue*

The Fifties . . .

It was a time of tranquility and prosperity. The nuclear family flourished, and everybody headed to the suburbs as the baby boom exploded. Cars had fins, the bigger the better. Everybody loved Ike, and the New York Yankees were a baseball dynasty. Kids stuffed themselves into phone booths, wore coonskin hats and twirled Hoola Hoops around their hips. Little girls witnessed the birth of Barbie, the symbol of the ideal woman, and future engineers spent hours in the dirt with their Tonka Trucks. Mothers stayed home and baked apple pies and fathers barbecued in the back yard. Elvis was raw Southern sexuality and Chuck Berry's searing guitar and lyrics about cars and girls were pure poetry. One hundred years after the first cattle drive, westerns dominated the television screen while in movie theaters and drive-ins *Ben Hur, Pillow Talk* and *Gidget* earned millions for the old

Hollywood system, a complex network of men that Valentina Manchester had finally conquered.

Rubbing the almond oil over her calf, Valentina called out from the bathroom with its long windows overlooking Hollywood Hills, "Carmela, I think I'll wear the yellow Edith Head, that new suit she's made for me. And the Dior shoes and bag I bought last week at Marabellas." She switched legs and remembered to add, "Thanks," while drizzling the scented oil over her skin. It was a routine that she had learned early in life at her mother's knee. She knew a female must take care of her body if she wanted anything in this world, and Val's body was her most valuable asset. It had brought her fame and fortune.

"I wish I could shoot you in this light, *mi tresora.* Right now. The way your fingers glide over your leg."

He called her his treasure. She looked up and smiled at the man still soaking in the tub she had shared with him. "I wouldn't dare let you take a picture of me without my makeup. I have an image, Johnny. You should know, you helped create it."

Johnny Cochran picked up a filter tip cigarette and lit it. Blowing a gush of smoke over the soapy water, he smiled. "Doing that first cover for *Playtime* launched a magazine and both our careers. You were magnificent, Val. Every man in America went wild for that body . . . that face."

Val screwed the top back onto the bottle of oil and stared at her reflection in the mirror. "That was eight years ago," she whispered, noticing the fine lines at the corners of her eyes. Thank God, makeup would cover them. Eight years and eight screwball comedies playing the silly blond bombshell. "I don't do cheesecake anymore. Those nude shots were my first and last."

"It's a pity," he murmured, looking at her with a photographer's eyes. "You still have a great body."

Val grabbed a thick, white terrycloth robe and wrapped it around her. She walked over to the tub and leaned down, as if to kiss him. Instead, she picked up one of his cigarettes and lit it with the end of his. Blowing smoke into his face, she smiled with a practiced seductiveness. "Then consider yourself lucky, darling, to have had firsthand knowledge of it."

Waiting until the smoke cleared, Johnny muttered, "Yeah, me and half the men in Hollywood. You aren't a starlet anymore, Val. You don't have to sleep your way to the top. You're there. At least you will be when you sign this deal."

She couldn't afford to get upset. Not today when she had to meet Harry, her agent, at the Brown Derby to sign the contract with Universal. She was signing to do a film about a woman, a real woman with depth, and it was her first chance to show everyone that she could pull it off. Taking a long drag from the cigarette, Val sighed. "Wasn't it Ben Hecht, the writer, who said that in Hollywood, 'starlet' is the name for any woman under the age of thirty not actively employed in a brothel?" She blew out the smoke and turned toward the tub. "I'm thirty-three, Johnny. And I've paid my dues. If you don't care for the way I've paid them, then you don't have to keep coming back here. You knew all of this before the first nude shot for *Playtime*. So why are you doing this now?"

"Is it true what they're saying about you and Barnie Milkin over at Universal?"

Val held his stare. "What are they saying?"

"That you gave new meaning to the term 'production head'."

Inwardly Val cringed, but she had been trained from the time she was five not to show her real feelings. Instead, she flicked her ash into a crystal bowl and laughed. "That's pretty good. I like it."

"Damn it, Val. Why do you keep doing this to yourself? You don't have to keep trying so hard. You tested for the part in a serious role, and you got it. You're beautiful and talented, and you don't have to prove anything anymore with every man you work with. What are you so scared of?"

It was a question she couldn't answer out loud. It was hard enough to figure it out in her mind. Walking back over to the huge tub, she flipped the plug and let the water begin to drain. "Maybe it's time you left," she suggested in a bored voice. "I have to get ready."

Johnny shook his head, as if defeated, stood up and grabbed a towel. Soap bubbles clung to his long body and Val felt a stirring of desire once more for the man who had captured her heart eight years ago. The pictures he'd taken of her for *Playtime* had been spectacular, not because her body was better than a hundred other hopefuls, but because she had fallen in love with the man behind the lens, and she was seducing him during the shoot. That's what men had seen when they'd bought out the first issue. Raw sexuality mixed with honest desire. Maybe the sex wasn't raw anymore, but she still desired him. Johnny Cochran was the only man alive that knew everything about her. And he still loved her. Oh, they never said the words aloud, not either of them. But it was love, or at least as close to love as she'd ever come. She played a part with other men, giving them the bombshell they expected. With Johnny, she could relax.

"Do you want to have dinner tonight?" he asked from behind her where he was stepping into his pants. "We could celebrate."

Still angry over their discussion, she said, "Universal wants me to go to a viewing of *Spartacus* tonight with Jeffrey Hunter. They're considering him or Laurence Harvey for my male lead."

"I'd heard Nicholas Ray had him signed to play Jesus in *King of Kings.*"

"I don't know," Val answered, sitting down at her dressing table and brushing out her long blond hair. "I'll ask him tonight."

Johnny was almost dressed. Tucking the tail of his shirt into his pants, he pulled up the zipper. "Go with Harvey. Jeff Hunter is probably one of the most decent men in this town, and he's almost as good looking as you are. The two of you will make for a great picture in *Photoplay* tonight, but not on the big screen. Those blue eyes of his are mesmerizing. I can see him as Jesus, but not a philandering husband. Harvey's got an edge to him. He'd be able to bring off a man cheating on his wife with a prostitute and falling in love with her."

Val looked at him in the mirror as he spoke. Johnny always had her best interests at heart, and that's why she had insisted that he take all her publicity shots for the last eight years. He was handsome enough to be the movies, looked like a young Bill Holden, but Johnny's real love was behind the camera, seeking and freezing the soul of his subject. And he loved her. He knew all the ugly secrets and he still kept coming back, making love to her as if she were someone precious and his alone. It was too bad that he wasn't visible enough to consider marrying. Marriage would fit the new image she was trying to create.

"I'll tell Harry your opinion at lunch," she said, pinning up her hair in a French twist.

He bent down and kissed her neck. "With your hair like that, you look like Grace Kelly—pure and regal."

Val snorted an unregal laugh. "That woman's slept around more than I have, and the whole world thinks she went to France a virgin! MGM's publicity department must have worked triple time covering up her appetite for men. Just goes to show you that nothing in Hollywood is real. They can create and destroy people quicker than McCarthy can find communists. By the way, remember to leave by the pool, okay?"

Johnny's face darkened with renewed anger. "What am I? Somebody you have to hide? For

Christ's sake, Val, I've been coming out of your bedroom for eight years now. Our relationship isn't exactly a secret, and I don't think Hedda Hopper is camped in your driveway waiting to break this story."

Val took a deep breath, determined not to create any more lines on her face with anger. "Why can't you understand that I'm trying to change my image? I don't want to be thought of as another brainless blond at thirty-three years old. I'll leave that for Jayne Mansfield, Anita Ekberg and Diana Dors. I have a shot at some serious work. If I can pull this off then I won't have to worry about good scripts. Parts will start coming to me."

She took out the huge bag of makeup and started applying a moisturizing base to her skin. "And I'm not taking any chances with the gossip mongers in this town. Look what they did to George Nader. Universal handed him over on a silver platter. They gave *Confidential* a story on Nader's sex life so the magazine wouldn't print what they had on Rock Hudson. Nader took the fall and Rock's still the all-American boy! It scares me. I didn't give a damn before, but now I have something really important—"

"Then explain Barnie Milkin," he interrupted. "If you really feel this way about changing your image, why would you let some old studio fart treat you like a ten-dollar whore?"

Her entire body froze and she had to force her mouth to move. "How dare you? You don't have the right—"

"No right!" he again interrupted with anger. "What am I to you, Val? A friend? A lover? Define this relationship, so I'll know what my rights are."

She held his gaze in the mirror. "I will not allow you to do this, Johnny. Not today. Please leave."

He grabbed his watch off the edge of the tub and turned. Before he left the bathroom, she added, "By the pool, please."

Stopping, he threw over his shoulder, "You really can be a bitch, Valentina."

She heard him slam the bedroom door and she closed her eyes briefly, trying to regain her earlier sense of peace. The moisture built up behind her lids and seeped out, running down her cheeks, and she quickly wiped it away. She could not afford to fall apart now. Today was too important. Taking a deep breath, Val straightened her shoulders and started applying her makeup as she'd been taught by the masters.

It was all part of the illusion, she thought. So many layers, disguising and concealing the imperfections, the true identity. Maybe that's why she never went out in public without it, for that truly would be naked and exposed . . . a nude shot even Johnny wouldn't want preserved.

Why did they keep hurting each other, she wondered, throwing a crumpled tissue onto the dressing table. She'd never slept with Barnie. He'd tried to cop a feel, but she'd stopped him cold, determined to make the man respect her. And if not her, then at least her talent, for she knew the test was good, damned good. But Johnny had listened to gossip and had thought the worst. And that had hurt. He didn't believe she had enough talent to get the role without sleeping her way to it. Feeling betrayed, she'd struck back by asking him to leave by the rear door. How childish she felt now.

Satisfied with her makeup, Val stood up and entered her bedroom. The yellow Edith Head was laid out on her bed, along with underwear and stockings. Thank God for Carmela. The woman was efficient, loyal and silent. The last attribute was the most valuable in this City of Rumors. Not for the first time, Val wondered what her devout Catholic maid thought of her employer's lifestyle. The only person Carmela showed any emotion with was Johnny. He spoke Spanish and teased her whenever he entered the house, making the old woman blush.

Johnny . . . Why did she always wound him when he tried to get too close? He was right, she thought, as she started to get dressed. She was a bitch. She'd been programmed to be one by Nora, her mother. Good old Nora Kobilik knew this day would happen, for she'd told the story so many times it was ingrained in Val's head, like the litany Carmela said at her morning masses.

Val's earliest memories were of sitting on a hard kitchen table and Nora telling her that on a hot sticky day in Pittsburgh, August 23, 1926, she had heard about the death of Rudolph Valentino. Nora, stalled in her own dream to become a silent screen actress by an unplanned pregnancy, went into early labor and named her daughter after her idol. Nora said it was a sign that Val was special. Her daughter would make the dream come true. So she was groomed with a passion.

Val's childhood was filled with voice and dance lessons and the importance of being pretty, instead of education and playmates. By the time she was six, she knew her left side was her best. She knew how to lower her chin and look up at a producer or talent scout, while slowly fluttering her eyelashes. She and Nora had practiced for hours in front of a mirror. If Shirley Temple was cute, Val was precocious. There were no friends, none that lasted, because Nora didn't want her picking up bad habits. They moved all the time. There was always another town, another opportunity, another contact, and they always moved west . . . heading toward Hollywood. Along the way Nora picked up a string of men, none of them lasting for more than a few months, but Val learned how to manipulate a male by watching her mother. Both of them aged while nurturing the dream, but as Nora's beauty decreased, Val's blossomed, and their interactions got ugly sometimes . . .

Val shook the thoughts out of her head as she bent over at the waist and let her ample bust fill the bodice of the dress. Straightening, she smoothed the pale yellow material over hips and slipped her feet into her pumps. Why was she filled with thoughts of the past, when her future was at the Brown Derby? Harry had the contract, just waiting for her signature, and all she had to do was show up and go on with her future. After spending a lifetime preparing for it, she was ready. Picking up white gloves, a scarf and her clutch bag, she left the room.

"Carmela?" Val walked through the sprawling Spanish rancher until she reached the front door.

The housekeeper appeared and silently waited.

"I'll be gone for a few hours, Carmela," she said while putting on her black sunglasses and picking up her car keys. "Don't bother with dinner tonight. The studio is sending a limo at six for the premiere. Could you check the black strapless, the one with the bugle beads at the top? See if it needs pressing."

"Si, Señora. It will be ready."

"Thank you," Val muttered, while checking herself one last time in the hall mirror.

Carmela walked over to the massive door and opened it. *"Vaya con Dios, Senora."* It was the religious woman's form of goodbye.

Val's heels clicked on the terracotta tiles as she left the house and absently whispered, "Same to you."

She walked to her car, passing palm trees and beds of flowers that normally gave her pleasure. But today she was preoccupied, and missed their beauty. The pale yellow Cadillac convertible, her signature car, stood waiting for her and she slid behind the wheel, anxious to get started. She let the car warm for a minute and wrapped the white chiffon scarf around her head, flinging the long ends back over her shoulders.

It was going to happen. She could feel it. Her life was going to be altered today. That had to be the cause of the strange feeling building up inside of her. Everything Nora had done, everything she had done to get to this day was worth it, she thought, as she drove down from the hills.

This picture was going to put her where she was meant to be . . . up there with the real stars. As soon as she had read O'Hara's book she knew she had to have the lead role, and had campaigned for it when she'd heard Universal had optioned the rights. Under Steiner's direction, she could win recognition, respect, maybe even an Oscar nomination.

Her full lips curved into a smile as she saw herself seated at the ceremony. She had been to the Academy Awards many times, but she'd been merely window dressing, not really part of the inner circle. Things would be different next year. She'd get Edith to design something truly spectacular and—

All daydreaming vanished as she rounded the curve on Mulholland, and saw the blue and white bus in her lane. She swerved to avoid hitting it but the Cadillac didn't seem to respond quickly enough! When impact was imminent, she panicked and instinctively brought her hands up to cover her face. Her brain wasn't screaming how unfair it was for it to happen on this day. She could only think of Carmela's words a few minutes earlier.

*Go with God . . .*

# Chapter 1

Present time . . .

It was a paradox, a riddle without an answer.

Nature had played a trick on her, leaving her confused and filled with questions. Why was it that men were at their sexual peak in their early twenties and women were supposed to hit it after thirty-five? Wasn't the basic purpose of life to procreate, to perpetuate the species? How many twenty-year-old males would really be interested in a middle-aged woman? And what in the world would a thirty-nine-year-old woman have in common with a man that was closer in age to her daughter than her? The question was moot since, outside of work, she didn't have much in common with any male, twenty, thirty or forty . . . Noise from the front office broke into her reverie.

"Thank God, it's Friday! I never thought this week would end."

"I know what you mean. Are you going to Happy Hour at Gallagher's?"

"Of course. Everybody's going. It should be a blast. 'Nite, Julia."

The women in their early twenties looked into their supervisor's office as they headed for the elevator.

Pretending to be absorbed in the paperwork on her desk, instead of trying to figure out her life, Julia Edwards lifted her head and smiled. "Good night," she called out. "Have a nice weekend."

"Thanks. You, too."

Julia watched as they stood in front of the elevator, two young women eager to begin the weekend. She unconsciously sighed. Once she had been like that, anxious to rush into life. But that was a long time ago—twenty years, to be exact. And that's what had gotten her in trouble. What a strange way society had of tagging an unmarried pregnant woman. Her daughter Paige had never been trouble or difficult. It was life that had been difficult.

She mentally shook the thought out of her head and concentrated on the report in front of her. Since Paige had left for college last year, she had been spending more time at the office than at home because home was too quiet, too lonely.

"You're still here? Again?"

Julia glanced up and smiled at the woman in her doorway who was holding a large bottle of glass cleaner and several rags. "Hi, Milly. I'll be out of your way soon. I just want to finish this."

"Well, it ain't none of my business, Julia," the woman said as she brought up her hand to rest on her hip. "But you've been spending way too much time here since your daughter went away to school. You finally did it. You did your job by that girl and now you've got your freedom back. You should be out enjoying life, instead of being here."

Still smiling, Julia said, "I'm just finishing some reports, not moving in."

"You might as well move in. Let me tell you . . . I can't wait for my kids to take off. I love 'em, but they're wearin' me out. Just this afternoon, when Martin came home from school, he started on me for new sneakers. Ninety-seven dollars they are. At Footlocker. Remember, Julia, when kids had school shoes and sneakers were for after school? And we bought them for five bucks at Woolworths?"

Julia laughed. "I remember. And they were canvas. Not leather. God, I must be getting old . . ."

"You're not old. What are you? Thirty-five?"

"Thirty-nine, going on sixty."

"I remember when I started here. Your Paige was about eight or nine, and you would run out at quittin' time to pick her up from your mother's. You were always on the move."

Shaking her head, Julia whispered, "There never seemed to be enough hours in the day back then. Now there seem to be too many."

"I'm tellin' you, Julia," Milly said as she pulled herself away from the door, "you've got to get out more. This is your time, woman. Find a man and kick up your heels. Enjoy it—you sure earned it."

"Good night, Milly," she called out to the chief

of the Maintenance Department. "Have a good weekend."

Julia shuffled the reports into a neat pile and filed them in her pending drawer. Nothing in them was vital and they could wait until Monday. The truth was she didn't want to go home. Work was the only place she felt needed.

It was a twenty minute ride from Coolback Industries to her house in Marlton, and in the last seventeen years the route had been indelibly etched into her subconscious. She knew how to time the lights, and usually her brain was planning out the rest of the evening. Questions used to fly in and out of her head as she started the second half of her day. Would Paige be over-tired when she picked her up at her mother's? What would they have for dinner? Should she stop at the store, did she have time? Or should she just take Paige to Taco Bell? Later she had gymnastics and soccer practice to fit in and trips to the library to research school reports. Doctor and dental appointments. Croup, chicken pox, braces; boys, dating, graduation . . . How had she ever done it alone? She had started out in the secretarial pool at Coolback when there were fifty employees and she was desperate for a job to support herself and her infant daughter. Now the company had grown into a leading lighting manufacturer and she was head of the Human Resources Department. Hiring. Firing. Health Insurance. Substance Abuse Programs. The business of life.

*Life.* How had hers become so quiet, so lonely? And how had it happened so quickly . . . ?

Was it the Empty Nest Syndrome? Dozens of books had been written about it; talk shows devoted programs to it, and Julia was shocked and embarrassed to find herself one of those lost, lonely, middle-aged women. She had become a statistic. Milly said to find a man and kick up her heels. Right. Great advice, and nearly impossible to follow through.

She had tried dating some years back, but found out that most men don't want to date women with children and Paige was always her highest priority. Over the last nineteen years she supposed she'd developed a slightly feminist attitude, from her experiences at work and her infrequent brushes with dating. She told herself that her life was full, that she didn't need a man to complete it. She had her daughter, her work, her home. Everything in her life was in order—until Paige had left for college, then the delicate, structured balance that she had worked so hard to achieve was destroyed. At times her body actually ached to hold her child, to feel her body next to her, her skin against her own. It was an indescribable bond that a male could never understand.

Okay, so she was lonely and depressed. She had tried getting involved, had even joined an exercise class, but it had only lasted a few weeks. Nothing held her interest anymore, and that frightened her. Now she went home, threw a frozen dinner into the microwave and watched TV until she fell asleep. What kind of life was that? She was speeding to-

ward forty, alone, and without the energy or knowledge to fix what was happening to her.

Her time was over, that special period in a female's life when she easily attracts attention. It was
now her daughter's turn, and she prayed each night
that Paige had the self-esteem and intelligence not
to repeat her mother's mistakes.

Julia turned the car into her driveway and realized her problem was easy to diagnose. She no longer knew her place in society. She had spent the last
nineteen years focused on her daughter and her job.
Now that she had lost one, the other was all she had
left. And it wasn't enough. Now that she had the
time and opportunity, she felt too old, too tired, too
foolish to go out with the younger women at the
office, and everyone else had stopped asking.

Julia opened the car door and stepped into the
early spring evening. She deeply inhaled and felt a
stirring inside of her as she walked up to her home.
Spring. A time for renewal, for rebirth. But how?
She had firmly believed the old proverb about reap-
ing what you sow, and had tried to sow good seeds
of love and responsibility with Paige, but now she
was alone. Her mother had died three years ago and
all her friends were married. Where could she turn,
without sounding foolish? She had a job, a house
and money to buy food. She was more fortunate
than many, but it seemed to her that by doing the
right thing by her daughter, she had set herself up
for this emptiness. She wasn't prepared. She simply
didn't know how to deal with it.

Think of the positives, she thought as she approached her front door. She had a beautiful, intelligent daughter who had made the transition into college with amazing ease. She had a good job and a certain amount of security. And she was proud of her house, a two-story, center hall Colonial that she and Paige had moved into the summer before Paige had entered high school. What more could she ask of life?

She unlocked the door, walked inside, and was surrounded by darkness and a depressing silence. Once Paige and her friends had greeted her. There had always been noise and music and laughter. Now there was only an emptiness that needed to be filled. Maybe she should get a dog. Maybe she should sell the house. Shrugging, Julia kicked off her heels, felt the cold tile beneath her feet and suddenly recalled Milly's advice. When was the last time she had kicked up her heels and was carefree? She couldn't remember. And where was she supposed to do this kicking up of heels? A singles club? The thought was even more depressing in a dark, empty house and she quickly flipped on the foyer light. Maybe she should just go into the kitchen and throw something into the microwave. If she was lucky, there might be a good movie on cable.

"Ain't life grand?" she whispered, feeling old, alone, facing a future that didn't hold any promise.

"Good God, I feel like Archie Bunker," Julia pronounced as she sat in the overstuffed chair that faced the television. Here she was, alone and depressed on a Friday night. She felt detached from the rest of the world, but comforted herself with the thought that millions of others must be just like her. At least she had lucked out with the movie. *Splendor In The Grass* was on A&E. Her feet were propped up on a matching ottoman and she was surrounded by the necessary tools of a true couch potato—food and the remote control. "And I'm talking out loud to myself. Archie had Edith. What I wouldn't give for the sound of another voice," she muttered. She opened her mouth to receive a handful of popcorn.

*"Then get up and get out of this house!"*

Julia's hand was frozen at her lips. She nearly choked on the popcorn while staring at the television. That deep, husky feminine voice had come out of the damned TV! How could that be? She coughed up the popcorn and continued to stare at the set as if it were possessed. A voice, a woman's voice, had called out to her! She watched as Natalie Wood and Warren Beatty walked hand in hand down a high school hallway. Everything sounded normal now. She had seen this movie at least five times and *never* had she heard any character utter those words!

Get up and get out of this house?

It was as if the television were talking to her!

Sitting perfectly still, Julia waited until her heartbeat returned to near normal. She tried to reason out how such a thing could happen, but there wasn't a suitable answer. She'd said she would give anything for the sound of another voice, and . . . and the TV talked to her!

Grabbing the remote control, she flicked the set

into silence and rose from her chair. "I'm having a nervous breakdown," she whispered as she picked up her herbal tea and turned off the light. "I'm talking to myself and the TV is answering me!" She started to giggle nervously as she left the living room and headed for the stairs. This was a sign, a frightening sign, that she simply had to start a life of her own.

Entering her bedroom, she immediately smelled something heavy and exotic and familiar. Perfume. Where was it coming from? She only bought light, flowery scents.

"I don't want to know," she muttered.

Too frightened to get properly undressed, she pulled her sweatpants off, slipped her bra straps down her arms and flung the bra onto a chair. A slight breeze seemed to pass over her and she shivered as she checked the window to see if it was open. It wasn't. Clad only in panties, socks and a sweatshirt, she hopped into bed and yanked the comforter up to her chin. She felt as scared as she had when she was a kid and had thought the bogeyman had been hiding in her closet.

Now he was in her television . . .

"Get your act together, Julia," she whispered. She was almost forty years old and should be above childish fears. But this was weird, beyond weird. She told herself that she was under stress, depressed, and had an overactive imagination. She simply thought too much about life. She had to give her mind a rest. Tomorrow she would clean the house, do the laundry, maybe check out some plants for the flower beds, and then she was going to go out to dinner. And perhaps a movie. She could do it. She had to do it. Her sanity depended on it.

Julia pulled off the gardening gloves and rubbed the ache in her lower back. Despite being dirty, tired and sore, she felt pretty good, for it had been a productive day. The house was clean. The laundry was finished, and she had planted geraniums and impatiens in front of the house. There was nothing like good old dirt therapy to get her back on track. Hungry, Julia decided to take a shower and get dressed for dinner. She was going to do it, no matter how awkward she felt about sitting alone. Passing the answering machine in the kitchen she saw the light flashing and her mood lifted. Someone had called.

"Mom, it's Paige. Call me as soon as you hear this. Don't worry . . . it's something great! Bye."

Immediately dialing the number in Ohio, Julia tried to imagine what her daughter's news could be. A great score on an important test? A new boyfriend? Dear God, don't let her think she's in love already—

"Hello?"

"Hi," Julia answered, smiling when she heard her child's voice. "I got your message. You sounded happy. What's the great news?"

"Oh, Mom, you'll never believe it!"

"Then tell me." Please God, Julia prayed, don't

let her throw everything away because of puppy love. *Don't let her repeat my mistakes.*

"Maria's parents came up yesterday for a visit. They're staying the weekend, and last night they took me to dinner with them."

"And?" Julia had met Paige's roommate's parents when she had taken her daughter to college. They seemed like nice people.

"And . . . they go to Europe every summer. They have relatives in northern Italy. And this is the part you're not going to believe. They asked me to go with them! Can you believe it? Me! In Europe!"

Julia was speechless. Her daughter didn't want to come home this summer? She had felt as if she were merely passing time until freshman year was over, until Paige was once more with her.

"Mom? Didn't you hear me? The DeMarcos want to take me to Europe. We'll be staying with their family, so all I have to do is pay for the airfare and bring spending money. And I've got most of that taken care of. You know I was saving for a car, but this is too great an opportunity to pass up. They told me they rent a car and we can drive to France and Spain and Germany. They do it every summer. Say something, Mom. What do you think? Can I go?"

She heard the excitement in her child's voice and she pushed her disappointment down to ask, "When are they leaving?"

"The second week in May. I'd only be home long enough to unpack from college and re-pack for Europe. I know it's not much time, but I'd have a

couple of days with you before school starts again.
So, what do you think, Mom? It's a great opportunity, isn't it?"

"It is," she said honestly, feeling the depression once more settle in over her soul. It was an educational and cultural opportunity that she could never give her daughter. "But I'll miss you, Paige. I was looking forward to the summer with you."

"I'll miss you too, Mom. I'll write every week. I promise. Mrs. De Marco said if you agree then you can call her to get all the details."

Julia picked up a pen and wrote down the number. "Won't you need a passport?"

"That's right. Maria said I can do it by mail if you send me my birth certificate. Does this mean I can go?"

She wanted to scream no, to tell her daughter that she had to come home to her, that she wasn't handling this separation well and didn't think she could make it through the summer alone. Instead, she cleared her throat and answered, "Of course you can go. I'll call Maria's mother sometime this week."

"Oh, Mom, thanks! You're the best!" Paige sounded ecstatic and Julia was even more depressed.

"Well, listen, I just came in from gardening and I'm a mess. I have to take a shower and get ready."

"Are you going out?" Paige asked.

"Ah . . . yes. I'm going out to dinner."

"Great! Who with? Do you have a date?" There was a teasing note to Paige's last question.

"Goodness, no. I'm . . . I'm going out with friends from work," she said, feeling even worse for lying.

"That's great. You should get out more, Mom." There was concern, maybe even pity, in her daughter's voice.

Unable to handle such emotions coming from her own child, Julia took a deep breath and forced her voice to sound cheerful. "I know you're right, but if I don't get in the shower I'll be late. So, I'll call you after I speak with Mrs. De Marco."

"Okay. Are you sure you're all right about this? I mean, it's been an adjustment for you with me going away to college and everything—"

"Hey, this is a terrific chance for you to see a part of the world and live in a different country. It'll be a wonderful experience. And I'm fine. Don't worry about me. Worry about keeping your grades up, or you'll be taking summer courses instead of seeing Europe."

"I know. I am working hard; I'm just so excited about this trip. Who would ever think *I'd* get to go to Europe? I still can't believe it. Thanks, Mom. Thanks for letting me go."

"Okay, I'll call you next week after I hear all the details."

"I love you." Paige suddenly sounded like a little girl in need of reassurance.

"I love you, too, sweetie. Bye."

"Bye, Mom. Have a good time tonight."

Julia hung up the phone and sat down at the kitchen table. She stared at the wooden surface, seeing fine scars cutting through the grain, scars that had come from countless school projects and the impatience of a little girl growing into a young woman.

*Paige wasn't coming home . . .*

Tears gathered at the corners of her eyes and she wiped them away with the back of her hand. Suddenly her eyes began to sting and she realized that, although she'd worn gloves, dirt was still on her skin. In real pain, she hurried to the sink and splashed water over her eyes. Grabbing a dish towel, Julia wiped her face and sighed. So much for crying. Maybe she would throw something into the microwave after all. It would take too much energy to go out. She could just call and cancel the reservation. From somewhere inside her head she heard the command to stop feeling sorry for herself and to get upstairs and get ready. She was alone, and it wasn't a temporary situation. This was it. Her new life. And she had better start getting used to it.

"Ain't life grand?" she muttered again, as she dragged herself toward the stairs. The sarcastic question seemed like her new motto.

Dinner at Martelli's had been painful. She hadn't been able to stop thinking about Paige. Instead of enjoying the wonderful chicken marsala, she had felt self-conscious sitting at a table alone, as if everyone's gaze were on her, as if they had known that she was unwanted and unloved. She had been surrounded by couples, laughing and talking, and had felt envious that everyone else had seemed happy.

But it had been her choice to remain single, not to date men who had thought of Paige as an intrusion, and she hadn't met any others. Her depression deepened and, when she left the restaurant, she drove to the Multiplex, needing to be with people, even strangers, rather than go home to an empty house.

The only movie that she was able to see from the beginning was a police drama, so she stood in line with couples waiting to purchase a ticket. It seemed to her that if she wasn't half of a couple, she was an outsider. She watched the way men and women related to each other as they queued up. Arms were laced together. Fingers were intertwined. Intimate looks were passed.

"How many?"

Julia took out her wallet. "One."

"I'm sorry? How many?"

Embarrassed, Julia leaned closer to the mesh microphone. "One, please."

"Seven dollars."

Julia handed over the money and a single ticket spat out of the counter. Grabbing it up, Julia muttered, "Thank you," and hurried into the lobby. There were fourteen movies showing and she searched for a sign that would point the way to hers.

The usher ripped her ticket in half and said, "To the left. Last one on the right."

She couldn't wait to find her seat. Only when she was concealed in darkness would she feel less conspicuous. The screen filled with images and Julia quickly realized it wasn't her kind of movie. She never went in for violence and gore, yet she was here and she was staying. She didn't really pay attention to the drama. Tears welled up in her eyes as she kept thinking about her daughter traveling to Europe, how lonely her own life was, and how much more lonely it was going to become.

*"You know you're bordering on pathetic, don't you?"*

Julia tried to focus her attention back on the screen. The scene was a court room and one of the women jurors was looking straight at the camera while delivering her lines. It must be one of those movies, like Woody Allen's, where the actor breaks character and speaks directly to the audience. It had always jarred her.

*"You were doing so well today, until that phone call, Julia."*

A queer feeling started in Julia's belly and she looked around her to see if anyone else thought it was odd. No one seemed to be as startled as Julia felt. Of course, how many could claim such a coincidence? A character named Julia was upset about a phone call . . .

*"Oh, stop it,"* the blond woman commanded. *"You know I'm talking to you, Julia Edwards!"*

She didn't move. She barely breathed. She had imagined that! No one was talking to her from a movie screen! Julia suddenly recognized the actress as Valentina Manchester . . . a blond bombshell who had starred in the comedies of her youth. The woman wasn't even alive! She had died in a car crash or something. How could she be in this movie, unless it was special effects? But how could anyone know her name, or how depressed she was over Paige's phone call?

*"That's right . . ."* Val said in that famous husky voice, as she ran her fingernail over her arched eyebrow. *"You're starting to get it now. I'm not really in the movie and no one can see me except you. We've got to talk, Honey. That kid of yours is going on with her life. Hell, she's going to Europe, and what are you going to do? Sit and cry like a baby? Face it. You did your job and it's over. I'd think you'd be glad. What about those two weeks when you missed work because she got chicken pox? You lost out on a promotion and it took three years before you were considered again. You never dated because of that kid, and—"*

Julia jumped out of her seat and ran from the theater as if the hounds of hell were at her heels. She was losing her mind; it was the only explanation.

*"Hey, wait a minute!"* the dead movie star shouted. *"We aren't through yet!"*

Val shrugged once and turned back to the other actors who seemed riveted to the defense attorney's opening statement. "I say the sucker's guilty. Let's fry 'em and get outta here!"

# Chapter 2

God watches over drunks and fools . . . and maybe those who have lost all touch with reality. How else could she explain sitting in her driveway? She barely remembered driving home from the movies. Her brain wasn't functioning at a normal level. She didn't think about what had happened. She *refused* to think about it until she was home, for she knew that if she did she would completely unravel and never make it to safety. Maybe she could see a doctor. Right! And tell him what? That the television talked to her? That old movie stars were appearing in new films and speaking to her? A straitjacket would be slapped on her before she ever left the office. No, she couldn't tell anyone about this. She would have to take care of whatever was happening to her. She was an intelligent woman; she could figure this out. Hearing voices, seeing visions . . .

She was either schizophrenic or . . . or a saint!

Saint Julia. Laughter bubbled in her throat at the

thought. Well, she certainly wasn't in line for canonization, and, if by chance God wanted to send a message to the world, He definitely wouldn't be using a 1950's sex goddess and a single mother to do it. It was stress, depression, and perhaps a chemical imbalance. Maybe she was starting menopause. That's it! Her hormones were fluctuating and she was a little unbalanced. Monday morning she'd take an early lunch and go to the bookstore. Menopause. Thank God for it. Thank God she was obviously starting to go through it.

Happy to have found *some* explanation, she got out of the car and walked to her front door. As soon as she was inside and turned the lock, she smelled it.

The same scent. Heavy. Exotic. Familiar.

What *was* it?

Before she had gone out to dinner, she'd left the foyer light on, and the one in her bedroom. Turning off the small chandelier in the foyer, Julia walked through the dark house toward the stairs and the dim light coming from her bedroom. The scent grew stronger with each step. She knew it was perfume, and also knew it wasn't hers. Just get into bed, she told herself. Read until you fall asleep. She'd bought two books earlier in the week, but hadn't gotten to them yet. Forget the mystery. This was not a night to be frightened any more than she already was. She would read the one about those covered bridges. A romance written by a man should be interesting, and temporarily take her mind off the crazy things in her life. Relieved to have a plan, Julia walked into her bedroom. She stopped dead in her tracks when she saw the apparition before her.

Valentina Manchester was standing in front of her closet and shaking her head.

"We really have to do something about your clothes."

"My God!" Julia was frozen in fear. Her heart was pounding in her chest, as if trying to escape. Her brain refused to work, sending only signals of dizziness to the rest of her body.

Valentina dropped a blouse to the floor and turned around. "So how'd you like my performance? Been a long time since I was up on the screen."

Julia stumbled to the bed and collapsed. She was breathing heavily and clutching the edge of her night table. "Please . . ." She swallowed several times, attempting to bring moisture back into her mouth. "Please, get out. Go away!"

"Sorry, toots. Can't do."

Julia starting shaking her head, as if the movement might bring some sanity. "You—you're not real! Valentina Manchester died when I was little. Whatever you're trying to do won't work . . ." It couldn't be Valentina Manchester. She had to be a kook, some obsessive person who went through plastic surgery in order to look like her idol. Didn't she see something like that on Oprah once? She should call the police, get some help.

Forcing her hand to move toward the phone, she whispered, "I'm calling the police, so if you want to avoid—" Words stuck in her mouth as the receiver lifted off the cradle and hung in the air, suspended in motion.

"I don't think that would be such a good idea, Julia. No one else can see me, and you'd look pretty silly trying to explain this."

Julia stared at the phone, incapable of speech. Suddenly her body started shaking and tears ran down her cheeks. She was certifiable! This sort of thing just couldn't *happen!*

Val watched the woman unravel and sighed with impatience. "Look, if it makes you feel better, I don't know why I was sent here. When they said Julia, I thought it was that Julia Roberts woman. Now, her, I could have helped. Or Princess Diana's mess, that's something I could've sunk my teeth into."

At Julia's look of horror, Val laughed. "No. I'm not a vampire. That's strictly low budget, B–movie stuff. Gloria Talbolt and Julia Adams were the innocent victims. And Marie Windsor. She was Queen of the B–movie. I may have been the brainless blond, but I never did vampires—although some producers I've known certainly qualify as blood-suckers."

"Who *are* you? Why are you here?"

"You know who I am, Julia. You said it yourself. Valentina Manchester died when you were a little girl." She walked around the bedroom, looking at pictures, smelling bottles of perfume. "Pissed me off, too, let me tell you. I'd worked so hard to get that part, and they gave it to Elizabeth Taylor. Anyway, that's not why I'm here. I was getting bored with eternity, at least that's the sensation I was getting, and then you became my mission."

"Mission?" Julia found it hard enough to believe that she was actually conversing with . . . with whatever was in front of her. Valentina Manchester? The *ghost* of Valentina Manchester?

Val nodded and patted her perfect blond curls. "I'm supposed to help someone in need. As soon as I saw you yesterday in front of the television, stuffing your face with popcorn and feeling sorry for yourself, I knew I had to get a little more direct."

"That was you? I thought I was going crazy." Julia almost laughed with hysteria. As if *this* was better!

"And all of it because your kid's gone away to college. Isn't it enough that you spoiled her for almost twenty years? Now that she's finally out of your life, you're ready to toss it away because you're lonely."

"Paige is not spoiled."

"Oh, yeah?" Val looked around her, as if assessing her surroundings. "Looks pretty damned good to me. Try growing up in cold water flats in more towns than you can remember. You gave that kid everything, and now she's going on with her life. Isn't that the way it's supposed to be?"

Something fragile snapped inside of Julia and she stood up, shaking with a mixture of fear and anger. "How dare you talk about me and my daughter? What do you know of us? Get out of my house! Get—"

"Oh, I know almost everything about you,

Julia," Val interrupted. "I know that you were a shy child, that your father walked out on you when you were five and you always felt it was your fault. I know that you wanted to go to college, but didn't have the money. So you met Jim Edwards and thought you were in love. You got pregnant and the two of you married, but Jim was just like your father and you knew the marriage wasn't going to work before Paige was born, so Jimmy boy packed up his marbles and left—"

"Stop it!" Julia yelled, too frightened to hear any more. She had to get out! If this . . . this *thing* wouldn't leave, then she would. About to run out of the bedroom, her shin connected with the extended phone cord and she tripped. She knew she was falling, yet a part of her was aware that the progress to the rug was much slower than normal. When she finally hit the ground, it wasn't with an impact, more like a soft landing, and she heard the voice over her.

"Maybe I'm going too fast for you. Why don't you get into bed and go to sleep? I'll leave you alone for the rest of the night. Promise."

When Julia looked up, the woman was gone.


Val walked around the daughter's room, seeing the mementos of a happy childhood. A bulletin board was a collage of memories, with pictures of friends, ticket stubs, prom trinkets, special things with a story behind each. The bed was large and inviting with a thick, downy comforter and Val found herself drawn to it. She lay down, running her hand over the soft material. Kicking off her heels, she wondered what it must have been like growing up in one house, making friends, going to dances and proms, having a normal life . . . This kid had it all. Julia gave her daughter stability, something Val never knew. Maybe if she'd had this, her life would have turned out differently. Maybe she would have married and had children, and . . . Suddenly, she stopped herself. What in the world was she thinking? She'd had a great life. Thousands of women had envied her lifestyle, her position. She'd had it all before it was torn away from her. Forcing herself to get up from the bed, she walked out of the room and its memories. It was better to sleep on the couch than compare herself to a teenager.

Reclining on the sofa, Val looked around the comfortable room. She supposed she could have done worse for an assignment. Julia wasn't ugly; she was . . . ordinary. A little on the skinny side, and not much on curves. But she had pretty blue eyes and nice hair, a natural brown that was straight and shiny. She just wore it too plain. And no taste in clothes. The closet looked like the wardrobe of "Our Miss Brooks". It was filled with stuff a teacher or librarian would wear. And not a single cocktail dress in the lot. No wonder the woman was bored. All of that could easily be fixed. It was what was inside of the woman that could be a problem. But Julia had some spirit left in her. That was obvious by her animated defense of her daughter. Val liked the courage and resilience she'd witnessed. Maybe there was something to work with, after all. Julia just needed some guidance to get back into life again. She'd had it drained out of her by responsibility and poor choices.

*Poor choices . . .*

Now that was something Val understood.


She awakened to the aroma of coffee and snuggled deeper into her pillow as she sighed with contentment. Dear God, what a night! What a dream! Dead movie stars and . . .

Julia immediately opened her eyes and stared at the phone on her night table. *Who* had made the coffee? Paige wasn't home. She hadn't done it herself, unless she'd been sleepwalking. She kept staring at the phone, picturing it rising and hovering in the air like in the dream.

Valentina Manchester.

She couldn't shake the name, the image of the woman.

Much more brave in the light of morning, Julia threw the covers to the bottom of the bed and got up. She grabbed her robe and wrestled her arms into it as she hurried downstairs. There had to be an explanation. Nothing had really happened last night. The movie wasn't her type, and she'd come home and gone to sleep. All the rest . . . an old movie star talking to her from the screen, and then in her bedroom . . . it never happened. It was stress, depression, menopause and—

Julia slid to a halt at the doorway leading into her

kitchen. She couldn't believe it. She wouldn't! Valentina Manchester was standing in front of the stove, wearing that tight yellow dress, and she was cooking eggs!

"You're still here!" The words rushed out of Julia's mouth in a terrified squeak.

"Of course I'm still here," Val answered calmly. "We have a lot of work to do. But first you need breakfast. Hope you like eggs over easy? Worked as a waitress during World War II and sometimes filled in as a short-order cook. Took me a while to figure out your coffee pot, but—"

"Why are you still here?" Julia interrupted while clutching the door molding for support. It wasn't a dream! She was here in the light of morning when ghost and goblins and scary things that go bump in the night should disappear! And she was in her home!

Val slid the eggs onto plates that already had wheat toast on them. Placing the plates on the table, she said, "I've already told you that last night. I've been sent on a mission to help you."

"I don't need your help," Julia protested, once more close to tears. "So you can just leave and go back to wherever you came from." That sounded stern enough. She had to take control back. This was her house!

Valentina stood with her hand on her hip, lifted her chin and stared at Julia. "Listen, toots, I *can't* go back. It isn't up to me. So, sit down and eat your breakfast, and we can get started."

"Started doing what?" Julia cried. "You're not real. You don't even exist."

Val sat down and pulled a napkin onto her lap. "Technically, you're right," she said as she reached for a piece of toast. "But, like it or not, I do exist for you." She bit into the toast and murmured with appreciation. "Ummm . . . this is delicious. I didn't even know if I *could* eat, but I woke up this morning and I was starved. C'mon, Julia. I'm not going anywhere, so you might as well accept it and have breakfast."

Julia watched as the woman attacked her eggs and she shook her head in disbelief. "This isn't happening," she muttered. "Valentina Manchester died in a car accident. You can't be here in my kitchen eating breakfast. You can't!"

Val sighed with exasperation and wiped her mouth. "Will you please stop saying that. Don't you think I know I'm dead? Don't you think I'm pissed off that it happened when I was only thirty-three, when everything was finally going my way? If *I've* accepted it, why can't you?"

Julia pushed herself away from the doorway. "You really are her?" she whispered, remembering the TV, the movie . . . good God, the phone!

Val smiled while slowly nodding. "Almost, but not quite. I have my limitations. Actually, Julia, I'm only here for you. I can't have my old life back. It doesn't exist, anyway. No one but you will know I'm here."

Julia reached the table and sank into an opposite

chair, still stunned. "But you look so real, as if I could touch you."

Val stuck her hand across the table. "Go ahead and try. Nothing's going to happen."

Julia stared at the perfectly manicured nails, the graceful arch of her fingers, the tiny blond hairs on her forearm. She looked so damned *real!*

"Go on. Even I don't know if you can."

She raised her hand, yet hesitated. If she did this then she was admitting that all of it was actually taking place. That Valentina Manchester was sitting across from her, looking as beautiful and as young as in her last movie. "What year did you die?" Julia whispered, still not touching the woman.

"1959. A month before *Crimson Tears* was released."

"I saw it," Julia said, trying to figure out the math. If Valentina Manchester had died in 1959 when she was thirty-three, then it meant the woman would have to be . . . God, she looked twenty-five, not sixty-eight. Tentatively, knowing that it would somehow change her perception of reality, Julia lowered her arm and let her fingertips touch the elegant hand.

*"You're real!"*

Grinning, Val pulled back her hand and picked up her fork. "As I've said, I'm real for you, Julia, and—"

"No, wait," Julia interrupted. "Are you like . . . a ghost, or something? I don't get it. I'm confused. I thought ghosts, if they existed at all, were ethereal, hazy vapors of energy, not substance."

Val quickly swallowed the eggs and answered, "I would imagine you are confused, and that's why I'm here to help you. Listen, have you ever heard of people seeing or talking to someone and then finding out later that it couldn't possibly have happened because that person had died?"

Julia continued to stare at her and chose her words carefully. "My great aunt, Cass, lived up the street from us and she used to watch me while my mother worked. I was little and I don't really remember her very well, but my mother said that one morning my aunt came to the house and said that she couldn't take care of me that day. After telling my mother that she loved both of us and that my mother was working too hard, she kissed her and left. Later that morning, my mother found out that her aunt had died during the night. It was weird. My mom told me that at the viewing, several people said they saw Cass walking in town."

Val's smile was serene. "There. You see? Your mother's aunt looked real, spoke to her, and even kissed her. Not all who die are—how did you put it?—ethereal, hazy vapors. Your great-aunt needed to finish something that was important to her."

"But why are you here?" Julia again asked in an earnest voice. "Why am I important to you?"

"I don't know. I can only say that you're my mission. I was sent here to help you. I can't remember anything about what happened after the accident, after I entered a brilliant white light. It wasn't as if someone spoke to me, like we're doing. It was just a sense . . . a strong feeling of unrest, of something unfinished, and that I was needed. Then I became aware of you, of your unhappiness and your own unrest. I didn't think I'd be this direct. I didn't even know if I could."

"But why me?"

Val picked up a cup of coffee and held it. "I really don't know. We can't have much in common. But I have been thinking about ways to help you."

As insane as it seemed, Julia actually believed her. It wasn't menopause, after all. It was what? Her guardian angel? A Fifties bombshell? Somebody up there had made one hell of a mistake. Without further thought, she picked up her own cup of coffee and drank from it. "This is good," she said evasively.

"Thanks. Try the eggs, though they're probably cold by now."

Not really hungry, Julia found herself eating only to be polite. "How long are you going to . . . be here?"

Val shrugged, causing the front of her tight dress to lift her breasts. "I really don't know. I suppose until I've accomplished what I was sent here to do."

She really is beautiful, Julia thought as she continued to eat. It wasn't just the perfect makeup, the silky blond hair or the sexy dress. Valentina Manchester possessed great beauty, the kind that doesn't really need help and is the result of great genes. It wouldn't have mattered if she had been a nun or a movie star, the woman had a perfection that couldn't be denied. Suddenly Julia was aware of her own appearance. She hadn't even washed her face.

"What do I call you?" she asked, wanting to change the direction of her thoughts. How futile to compare herself to a legendary beauty.

"I would think you'd call me Val, since we're going to be spending a lot of time together."

"We are?"

"This isn't a visit, Julia. I'm going to be here, in one form or another, until this mission is accomplished."

"And I suppose I don't have any say in the matter?"

"Afraid not."

"What if I told you that I don't need help, that I realize my problem and I'll find the solution?"

"And what is your problem?" Val asked, sitting back in the chair and relaxing. "By the way, you don't happen to have any cigarettes around here, do you?"

"I don't smoke. It's unhealthy."

Val raised her eyebrows, as if to say that no longer mattered. "I just always enjoyed a cigarette after breakfast. I'm sorry . . . you were about to tell me what you thought your problem was."

Trying to avoid that subject, Julia said, "If you want, I suppose I can buy you a pack of cigarettes, but you'd have to smoke outside. Secondary smoke is just as bad."

"Secondary smoke? What do you mean? Doctors were in ads and in television commercials saying that smoking, especially menthol cigarettes, calms the nerves and soothes the throat."

"That was in the fifties. Today we know it causes cancer. It's dangerous."

"Really? I guess I have a lot to catch up on." Val stared into her coffee cup, knitting together those perfectly arched eyebrows as she thought over Julia's words. "But since it can't hurt me then I don't mind going outside." She looked up. "Now let's get back to you. Your problem?"

Julia wiped her mouth and stared at the smear of eggs on her plate. "I . . . I'm experiencing what's called the empty nest syndrome, when a child leaves home and the parent is alone. I just need time to make the adjustment."

"You've had since September. That's seven months, and you're worse now than when Paige first left."

"Did you ever have children?"

Val shook her head.

"Then you can't possibly understand," Julia said. "It isn't just the energy and the love invested in them. There's a bond so strong that time or distance can't break it. I miss my daughter. Is that so terrible?" Julia ran her fingers through her tangled hair. "I miss the sound of her voice, her laughter. She filled this house with life. And now? Now there's silence and emptiness."

"Now there's me, Julia. You're not alone any more. And I have plans."

She raised her chin and looked at the glamorous woman across from her. "What kind of plans?"

Val smiled. "Finally, we're on the right subject. Last night I did some thinking about this situation.

I mean, why would I be sent to you? As you've mentioned, we're an odd match. Now, either some-one's made a huge mistake, or I've been sent here to teach you what I know."

"What you know? Acting?" Julia's disbelief turned into laughter.

Val waited until the laughter subsided and then said in a patient voice, "No, Julia. Not acting, though I think at least half of life is acting. Pretend-ing to be happy when you're hurting. Not letting others see who you really are. You need to get back into life, to regain your vision of who you really are and what you want. You have the time now to do whatever you choose. Instead of thinking that ev-erything's over, you need to look at it like a whole new exciting chapter is beginning. You have free-dom again. It's like starting over. How many people have that chance?"

"Freedom to do what? I don't need freedom. I need my daughter."

"What would you like to do? Travel? Find a man? Get married again?"

"Good Lord, no. A man? I don't need a man. What can a man do for me now? I'm independent. I have a good job. I have this house. A man isn't the answer to everything."

"No doubt. But wouldn't you like the . . . com-panionship?"

"Well, Val," Julia said, using the woman's name for the first time. "I think I have a few things to teach you. A great deal has happened since 1959. Marriage isn't always the ultimate goal of a woman anymore. In your time, men held all the power. We women still don't have our share, but we are making progress. There are now two women on the Supreme Court. Our ambassador to the UN is a woman. So are the prime ministers of several countries. There are women who head large corporations. And you might be happy to know that there are even female directors and producers. One woman I remember reading about, Sherry Lansing, actually ran an entire studio."

"You're joking? A woman was the head of a studio?"

Julia nodded. "There are laws now that protect women against discrimination and sexual harrassment. A male in the working environment can't pressure a woman anymore with sexual innuendo without the threat of a lawsuit."

Val was listening with an intense interest. "Against the law, huh? There's actually a law that protects women from sexual intimidation? I spent my whole life fighting it and then finally using it. But what I was talking about, Julia, is the comfort you can find with a man. When was the last time you were with one?"

Julia laughed and looked away with embarrassment. "I don't see what that has to do with our conversation."

"Why can't you answer me?"

It was a challenge. This woman—this *ghost*— didn't think that she would tell the truth. Turning back, Julia held her chin high and said, "I can't remember exactly. Probably around nineteen, twenty, years ago."

"No kidding." Val seemed to move further into her seat, as if taking a step back in shock. "Damn, Julia, I didn't think anybody had been without sex longer than me."

After a startled moment, Julia burst into laughter. Val joined her and, when they stopped, their gaze caught in a moment of connection. It was the beginning of acceptance for both of them.

"I can't believe I'm about to ask this. It's all so crazy, but right now it seems, well, sort of okay."

"Good. What's your question?"

"I guess I'm curious. So what are your ideas, Val? If you're my fairy godmother, how are you going to straighten out my life?"

Val smiled and said, "You're willing to change?"

"I'm willing to listen," Julia said cautiously.

Val nodded. "It's a beginning."

# Chapter 3

Pulling into the parking lot of Coolback Industries, Julia thought how bizarre the weekend had been. The further she got from her house, the more unreal it all seemed. It couldn't have happened! Maybe she should call her doctor this morning and make an appointment for a check up. She had to have been grasping at figments of her imagination. Good Lord, she thought as she pulled into her parking space, having dead movie stars living with you is certifiable. Shutting off the engine, she looked into the rearview mirror. Valentina Manchester plucked her eyebrows? Try telling *that* to a physician! Oh yes, Doctor, this dead glamour queen has taken up residence in my home and insists that I need a makeover. She said my eyebrows looked like caterpillars, that my skin was beginning to resemble a dried-up creek bed, that I had let myself go . . .

Right. She couldn't tell a soul about this insanity. She might be confused about *a lot* of things that were happening in her life right now, but her survival instinct was still strong. This . . . this meno-pausal madness must remain secret. She had a child, a job, responsibilities.

Grabbing her purse, Julia got out of the car and locked it. As she walked toward the office portion of the huge factory, she promised herself not to think any more about it. Here, she was safe. There wouldn't be any ghosts nagging at her about her life and her appearance. Here, at Coolback, she was in charge.

"Julia, wait up. I need to speak with you."

She turned and saw Peggy Morrison hurrying to catch up to her. Mentally, Julia switched into her manager mode. She prided herself in remembering the vital statistics of the office personnel. Peggy was a secretary to Vince Demicci, Senior VP. She was divorced, two children, enrolled in HMO and profit sharing.

"How was your weekend?" she asked the ap-proaching woman. It was the automatic Monday morning question.

"Oh, great," Peggy answered, as she shifted her purse strap back onto her shoulder. "I spent all day Saturday and Sunday on baseball fields for Spring tryouts. Why do males put such importance on this ritual? If neither kid makes the A team, it's going to be up to me to restore their self-esteem. How do you convince an eleven-year-old that he'll have more use for math than baseball?"

Julia smiled sympathetically as they walked to-ward the entrance. "My daughter played soccer, but boys are so much more competitive. Where's the fun when there's that kind of pressure?"

"Listen, Julia," Peggy said in a rush, "I need to talk to you. I would have called over the weekend, but your number is unlisted."

Julia stopped. "What's wrong? Are you okay?" People usually wanted to speak with her when there was a medical or financial crisis.

"I don't know if I'm okay. I was hoping you could tell me."

"I'm confused. I don't know what you mean."

Peggy crossed her arms over her chest, as if for protection. "Look, I don't want you to take this the wrong way and I hope I'm not speaking out of turn, but I figured you'd be the person to ask. Last week Vince had me make reservations at the Embassy Suites for three men from Amalgamated Energy. When I asked him how long the suites would be needed, he said at least a month, maybe indefinitely. Then Marie said she had just sent messenger-delivered letters to the board of directors requesting a special meeting on Saturday. I guess what I'm trying to ask is if there's any truth to the rumor that Amalgamated is taking over Coolback. And if there is, what's going to happen to us?"

Julia was stunned. The secretaries always knew industry rumors before anyone else. If the CEO's assistant had sent out letters for an emergency board meeting, on a Saturday, then something was obviously up. "I don't have any idea, Peggy," she said honestly. Coolback had gone public two years ago and the stock had already split. Everyone in the company had been ecstatic, and the picture seemed even brighter since the lab had come up with a filament that increased the life of a bulb up to seventy percent. If Amalgamated wanted to take them over, it had to be because of the filament. "Maybe we're jumping to conclusions here. But I'll see what I can find out and get back to you."

Peggy nodded as they both entered the huge building and headed toward the elevators.

"I'm scared, Julia. Amalgamated is one of the biggest companies in the country. If we're being taken over, you know they're going to bring in their own people. I've got two kids and an ex–husband that can't be depended on to make child support payments."

Julia pressed the up button and whispered as others joined them, "Let's not get worried about rumors, okay?"

Peggy nodded and, as the elevator ascended, Julia wished she could follow her own advice. A takeover would be disastrous for her department.

As she walked to her office, several people called out good morning and she forced herself to give a cheerful reply. Her assistant, Meg, was just getting to her desk when Julia approached. She took notice of Meg's short, tight skirt and was going to again remind the young woman about the dress code and being professional, when she thought that Meg really looked cute. What's wrong with self-expression, she thought, and almost laughed out loud. My God, the ghost is getting to me!

"Morning, Meg. See if Larry Millborne's in yet. I need to speak with him ASAP."

Meg glanced up and nodded. "Sure. How was your weekend? Do anything interesting?"

Julia stared at the younger woman. "My weekend?" she asked stupidly, as if somehow it showed that she had spent the last two days skirting insanity.

"Yeah. I went to a reggae concert at the Mann with Tommy and we started arguing. Typical. How about you? You do anything?"

"As a matter of fact I went to the movies."

"Really? Was it a good film?"

"I . . . I left before it was over. Police dramas aren't my thing."

Meg nodded as she handed her a pile a letters and memos. "I know what you mean. I feel the same way about reggae. Say, what is it about you? There's something different."

Meg stared at her face so long that Julia was embarrassed. "It's my eyebrows," she finally admitted. "I plucked them." It was a small lie. Val actually tore each and every offending hair from her forehead with relish.

Meg's expression changed. "Right. It makes you look . . . I don't know, younger, maybe."

"It would take more than the removal of a few hairs to accomplish that," she said, turning to her office. Yet once inside, she closed the door and ran her fingertip over the trim, silky hairs above her left eye. Good God, she thought, as she touched the still-tender skin, how much more torture would she have to endure?

The pager on her phone rang and she pressed it down. Meg's voice told her Larry Melbourne was on the line.

"Thanks, Meg." She pressed the button for her telephone and picked up the receiver. This was not a conversation for the speakerphone. "Larry?"

"Morning, Julia. What's up?"

Larry had been her mentor as they'd both risen in the company. She respected his many years as a manager and an executive. He had encouraged her and supported her when others, like Vince Demicci, had thought she didn't have the education or ability to handle an entire department. And Larry was the soul of discretion. He was the only one she could go to on this one. "Good morning, Larry. I'm sorry to call you first thing, but I've just heard a disturbing rumor and I was hoping you could dispel it before it spreads to the rest of the company."

There was a pause, and it was significant enough to make the muscles in her stomach tighten with apprehension.

"Don't tell me," Larry finally said. "Amalgamated Energy is buying us out."

"So you've heard it, too. It isn't true, is it?"

He answered her question with one of his own. "Have you looked at your morning mail yet?"

Julia glanced down to the pile in front of her. "No, not yet. Should I?"

"There's a confidential memo in a sealed envelope telling you about a meeting at ten o'clock for all administrative department heads. I think we'll get our answer there."

Julia found the envelope and ripped it open. Ten o'clock. In the CEO's conference room. Jesus! Something *big* was up. "What do you think, Larry?" she persisted. "Can this happen so quickly? Amalgamated already has most of the market. Isn't there something about anti-trust laws or monopolies?"

"Amalgamated has the best lawyers in the country. They're like Westinghouse or General Electric. They're so diversified, that lighting is only a small market for them now. We have a niche in that market and it's already developed. It has to have something to do with the Bradford filament. They either want to capitalize on it, or bury it so it doesn't put their own lighting division out of business. Rather than compete with us, they'll buy us out." There was a long pause before Larry expelled his breath in a rush. "I guess we'll find out at the meeting."

"God, Larry. What's this going to mean to us, to Coolback?"

"Depends on what Amalgamated wants to do. I would say that when and if a buyout occurs, some of us won't make it through the fallout. The work force in the factory is probably safe, especially if Amalgamated wants to use the new filament. Those of us in the Ivory Tower, however, may lose our heads when the henchmen come. At least some of us."

Julia was thinking about her job, her home, Paige's college tuition. "I think they're already here.

I'd heard they had arrived this weekend and were staying at the Embassy Suites for an indefinite period of time."

"Then hold onto your seat, Julia. It looks like we're in for a bumpy ride."

Knowing there wasn't anything more to discuss, she thanked Larry, told him she'd sit with him at the meeting, and hung up. She couldn't concentrate on her work. She kept looking at the clock on her desk, then at her wristwatch, dreading the meeting, yet wishing that time would pass more quickly so she could at least know for sure.

Wasn't it just Friday that she had thought her life was boring?

Val checked her makeup in the hall mirror, as she had always done before leaving, and smiled at her reflection. Even if no one but Julia could see her, Val was determined to keep up appearances. Habits were always hard for her to break. Like smoking. Why couldn't she just find a store, instead of waiting for Julia to come home from work? Then she could check out makeup and styles. It *had* been thirty years, and Julia desperately needed help.

When Val opened the door and attempted to leave, she was stopped, as if by an invisible wall that she couldn't penetrate. She pushed against it, but to no avail. What was wrong? She wasn't supposed to leave the house? But she had gone to the restaurant and watched Julia eat. She had appeared in the movie. Was it that she could only leave the house with Julia? Oh, no . . . how in heaven's name was she supposed get through the day stuck in this house?

Defeated, Val closed the door and turned back to the foyer. What could she do to pass the time until Julia came home? She walked into the living room and looked around. Television. She'd watch television and catch up on what's been happening in the world.

The screen came alive as a middle-aged man with white hair was running up an aisle into the audience and giving the microphone over. A young woman asked, "I'm just curious, are the two of you thinking about marriage?"

The camera then showed two men sitting in chairs on a stage. And they were holding hands! The dark-haired man answered with a grin, "Well, *I* want to get married, but David is still holding out. I guess he thinks Prince Charming is around the next corner."

Val gaped at the TV set. It couldn't be! Homosexuals were on television? Thirty years ago, they couldn't even hint at it on the movie screen. Where were the censors? Didn't they exist anymore? Fascinated, she sat back on the sofa and listened. What in the world would make people, real people, get up on a stage and reveal such personal things about themselves? Had they no self-respect? And then it came to her. They wanted attention and notoriety, and that was something she understood. It was something she herself had craved like a hungry child. But this? This was stripping naked before strangers, opening oneself up to ridicule. She may have led an unusual life, but she would never have answered questions about sex or her partners. Nor would anyone have had the audacity to ask. What had happened to privacy in the last thirty years? When the program was over, she glanced at the clock. Julia would be home in seven hours, and she'd ask her to explain.

The minute she walked into the conference room and saw him, she didn't like him. He reminded her of the character Michael Douglas had played in *Wall Street*—all spit and polish, the perfect haircut, the impeccably tailored suit, the calm assurance, the riveting eagle eye. The head henchman. She knew he could sense their confusion and fear and resented him for not breaking his chiseled expression. What would it cost him to smile and reassure them that they weren't about to be put into the street?

There were eleven of them, sitting nervously, waiting for the meeting to begin. Department heads from production to payroll were present, trying hard not to fidget, or to be caught in the direct gaze of Amalgamated's top assassin. Everyone was there, except Rob Otto, the comptroller. It wasn't reassuring that the numbers man, the financial brain at Coolback, was conspicuously missing. Julia looked at Larry, seated next to her, and forced a smile. She could see that he was attempting to play the corporate game of waiting, but she also knew that Larry was fifty-nine years old and, as in nature, these carnivores would go after the old and the vulnerable first.

Richard Massey, Coolback's President and CEO, strode into the room and smiled broadly at everyone. It should have been a good sign. It wasn't.

"I would like to thank everyone for rescheduling their day for this meeting. It's quite important." Massey took a deep breath, looked around the huge table, and then said, "Negotiations between Coolback and Amalgamated Energy have been taking place for the last month. I would like to announce that they have been successfully completed. Beginning immediately, Amalgamated Energy will be taking over the running of Coolback Lighting."

Gasps of shock came from those who hadn't heard the rumor. Questions were fired at Massey about job security, benefits, promised promotions.

The CEO held up his hand to stop the fire of demands. "Please, hold your questions until the end. This is a wonderful opportunity for us and for our stockholders, and now I'd like to introduce Steve McMillan. Steve is Amalgamated's senior vice president, and will be in charge of the transition."

She watched the man rise and walk with confidence toward the head of the table. He shook hands with Massey and smiled professionally as he turned to those seated in front of him. While remaining standing, he placed his palms on the table, as if taking ownership of it, and began speaking.

"I realize, for most of you, this is a shock. My job will be to make the transition as smooth and as painless as possible. Assisting me will be Mike Kerlocki and Garrett Morgenstern."

Each man nodded as McMillan called out their name.

"Garrett will assume the position of comptroller immediately, as Rob Otto has accepted an early buy out this weekend and is no longer with Coolback." He ignored the murmurs of discontent and, nodding to Mike Kerlocki who got up and turned off the lights, he continued. "If you'll bear with me, I'd like to introduce you to Amalgamated Energy and our long term objectives." With the grace of an actor, he moved to the side as the wall behind him became a screen on which slides and transparencies were shown.

"Coolback was a very desirous acquisition for Amalgamated," he began in a smooth baritone voice. "You have secured an impressive hold in a market that's already developed and have a loyal customer base. We were competing against you and, quite frankly, your aggressive advertising campaign made us sit up and take notice. When word came to us of your development of the Bradford Filament, we had some serious decisions to make. Do we continue to compete with you, and risk our own lighting division—the mother company that was the foundation for Amalgamated? Or do we join forces, since Coolback is already tooled up with a trained work force?" He paused for effect. "The decision was made to begin negotiations to acquire Coolback, a successful company, yes, but a one-product industry that might not continue to grow in the economic climate of the next ten years. Ladies and gentlemen, I'd like to present you Amalgamated's plans to take Coolback into the Twenty-first Century."

He was a polished showman, Julia thought as she listened to him talking numbers in domestic and foreign markets. Her heart sank as she studied the transparencies and heard Amalgamated's goals and objectives and their five-year company profile. She tore her gaze away from the screen and looked at the people seated around the table. They appeared shell-shocked. She wondered how many of them would survive the fallout.

Damn Amalgamated. And damn Steve McMillan and his smug assurance. He was talking numbers and percentages. She was the one that was going to have to deal with people's lives. She tuned the man out and remembered pulling into the parking lot less than two hours ago, glad to be away from the craziness at home. She had actually thought that here, at work, she could be safe and in control. What a laugh. Her life, it seemed, was completely out of her control. Sighing, she stole a glance at Larry. His expression was calm, but there was fear in his eyes, the same fear that she and every other person at the table was experiencing. Who was going to make the cut? And who was going to be cut loose? Rob Otto had only been the first.

Turning her attention back to the front of the room, she was startled to find McMillan staring at her as he spoke. Feeling guilty, as though she were a child in school that hadn't been paying attention,

Julia forced herself to meet his gaze. He's like a cobra, she thought, mesmerizing and just as deadly.

When the slide show was complete, McMillan handed out statements about the friendly takeover and transition that each were to read to their departments, in order to contain negative rumors that may be circulating. He told them that in the coming week he planned to meet with each of them personally and at that time there would be a departmental review. Thanking them in advance for their cooperation, he turned the meeting back over to Massey who tried to answer their many questions. In the end, they were left with no promises, only more questions, and everyone knew their job was on the line.

She and Larry walked back to their offices together. "I fastened my seat belt," she whispered. "I just didn't expect the Tilt-A-Wheel, ready to hurl me out into space. Who was he kidding? *'Ladies and gentlemen, here's our plan to take you into the 21st Century!'* The guy's a viper."

Larry kept his gaze straight ahead. "I'm not ready to pass judgment yet. McMillan has the power now; we'll just have to wait and see if he knows how to use it properly."

Julia was surprised. "Properly? He's Amalgamated's hatchet man. He takes orders and carries them out. He's completely void of emotion."

"No, he's not. He's just learned not to show it."

"I can't believe you're defending him."

Larry almost smiled. "I'm not defending him. I'm just saying that some of what he was saying made sense. Coolback *is* a one-product company and we should have been thinking long term. How long have I been trying to get Massey to penetrate the foreign market? With Amalgamated's resources it'll become a reality."

Julia reluctantly admitted Larry was right, but she still didn't change her mind about Steve McMillan. The man was a snake in the grass, waiting to strike, and she couldn't help but wonder who would be his next victim.

After she gathered her staff together, she passed out copies of McMillan's letter and tried to answer as many questions as possible. She realized everyone was upset and spent more time than she wanted attempting to reassure them. When she finally got back into her office, she closed the door and collapsed into her chair.

What a morning! What a life! If she could just run away somewhere, somewhere calm and peaceful, somewhere where there weren't any glamorous ghosts trying to rearrange her life or pompous corporate executives trying to rearrange her job. She needed a vacation, a—.

Suddenly she remembered that she hadn't called the DeMarcos about Paige's trip to Europe. Ripping off a piece of paper, she jotted down a reminder and was putting it in her purse when someone knocked on her door. She thought it was odd, since Meg always used the pager, but she called out, "Yes?" expecting to see her assistant's face looking in.

It wasn't Meg.

It was the snake. In her office. She felt like a cornered rabbit and forced her accelerated heartbeat to slow down.

"Am I disturbing you?" he asked, standing there looking like the cover of *Gentleman's Quarterly*. How she resented his perfection.

"No. I was just making a note to remind myself to call my daughter's roommate's parents," she said nervously, hating the reaction she had to him. Realizing that he was now her employer, she hurried to add, "They've invited my daughter to Europe this summer and I need to call them when I get home." Damn, she was rambling! What did he care about her problems? She just wanted him to know that she wasn't planning on calling during company hours. Why didn't she just say she wasn't busy. Period. What did he want? Was he going to fire her now? God . . .

"Europe?" He smiled and closed the door. Pulling out the chair opposite her desk, he sat down and asked, "Where in Europe?"

"Italy. Northern Italy, I think. I just heard about it this weekend and I have to call for all the details."

"It's a great opportunity for your daughter. How old is she?"

Why was he trying to be friendly? Why didn't he just say what was on his mind? "She's nineteen."

"In college?"

Julia nodded, not comfortable talking about Paige to this carnivore. "Ohio State."

"Good school."

"Thanks." What was with the small talk? Did she

have a job, or not? Determined not to crack, Julia waited for his next move. It was unexpected.

"I have a farm in the south of France. A small vineyard, actually." He looked out her window, as if daydreaming. "It's an enchanted place, quite beautiful, and I never spend enough time there."

She had no idea how to answer, or if one was expected. Instead, she said the first thing on her mind. "How fortunate for you. The furthest I've been from New Jersey is Florida. I took my daughter to Disney World seven years ago." As an after thought, she added, "Actually, it's an enchanted place, quite beautiful, and I didn't think we spent enough time there, either."

He stared at her and the corner of his mouth lifted, as if amused. "Touché, Ms. Edwards. I appreciate the irony."

She continued to return his gaze, even though her stomach was now churning. She should have been thinking of how to answer him. Instead, all she could picture was the Tilt-A-Wheel spinning and spinning her around, until she was dizzy and sick to her stomach. Convinced she was about to be hurled out of a job, she realized she hadn't fastened her seat belt for the crash landing.

"Can I help you, Mr. McMillan?" There. That was getting the conversation back on a professional level.

"Steve, please," he said, crossing his legs and sitting back in the chair. "I came to speak with you because I noticed your reaction in the meeting."

"My reaction?" she asked, sitting back in her

chair and crossing her hands in her lap. How she hated these power games men loved to play.

"You were observing the others at one point, and I need to know if I can depend on you during this transition. You and I will be working closely together for the next month or so, and I need a manager that can keep her emotions in check."

"Are you saying that my emotions were revealed in the meeting?"

"I thought you showed concern."

"As head of Human Resources, I am concerned. The bottom line for me isn't always the numbers or percentages. The bottom line is people. Their lives. Their health. Their futures. Amalgamated's takeover is going to be throwing people's lives into chaos. Do you realize that by now everyone in this company is worried about their future?" She didn't wait for an answer before continuing. "Yes, Mr. McMillan, I *am* concerned. And that's the reason I'm good at my job, whether it's hiring or firing, or personally driving someone to a detox center so they can dry out and try again. If you're asking whether I can do my job, the answer is yes. If you're asking whether giving the axe to people that I have worked with for years is going to bother me, then I have to be honest and say the answer is also yes. I'm a human being, Mr. McMillan, not a robot. If you want someone with ice water in their veins, then perhaps I should be the first to go." She raised her chin and smiled sadly. "But then Rob Otto was the first, wasn't he?"

His face showed no emotion. He could have been

listening to a production report. In the ensuing silence she realized that she had probably just shot herself in the foot. Her anger had overridden her common sense. She had answered honestly instead of judging her words. Part of her wanted to apologize because she had a daughter in college and she needed this job, yet another part of her felt alive for the first time since Paige left.

"You know," he finally said in a low voice, "when I accepted this position years ago, I knew I wasn't going to make friends. I realized that when I walked into a newly acquired company I wouldn't be liked. But you *really* don't like me. Do you? And I don't think it has anything to do with the takeover."

She stared at him, startled by his response to her outburst. His brown eyes pierced hers, as if demanding the truth. She broke his gaze, thinking he must one hell of a negotiator, and glanced at the perfect, razor-sharp pleat that fell from the bottom of his knee to the tip of his shoe. Slowly looking back up, she said, "I'm afraid I don't know what you mean."

He hesitated, for only a moment, and smiled politely. "Then I apologize, and I will repeat my original question. Can I depend on you during this transition?"

"Yes." Her response was immediate. At least she could try to protect those who were under question. Without her, who would fight for a fair severance package?

He considered her answer for a few seconds, nodded, and reached into his pocket for a piece of paper that was folded in half. Handing it to her, he said, "Good. Our first meeting will be tomorrow morning at nine-thirty. Please bring the personnel files on these people to the conference room." He straightened and added, "Thank you," before turning and walking out the door.

Julia looked down and slowly unfolded the paper. There were six names listed next to their positions in the company.

Larry Melbourne's name was third.

# Chapter 4

"Thank God, you're home!"

Julia closed the front door and clamped her eyes shut at the sound of Val's voice. She was still here, invading her life and her peace of mind. How could such a thing be possible? A ghost, a very real-looking ghost, was living with her? If such a thing had to happen, if someone up there had decided she needed celestial help, then why couldn't it have been a little less intimidating than a glamour queen? Sighing, Julia turned around and walked toward the kitchen. When she reached the entrance, she stopped and stared at the disaster in front of her. Pots were boiling over onto the stove. Dishes were thrown into the sink. An onion peel was on the floor and Val was standing by the counter with a towel in her hand, holding something gray and disgusting.

"What happened?" Julia whispered, suddenly drained of all energy. It had not been a good day.

"I'll tell you what's happened," Val said in a frustrated voice. "I tried to cook dinner and your—

your oven did this!" She stuck the platter out for Julia to see.

"What is it?" Julia asked, avoiding a closer look.

"It *was* steak." Val picked up a fork and tried to pierce the meat. "Now it's garbage. Petrified garbage. What's wrong with your broiler?"

"Nothing's wrong with my broiler," Julia answered and dropped her briefcase onto the kitchen table. "Tell me what you did."

Val put the plate on the counter and wiped her hands down the front of Julia's good Battenberg lace apron. Julia's teeth clenched at the streaks of brownish gray grease that now stained the expensive material. She had only used the apron on Christmas and Thanksgiving.

"I defrosted these steaks and put them in your broiler. I figured out how to use it and when it asked for the time I punched in fifteen minutes. It didn't look done. It wasn't even browned, so I punched in fifteen more minutes." She waved her hand dramatically toward the meat. *"This* is the result."

"Show me the broiler," Julia said, trying to be patient. Val walked over to the built-in oven and pointed to the rectangular box above it. "That isn't a broiler. It's a microwave. The broiler is inside the oven." And she opened it to show her.

"What's a microwave?" Val muttered.

Julia sighed and ran her fingers through her hair. She didn't need this, not after the day she'd had. "A microwave is . . . it's something that cooks certain kinds of food extremely fast. But not meat. It doesn't brown. I use it mostly for heating things up."

Val examined it more closely. "How fast?"

Julia thought for a moment, wondering how to make her understand. "Buck Rogers fast. Space-aged fast. A baked potato in six minutes."

"No!" Val stared at her in disbelief.

Julia nodded. "I'll show you tomorrow night. I'll cook dinner." Turning off the flames under the pots, she walked over to the kitchen table, kicked her heels into the corner, and sat down. "I've had a really bad day."

"You've had a bad day?" Val asked in a frustrated voice. "I can't leave this house. I tried, but something stops me." She sat opposite Julia and leaned her elbows on the table. "There are no bath oils in this place and I need Shalimar. And a good cream. Julia, I swear my skin is aging!" Rattled, Val waved toward the living room. "I watched TV and the Guiding Light is still on after thirty years! Then there're all these shows where people talk about their personal lives. It's embarrassing. And then I found out that Jack and Bobby Kennedy were murdered. That Elvis is dead and so is Bill Holden and Monty Cliff and Marilyn and I don't know how many others. You want to talk about a bad day? And what the hell is MTV? And rap? I feel like I've landed on another planet!"

Despite everything Julia burst out laughing. Shaking her head, she managed to say, "I'm sorry . . . sorry that so many people have died in the last thirty years. I'll go shopping tomorrow and get you bath oil and Shalimar. I should have recognized the scent. What else? Oh, yes, MTV. It's modern music combined with video. Paige was addicted to it. And rap . . . well, I guess the best way to describe it is urban poetry set to a beat. It takes some getting used to."

She looked at Val and smiled. "What do you say we just order pizza and clean this kitchen?"

Val smiled back. "It's been a while since I've cleaned a kitchen, but I suppose I can. And then we can start your lessons. I want to give you a facial and teach you how to care for your skin. But we're going to need a very good base to bring moisture back. You really should have been doing this for years. Now we can only hope to cover the damage—"

"Excuse me?" Julia interrupted. "Damage? Are you saying that my face is damaged?" How could this woman be so conceited?

Val evaded her direct gaze and looked out to the kitchen while shrugging. "Well, you have to admit that you don't take proper care of your face. You have . . . wrinkles. We're going to have to work to counter the years of neglect." She looked back at Julia. "I'll bet you've gone to bed some nights without removing your makeup."

Julia didn't answer her. In truth, she rarely performed any cleansing ritual before bed. Most nights she was too exhausted and could only think about sleep. "Okay, some nights I didn't."

"And frankly, Julia, you have the most unfeminine walk. You're always in such a hurry. I can give you few pointers in that area, too. You're never going to catch a man if you stride like that. You have to glide, very slowly—"

"I don't want to catch a man." Julia's smile had quickly disappeared. "I told you yesterday that a man isn't the answer to everything."

"Of course you want a man. You're just afraid because it's been so many years. But I'm here now. I'm an expert on men, and how to get them. If you don't like them, getting rid of them is your problem. I was never very good at that."

"You are absolutely amazing," Julia said very slowly.

Thinking it was a compliment, Val smiled. "Why, thank you. But you must remember I've had years of practice."

Julia tried to control her growing annoyance. It didn't work. "Geez! It's like you were thawed out of the Donna Reed Ice Age. Let me tell you for the last time—getting a man and then spending my time serving him and keeping him happy is not in my plans. Men! My God, they're at the root of every rotten thing that's ever happened to me."

Val raised her eyebrows in question, but Julia refused to elaborate.

"I think you've misunderstood me," Val said in a calm voice. "I wasn't talking about becoming a slave to a man. I never did that in my life. But I understood them and I used that knowledge to get what I wanted from them."

Julia stood up. "I don't want to talk about this anymore. Do you want anything on your pizza?"

"Plain cheese would be fine," Val answered as Julia picked up the phone and punched in numbers. When Julia finished ordering and replaced the receiver, Val continued the conversation as if it had never been interrupted. "Isn't there any man that you've been attracted to over the years?"

Julia pictured Steve McMillan and immediately banished him from her thoughts. "No. I've been too busy to think about men."

"Too busy? In what, twenty years? Come on, Julia. That's hard to believe."

Julia unbuttoned her jacket and slipped it off. Placing it on the back of a chair, she said, "Well, Val, here's the scoop on what life is like, in this time, for a single mother. First you wake up at six o'clock in the morning to get you and your child off for the day. Then you work for eight to ten hours, trying to juggle the job, your child, school, and babysitters. When she gets sick, everything's thrown into chaos. If the day goes without a hitch, then you pick up your kid at the babysitters and take care of dinner, homework, housework and laundry. By the time you bathe the child and put her to bed, it's nine o'clock and you collapse into bed only to wake up and do it all over again. Where in that day do you think a woman can find time to worry about her skin and moon over a man?"

Val listened without interruption. "But it's, I don't know, it's natural to think about men and companionship. And sex."

"It isn't sex that I think about after all these

years," Julia said as she dumped the steaks into the garbage container. "I don't miss it."

"Really?" Val's expression showed her shock. "I can't imagine."

"I'm sure you can't," Julia said with more than a hint of sarcasm. "Whereas your life centered around sexuality, mine has been devoid of it." She gestured to the stove. "Since you made this mess, I would appreciate some help."

Val stood up. "Are we having our first fight?" she asked, as she picked up a pot and dumped its contents into the garbage.

Julia sighed. "Look, you came into my life uninvited. I would like you to return to wherever you came from, but you say that's impossible. You can't leave until you complete your mission. Well, I didn't ask to be your mission. I didn't ask to have my life invaded."

"You're angry because I messed up your kitchen?"

"I'm not angry about the kitchen. Actually, it's kind of funny. It shows you aren't perfect."

"Then what is it?"

Julia turned on the hot water and squirted dish liquid into the pots. "I'm angry because I'm standing here talking to a ghost, and I know they don't exist. I'm angry because I'm questioning my sanity and my belief system. I'm angry because my daughter is going to Europe this summer and because my company has been gobbled up by a bigger one and the power-crazed henchman that arrived today is going to fire my friends, and possibly me." She slammed the hot water faucet into silence and gripped the edge of the sink. In a low voice, she admitted, "And I'm angry because you're making me think about issues that I had successfully put out of my mind." Shaking her head, she muttered, "Men and sex . . . I'm not very good at either one of them."

Val came up behind her and touched her shoulder. "But don't you see, Julia? I am." Val's laughter was almost shy. "I couldn't cook worth a damn. I couldn't clean a house properly. I couldn't hold down a job in the business world. But I understood men."

"You used them," Julia whispered, staring down at the soap bubbles. "You used them to get what you wanted."

"I used them as they used me. And in the end, everybody got what they wanted. So what's the name of the power-crazed henchman?"

Julia turned her head and laughed. "You really do have a one-track mind, don't you?"

Val smiled and ignored the remark. "His name?"

"Steve McMillan." Julia felt her stomach muscles tighten. Surely it was a mixture of hunger and dread. Tomorrow she had to face him with Larry's personnel file.

"Tell me about him. Is he married?"

"Who knows," Julia snapped. "Who cares?"

"Strong reaction," Val observed.

Julia was saved by the door bell, and the prompt arrival of the pizza.

\*  \*  \*

"I'm not doing this!" Julia insisted. "You nearly cracked my face with egg whites and oatmeal, and then scrubbed it raw. Now you want to teach me how to walk? Thank you, but I've been upright and walking for almost forty years."

Val sighed with impatience. "You walk like a man. You're too hurried and you swing your arms too much. Now look at me, and learn."

Julia watched as Val gracefully walked across the bedroom. The tight yellow dress clung to her hips, and her rear end slowly undulated beneath the material. "The only way I would walk like that was if I were standing in front of a casino in Atlantic City trying to earn a living."

"What's that supposed to mean?"

"It's too seductive. I can't walk like that."

"Yes, you can. Get up and try."

"I don't want to. People would think I've lost my mind. I didn't do that when I was twenty. Doing it at forty would look ridiculous."

"Julia . . ." Val's tone was threatening. "I'm not giving up tonight until you try."

Tired, and knowing Val meant it, Julia pulled herself off the bed and reluctantly stood at the doorway with her fist on her hip. "This is stupid."

Val waved her hands, as if she were an instructor at John Powers. "Head up. Chest out. Stomach in. And . . . glide."

Julia walked across the room and turned back to her tormenter. "Well?"

"You looked like Charlie Chaplin. Lose the over-exaggerated movements and do it again."

"I'm tired, Val. I just want to go to sleep."

"Then do it right, and you can."

Julia deeply inhaled, attempting to control her patience. Who would believe this? At forty years old, she was being taught to walk seductively by the ghost of a sex goddess? She was obviously having a nervous breakdown. No question this time. Suddenly, she thought of all the sorry people she had passed on the streets of big cities, the ones that seemed to be talking to themselves. Maybe they were talking to ghostly manipulators on a mission. She didn't need this in her life. Not now, not tonight. She should be preparing for her meeting with McMillan in the morning. She should be sleeping. Anything but *this!*

"Julia?"

"All right! One more time, but that's it." Taking a deep breath, she slowly walked back to the door.

"That was better and you didn't swing your arms as much."

Julia sighed with relief. "Great," she pronounced as she walked to her bed and threw back the comforter. "Now can I go to sleep?"

Val smiled. "Good night, Julia. Tomorrow morning I'm getting up with you and showing you how to apply makeup. You won't believe the difference it will make."

Julia stared at the closed door in terror.

\* \* \*

"I don't have time for this!" Her voice was a shriek of annoyance. "I have a very important meeting this morning and I can't be late."

"Then shut up and stop interrupting me," Val answered, as she applied blusher to Julia's cheeks. "It's really disgraceful how little makeup you own. I found most of this in Paige's room. Tonight, you simply must take me to a store. I'll make up a list."

"Anything," Julia promised. "Just let me get out of this house."

"In a minute," Val whispered, while critically surveying her work.

Looking up at Val, dressed in Paige's old robe and a blue scarf tied around her blond curls, Julia wondered if makeup really was magic. Without it, Val did seem older. There were lines in the corners of her eyes, lines she hadn't noticed before. And she seemed tired. Did ghosts get tired?

"All right. Finished. What do you think?" Val stood back and watched as Julia got up from the chair and looked into the bathroom mirror. "Well?"

Julia's lower jaw hung down in obvious shock.

"See the difference? Don't you look wonderful?"

A strangled sound came out of her mouth, and she cleared her throat before she could speak. "I . . . I . . . The difference is I now look like a hooker! I can't go to work like this!"

"Excuse me? A hooker? Are you saying I look like a whore because I wear makeup?"

Frantically grabbing a handful of tissues, Julia tried not to cry. "You can wear as much makeup as you want, but I don't. The people at work would think I've had a nervous breakdown if I walked in like this. That, or I'm going through a mid-life crisis. Maybe I am," she cried, clutching the tissues. "Maybe that's why this is happening to me!"

"You look pretty," Val insisted. "Glamorous."

"That's you, Val, not me. I'm not glamorous. I'm . . ."

"You're what?"

Julia bit the inside of her cheek to stop the rush of emotion. "I'm late," she said, and then wiped the cherry red lipstick from her mouth. The rest she'd have to fix at work.

As she ran out of the house, she heard Val reminding her that they were going shopping tonight. "I'm losing my mind," she muttered as she fumbled with the car key. "That woman is driving me crazy!"

Val wasn't sure if anyone else could see her reflection in the mirror, but she did . . . and something was wrong. Leaning closer to the glass, she brought her fingers up to her face and touched the lines at the corners of her eyes and mouth. They were more visible than before, deeper and defined. She looked as if she had aged ten years. Even though no one, except Julia, could see her, Val was filled with dread. This couldn't be happening to her. Not now! What kind of cruel joke was this, to die young and beautiful and then age in the afterlife? She didn't want to grow old and ugly. The thought terrified her.

* * *

She looked like a bad cliche. With her collar turned up and wearing sun glasses, Julia felt like a reject from spy school as she sneaked into work. Making it to the elevator, she felt she was almost safe. Almost. Vince Demicci hurried inside, just as the doors were closing.

" 'Morning, Julia."

Defeated, her shoulders sagged. "Good morning, Vince." She saw him looking at her, but kept her gaze directed on the closed doors.

"You look different."

Was it the tousled hair? An overabundance of blusher? The near hysteria that was bubbling at the surface? "Really?" Her tone was defensive, not exactly inviting a response.

"I don't know what it is," he mused.

"I'm sure I don't either."

There was a moment of silence before he cleared his throat. "Has McMillan descended on you yet? We figured personnel would be first."

"I have a meeting with him this morning," she answered, watching the numbers light on the panel above the door. One more and she'd escape.

"Has he made any decisions yet? Asked for any files?"

Too late. Knowing everyone wanted that information, Julia realized what an uncomfortable position she was in. Should her loyalty go to her friends, or her job? Since Vince never was a friend, she answered, "I'm sorry. I'm sure you realize that information is confidential." The doors opened and she smiled tightly. "Right now, your guess is as good as mine, Vince."

She walked through the offices, desperate to get to her own. Self-conscious, she believed everyone was looking at her and hurried past them.

At Meg's desk, she muttered a quick good morning and rushed into the safety of her own office. Ripping the sunglasses from her face, she threw them down on her desk and spun around at the sound of Meg's voice.

"Julia, are you okay? Hey—you look great! What did you do?"

Running her fingers through her hair, Julia tried to smile. "It's . . . so silly. A friend spent the night and this morning she insisted I needed a makeover. I don't know why I even allowed her to talk me into it, but I was running late, and . . ." She stopped rambling and asked, "Do you have a mirror, so I can fix this? I have a meeting in less than twenty minutes and—"

"No." Meg interrupted her while shaking her head. "You look terrific, maybe a little more lipstick. It's . . . I don't know. You look younger, healthier, more professional, more in charge. Don't take it off."

Julia stared at her. "Are you serious? I feel like a clown in the circus. This isn't me!"

Meg smiled and came closer. "You're just not used to it, that's all. Take my word for it—you look wonderful."

Julia didn't know what kind of judgment that

was, since she had thought that Meg overdid her own appearance. "I normally don't ask this of you, Meg, but would you get me a cup of coffee? I need to get my act together before my meeting with McMillan."

"No problem. Just sit down and relax. I'll be back in a minute."

Alone, Julia walked over to her chair and sank into it. She picked up the silver letter opener Paige had given her three years ago and held it up in front of her, seeing her reflection. Immediately she opened a drawer and brought out a comb. She pulled it through her hair, straightening it into her usual style. "This is stupid," she muttered, just as Josh Wilkins came into her office.

"Hey, Julia, glad you're here. I have two guys in production, Pouland and Young, who got into a fight on last night's shift."

She quickly threw the comb into the drawer and shut it. "Were they hurt?"

Wilkins shook his head. "From the supervisor's report, their egos were bruised more than their faces, but I have to fire them. Company policy. I fire them. The union demands a hearing and then we agree on suspension without pay. We all know how it works, but I still have to do the paperwork. I'm all out of WC42's. Do you have any, or should I ask someone else?"

Julia rose to get the necessary forms from her filing cabinet. Handing them over, she said, "As soon as you finish I can notify payroll."

Wilkins took the papers and stared at her, longer

than necessary. "You look really pretty this morning, Julia. Ah . . . thanks for the forms."

"You're welcome," she whispered to his back. Josh Wilkins was ten years younger than she and the company Don Juan. His exploits with the women at Coolback, especially the young and pretty ones, fueled the office grapevine. This was the first time since he'd started at Coolback that he'd said anything personal to her. What was it with this makeup? It seemed as though no one had ever noticed her before, and now . . .

"Here's your coffee," Meg announced as she hurried into Julia's office. "What else do you need for your meeting?"

"Thanks for the coffee, Meg, I just need a few minutes to get my thoughts together. Will you hold all calls?"

"Sure. No problem," she answered, and closed the door behind her.

Alone, Julia pulled the files from her drawer and looked at the names of the people she would be discussing with McMillan. How could she fight for these men, all in their fifties? Would anything she said be considered by a person like McMillan?

Sighing, she opened the first file and studied it.

Twenty minutes later she applied a light shade of lipstick, took a deep steadying breath, and left her office.

One way to control a snake was to mesmerize it. Another was to confront it. Since she had never mesmerized anyone in her entire life, she was prepared for a fight.

# Chapter 5

"I have the files you requested."

He seemed surprised as he looked up from the neat mounds of paperwork in front of him. Rising, a smile appeared at his lips. "Good morning, Julia," he said smoothly, walking around his desk and closing the door behind her. "Have a seat. Would you like a cup of coffee?"

"No, thank you. I've already had a cup." She wondered how anyone could look so perfect this early in the morning. It wasn't that he was exactly handsome. He was just so *perfect,* so impeccable, that it set her teeth grinding. His navy pinstriped suit, snowy white shirt and burgundy patterned tie was the perfect corporate image. He probably had all his suits custom made and hanging in a neat row, next to coordinating ties. Anal retentive, she decided. Cold and orderly. His emotions, if they existed, were always in control. Her exact opposite.

He sat down at his desk and nodded to the files that she was clutching to her stomach and reluctant to let go. "Of course," she finally muttered, handing them over. Sitting back, she straightened the skirt of her beige gabardine suit and forced her hands to relax as she folded them in her lap. "All of the men have been with Coolback for an average of fifteen years. Larry Melbourne has been with us for twenty-one. He was one of the first employees."

He again nodded and opened the first folder. Julia continued to sit with her hands folded, as if she were a child called into the principal's office, and watched him silently go over the contents. Leaving it open, he picked up the next. And then the next. She could feel perspiration starting in her armpits and at her shoulder blades. Soon a drop slowly ran down the center of her back and pooled at the waistband of her skirt. It took every bit of concentration that she could muster not to scratch at it. But—like the commercial said—never let them see you sweat. So she stared at the straight line of his nose. Tried to count the gray hairs at his temples. She decided he didn't look like Michael Douglas; more like an older Alec Baldwin, with that dark hair combed back and those intense brown eyes . . . eyes like a snake, she reminded herself.

He never said a word until he finished reading all of the files. Sitting back in his chair, he finally looked up at her and said in a solemn voice, "This is the hardest part of this job. But it's my job to make decisions. We're prepared to be generous, and—"

"You're *terminating* them?" Julia demanded, shock and anger racing together through her body.

"The official term is furloughing them," McMillan answered.

She sat up straighter, preparing for battle. "Excuse me, but I thought a furlough was time off, a sabbatical. Are you saying that you're going to bring them back to work at some future time?"

"No, I'm not. Would you be more happy if I said corporate downsizing? And we aren't speaking about all of them yet. Waller and Melbourne will be furloughed. I haven't decided about Demicci and the others."

She felt as if someone had punched her in the stomach. Swallowing back the emotion, she tried to speak in a steady voice, "Larry Melbourne has devoted almost half his life to this company. He has six years until retirement, and you won't find a more competent manager. He has the respect of the work force and his subordinates, and almost always meets his quota without going over his department's budget. I ask you to reconsider."

He steepled his long fingers together and brought them to his chin, as if thinking. "I'm sorry, Julia. I wasn't aware that Coolback's management had a union representative."

"Management doesn't have a union."

"It would be unusual if it did, yet that's exactly how you sound. I asked you yesterday if you would have a problem in this area and you assured me you wouldn't."

Now her own job was on the line. Deciding to be honest, she said quietly, "Larry Melbourne was my mentor. He took me under his wing and supported me. I will admit I'm having a hard time where he's concerned. It just doesn't seem fair."

Standing, McMillan took off his jacket and slipped it over the back of his chair. When seated, he crossed his arms at the edge of the desk and said, "Let me tell you my problem. Amalgamated has twenty-two thousand employees, and I've been handed a list from my superior to find jobs for sixteen of them. One is a thirty-three year old man. Married, with four children. He's proven himself a valuable asset to the company in production at our Virginia plant. But he's never going to go anywhere, or be promoted to where he can do the most good, because his boss is only four years older than him. So he's stuck in a job that isn't challenging anymore. Unless an act of God removes his superior, this man is either staying put or will look outside the company for another job. With the acquisition of Coolback, I was assigned to assess the management team and see where personnel can be realigned. Larry Melbourne is fifty-nine years old. He's done a good job and will be rewarded. That's my job, Julia. The decision has been made. Your job is to assist me during this difficult transition period."

She swallowed down the bitter taste of tears at the back of her throat and nodded. "And what would you like me to do, Mr. McMillan?"

He caught her gaze and held it. She refused to look away, knowing he was testing her. Any quick movements, even blinking her eyes, and he would sense her weakness and strike. Finally, he blinked and picked up a notebook and pen from his desk.

Handing them to her, he said, "I'd like you to take notes, and later you can prepare a detailed severance package that I can present to the men."

She opened the notebook and waited for him to begin.

"I know you're not a secretary, but I'll be using you as my assistant. I don't want word of this to get out through the grapevine until I speak with these men, so I'll ask you to personally type up the packages."

She knew he was right. Any secretary he used would have to tell someone, maybe even the men, and the resentment would spread through the company. "Fine."

"We'll start with Larry. Since he's been with the company for over twenty years, we'll give him one year's salary in a lump sum. Full medical benefits will be carried for one year, then he can switch to COBRA, and pay his own at the corporate rate. We'll also make a generous settlement of so much money for the number of years of service. I'll decide on the amount later. I see that he's contributed the maximum into his Savings and Investment Plan. The company will carry his 401K for two years and then roll it over into his own KEOGH. Make a special note to send him letters in fifteen months to establish one."

He went on, talking about retirement and medical benefits, and Julia thought that it was one hell of an attractive package. If Rob Otto's was similar, no wonder he'd packed up his calculator and gone on with his life. Amalgamated was certainly being generous. Quick mental arithmetic told her that Larry could walk away with two hundred thousand, maybe more. He might come out of this financially ahead of the game, but what would losing his job do to him psychologically? She couldn't think about that now. Now, like it or not, she had to do her job.

They spent the next two and a half hours putting together the severance packages and she developed an annoying headache. When McMillan started talking about the others on his list, going over the pros and cons, she felt her back teeth once more grinding. Would this meeting *never* end?

"Herb Grill . . . Looks like he's missed a lot of time at the beginning of the year."

She watched as he put Herb's file on the pile of those to be replaced. It was so simple for him. He was like some god with the power over lives. One person's life stays the same; another's is turned upside down, all by the direction of his hand. Something fragile inside of her seemed to strain, like a rope with too much tension. Before she could stop herself, she snapped.

"Look," she said in an angry voice. "If you had bothered to read his entire file, you would have seen that his wife died of cancer in March." The tears were back at her eyes, yet this time she didn't care. "How can you be so callous?" she nearly yelled. "The man's wife was dying of a hideous disease and because he took the time to comfort her, to be with her, like any decent human being, you're going to take away his job? Where is your compassion? Your own decency? He's just starting to make the adjust-

ment and come out of the depression, and if you do
this you'll throw him right back in. I don't know if
I can be a part of all this!"

Her hands were shaking so bad that she closed
the notebook and clutched it in her fingers. She was
scared. Something was happening to her. Dear
God, why was she doing this? Why was she so emotional? Maybe she really was cracking up. Everything in the last week was catching up to her.
Thinking of Val, she wondered how the glamour
queen who understood so much about men would
play this one. She'd probably bat her eyelashes and
pout her mouth, and become a weak, silly, emotional female while begging him to forgive her outburst. Julia knew she could never do it. That wasn't
her style. Hers was straightforward, no nonsense,
and keeping intact as much of her integrity as possible.

Straightening her shoulders, she tried to sniffle
back the tears and look at the surprised man across
from her. "Perhaps I should be on your list, Mr.
McMillan. I can't play with people's lives like this."

He closed Herb Grill's file with a quick snap of
his wrist and stood up. "All right. Time out. We're
taking an early lunch. Go get your purse and whatever else you need and meet me in the parking lot."

Shocked, she stared up at him as he pulled his
arms through the sleeves of his suit jacket. "I . . . I
don't think that's such a good idea," she managed
to say.

"Well, I do," he answered, clearly trying to keep
his anger under control. "As your superior, I'm

telling you that it would be in everyone's best interest for you to attend this business lunch. Now, if you'll excuse me, I'll see you in the parking lot in ten minutes." Without another word, he walked out and left her in his office.

Julia stared at the doorway for thirty seconds, trying to get her brain working again, and then walked out. She was immediately aware of faces turning in her direction as she passed. Did anyone overhear them? What would they think of her going to lunch with McMillan? Would she be considered a traitor, or a martyr? There were too many questions weaving in and out of her head, so she went to her office, grabbed her purse and two Tylenol, and told Meg she was taking an early lunch.

Was it only last week that she had thought her life was so predictable?

He should have fired her, he thought as he left the engine of the rental car running. Never, not in eleven years, had anyone challenged him like that. He was shocked by her emotional criticism. There were always bad feelings when he made changes in a company. He could sense it, see it on the faces of the employees, but most realized he was only doing a job and accepted his decisions. Julia Edwards not only challenged him, she didn't like him—and he'd only met her yesterday. Here was a person that he couldn't manage by the normal methods of corporate structure. And that bothered him, because he was a damn good manager. He'd built his reputation on it. He'd even been featured in *Money* magazine last year!

Eyeing the glass front doors, Steve blew his breath out in a frustrated rush as he waited for her. He knew what the problem was, at least on his part. She challenged his value system, and fissures of insecurity were cracking into the wall he'd built around himself. He didn't want to remember growing up in concrete and high-rises, fighting the subway, the bums, even his own parents to get an education. There were winners and there were losers. He didn't use alcohol like his parents, or drugs, to escape. He'd used education. And he wasn't going to allow anyone to make him feel guilty for being a winner. What he couldn't figure out was why he'd cut off the meeting with asking her to lunch, instead of firing her.

He told himself it was because they needed fresh air, a change of scenery, a place to calm down. He didn't like what she did to him. He was trained in rational thinking and making sound judgments. Somehow, now, eating lunch with Julia Edwards didn't seem rational.

He had sensed she was a challenge from the time their gazes had locked in the board room. Even before meeting her he had checked out her file over the weekend for, as personnel director, she was an integral part of the transition. His mind went over the facts. Single mother. A woman who rose through the ranks. Profit sharing. Homeowner. Daughter, Paige, in first year of college. This was supposed to be a stable woman, a woman who had conformed to the corporate structure, a woman who couldn't afford to put her job in jeopardy because of emotions. He had long ago realized that emotional things weren't really that important, and they weren't lasting. What lasted were tangibles, things that were built through his efforts, things that would remain after he had moved on.

When he saw her walk out of the building, he drove his car up to the entrance and reached across the seat to open the door for her. She looked nervous, yet he watched her straighten her shoulders and walk up to his car. That was it. That was what he liked about her. She was a fighter. And even though he might disagree with her principles, he had to admire her spirit.

After she closed the car door, she held her purse on her lap, as if for protection. Sensing her unease, he said casually, "Where should we go? I haven't checked out the restaurants in the area yet."

Shrugging her shoulders, she answered, "I don't know—what would you like to eat?"

He pulled out of the parking lot and onto the main street. "It doesn't matter. Just point me in the right direction."

"Make a right at the next light. There's a little cafe a few blocks down."

Grateful that the awkward silence was short-lived, he parked the car in front of the restaurant and got out. Before he walked around to her door, she had opened it and was standing on the sidewalk, waiting for him. For some reason, even that seemed like a challenge.

When they were seated at a small table in the corner, he was finally able to relax, to once more feel in control. They each ordered mineral water, soup and a salad. "Well, at least we agree on something," he said as the waiter left their table.

She almost smiled. "It's light, and I usually don't go to lunch this early."

He nodded, and watched as she looked around the nearly deserted restaurant. Deciding to get right to the issue, he asked, "You think I'm a real hard-ass, don't you?"

She seemed startled, but not offended. Recovering quickly, she answered, "I'd like to apologize for my outburst in your office. It was unprofessional, and I've worked too hard to be a professional, Mr. McMillan."

He nodded, noticing that she didn't say it wouldn't happen again. "It's over, but call me Steve. Mr. McMillan sounds like a high school science teacher. We're all in this together and we're all adults, Julia."

He stared at her, sensing the fight that was taking place in her mind. Finally, she seemed to come to some decision. Her smile was strained as she said, "All right, Steve. And, yes . . . I do think you're a hardass."

Laughter followed his startled three–second stare. "Okay. That's fair. You're entitled to your opinion, but I don't think you're looking at the big picture. Even if you discount the global economy, and add the Bradford filament, your stock was bound to go down in five years because you couldn't diversify. So does Coolback make a few changes now, or wait five years and then slowly go down the tubes? How many jobs would be lost then?"

She was saved from answering by the arrival of the soup. He watched her manners and saw they were impeccable and natural, as if she were born with them. He'd had to wait until high school and college to acquire them by watching those around him.

"Since you brought it up, what is Amalgamated planning to do with the Bradford filament?"

How had he walked into that one? Lightly touching the linen napkin to his mouth, he placed it back on his lap and said, "I really can't answer that. Production isn't my department."

Now she was staring at him, and he wasn't sure if he liked it. Finally, she said, "Are they going to keep it off the market?"

"I don't know, Julia."

She waited a few seconds. "Planned obsolescence . . . This country has developed tires that will never wear out for the life of the car. Batteries that won't die. And God knows what else, but they're kept off the market and away from consumers."

"To keep the economy strong," he countered. "To keep jobs for tens of thousands of workers. As I said, Julia, you have to look at the big picture."

"Gee, *Steve.*" and she emphasized his name, "are you being condescending to me because my world is so small? Remember, I've only been to Disney

World. Or could it be because I'm a woman, and I just can't understand the global economy?"

She ended her statement with a pretty good imitation of a wide-eyed innocent, batting eyelashes and all. Weird thing was, it actually turned him on. Not the batting eyelashes, the discovery that she wasn't afraid or intimidated by him any more.

Grinning, he said, "Very good, Julia. But you're wrong. I wasn't being condescending toward you. I happen to think that women make very good managers."

"Really?" She wore a look of disbelief.

Still smiling, he nodded. "Women have very distinctive managing styles, though different from men. Men will work out all the logistics of a situation and say okay, that's it. Let's move forward. Women will say all right, now let's find out what impact this will have on people. How are people going to react to it? How will they respond? How can we get people ready to implement it? They think the human process through, and then they modify the plan based on that."

The salads came and Julia didn't seem interested. He could see that, instead of food, she was digesting his last statement.

"Are you admitting that men are unemotional in the workplace?"

"I'm saying that men have a mechanistic view of the world—this is wrong. Let's fix it, and move on. Women understand the mechanistic, and the human side. They understand that human beings have to implement a great plan, so how can they get the humans to accept it? Men are more hostile to change. Somebody's got to be right. And somebody's got to be wrong. Men just don't want to be wrong."

"That's very honest of you," she said quietly, and they both started to eat their salads.

After half a minute, he wiped his mouth. "I just observed and learned. That's why you're a good manager, Julia. You really care about the people at Coolback. You just have to learn to accept decisions that come down from your superiors, especially now that Coolback's part of Amalgamated. Pick your wars and fight those that you have a chance at winning. This war's over. The treaty has been signed, and now it's up to people like me, the negotiators, to divide up the spoils."

Their gazes locked. Hers was filled with fire and challenge. "And can we expect the conqueror to have compassion?"

He knew exactly what she was talking about and gave her the answer she wanted. "I'll take another look at Herb Grill."

"Thank you." Her voice was low, almost a whisper. Finally backing down, she lowered her gaze and concentrated on her salad.

Satisfied, Steve speared the romaine with his fork, knowing that if they weren't quite friends, at least they had a better understanding of each other.

It was a beginning.

* * *

"I do not believe civilization has gone to ruin like this!"

Julia had to bite the inside of her cheek not to laugh at Val's shocked expression as she stared into the crowd milling about the Cherry Hill Mall.

"Look! Just look at that kid!" Val exclaimed while pointing to a teenager who had chosen to express his independence by shaving off his hair, all except a small portion over his left ear that was gathered into a long ponytail. "And that one—he's got an earring. And one in his nose! So does that girl. And you thought *I* dressed like a street walker? Look at it, Julia. It looks like the set from a horror movie where everyone has gone crazy. Can you believe all this?"

"Yes," she whispered out of the corner of her mouth. "Don't ask me questions I can't answer right now. I know it's confusing. Just wait until later. C'mon."

"But they look like they're from a different country. Hell, a different planet! What's happened to the kids today? We had a few beatniks in Hollywood, smoking reefer and reciting poetry no one understood, but this! This is madness! What the hell happened?"

"Calm down. It's called history and I'll try and explain it when we're alone. Right now, to everyone else, I look like I'm talking to myself. Let's get on with it. And no more questions."

Tired, she led Val into Macy's.

Val immediately rushed up to the perfume

counter and started spraying expensive scents. "Shalimar! I have to find Shalimar!"

"All right, all right!" Julia muttered, while frantically searching for the Guerlain perfume. While she was paying for it, Val wandered off and it was only when the saleswoman was handing back her charge card that Julia noticed her unwelcome house guest trying on a large picture hat.

Rushing over to Val, she snatched a deep green creation off Val's head. "Don't do that," she reprimanded, feeling like the parent of a hyperactive kid, as she placed the hat back on its pedestal. "No one can see you. They will only see hats hovering in the air."

Julia noticed one older woman staring at her with a confused expression. Julia smiled politely, but the woman seemed worried as she removed her glasses to clean them on her chiffon scarf.

"Oh, Julia, please . . . Let me try on something. I've been in this dress for . . . it feels like forever. A dress. One dress. Please?"

Worn out from the stressful day at work, Julia sighed and fought for some patience. "One dress," she whispered. "And that's it."

Like a child let loose in a candy shop, Val ran through the departments while trying to make her choice. Julia didn't attempt to keep up with her, but merely hugged the small shopping bag with the perfume to her waist as she waited.

Finally, she heard Val's shriek of pleasure as she called out to her. Walking into the exclusive department, Julia should have known that Val's choice wouldn't be off the rack. She'd selected an Ungaro gown of black jersey with a halter top, clinging bodice and a graceful flare below the knee.

"Isn't it beautiful?" Val asked, while lovingly touching the material. "Simple and seductive."

Julia nodded, knowing that she could never wear a dress like that. You had to have the right body—the right breasts, to be more accurate. And Julia felt almost adolescent next to the voluptuous figure standing beside her. "It's lovely," she murmured.

"Why do they have these wires threaded through them?"

"So no one will steal them. Look at the price tag. They're expensive."

"But they're locked. This is so . . . I don't know, drastic, isn't it? How do I try it on, if they're locked together?"

"May I help you?"

Julia turned toward the saleswoman who was assessing her good suit and, apparently, finding it lacking. "Ah . . . yes, I'd like to try this on."

"Of course, what size?" the woman asked, as she fished around in her skirt pocket for keys.

Julia looked at Val.

"Twelve."

"Twelve," Julia said to the sales clerk.

The woman stared at her. "Really? I would have thought an eight, maybe a ten."

"I, ah . . . I like it big."

"But this style should be worn close to the body and—"

"That's all right, I like loose clothing."

The woman seemed annoyed, as though she knew fashion and Julia was a borderline idiot for arguing with her.

"Twit," Val proclaimed, giving the woman a withering, superior glare. "Ask her if she realizes she's wearing lumber jack boots with that outfit."

Julia had to smile at Val's comment. She'd have to tell her about the current fashion of coupling feminine attire with masculine boots. Surely, that would confirm her fear of landing on another planet.

The clerk unlocked one of two dressing rooms, hung the gown on the hook and then walked out. Seeing that the woman was waiting for Julia to enter, Val stepped inside and said, "Well, do come in, Julia, or she'll never leave."

Feeling awkward, Julia walked into the dressing room and the clerk shut the door behind her. She saw an upholstered stool in the corner of the large room, but wasn't sure what to do. "I can wait outside," Julia whispered.

"I beg your pardon . . . I didn't catch that."

Julia snapped her head toward the voice on the other side of the door as Val pointed to the stool.

"Oh, for God's sake, sit down."

Julia rushed over to it and obeyed, clutching the shopping bag to her stomach. "No, nothing! I'm fine, thank you." She hoped the clerk would just leave them alone.

"I'm certainly not shy," Val said with a laugh as she kicked off her heels. "Geez, I remember sitting in Jack Dawn's chair for over two hours at Metro, while the entire makeup department went over every inch of my face with a magnifying glass. They criticized everything and talked like I wasn't even in the room. 'The nose is narrow. We'll have to use dark on her.' '' The zipper came down on Val's dress.

"The eyes are sunken. White under them." The dress fell to a puddle at her feet.

"Lips are too large. Bring 'em down with liner." A wispy half-slip followed the dress.

She had her hands on the clasp at the back of her bra when she said, "And that was just the face. Between makeup and wardrobe, I've had more people examine my body than King Tut's. Modesty is not one of my virtues."

And, following a snap, she slipped her bra down her arms. Hanging it on a hook, she started to unbutton the gown.

Julia tried to swallow down her embarrassment and immediately looked to the thick rug beneath her feet as she brought the shopping bag higher to cover her own chest. Valentina Manchester was standing practically nude in front of her! This body that men had fantasized about for decades was displayed without any sign of modesty. But the image of Val had been imprinted on her mind before her own embarrassment had kicked in. Val was lush. Ripe. Fertile. Her body was round, soft and womanly. Almost plump. She thought of the firmly muscled models and the skinny waifs that were the current rage, and wondered why women were always trying to resculpture their bodies. Who were they doing it for? Was it for men or, like mindless sheep, were they being led to the slaughter of self-esteem by the advertising gods? It really didn't matter, since Julia could never hope to be either lush or sculpted. For the first time in years, she felt inadequate. It had been many years since she had compared her body to another's, having long ago pulled herself out of that loop. Not having dated since forever, she thought she was over such competitive feelings.

"Oh, look at this." Val breathed a sigh of pleasure as she buttoned the halter behind her neck and then ran her fingers over the soft jersey material.

Julia looked up and her breath caught at the back of her throat. Val looked magnificent. She possessed a quality of glamour and sexuality that today's movie stars seemed to lack.

"You . . . you're beautiful," Julia whispered in awe.

Val smiled. "Thanks," she whispered back and stepped closer to the mirror. She wasn't looking at the dress. She was staring at her face, smoothing the fine lines at the corners of her mouth. Quickly, as if she had seen something troubling, she unbuttoned the dress and stepped out of it.

Handing the designer gown to Julia, she said, "Thanks for letting me try it on. Here's the hanger. Didn't we come into this place for makeup?"

Julia took the dress and hanger and opened the door. "That's right. I'll give this back to the sales clerk and wait for you outside."

"Okay," Val answered, already back into her bra. "I'll be out soon."

Just before she turned around, Julia saw Val stare at her reflection in the mirror. The painful expression was too private, too intimate, and Julia hurried out of the dressing room.

Ten minutes later, Julia led a subdued Val through the store and up to the Lancôme counter. "Okay," she whispered when she thought no one was looking. "As we say in this time, do your thing."

"I'm in heaven," Val breathed, taking in the seductive displays and the exotic colors reflected in the samples of lipsticks, blushers, pencils and creams. For an ex-Miss Tuna Fillet, it was a beauty queen's Valhalla. "Where do I start? I need this and this and . . ."

By the time Val was finished or, more accurately, by the time Julia put a stop to Val's purchases, they had spent over two hundred and eighty-seven dollars. Even though Julia was happy to see Val's mood change, she still cringed as she handed over her Visa card. Beauty, at least Val's version of it, sure as hell didn't come cheap.

"Julia, I don't understand," Val said as they drove home in the dark. "Why did that twit think a size twelve was large? *I'm* not large."

"Oh, Val, it's too hard to explain."

"Try."

Sighing, Julia passed a van. "Every couple of years the ideal body shape of a woman changes. This year, it's supposed to resemble a fifteen-year-old girl, with no breasts or hips. It's called the waif look. A few months ago, Paige told me that one of the top models was a girl still in high school."

"That's crazy," Val pronounced.

Julia agreed. "Of course it is."

"Then why do women put up with it?"

Julia shrugged. "Why did women put up with trying to look like you thirty years ago? It's the same thing now, except in reverse. Women are constantly trying to conform to an ideal that's impossible to meet. Only I guess it's more dangerous now."

"What do you mean?"

Stopping for a red light, Julia glanced at her passenger. At least at night no one else could see her talking out loud. "A couple of years ago, when Paige was a junior in high school, I started to notice that she was skipping meals. After a few confrontations with me, she would eat dinner and then immediately go into the bathroom. It didn't take me long to catch on that she was throwing up."

"Why? Why in the world would she do that?"

"So she wouldn't gain weight." The light changed and Julia pressed her foot down on the accelerator with more force than usual. "She's fine now, but it still makes me angry. My daughter had a beautiful, normal figure. She wasn't overweight. But all the fashion magazines, all the commercials on television, showed a standard of beauty that rarely exists in real life. I got scared and I called our family doctor. He put me in contact with some people and I did a little research on my own. What I found out made me really angry."

"What was it?" Val's voice was hesitant, as if she were afraid of the answer.

"That the average American female has low self-esteem. It doesn't matter if she's twelve or fifty. She always feels like she can't measure up to what she's seeing in the media. Women spend fifty *billion* dollars a year on diet and cosmetics. It's a major industry in this country. If you look in a fashion magazine, the majority of the ads are for products that promise they'll make you look thinner or younger or prettier."

Julia looked for her turnoff before continuing. As the anger built inside of her, she felt a tightness in her chest. "Women are being manipulated, and it's all about money. To keep this fifty billion dollar industry going they must convince us through ads, models, and attitudes, that we must fight aging or weight gain and buy their product. So we continue to buy the magazines, see pictures of models that are enhanced through computers to make cheekbones higher, waists thinner, legs longer, and go out and buy the products so we can strive to look like something that isn't even real anymore. It's crazy. Even fashion magazines aimed at a more mature woman admit they air brush out the wrinkles on their models."

From the corner of her eye, she saw Val cringe and reach up to touch the tiny lines in her own face.

"What's worse is that men now expect the same thing, and it's an impossible goal. We are going to age, just like men, and our bodies are going to change. What's so harmful is that we don't look at a women and see her worth in society. First, we see whether she's thin and pretty. It's a shame, but that's what's valued in this country."

"You sound so angry," Val whispered. "It's just lipstick and cream."

"I guess I am angry, but not at lipstick and cream. I'm angry that millions of women, and men, have bought into the myth and have a distorted sense of what a female should look like. I'm angry because the new waif models look like they were in concentration camps, and young women are thinking that they weighed more than that at thirteen, so they engage in dangerous dieting. I'm angry because women are making rich the very individuals that are making their lives miserable. And I'm angry because I saw the pain you experienced in that dressing room when you saw the wrinkles on your face. It's so wrong. It isn't that we're grieving the loss of our youth. That's a normal process. We're grieving the loss of youthful beauty. And that's sad, and dangerous."

"So you're saying that I've contributed to this, and now you think I'm vain because of what you believe you saw in the dressing room."

Julia weighed her response. "I think you're scared, Val, because if your beauty fades you're not sure what you'll be left with. I don't think you ever got the chance to know yourself."

"That's ridiculous!" Val's voice was defensive. "I knew exactly who I was."

Julia shrugged. "If you say so." Neither of them spoke for some time. Julia figured Val was angry with her and she supposed she should apologize. She did sort of go off on a tirade, never giving Val a chance to get a word in edgewise about the subject. It was just that she was so angry about what had almost happened to her daughter and—

"I think I'm getting older here in this time," Val murmured, her voice low and thick with emotion. "Every day I can see it getting worse."

The pain in Val's voice was so raw that Julia reached across the seat and grabbed her hand. Squeezing it tight, she whispered, "I know how hard that must be for you, but maybe, it's a chance, a gift of time, so you can discover something important about yourself."

"If I have to find out like this, I don't want to know."

Julia smiled sadly. "Maybe it's something you have to know."

Val tightened her hold on Julia's fingers before slowly letting go. "Is all that, about Paige and your research, what made you so tough, so angry?"

"Is that how you see me?" Julia asked, as they turned onto her street. "Angry and tough?"

"Sometimes. Especially when I try and help you."

"I'm sorry for that. I guess, since Paige, I don't have much patience with the other side of the argument."

"And I'll bet you're angry that we spent so much on cosmetics tonight."

Julia grinned as she drove into her driveway. "Just don't expect me to wear it."

"Not all of it," Val answered. "I'll bet you got compliments this morning when you went to work." When Julia didn't reply, Val prodded, "Am I right? You did, didn't you?"

Turning off the car, Julia reluctantly said, "Yes, Val. I did."

"Hah! I knew I was right. See, Julia, you have to give a little. Some things are just too big to fight."

Didn't Steve McMillan say almost the same thing to her at lunch? Trying to regain some ground, Julia opened the car door and answered, "I don't want to wipe out makeup, Val. I'd look pretty sorry without it. I just wish we'd learn moderation, to think for ourselves. I wish women would say, *That's enough.* I am who I am, and I don't have to accept what advertising says I should look like, just so someone else can make a buck. I should say make a billion, because that's what they're doing. Fifty times that. And those figures don't include the fashion industry."

"You sound so angry, Julia. What's wrong with looking pretty?"

Julia smiled. "Nothing would be wrong with it, except seventy-five percent of all women don't like the way they look. That's self-hate, Val—the death of self-esteem."

Later that night, as Julia passed the hall bathroom on her way to bed, she saw Val through the crack in the door. Val was standing in front of the mirror, desperately rubbing the expensive anti-aging cream onto her face, over and over and over again. It made no sense. How could a woman that was dead, a ghost, think some fake cream was going to work?

Vanity . . . the price was frightening.

# Chapter 6

Larry Melbourne said his goodbyes like a gentleman. He understood the corporate structure, took his early retirement and trained his replacement. He also looked like he had aged five years in the last few weeks. Steve wondered why this termination was any different from the hundreds he had settled in the past, and why it was bothering him. Perhaps in Larry he had recognized himself, someone who was consumed with work. When work is the driving force in one's life, the reason to get up in the morning and get dressed, what happens when it's taken away? Steve couldn't imagine waking up jobless, without direction, because always lurking in the dark corners of his mind was his fear of failure, of winding up like his parents. Dead before sixty and with nothing to show that they ever existed on Planet Earth. He would do just about anything to avoid that, working harder, longer, covering all the bases. He remembered his professor in first year law telling him that the best protection against failure is preparation. But how could you protect yourself against getting older?

"Can I get you another?"

Steve looked up and nodded to the bartender. And this . . . stopping at a bar after work. It wasn't like him. He rarely drank anything but wine. Three scotches, and he was still depressed. It was Julia's fault. He had never questioned his judgment until she'd stood up to him and had forced him to take a look at the human side. But he had offered Larry a good package, and the man had understood the decision to bring in someone younger. If he had done his job, and had made the right decision, than why the hell was he feeling this depressed?

The bartender placed his scotch and soda in front of him and slipped a ten dollar bill off the pile of money on the bar. Steve picked up the glass and took a sip, trying not to wince as the strong alcohol slid down his throat. It was Julia's fault, he reasoned. She was the one that came into his life three weeks ago and started trouble by questioning his value system. And why should he care what Julia Edwards thought? She certainly wasn't his type, so he wasn't interested in her that way. Maybe it was because she was a good manager, and she wasn't afraid to speak her mind. He respected her. She had made her way alone, without help, without college, along with being a single parent and raising a daughter all those years. He wondered if she dated.

Now where did *that* come from?

It must be the scotch. Why should he care one way or the other? Julia Edwards was not the kind of

woman he could get involved with. He liked them
. . . How the hell did he like them? Intelligent. Julia
was intelligent. Funny. She had certainly sent her
piercing wit in his direction more than once. Pretty.
When he had first seen Julia he had thought she was
kind of plain, but in the last three weeks she had
sort of blossomed into one hell of an attractive
woman. She had intense eyes that couldn't disguise
how she was feeling, whether it was amusement,
anger or admiration. The admiration had been directed toward others, particularly Larry Melbourne, but not himself. He had been the recipient
of her anger, and her amusement. The anger he
understood, but not the amusement. What did she
find so damn amusing about him? That's what
bothered him about her. It was as if she knew some
secret about life that he hadn't even glimpsed yet—
that mystical aura some women had around them
that said they knew the secret and men were just
spinning their wheels trying to gain power and control. What did she know about life, a woman that
hadn't been further away from her home than Disney World? And he liked them tall, anyway. Julia
Edwards was short and skinny, and her utilitarian
clothes seemed like they were still on the hanger,
without any indication of what was underneath. No
panache.

He looked to his side and saw a well-dressed
woman sitting three bar stools away. Now that was
his type. Tall. Blond. Sophisticated. How long was
it since he'd been with a woman? He stared into his
drink, trying to remember. A couple of months, at

least. It was before he'd left New York and had come to Coolback. Right. The lovely Lorraine, an art dealer in the city. Maybe he should call her and drive up this weekend. He mentally shook his head. It had been too long, and she'd be ticked off about not hearing from him since he'd left her bed.

Suddenly he knew he shouldn't have dragged up memories, especially that one. Something had happened to him that night. After dinner, they had gone back to her apartment and had made love. Sex was a release for him, like exercise, and he gave it the same amount of attention as anything else of importance in his life. Some people coped with the stress of being successful by drinking or doing drugs. He preferred a healthier outlet. But that night, afterwards, instead of feeling a normal release, he had felt empty and hollow inside. He remembered wondering how long he had to stay in bed without insulting Lorraine, because all he'd wanted to do was jump up, get dressed and get the hell out of there. For the first time he felt something was missing, and he couldn't figure out what it was, so he'd dismissed it. Until tonight.

Determined to put negative thoughts out of his mind, he again looked to the woman on his right. She turned her head and smiled at him. Perfect teeth. Perfect smile. Perfect complexion . . . So why was he thinking about the faded freckles sprinkled across Julia Edward's nose and cheeks?

Damn, he must be getting drunk!

* * *

"I can't believe you actually did this! It's torture!"

"Oh, shut up, and stop complaining," Val ordered as she applied the last of the mud pack to Julia's chin. "If you keep talking, you'll ruin it and we'll only have to start again. Just relax and enjoy it. People pay a lot of money to have this done." She stood back and examined her work. Grinning, she said, "I know some people that would pay a small fortune to have me do this to them." She shrugged and added, "Of course, most of them are dead. Anyway, it'll clean out your pores, tighten them up, and fade those freckles. I thought most women outgrew them."

"I like my freckles," Julia muttered, trying not to disturb the quick-setting mud. God knows, she wasn't about to go through this again. "How long?"

"I told you. Twenty minutes. Starting now."

Julia sat on the toilet seat and watched as Val opened the bathroom window. Reaching into the pocket of her robe, she withdrew her pack of cigarettes.

"Don't start," she said, as she lit one and stood with her elbow resting on the window sill. "I'll blow the smoke outside. You know, this reminds me of the makeup department at Metro. Bebe Wakefield always had the best gossip. That's where I first learned about Rosebud."

"Rosebud?" Julia mumbled.

"Don't talk," Val ordered. "Yes. Rosebud. You know, from Citizen Kane. You did see it, didn't you?"

Julia merely nodded, not wanting to risk another scolding.

Val deeply inhaled. "Well, you know it's based on William Randolph Hearst's life?"

Again Julia nodded as Val exhaled out the window.

"That was before my time in Hollywood, but everyone knew of his affair with Marion Davies. They weren't exactly discreet, were they? God, I can still picture Bebe telling me . . . Anyway, Willie and Marion met at the Follies when she was sweet sixteen and he was almost sixty. The little innocent and Daddy Warbucks made quite a pair up at San Simeon, but one house guest, Herman Mankiewicz, loved to tell tales out of school. Especially to his friend, a radio man named Orson Welles. Get this—Hearst's pet name for his little girl's . . . ah . . . love bump, you know, *the* hot spot for a woman, was none other than Rosebud. Kinda graphic, huh?"

Julia sat on the toilet seat and attempted to open her mouth. The mud had hardened, yet she tried to move her lips. "Rosebud wasn't a sleigh?" she managed to get out in disbelief. "It was Marion Davies' clitoris?"

Val stopped laughing and said, "Well, I don't know what that is, but if it's what I think, then yes. That's what old Willie called it. Half of Hollywood was scratching their heads, trying to figure out the end of the movie and its significance, and the other half was laughing at that old fart, Charlie Kane, dying with Rosebud on his lips." She giggled again and took a drag on her cigarette. "For that reason, and the fact that Mankiewicz and Welles got away with it without Hearst killing them, I consider that scene one of cinema's greatest moments. No wonder Welles was banned from the studios."

*Rosebud, rosebud* . . . Picturing the final scene of Citizen Kane in her mind, Julia giggled. Who'd believe it? She hated to admit it herself, how fascinated she was with insider's gossip about the famous.

Julia felt the mud crack around her lips, but saw Val grin at her muffled giggle.

"You liked that one? Okay, don't smile anymore or you'll ruin the mudpack."

Somehow that admonishment made her want to laugh all the more. It was like being in church and forbidden any outlet.

"I'll tell you another while you're sitting there. We've got fifteen minutes. You may not believe this, Julia, but I've never really had a girlfriend before. I know I've never spent this much time alone with a female. We are getting on much better, don't you think?"

Julia nodded. Why remind Val of all the arguments about clothes, makeup, hair, politics, religion . . . the list was endless. If you hadn't lived through the last thirty years, how could you expect to understand it? Val came from a time when you either looked like Val, beautiful and glamorous, or Aunt Bea in Mayberry. All those women in between didn't have a voice. Feeling the mud pulling at her skin, Julia figured it must have been a heck of a lot easier to be Aunt Bea—normal, natural, and respected.

"Okay, how about this one? I heard it from Joey Abrams at Fox. It's about Loretta Young. Her real name's Gretchen, so she was called Gretch the Wretch, The Steel Butterfly or The Manipulator behind her back. I never met her personally. Can you imagine Saint Loretta and me in the same room?" Val laughed. "Anyway, I heard enough stories about her holier-than-thou attitude to stay clear of the woman. I guess that's why she was so disliked. It isn't as if her own past was pure as the driven snow, although that's the image she sought. Joey was friends with a guy named Wellman, who had directed Loretta Young and Clark Gable in a movie called *Call of the Wild* in '35. He said that the romance between them was so intense it interfered with his production schedule. Everyone thought the affair would end in marriage but it didn't happen. Then the gossip columns reported that Fox was retiring Miss Young for one year citing health problems. Two years later, in 1937, still unmarried, she adopts a two-year-old girl, born a few months after production ended and when she was on her leave. There was a great deal of speculation, especially since California had laws prohibiting adoption by a single person. Wellman could only say that when the film was finished she disappeared for a while and later showed up with a daughter with the biggest ears he ever saw, except on an elephant. Everyone knew Loretta saw to it that the child had surgery to flatten her ears. I saw the daughter once, very pretty, with a remarkable resemblance to her adopted mother."

Val sighed and stared out the window into the night. "All that cover up. It wouldn't be like that today, would it? I saw on television that having a child out of wedlock is now almost accepted. Strange, isn't it? Sixty years ago a woman went into hiding. Now she appears on TV and tells everyone."

Julia wasn't really listening. Did Loretta Young and Clark Gable have a love child? Loretta Young? Julia remembered the woman as being a devout Catholic, almost zealous. She had a swear box on the set of her TV series and holy water fonts at the doors of her home. She even wrote a column for the lovelorn in a Catholic newspaper that Julia had been forced to read in high school. Maybe it just showed that famous or not, she was only human. After listening to Val's stories, Julia wondered why the public placed actors on such high pedestals. Was it because we had no real heroes anymore, so our role models were movie stars and athletes?

"Who's this?" Val asked, sticking her head out the window as she exhaled smoke into the night air. "Somebody's driving up to the house."

"Huh?" Julia was brought back to reality. Who would be coming to her house at nine o'clock at night? A mother's instinct kicked in. Paige. Something might have happened to Paige! Jumping up from the toilet, she ran down the hall and took the stairs two at a time with Val calling out to her. The doorbell had barely rung when Julia flung it open, half expecting to see a policeman standing on her front porch.

"Julia? Is that you?"

"Ohmygod!" A large chunk of mud cracked off her chin and fell to the foyer floor as Julia stared at Steve McMillan's shocked expression.

"Well, well, well . . . and who is this gorgeous man?" Val's grin widened with mischief as she leaned against the door.

"Steve McMillan," Julia muttered, bending down to pick up the dried mud.

"Yes," he answered, as if she had spoken to him. "Well, it seems I've come at a bad time."

"This is the guy from work? The vampire who sucks out all enthusiasm?" Val asked in a surprised voice. "I do believe I should have worn something strapless to expose my neck."

"Oh shut up," Julia muttered as she stood up.

"I'm sorry? Maybe I should leave." Confused, Steve's hands were jammed into the pockets of his jacket as he watched her rise. "Obviously, this isn't a good time."

"No, I didn't mean you." Julia mumbled. Again, more mud hit the floor as she spoke. "Please, come in. I . . . I'll be right back." Without waiting for an answer, she ran for the stairs.

Within moments Val was at her side in the bathroom as she started to frantically pick the mud from her face.

"Don't do that. You have to wash it off with warm water."

Julia turned on the faucets and stared into the mirror at the frightening reflection. "I can't believe this! Look at me! *Look!*"

"I tried to stop you, but you wouldn't listen."

"I thought it was about Paige. I was scared. God, now what? How can I go back down there?" Testing the water, she decided it was warm enough and began scrubbing her face with a washcloth.

"It's kind of funny, Julia, when you think about it. I mean here you are so opposed to cosmetics and when Mr. Perfect knocks on your door you're—"

"I am not opposed to cosmetics," Julia interrupted in an angry voice, as she scrubbed away at the thick mud. "And he is not Mr. Perfect, not by a long shot. I'm just embarrassed. I'm beyond embarrassed. Humiliated is more like it. What does he want? Why is he here? Why tonight, when I look like *this?* My God, this stuff has turned into plaster!"

"Just keep putting water on it, and don't scrub so hard. I'll go find you something to wear."

Julia was about to tell her that she didn't need new clothes when she looked at herself in the mirror. She was wearing gray sweats, and the top was now stained with mud. She almost started to cry. How could this happen? Why did it happen? Watching rivulets of mud slide down her cheek, she quickly leaned back over the sink and continued scrubbing.

"You still have some mud on your face, around your hairline," Val advised as Julia hurried into the bedroom. Julia swiped at her forehead and took the dress Val handed her. She tore her sweats off and was about to lift the dress over her head when she stopped.

"I can't wear this. Why would I put on a dress?"

Tossing it onto the bed, she decided on jeans and a white silk shirt. "This is more like it. Casual, yet . . . nice. Okay. I can do this. I'll just go down there and apologize and find out what he wants."

As Julia buttoned the blouse, Val tried to rearrange her damp hair. Fussing over her like a mother hen, she said, "Run in and put a bit of lipstick on, and some rouge. There. You look very nice."

"And casual? I want to look casual. Is the silk too much? Maybe just a cotton blouse?"

"Stop it. You look . . . very nice. Now don't keep that man waiting. Normally, I would say anticipation is more sweet than punctuality, but in this case I think the quicker you make an entrance, the better."

Julia nodded. "Right." She took a few steps and stopped. "What do I say? How can I explain what happened."

Val rushed up and pushed her toward the door. "Just say that you were indulging in a beauty ritual as old as the Queen of the Nile. It might help if you ran the back of your hand over your cheek while you gave him a deep, soulful look."

"Oh, for God's sake!" Julia threw off Val's clutches and walked ahead of her. "Great recovery. First I open the door looking like The Mummy, and then I turn into Marilyn Monroe in the *Seven Year Itch*. I'll be fired and spend the next two years in a mental facility."

From behind her she heard Val yell, "Well, the least you could have done was name one of *my* movies!"

* * *

He stood in the foyer, not sure what he should do. He looked down to the floor and stared at the clumps of mud and brown dust. Should he clean it? Maybe that was pushy. This was her home. He couldn't just go wandering around, looking for paper towels.

He shouldn't have come. This was a major mistake. Now that he was here, he couldn't remember what excuse he had made up in the bar to justify this visit. When she had answered the door, he'd been so shocked that all rational thought had fled his brain. And then she had told him to shut up, but said she wasn't speaking to him. No one else was there. He had actually looked!

Then she ran away, and he was grateful for the chance to pull himself together, to try and get his brain working again. She had on a mud pack. Women did that sort of thing. He had simply caught her unawares and she was embarrassed. Now if he didn't want to embarrass himself any more than he had already, he was going to have to come up with one hell of a good excuse for being here.

It had to be something to do with work. The takeover. The furloughs. Damn, why couldn't he think of something? And who was she talking to up there? He thought she lived alone now that her daughter was in college, but it sure as heck sounded like she was speaking to someone. Maybe he should just get out before she came down.

"Steve. I must apologize for leaving you here alone. Please, come in and sit down."

Too late to run, Steve squared his shoulders and tried to sober up as he entered her living room. "Hey, I'm really sorry, Julia. I didn't mean to disturb your evening."

She ran her fingers through her hair in a nervous gesture. "I was just surprised. A friend insisted that I try this new mud pack and . . . well, you caught me."

"I'm sorry."

"Don't apologize anymore. Please, sit down. Can I get you something to drink?"

Sinking into the nearest chair, he swallowed deeply. "No, thank you. You have a lovely home." It was nice, comfortable and homey, completely different from the modern gray and white corporate apartment he was using. He watched as she sat down on the sofa and looked at him expectantly.

He cleared his throat and said, "I guess you're wondering why I'm here."

She nodded.

"To be perfectly honest, I can't remember the reason." He figured honesty was better than bluffing in this case, especially since he hadn't come up with anything plausible. "You see, I was sitting in a bar having a couple of drinks and I was thinking about Larry Melbourne. A half hour ago, I had a good reason for barging in on you this late at night but, for the life of me, once I got here I couldn't remember what it was." As he was speaking to her, he noticed that she had a ring of brown starting at her hairline and following the line of her jaw. Mud.

"Well, can I get you coffee?" she asked, looking as confused as he felt. "Or tea?"

"Please, don't bother." God almighty, how was he going to get out of here? He felt as nervous as a kid in high school.

"It's no bother, really," she said and jumped to her feet. "I'll be back in a minute."

Left alone in the living room, Steve got up and walked over to the bookshelves that were built on either side of the fireplace. There were several books on psychology, a couple of coffee table books on art, mostly Impressionism, amid the hard–cover fiction. He even found a first edition Nancy Drew. It seemed Julia's love of mystery started at a young age. But what really had made him walk over were the pictures nestled among the books . . . Julia holding a baby and laughing into the camera. The same baby, as a toddler, being held by an older woman, probably the grandmother. School pictures. Her daughter playing soccer. Her daughter going to a prom. Graduation. A whole life was represented here, lovingly preserved.

Steve tried to remember his parents taking pictures. Other relatives had, at rare family gatherings, but he had never seen them. And his parents had never bought the school pictures, telling him it was a waste of money. The history of his days before college was in his memory only, and he had blocked out most of that.

He turned back to the first picture of Julia holding her daughter. She looked so young, almost like her daughter's graduation picture. Suddenly he wanted to know what happened. Did she marry the father? Did he abandon her and the child? Did she hear from him? How did she ever work and raise a child alone?

As he stood before the shelves, he thought he heard Julia's voice. Turning around, he saw the room was empty. There . . . he heard it again. She was talking to someone in the kitchen, whispering was more like it. He decided to tell her that he was sorry for intruding on her and that he should leave. Obviously, she was busy and had company.

Maybe it was a man. Why hadn't it occurred to him that Julia Edwards might be involved? And why was that thought so disturbing?

# Chapter 7

"Will you go upstairs, please, and leave me alone?"

"This is the first man that's walked into this house in the month I've been here, and you've still got mud on your face." Val tried to wipe Julia's jaw, but she quickly turned her head. "If you would just listen to me, I could help you with him."

Waiting for the water to boil, Julia rubbed her forehead. "How many times do I have to tell you that I don't want him, that I don't want any man? I'm not you, Val," she whispered. "I'm comfortable with who I am, and if I have to live the rest of my life alone then I'm prepared to do it. Now go away before he hears us."

"He won't hear us, he'll hear you. So lower your voice. And don't lie to me. You forget, I know what you're thinking. You are so interested in this Steve McMillan. Who wouldn't be? He's not exactly Lon Chaney—"

"Oh, will you knock off the movie references?

Not everything in life can be compared to a Hollywood script. This is real life."

"Then why are you nervous?"

"Because he's my superior, my boss. I have a job to protect, a daughter to put through college, a mortgage to pay. I've had enough changes in my life. I don't want to have to look for a new position. Why can't you just go away?"

"Because I have a mission and you're fighting me. I have to help you."

"Oh, thank you very much for your help. Obviously, I didn't fight hard enough, or I wouldn't have been caught with a mud pack on my face."

Val put her hand on her hip. "Why do you have to be so stubborn? Julia, I'm the only friend you've got. Who else comes here to visit? You have no one. I've been here for a month now, and this is the first person, male or female, to knock on your door. I may not have had many women friends, but there were enough men around to keep my social calender full, and—"

"Oh, good for you," Julia interrupted in a heated voice. "Well, I don't have a social calender." She took two cups out of the cupboard and placed the tea bags in them. "Maybe you should just go back to wherever it is you came from and try and find some of these Romeos. Didn't you say you had dated James Dean? Well, he's up there in the stratosphere somewhere. Why not look him up and get off my back?"

"You really are going to make this difficult, aren't

you? I'm warning you. If you don't at least cooperate, then I may have to be more forceful."

"Julia?"

Both women turned at the sound of a male voice. Steve was standing in the doorway, looking at her and then searching the room for another presence. Julia knew in that instant that he had heard her whispering. Now what? How in the world was she supposed to explain *that?*

"Steve. You startled me. Don't mind me. Ever since my daughter left for college, I seem to talk to myself. I guess it's rattling around in this house alone that makes me want to fill it with noise." Dumb. She sounded like a mental case! "Here's your tea," she said, pouring the boiling water into the cups. Would this fiasco never end?

"Listen, Julia. I think I should go. I'm really embarrassed and I shouldn't have come here. I don't usually stop off at a bar after work and I guess, to be honest, I had one too many. I can't think of any other excuse for showing up on your door step like this."

"Make him stay," Val warned.

Ignoring Val, Julia placed the cups on the table. "Well, if you're sure you want to go. Are you okay to drive?"

"I'm fine. Just embarrassed."

"Julia . . ." Val called out. "I've warned you. This man came here to see you. It had nothing to do with work."

Julia pretended that Val wasn't in the room. "If you're sure you'd rather leave . . ."

A crash exploded behind her and Julia spun around as Steve grabbed the edge of the counter.

"Did you see that?" he demanded in a shocked voice. "My God, the teapot just jumped in the air about two feet and then slammed back to the stove!"

Julia glared, as Val said, "I did warn you."

Pushing a stray lock of hair back off her forehead, Julia said in a tightly controlled voice. "It was nothing. I've been meaning to call the gas company about that. It seems a . . . ah, a jolt of gas will sometimes burst from the jets and—"

"Julia, that's dangerous! You shouldn't even touch the stove until it's serviced. It could explode." He straightened his shoulders and added, "Maybe I will have that tea since you've already poured it."

Julia gritted her teeth as she placed spoons on the kitchen table. When Steve left, she was going to get Valentina Manchester out of her house even if she had to find a priest to perform an exorcism! This was too much!

"In fact, why don't you call them now. Gas companies have twenty-four hour emergency numbers. You shouldn't put this off. I can wait with you." Obviously shaken by the experience, Steve lost his embarrassment and sat down at her table. If Val wasn't already dead, Julia swore she would kill her for this latest prank.

"It's okay," she said, sinking into the chair opposite him. "I'll call tomorrow morning. Don't worry about it. And I certainly wouldn't keep you here. They could take hours."

"Julia," Val called out. "Don't try to push him out of the door. He wants to stay."

It took every ounce of will power she possessed not to tell Val to shut up. Instead, she smiled tightly and asked, "Do you take cream and sugar?"

"Just sugar, thanks."

Before Julia could rise from her chair, the glass sugar bowl started to float across the room! Both she and Steve bolted out of their chairs. He flattened himself against the wall, while Julia raced for the bowl and grabbed it out of Val's hands.

"Do you realize what you've done?" she demanded of the laughing matchmaker.

Val smiled with that all-knowing huntress expression. "Of course I do. Now you and the vampire have something in common. Me."

Julia turned away from her and looked at Steve. He hadn't moved a muscle, except for his eyelids. In a flash of seconds she remembered her first impression of him when he had walked into the company boardroom. Only Val could have turned that self-confident man into a jelly fish that was stuck to her kitchen wall.

"Steve, let me try and explain," she began as calmly as possible, since he seemed to be having trouble swallowing his own saliva and he hadn't yet let go of the wall. "You see, about a month ago, actually right around the time you came to Coolback, I . . . ah, well, someone, or some*thing,* came into my life. Sort of a ghost, I guess you could call her. A friendly ghost, so you don't have to be fright-

ened. Okay? You can sit down now if you want."
She walked over to his chair and straightened it.

He continued to stare at her, as if she'd lost her
mind. And could she blame him?

"You . . ." He swallowed and tried again. "You
call that an explanation? *Sort of a ghost!*"

"I can understand why you don't believe me.
Please, if this was happening to anyone else, I'd feel
the same way. But it's happening to me. I have no
choice. I have to believe. I can see and hear Val. As
crazy as it sounds, she's as real to me as you are."

"Val?" He pushed off the wall and held onto the
back of his chair.

It was Julia's turn to take a deep breath and
swallow. "Yes. Valentina Manchester."

He didn't say anything for a few seconds. "Valentina Manchester? Not Elvis?"

Val, standing by the stove, laughed. "Now that's
a good one. Tell him this is definitely not an Elvis
sighting."

Julia glanced over her shoulder and shot Val a
look of contempt, as if commanding her to keep
silent.

"Do you seriously expect me to believe that
Valentina Manchester is a ghost living in your
house?"

Sighing, Julia bit the inside of her cheek. How
could she expect him to believe anything right now?
"Okay, then how do you explain the tea pot jumping two feet in the air? And the sugar bowl? When
was the last time you saw a sugar bowl suspended
midair in the center of a room?"

"I've got to go," he said, and straightened his jacket and tie. "Again, I apologize to you for coming to your home."

"Are you okay to drive?" Julia asked as she watched Val moving to the foyer.

His laughter was sudden and cynical. "I don't think I've ever sobered up more quickly. I . . . I think I need to sleep."

She followed him to the foyer, wanting to tell him that she wasn't crazy, but she knew he needed to get out of her home and away from her. Hadn't she felt the same when Val came into her life? Denial was a normal reaction.

He reached for the door knob and said, "I guess I'll see you at work tomorrow." When he opened the door, it was immediately slammed shut by Val.

While Steve gasped in fright, Julia sighed and then said in a tired voice, "Val, let the man leave."

Standing with her hand on her hip, Val answered, "Not until he acknowledges that I'm here, otherwise he's going to think you're crazy. Tell him not to be rude. Tell him to say goodbye to me."

His voice was a whisper. "What's going on, Julia?"

"Val wants you to say goodbye to her. She thinks it's rude if you don't."

"Are you serious?"

"Steve, it isn't me. Please. If you want to leave just say goodbye to her."

He stood in front of the door for a few seconds, as though contemplating such bizarre behavior. Finally, he muttered, "Goodbye, Valentina. May I leave?"

The door opened slowly and he darted out into the night. Reacting instinctively, Julia followed him and shut the door behind her, securely locking Val in the house.

"Steve," she called out while running behind him as he hurried to his car. "Can I talk to you? Please?"

He opened the door to his car and stood with it between them, as though it might protect him from her. "I have to go. I need to get some sleep, Julia. I can't be talking to . . . to anybody right now."

She nodded. "I understand how you feel. Val isn't here. She can't leave the house without me and I got past her. Please, don't think I've lost my mind. I didn't ask for this to happen, and I don't know how to get rid of her. I need my job. I have my daughter in college and she's coming home in less than a month. I don't know what to do."

He ran his fingers through his hair and scratched his scalp, as if the action might stimulate his brain. "Look, this has nothing to do with your job. Let's forget I ever came over here tonight. I don't know how any of it happened, but we'll never talk of this again. Now, I really have to get some sleep. Good night, Julia." He got in the car, shut the door and started the engine.

After she watched him drive away, Julia turned back to her home. The muscles in her face tightened. Her fingers curled into her palms in fists of anger. Val had gone too far. It was time to take back her life, and her home. As soon as she was inside, she called out, "Val? Where are you?"

That deep silky voice came out of the kitchen. "I'm in here. I thought I might as well have some tea, since no one else seemed to want it."

Julia stood at the doorway. "I want you to listen to me. This is my life and my home. I'm through with you running roughshod over me. I have tried to be open-minded and patient, but you went over the top tonight."

Val held up a mug. "Do you want your tea now?"

"I don't give a damn about tea. Are you listening to me? That was my boss you scared out of here. You, Val, not me, made him leave. How do you think I'm supposed to work with him every day when you've made him think I belong on a psychiatrist's couch? You are screwing up my life, not helping me." Never giving Val the chance to respond, Julia continued, "I want you to leave. I want my life back."

Sitting at the table, Val held the mug, warming her well manicured fingers. "You're just mad because I forced your hand. Now you'll have a relationship with this man, and you will have bypassed that awkward stage in the beginning."

Julia stared at her with disbelief. "Excuse me? How can you even suggest that what you've done isn't going to make our next meeting awkward? The man thinks I'm crazy! That my house is haunted! I'm going to be hiding from him at work and—"

"No, you're wrong, Julia," Val interrupted. "If you had just told him about me, then I might agree with you. But Steve McMillan saw with his own eyes that something unexplainable is happening, and he's too intelligent to ignore it. Take my word for it. You may hide from him, but he'll be the one to seek out an explanation. And the only way to that is through you."

Julia pulled out the nearest chair and sank into it. "Why are you doing this to me? Haven't I gone along with everything you've asked?"

"Look, Julia," Val said in a soothing voice. "We weren't making any real progress. If I left it up to you, I could be here forever. And you want to know something? I'm ready to get out of your life. I can't stand waking up and looking at myself in the mirror and seeing more lines and wrinkles. I had to do something. Steve McMillan came here. I didn't go out looking for him. And as much as you might want to deny it, he's interested. The way I look at it, that man is my ticket out of here."

"Are you saying that if I date Steve McMillan, you'll leave?"

Val pushed a mug in front of her. "Have your tea. It's still warm. I'm saying that if you get your life back on track, if you're happy, then my mission is finished and I'm gone."

"You simply can not understand that I can be happy without a man."

"Maybe that's so, but let's face it, Julia, it's been twenty years since you've had a man. So how do you even know anymore? I had to do something to get things started, and he's the first candidate that's come along. What are you so afraid of? He's just a man."

Julia swallowed her tea. "He's also my boss."

"So? Plenty of women marry their bosses and live—"

"Marry?" Julia interrupted in a horrified voice.

"Okay, date their bosses. It's one way of getting back into the swing of things."

"I haven't even decided if I like him. He's so, I don't know, aggressive and ambitious. Our values are totally different."

"Then we'll find someone else."

Julia glanced up from her tea. "Oh, really? And how would we go about doing that? Lure men into the house so you can scare them into dating me? I don't think it will work."

"Very funny. There has to be someplace where you can meet eligible men. Some restaurant or night club."

Shaking her head, Julia said, "There are plenty of clubs around. I hear the younger women talking at work. But I couldn't go into one of them, especially alone."

Val grinned. "But you wouldn't be alone. You'd have me."

Julia rolled her gaze toward the ceiling and spotted a long cobweb in the corner. "Is that supposed to be reassuring? I wouldn't dare let you loose in a nightclub." She wondered if Steve saw that cobweb. It certainly was in keeping with a haunted house, and she supposed her house was definitely being haunted. Strange that she wasn't scared any longer, merely annoyed.

"I'll be good. And remember, Julia, the sooner you find a man the sooner I leave."

Sighing with defeat, Julia closed her eyes briefly. "So when do we stalk this poor, unsuspecting soul?"

Val laughed. "What a way to put it. Let's do it this weekend. Friday night. You can wear that sexy black dress that I found hidden in the back of your closet. The one with the dust on it. When did you buy it? And why, if you haven't dated in years?"

"I bought it for an office Christmas party about six years ago. I don't even know if it still fits."

"We'll make it fit. And I'll wear . . . hmmm, what will I wear?"

In spite of everything, Julia smiled. "Val, no one will be able to see you."

"I know, but that doesn't mean I'm going to miss a chance to dress up for a change. Don't worry about me. I have a few days, and I'll think of something."

"All right. Then we have a deal? I will attempt to find a date and, when I do, you'll leave?"

Val nodded. "When you find happiness my mission is complete."

Julia held up a warning finger. "But if I don't find happiness, whatever that is, before Paige comes home, then you have to promise me you won't play any tricks while she's here. I do not want my daughter leaving for Europe thinking her mother is having a nervous breakdown."

"I promise."

"Solemn promise? I forbid you to play any more of your pranks."

Val looked annoyed, but finally stuck out her hand. "Okay. Solemn promise."

They shook hands and when Julia picked up her mug she noticed Val's left hand. Was that a freckle she hadn't noticed before? Or was it an age spot? Although she was still a beautiful woman, Val looked like she had aged twenty years in the last month. For someone who took such pride in her beauty, it must be painful to see the rapid deterioration each day.

"See? So who needs the vampire? Everything will work out for the best."

Julia nodded. "I wish you'd stop calling him that. I suspect that underneath all that male bravado, he's really a nice person."

"Having second thoughts? We can always lure him back."

"No second thoughts. He's not my type, though I don't know who is . . ."

"Not to worry. Now that I finally have your full cooperation, we'll find him. You pick him out and I'll figure a way to snare him."

Julia shuddered. "Good Lord, I can't believe I've agreed to this. It sounds like we're hunting bear."

Val's smile was almost brilliant. "Now you're getting the idea!"

* * *

She was avoiding him, and he couldn't figure out why that was so disturbing as he had made a point of avoiding her since the crazy scene at her house. But now it was obvious she was doing it to him. Several times he had seen her in the hallways before she'd ducked into an office. He felt silly, embarrassed, like a kid with a crush. He didn't know what to make of her . . . or what happened at her house. He'd told himself over the last few days that he'd been drunk. He'd imagined the entire thing. There was no other rationalization for the weird stuff he'd seen, especially Julia's explanation.

Valentina Manchester.

He was twelve years old when he had gone to the movies and had seen Valentina Manchester in *Nobody's Fool*. He remembered sitting in the dark watching her on the screen, the exciting way her voluptuous body moved, the fascinating way the light caught her blond hair, the flirtatious expression on her beautiful face. It was a sexual awakening, his first conscious erection, and was both exciting and embarrassing. And now he was expected to believe that the ghost of that woman was living with Julia Edwards, a manager at Coolback Industries?

*I don't think so . . .*

His pragmatic mind told him there was an answer to everything; he just couldn't think of one yet. He rejected the New Age subculture, regarding those that embraced it as optimistic dreamers. He had always believed that he was grounded in reality. But reality, as he knew it, renounced teapots jumping off the stove and sugar bowls flying through the air. That was the scotch. And if he'd been that drunk, was he the one to bring up Valentina Manchester, the cause of his sexual awakening? What else had he done? He had been thinking about Julia in the bar and had rejected another woman's attention to seek her out. Then he couldn't even muster a plausible explanation when he got to her door. What the hell did he do? For the first time in his life he was questioning himself, not concentrating on his work and having trouble falling asleep.

He needed answers.

And Julia Edwards was the only person who could supply them.

There was only one thing to do. He had to find a way to talk to her outside of work, because he wasn't going to go to her house again. Maybe he could invite her to dinner. It would be awkward and embarrassing, but it was the only way he could get his life back on track.

His opportunity came less than an hour later when he saw her leaving the ladies room with two other women.

"Excuse me, Julia. May I speak with you in my office for a few minutes?"

She appeared embarrassed, but merely nodded as she left the others and followed him down the hallway. When he shut the door behind her, he watched as she stood and waited for him to begin.

"Please, be seated," he said, walking around the desk.

He sensed that she was uncomfortable and

figured she knew he was feeling the same way. There was a sticky moment as he waited for her to sit down.

He cleared his throat before speaking. "I wanted to talk to you about this . . . situation."

She continued to stare at him. "I beg your pardon? What situation?"

He knew she was trying to play it off, and was grateful that she was allowing him his dignity by denying anything happened. Maybe he hadn't behaved as badly as he thought. "I want to apologize for invading your privacy. You don't know me well enough to understand that type of behavior is very out of character. I normally never drink anything but wine. This isn't an excuse. I've done a hundred of these downsizings, but something about Larry . . ."

He glanced at a filing cabinet. "But something you said must have gotten to me. I never really thought about the lives behind the statistics before. It was all just numbers and efficiency ratios. Maybe none of this is making sense to you, but Larry Melbourne put a face and a family to the numbers. Maybe that's what I came over to tell you. And to tell you that I'm sorry, truly sorry, that he got caught in the rift."

Still silent, she continued to stare. He couldn't tell if her look was understanding or disdain. "I embarrassed myself. I can't remember exactly what took place, and what I do remember is so bizarre." He shook his head in disbelief. "And to have invaded your home like that . . ."

Julia raised her hand, stopping the random thoughts that were spilling out in a senseless stream. "No harm: no foul. I knew something was wrong. I was just relieved it wasn't a state trooper telling me to come down and identify a body. You have no idea what a mother goes through when her child is no longer within her protection."

It was his turn to stare as he realized that thought never occurred to him, that she could be scared, worried, a mother . . . It made him wonder if his own mother ever came out of her drunken stupor long enough to have those same worries. His mother would turn him out into a battlefield, the streets of New York City, every day, so she could spend an uninterrupted morning with Jim Beam. And here was his efficient, professional colleague, living a double life—a robot by day and June Cleaver at night, terrified that a cop would be asking her to read the tag on her daughter's toe.

He stood up and looked out the window to the parking lot beneath him. There was more to Julia Edwards than met the eye. The astonishing revelation was that he wanted to know more. The risk pulled at him. He had just recovered from the greatest faux pas of his career, and now he was thinking of chancing another blunder. Would asking her to dinner be yet another invasion of her personal space?

All the questions that loomed before him while he waited in the foyer of her home came back, questions that made him examine his own life. He had obviously been drawn to her that night because he had wanted to know her better. If her maternal instincts never occurred to him, what about the rest of her private life? Surely someone as attractive and well-grounded as Julia would probably have a steady relationship. Though startled, she had graciously accepted him into her house—no, her home. He may not have remembered everything correctly that night, but it was most definitely a home. Pictures. Memories. Comfortable, lived-in furnishings. A place that immediately welcomed. On her own, Julia Edwards had built something of worth.

He had the vineyard in France, but was it a home?

Realizing how long he'd been caught up in his own thoughts, while staring at all the cars in the manager's parking lot, he said in a voice distant to himself, "I want to know more about all of them."

"I'm sorry?"

He turned back to her with a sad smile. "Maybe that's who was haunting me that night."

Her eyes widened with surprise, and he rushed in to explain. "Perhaps it was the ghosts of all the lives I've affected. I need you to tell me about them. Somehow, I don't think I can do this by the numbers anymore."

"Steve, I don't know what to say."

"Say you'll have dinner with me Friday night and you can begin there."

She appeared flustered by his proposal and rose awkwardly to leave. "I . . . ah . . . I have plans Friday night," she said, nervously turning her watch around.

"I'm sorry." The realization hit him. Of course she would. Trying to recover, he said, "Well, it seems all I do lately is apologize to you. I don't want dinner to cause a problem in your relationship, I only wanted—"

"Oh, no," she rushed in. "It's not like that. It's just that I promised my friend that I'd start getting out more. She won't leave me alone until I go with her to Weatherby's . . . and I did promise her."

"I wouldn't want you to change your plans, or anything," he hurried to add, adolescent relief washing over him. "Would Saturday be better?" He held his breath as he watched her retreat toward the door.

Bewildered, she stammered, "Ah . . . ah . . . well, yes, fine. Maybe. I should return to my office. How about I get back to you by the end of the week?"

"That's fine. I really needed to clear the air this morning."

Already opening the door, she answered quickly while making her exit, "Me, too."

The door shut behind her.

Steve stared at the wooden panel.

Weatherby's . . .

# Chapter 8

"I don't believe I'm here. I wish I were a ghost too, and invisible." She felt a headache chiseling away at the back of her skull from the pulsating, aerobic-length music that assaulted her senses.

"How could you pick this place, Julia? I thought we'd be going out to an elegant nightclub where we could sit and be observant. Not standing at a bar like meat on the hoof."

"So now you know why I haven't been out in twenty years? Places like you're describing went out of business twenty years ago. Welcome to the nineties. *This*, Val, is the result of the sexual revolution, the one you missed. There was something to be said for the social customs of your time. At least a woman could maintain her dignity," Julia muttered as she watched a man rudely place his drink order ahead of her.

"And chivalry wasn't dead," Val added as she glared at the man. "But there's got to be a better place."

"I heard the single women at work talking about it. They said it was the nicest club in the area."

Val looked at her in total disbelief. "You have got to be kidding. I wasn't expecting the lounge at the Beverly Hills Hotel, but this is a joke, almost like the set of a bad B–movie."

Julia saw a look of understanding pass over Val's face for the first time. "Do you want to leave?" she offered in a hopeful voice.

Val straightened her shoulders and looked around. "Absolutely not. We're here on a mission. And, considering the competition, no man in his right mind would pass us up. Will you look at these dolls? And you thought *I* was vulgar? Is that supposed to be a skirt that ends at her crotch?"

"It's called Spandex, Val. It wasn't invented in the fifties. And what do you mean, pass us up? They can't see you. All they see is a forty-year-old woman talking to herself over a drink. I can just see the line of interested eligibles forming now."

"What are you talking about? That knockout black dress is timeless. Of course it would have looked better with the black stockings with the seams up the back, but you thought that was over-kill. Look to your left. I would define overkill as a blouse so sheer you can see a woman isn't wearing a bra."

Julia found it funny that Val was actually offended.

"These babes leave no mystery. Men don't want everything shoved in their faces. And the ones who do, you don't want." She lifted her chin and tossed her hair. "Though it is a shame they can't see me."

Julia couldn't help laughing as she watched Val. In the dim light, most signs of age had been flawlessly covered by makeup. Val had obviously learned the subtle art of female transformation at the hands of experts. Julia wanted to compliment Val on that, but knew she couldn't. Any reference to Val's deteriorating condition was met with hostility. And the last thing she needed this night was a ghost causing a spectacle in a public place!

"Let's get this audition going." Looking across one of the circular bars, she said, "Starting at the first man on the left, let's work our way down."

Julia rolled her gaze reluctantly toward the first candidate, a nerdy man in his forties who thought that dressing up was unbuttoning his shirt and spreading his collar over the lapels of his suit to reveal his chest hair. She almost spit out her wine as Val commented, "Do you think that bulge in his pants is his clip-on tie?"

Waiting for her to recover, Val added, "Be careful, Julia. No one can see me. You just looked like you found a fly in your drink."

Val was right. If she ever hoped to entice any man into a date, she'd have to appear reasonably sane. Collecting herself, Julia looked to the next man a few feet down the bar. When Val's line of vision caught up to hers, both of them turned to each other and said simultaneously, "Married!"

"This is hopeless," Julia whispered, doing her best ventriloquist impression.

"We're not giving up." Val sounded skeptical,

but not discouraged. "Okay . . . how about him?"

Val pointed to a man that reminded Julia of Andrew Dice Clay. He had that leering, overblown machismo look, and it made the hair on Julia's neck rise when he caught her looking and winked.

"Oh my God . . ." To Julia's horror, she watched the man walk around the bar in her direction. "Please, God, let him be going to the men's room!"

"Oh, now stop it. He's a little rough around the edges, in a Jimmy Dean sort of way. Of course, James preferred men, so you may be right. He might just be going to the men's room."

Unfortunately, her worst fears were realized. It was a nightmare and she wasn't waking up. Dice Clay/Dean was making a beeline toward her.

"Hey, baby, were you looking for me?"

She felt her stomach muscles tighten in revulsion. In reflex, her head was shaking no. This couldn't be happening.

"Cat got your tongue?" If possible, he leered even more. "Wanna borrow mine?"

Before Julia was capable of responding, she watched in horror as Val bumped his hand, causing the foam of his beer to attach itself to the gaudy medallion that hung at his chest.

"This loser is disgusting," Val pronounced. "You can bet he won't be dying with Rosebud on his lips."

Her composure in shreds, Julia bit the inside of her lip as Val's last comment proved too much. Erupting into laughter, it was all Julia could do to hold onto her own drink. "No more," she pleaded, as she unsuccessfully tried to control herself. "I can't take it anymore."

Clearly indignant, her nightmare shook excess beer from his fingers, turned on the heels of his riding boots, and stalked away.

Still offended, Val glared at the man's retreating back. "This might be harder than I thought."

"Okay, so we agree. This is hopeless. Now can we go home?"

"For the love of Pete, there must be somebody in here halfway decent. At least somebody we can practice on."

Julia groaned.

"I'd give anything for a martini right now. It might improve this lot of prospects."

"Prospects? Like the charmer that just walked away? Now can you understand that I'd rather be alone than with something like that."

"Listen, Julia, a nymphomaniac would rather be alone than with that creep. Wait a minute, hold your horses . . . a reasonable candidate just walked in."

Julia let out a sigh of exasperation. "Okay, I'll look. But this is the last one and then I'm out of here."

She turned to the clean shaven, attractive man who sat down on the other side of the bar. He seemed mid-fortyish, dressed in a suit, as if he had stopped in on his way home from work. That was a plus. And his expression looked normal. He didn't appear to be on the prowl. Simply a man comfortable in his surroundings unwinding over a drink. It was a refreshing change.

"See?" There was triumph in Val's voice. "You just had to be patient. Now here's what I want you to do?"

"I have to do something?"

"Julia, Julia, Julia . . . if a woman had to wait for a man to make the first move, it would all have stopped with Adam and Eve."

"I'm not going to make a fool out of myself."

"A little eye contact won't kill you. Let's start by looking at the man. At least this time there's something worth looking at. Go ahead. Let him know that you noticed him since he's sitting right across from you."

Julia glanced up quickly. He caught her interest, but she immediately looked away feeling nervous and unsure. This was treading on foreign ground.

"That was a good start," Val said with encouragement. "He knows now that you saw him. Now let's see if you can walk and chew gum at the same time. Can you look at him *and* smile?"

Julia felt her shoulders slump with weariness. If she didn't do this now, Val would never give up. This was like going to the dentist. At least the man looked reasonable, and he probably wouldn't strut up to her and make a spectacle of himself. Reinforced with that thought, she raised her chin, looked at the man and offered a hesitant smile. To her surprise he returned it.

"Perfect!" It was obvious Val was in her glory. To Julia, it seemed that Val was an odd cross between a mother hen and a Little League coach, full of pride and expectation.

"Okay, now give him a slow bat of the eye. But make sure it's done slow and sexy."

Julia stared down into her wineglass and spoke through clenched teeth. "I can't do that!"

"Of course you can, and you will. Take my word for it. I know how this is done. I'm in my element here."

Julia shook her head and muttered a forceful, "No."

"You're talking to yourself again. C'mon, Julia. Just do it and watch the results."

Taking a deep breath, she raised her head again, smiled at the man and performed the task slowly and as sensuously as she dared. To her horror the man broke eye contact abruptly and turned his attention to the woman who appeared at his side. She threaded her arm through his while giving him a quick kiss of recognition.

Dear God, he was waiting for someone, and she had just made a supreme fool out of herself. The muscles of her face tightened with humiliation and she could feel hot tears gathering at her eyes.

"Okay, okay . . . so we made a mistake. Don't cry or you'll mess up your makeup. But it would've worked if this dame didn't show up."

Julia didn't care who was around her. She looked directly at Val and said, "Don't call her a dame. She doesn't look cheap, and they must have a relationship. I've had it, Val. I can't do this anymore. I want to go home." Angry that she had gone along with this fiasco, she wiped away a fat tear that was rolling down her cheek.

Val placed her arm around her and said, "All right. I didn't want you to be hurt by this. It was supposed to be fun. I just wanted you to see how pretty you are, and you have just as much right to a relationship as that woman."

Val's voice sounded distant, for Julia had closed herself off as the misery wrapped around her forming a barrier. She needed to get to someplace safe. Home.

"C'mon," Val urged. "We'll take the long way out. Just in case . . ."

As they threaded their way through the crowd, Julia felt Val come to a quick halt.

"Hallelujah! I knew my instincts were right!"

Julia was roused from her state of despair enough to find out the reason for Val's sudden excitement.

It couldn't possibly be! She blinked several times, trying to deny the name her brain was screaming. Dear God in heaven, the nightmare continued with a vengeance. This couldn't be happening to her.

Standing a few feet away was Steve McMillan, with a knowing smile on his face. She knew he had seen it, and her humiliation was now complete.

She wanted to die.

Turning away, hoping to lose herself in the crowd, Julia ordered, "Hurry, before he sees us!"

Val resisted her. "No, he's already seen us. Look, he's coming."

"Damn it! I've got to get out of here." Julia left Val and tried to weave her way to the exit.

Freedom in sight, she suddenly felt a strong grip on her elbow and, with a sickening feeling, she realized that she was trapped.

"Julia? Wait a minute."

She didn't want to turn around. She didn't want to see that knowing smile on his face again. And the very last thing she didn't want was to explain that scene he'd witnessed.

"Please, Julia, where are you going?"

Humiliation was replaced by swift anger as she spun around to face him. "I'm going home. This wasn't my idea in the first place."

Apparently taken back by the unprovoked hostility, Steve dropped his hand. "Look, I wasn't spying on you."

"Then what are you doing here?" She heard the anger still in her voice, but didn't care.

He seemed embarrassed by the question. "I don't know—it was Friday night. I'm by myself. I don't know the area that well, and I remembered you said something about Weatherbys."

His voice was gentle, there was almost a pleading quality to his explanation. Neither of them said anything for a few moments.

"Don't leave, Julia. At least not yet."

The anger started to dissolve as he softly touched her arm. "Will you come sit down with me for a few minutes? We're blocking traffic standing here."

With a sigh of resignation, she conceded and followed him to a small table away from the crowd. What was the point of avoiding him now? She had already made a fool of herself and creating a scene at this point would only make it worse. She might as well deal with him quietly and then get out of this place.

Reluctantly taking a seat next to him, she made sure she left a protective barrier of space between them while he ordered two glasses of wine. It didn't help that Val appeared at the table and slinked into the chair on the other side of Steve.

Leaning close to the man and striking a particularly provocative pose, Val grinned and said, "My, isn't this a cozy threesome?"

Julia couldn't even dignify the comment as the waitress brought their wine. She was livid, feeling the muscles in her jaw clench as she looked out to the crowd. Every embarrassing scene with this man was Val's fault, and now she had the gall to sit there vamping and practically draped over his shoulder. She wanted to slap her face, and that thought shocked her since she had never been a violent woman.

Breaking through her fury was Steve's voice. It was low and sympathetic. "Julia, I hate these places, too. Even though they're loaded with people, you can still feel lonely."

It was too much. He felt sorry for her!

"Look, I told you before, this was not my idea. It was hers!" Julia pointed to the space at his left. "This is the last time one of Val's harebrained schemes is going to explode in my face!"

Steve looked over his shoulder and then back at her with a strange expression. "Val? You're not saying . . .? I thought I was drunk."

"You were," she snapped. "It's probably the best way to deal with her. That way you don't have to question your sanity."

"Now wait a minute," Val interjected. "It wasn't that bad. Look how it turned out."

Julia couldn't believe that Val had the audacity to think this night had turned out okay. "Wasn't that bad? I was completely humiliated!"

Steve grabbed her hand tightly. "Julia, will you look at yourself? What's wrong with you? You're talking to an empty seat."

"Oh, you think it's empty? I wish you could see her. How I wish . . . She's sitting there with a smug grin on her face like she's just done something wonderful when she's ruining my life."

"You're overplaying the scene, Julia. Relax. This isn't method acting."

"Val, shut up!"

Steve seemed nervous as he tightened his grip on her hand. "Julia," he began firmly, "There isn't anyone with us. The chair is empty."

No sooner had the words left his mouth when his wineglass slid six inches across the table. Julia groaned. "Don't you ever stop?"

Frozen in shock, Steve stammered out a question. "How'd you do that?"

Julia shook her head in disgust. "It wasn't me. It was the blonde bombshell. She's really enjoying this, at both of our expense."

"What expense?" Val asked with a laugh. "You haven't even sported for a martini yet."

Steve's expression was incredulous. After a long

pause, he murmured, "This is either the best parlor trick in the world, or I've lost my mind."

"Neither," Julia answered. She was impatient with his steadfast refusal to accept her bizarre reality. At any other time, she would have been more understanding, but she was at her wit's end. "Hey, I didn't pick this table. And it's not like you're in my house, where there could be wires or mirrors. Just buy her the damn martini and see what happens."

"Are you serious?"

She glared at him. "Quite serious."

He signaled the waitress and ordered the martini. Julia quickly added, "And with a short straw." She looked at Steve after the young woman left and said, "Unless you want to see a glass floating in the air."

Val giggled in delight and, to Julia, it sounded like fingernails scratching across a blackboard. "Now are you satisfied?"

Val nearly purred. "Absolutely. Isn't this turning out to be a great evening?"

Exasperated, Julia said, "You'd better behave yourself."

Steve was silent through the entire exchange. He had let go of her hand and was sitting back in the chair, as though distancing himself from the conversation. When he spoke his tone was serious and clinical. "Julia, I'm worried about you. I know these negotiations were stressful, and probably tougher for you because some of those people were your friends . . ." His voice trailed off as the waitress brought the martini and placed it before him.

Julia reached across and pushed the drink in front of Val. "Knock yourself out." Sitting back, she folded her arms and waited for the show to begin. Knowing Val, she wondered whether the actress could resist the drama of lifting the glass before such a captive male audience.

It was with relief that she watched Val take a sip of her drink without incident.

"This is so tacky," Val whined. "Drinking a martini with a straw!"

As the level of clear alcohol slowly descended into the V of the long-stemmed glass, Steve's jaw lowered in astonishment.

"Okay, believe me now?"

Julia glanced over as Val took a deeper sip of the drink.

"My God, this tastes wonderful. It's been over thirty years since I've enjoyed one of these. We've got to get some liquor in the house. A martini is the perfect aphrodisiac," she cooed while looking at Steve. "And it's been thirty years since—"

"Don't even think about it," Julia ordered.

"Well, if you're not interested . . ." Before Julia could stop her, Val's hand disappeared under the table.

Steve's body jerked, jarring the drinks. "I felt something on my leg! I swear I did!"

"Good muscles," Val commented as she took another healthy sip of her drink.

"Knock it off. You're scaring him." Julia turned to Steve. "It was Val. She's trying to show you that she really is here with us."

"I thought you said you could lock her in the house. My God, I don't believe I even said that! What's happening?"

It was Julia's turn to offer reassurance. She took both his hands in hers and stared at him squarely. "I know you're frightened. I tried to tell you when you came to my house. She can only come out when I invite her, but how could I tell my boss that I'm going out with a ghost because she's determined to fix me up with somebody? She has the crazy idea that her mission is my happiness. And Val's definition of happiness is a man."

Steve merely blinked. "I don't get it. I don't . . . This kind of thing just doesn't happen."

Julia almost smiled. "I know. But you saw the sugar bowl and the teapot. You watched the martini disappear. And you even felt her. What more do you need?"

He jerked his hands away from hers. "I don't know!" he nearly yelled. "None of this makes sense. There are no such things as ghosts!"

Val noisily sucked the last of her martini up through the straw and turned to the man on her right. "Oh, really? No such things as ghosts, huh?" Giggling with mischief, she reached for the buckle on his belt and pulled the leather through the side strap.

"Val!" Julia was horrified.

Steve pushed his chair back and looked down at his waist as the expensive leather snaked itself out of the buckle and the center pin moved away from the first notch. "Stop it, Julia! This isn't funny!"

"It isn't me. I can't control her. She wants to be acknowledged. It's just like the door, Steve. You'll have to ask her to stop."

"Okay, stop then!"

Val grinned. "Say my name."

Julia sighed. "She wants you to say her name."

Val was not about to stop until she got what she wanted. Steve grabbed the top of his pants as the length of leather fell between his legs. Julia merely shook her head in disgust.

"Okay," he said in a frantic voice. "Please stop, Val. What more do you want?"

Julia watched as Val immediately removed her hands, leaned into Steve and said in a husky voice, "Another martini, for starters."

Confusion and anger raced inside of Julia. Val's actions had been too aggressive and much too intimate. "I think you've had enough. Another drink is totally out of the question."

Val glared at her. "Fine then. I'll just have to go get it myself."

"Oh, no you don't."

"Don't what?" Steve demanded, looking frightened as he hastily fastened his belt. "What's she going to do?"

Knowing what he must be thinking, Julia said, "She's not going to do anything to you. She wants another martini."

"Then let's get her one," he offered in relief. "Anything to keep her away from me." Again, he signaled the waitress and pointed to the empty martini glass.

No one said anything for a full minute. The music turned into slow ballads and couples started filling the dance floor.

Steve finally broke the silence. "This is so bizarre. I don't know what to say, or how to react. It goes against everything I believe."

Julia returned her gaze to Steve's. "So you finally believe me?"

He stared into her eyes, as if searching for answers she couldn't give. Hadn't she also had to suspend her own disbelief in order to accept this new reality? It was something he had to come to on his own.

"What choice do I have? I'm afraid of what would happen if I said no."

In spite of everything, Julia smiled, though Val's laugh of triumph grated on her already frazzled nerves.

"Julia, tell him to keep his pants on. I'm not going to bother him anymore tonight. I've got what I wanted," Val said as her martini arrived.

Watching the second drink disappear, Steve turned to Julia and asked in an awed voice, "How did this happen? I mean, did she just appear one day?"

"Sort of." Julia reflected on the long chain of events leading up to this night. "I had been really down since Paige went to college. Everything that was dear to me was changing and I couldn't stop it. I wouldn't want to stop it, because that's life and its normal progression. I raised my daughter to be strong and independent and was proud when she took that step. But I never counted on the loneliness I'd feel. I thought my work could fill my life, but even that was changed with Amalgamated's take-over. Home wasn't home anymore. Work wasn't work anymore, and I guess, quite frankly, I was at a loss for what to do next. My life had always been so structured. Paige and work. That was it. And when Val arrived, nothing made sense. I was sure I was having a nervous breakdown."

"I know what you mean," he muttered. "Weren't you terrified?"

She let out a short laugh and shrugged her shoulders. "Of course—at first. But Val wasn't threatening. Just persistent." She looked at Val, who appeared extremely happy with her surroundings.

"She seems like a real character. What did she do?"

Taking a noisy sip of her drink, Val turned to Steve. "Hey, sweetie, I'm not a character. I'm an actress."

Julia noticed that Val's words were slurring. Was it possible that a ghost could get drunk? "Remember, Steve, she can hear everything we say. And sometimes she can read my mind."

Steve looked to his left and whispered, "I didn't mean to offend you."

Val straightened her posture, thrust her breasts out in Steve's direction and ran her fingers through her hair. Her eyes were heavy-lidded and her speech low and deliberate. "I'll let you make it up to me later, hon," she purred.

Julia drew a sharp breath, and Steve turned back to her. "What did she say?"

"Never mind. She's drunk."

"I am not," Val protested. "I just know what to do with a good looking man on a Friday night. Unlike some I could name."

"Really, Julia. What's she saying?"

"She says you're good looking."

He smiled. "Tell her she was something in her heyday. I had the biggest crush on her as a boy."

"Tell her yourself. She can hear you."

Val preened with the attention. "I knew I liked this guy for a reason. He has excellent taste."

"She says you have excellent taste."

Steve turned to the chair at his side and shyly whispered, "I'm sorry you didn't get to do more movies. I watched every one you made."

Julia wondered at Steve's acceptance. He didn't seem worried that the people around him might be watching him talk to an empty chair. It was funny how men reacted to a compliment from a woman— even a dead woman.

Val looked at her and smiled drunkenly. "Isn't he sweet? Why don't you dance with the guy?"

"I don't think so."

Steve turned to her. "What did she say?"

"Oh, please . . ."

"No, tell me."

"She wants us to dance. Don't pay attention to her. She's had one too many."

Val leaned her elbows on the edge of the table, while resting her chin on her laced fingers. "Where's your sense of romance, Julia? I'd give anything to be held in a man's arms again. Remember, the faster you get this over with, the faster I go away."

Julia considered the tempting thought. To have Val out of her life all she had to do was make it seem like she was happy. Suddenly, it was clear and easy.

"Well, then, shall we?" Steve asked, nodding to the dance floor. "Let's make Miss Manchester happy."

"Don't worry, Julia. I'll be a good girl while you're gone. You children run off and play."

Without resistance, Julia rose and walked toward the dance floor. When she reached it Steve was behind her and they hesitantly walked toward each other, finding their places while slowly moving to the ballad.

"This has been the most incredible night of my life. I still can't believe it." He looked down at her and smiled. "But I'm actually glad it happened. I can't tell any one, can I? They'll think I'm crazy, right?"

"Right." Julia pulled her gaze away from his and looked at his necktie. "I have to say that I'm surprised at your acceptance. And relieved. I don't feel like I'm alone with this anymore." As they moved to the music she realized she wasn't alone. For the first time in years she was in the arms of a man other than a male relative at a wedding. Even if he wasn't a love interest, it still felt good. She was aware of his scent. It was clean and masculine. His cologne had a dark, mysterious quality to it that evoked thoughts she had buried long ago.

A slight panic raced through her. She didn't want to feel this way. It was pathetic. Yet the warmth she could feel through the material of his suit felt wonderful. She hadn't had this close contact with another living soul in months, not since Paige had left. He held her gently, but securely, and she experienced a sudden sense of well being. She should have felt awkward and stiff. She shouldn't be enjoying this so much; hadn't she already made a big enough fool of herself this evening?

With that thought in mind, she checked herself and withdrew slightly. It would have been so easy to pretend that he felt the same way. Wasn't that a crazy thought? This sophisticated man probably held glamourous women in his arms on a regular basis. She was sure for him it wasn't once every twenty years. Perhaps that's why Val's flirtation got to her. It was so easy for women like Val, women who were voluptuous and sexy, always secure in their ability to attract a man.

He wouldn't have danced with her if *Miss* Manchester hadn't insisted. If they had somehow wandered into this strange place at any other time, he never would have picked her out of the crowd. She simply had to remember it was Val's manipulation that had caused this situation.

But it was hard to ignore his steady, even breath on her temple. It was soft and warm, and causing pleasant shivers to race through her body. His hand rested easily on her lower back and, to her horror, it seemed to generate an embarrassing heat that spread to her thighs. How in the world was she supposed to get through this dance, especially when she felt him deeply inhale, as though breathing in her scent, and move in closer? How could she have allowed Val to put her in this position? This was how Val would have gone about getting a man, but it wasn't her style. Over Steve's shoulder, she looked toward the table the three of them had shared and her body immediately stiffened.

Steve pulled back and looked down at her. "What's wrong?"

"She's gone!"

"Gone?"

Julia frantically searched the crowd. "Val! She's not at the table. Damn it, she promised!"

Steve shrugged as he looked around. "Maybe she just went home."

Impatient, Julia pulled away from him. "No. You don't understand. She can't get home alone. She needs *me*. My God, what has she done?"

From behind, she felt his hand on her arm. "How can I help you find someone I can't see?"

"Don't you understand? She's drunk!"

Steve laughed and Julia spun around on him. "I've got to find her. I don't know what she could do . . ." Her words trailed off as she spotted Val amongst the abandoned tables lining the dance floor.

She couldn't believe her eyes.

Val was going from table to table, sampling the dancer's drinks with her short white straw! Julia stood for a moment in total disbelief, watching Val giggling with mischief after each sip.

"My God! C'mon. I've got to get to her before the dance is over! Now she's stealing somebody's cigarettes!"

Julia made a beeline in Val's direction.

"Wait up. What am I supposed to do when I can't see her?" Steve asked as he matched her stride.

Julia didn't stop. "Just follow the straw."

She felt him slow down and urged him, "Come on!"

For a moment he hesitated, seemed to focus on the straw, and then muttered, "Oh, shit!"

Julia raced ahead of him until she reached Val who was obviously having trouble with her hand-eye coordination as she dropped a pack of matches. Snatching the cigarette from Val's mouth, Julia threw it on the table and demanded, "What do you think you're doing?"

Val looked up at her with a drunken smile. "Wait . . . wait. I can do this," she mumbled as she tried once more to strike the match.

Grabbing the matches from her, Julia said, "I trusted you and you promised not to make a scene. Now, get up. We're going home."

Steve stood beside Julia with a bewildered look on his face. "What can I do?" he asked quietly, spotting a woman who was squinting in their direction.

Julia didn't answer him. She didn't care what anyone thought at the moment. Instead, she kept her attention on Val. "Val, we're leaving. Now stand up!"

"Aww, party pooper . . . okay." Val made a

wobbly attempt to stand, almost knocking over the table.

Steve grabbed the table and righted it before it crashed to the floor. "We've got to get her out of here."

"Put your arm around my waist and let her lean on us. That way, people will think that I'm the one that needs help walking."

Val looked up at them as they neared the exit and slurred, "You guys are great . . . Didn't we have fun tonight?"

Julia was beyond comment. *Didn't we have fun tonight?* First, the woman forces her into a singles bar, makes her endure a barrage of creeps, encourages her to flirt with an unavailable man and humiliates her in front of her boss, and now this! God in heaven, we sure did have fun!

A half hour later, Julia managed to get Val into the bed in her daughter's room. The car ride home had been a trial of patience. Steve had insisted that he follow them home, and she'd been grateful for his help getting Val into the house and up the stairs.

Covering Val with the quilt, she whispered, "Try to get some rest. We'll discuss this in the morning."

"Oh, don't be mad," Val mumbled, close to tears. "You have no idea what it's been like for me. I used to be beautiful before I came here. Every morning when I wake up I look like I've aged another year."

A fat tear rolled down her face and Julia reached over to wipe it away. "Just get some sleep," she soothed, anger quickly fading. "Don't think about it now."

Val opened her eyes and sniffled. "You didn't know me, Julia. I used to have such fun. I—I lived every precious moment of life to its fullest. And to come back here and . . . and to be stuck in this house with someone who doesn't even appreciate that gift of life . . ." Fresh tears shimmered at her lashes and she closed her eyes. "Do you know how long it's been since a man has held me in his arms? You might not have had a man, but at least you had a child. Somebody loved you for all those years. I . . . I can't think of anybody. Except Johnny. Yeah . . . Johnny loved me."

Julia leaned closer to hear her slurred words. "What was that, Val? Who loved you?"

Near sleep, Val whispered the name. "Johnny Cochran . . . maybe he loved me."

Julia was so moved by Val's confession that she automatically reached down and smoothed back Val's hair from her forehead, the same way she would have comforted Paige. "Rest now," Julia murmured.

She turned off the light and walked out of the room while reflecting on Val's words. She had spent so much time angry over the intrusion into her own life that she never really considered how horrible all of this must be for Val. To have it all, and to have been so full of life, then to have it all taken away by some cruel twist of fate . . . It was adding insult to injury to have been given a mission of helping some ordinary, boring person.

Taking a deep breath, Julia headed down the

stairs. This had been one hell of a night. Now that one crisis had been settled, she supposed she might as well move on to the next.

Steve McMillan was waiting in her living room.

# Chapter 9

Standing once again in front of the pictures in her living room, Steve picked up the small oval frame that held a photo of Julia with her baby. The same questions came back at him. Who was the father? Did he die? Was this why a ghost chose to haunt her? And if so, why not the husband? Did she love him so much that she couldn't bring herself to re-marry? These questions collided with new ones about Valentina Manchester. He had always considered stories of ghosts and spirits as fairy tales. At best, he'd thought those superstitions man's way of explaining what couldn't be answered by the science or technology of that time. Before man understood precipitation, storms were thought to be the wrath of the gods. Common illnesses, treatable today, were thought to be signs of spiritual possession. For someone so grounded in reality to actually witness spiritual phenomena was extraordinary, and was a massive challenge to his belief system. But he could no longer deny what he had seen.

"Steve, can I get you a cup of coffee?"

Newly awakened to the possibilities, he turned with a start. "Oh, Julia," he said with relief as he placed the picture back on the shelf. "Sure. Coffee sounds great. Can I help?"

She smiled, as if knowing he was like a little kid that didn't want to be left alone in the house, and said, "Sure. I'd love some help."

He followed quickly behind her, noticing that she had taken off her heels and was in her stocking feet. Could he take that as a sign she was becoming more comfortable around him?

She filled her coffee maker with water and began rummaging around for a filter. "I usually drink tea."

"Well, then, tea's fine," he said while looking at the teapot, half expecting it to move again.

Julia glanced in his direction and grinned. "Val's sound asleep. Or passed out."

"I didn't know ghosts had to sleep."

"Neither did I. And I certainly didn't know they got drunk."

They both laughed and a moment of familiarity passed between them. They shared the same awareness. Julia was the first to look away as she opened a cabinet to get out the coffee. "I didn't know ghosts would smoke and need food or indulge in makeup and perfume and mud packs."

Steve couldn't help chuckling. "You really did scare the hell out of me the other night, Julia."

She joined his laughter. "If you think that was bad, you should have seen her at the mall."

He was surprised. "What would possess you to take her to a mall?" Pausing for a moment, he again laughed. "I guess that was a poor turn of phrase."

"It's a long story. I'll tell you in a minute. Do you want to wait in the living room for the coffee to perk, or would you like to sit at the table?"

Julia leaned back against the counter and he couldn't help noticing how pretty she was. Even after such a horrendous night, she still looked great in that classic black dress that bared just a hint of shoulder. He was immediately reminded of dancing with her and holding her in his arms. The way she had fit with his body was electrifying. He had been glad she'd maintained a safe distance between them, as he was afraid she would have been offended by his physical reaction to her. She was soft and warm and feminine and real . . . unlike the artificial women in his past that were so protective of their hair and makeup.

Realizing that he hadn't answered her, he tore himself away from his thoughts and said, "The kitchen will be fine." As he seated himself at her table, he realized how much he liked the cozy environment that the room offered. He saw scratches on the table that could have been made by her daughter doing a school project. It was a welcome change from the formality that normally surrounded him. He realized in that moment it was because her home reminded him of the comfortable kitchen in the old farm house at the vineyard. Now he found himself wondering what souls had passed through that house to have given it the same warmth he found here.

"Val's signature scent, if you could call it that, is Shalimar. I noticed it for days before she appeared. When she realized I didn't have any, she harassed me into taking her to the mall to get some."

Julia sat across from him and smiled. "I know this is still hard to believe."

"I'm so confused," he said honestly, "I don't even know what I believe in anymore. Everything I used to believe has been turned upside down."

"I know how you feel. Val has a way of doing that, but you know something? She means well. It's just that her intent and the results don't match. She was really upset when I put her to bed. For a woman who acts so tough to shed tears . . ."

"She was crying?"

"The other reason we were at the mall was for makeup. Every day she remains here, she's aging. You said how beautiful she was, that's how you remember her. But each day she stays with me she's being robbed of that beauty. To me, Val now appears like a middle-aged woman. I hope she completes this mission, no matter how crazy it is, before all her beauty fades. Poor Val never realized that there was anything more to her than her physical attributes. It means so much to her. She believes that everything she ever achieved in her life was because of the way she looked. Take that away, and what does she have?"

Steve thought about it for a moment. "But she was funny, and a good actress."

The coffee finished perking and Julia rose from her chair. "Right now none of that matters. All she can see is that she's getting older every day."

Steve watched as she poured the coffee and brought the cups to the table.

Her smile was teasing. "I'll bring the sugar and cream."

"That did it for me, you know? I tried to tell myself that I was drunk. But even in my younger days, I never got so drunk that I saw things flying through the air."

Julia sat back down. "What were you like when you were younger? Do your parents still live in New York?"

He didn't want the mood to change, but he had to answer her. "They're not living."

"I'm sorry."

He nodded, not wishing to elaborate. "How about yours?"

Sighing, she sat back in her chair. "My father left when I was a child. I never saw him again. My mom died a few years ago."

"Is that her picture in the living room with your daughter?"

Julia smiled. "She loved Paige, and watched her while I worked. I depended on her so much. It was hard when she passed away."

"From the photos it looks like such a happy family. It must have been hard to lose your husband."

Julia looked down to the table. "He didn't die," she said in a low voice. "He left after Paige was born."

Steve was both shocked and embarrassed. "I'm very sorry. I shouldn't have asked. I just assumed . . ."

She looked up and smiled sadly. "That's okay. Don't be sorry. It was all for the best."

Once again, he had to re-evaluate his impression of her. Nothing was as it seemed. Knowing he had to say something, he said the first thing that came into his mind. "Well, it looks like you did a great job with your daughter."

"Thanks. That means a lot to me."

"It's none of my business, but wasn't it hard? Doing it alone?"

Sipping her coffee, she took a moment to respond, as though contemplating his question. "I don't know if I could have done it without my mother's help. She not only took care of my daughter during the day, but was there for support. I think that's the hardest part. Not having anyone to help make the big decisions. It's an awesome responsibility to shape someone's life. How do you know if you're doing it right?"

Her comment made him think about his own childhood. "I had two parents who never took on the responsibility of parenting."

Julia looked at him with a surprised expression. "I guess it's true. You never know what people have been through. I assumed you came from a model family. President of your class. Prep schools. All the advantages."

He laughed. "I suppose that's what I've been trying to create. When your parents are alcoholics, showing up at PTA meetings isn't a priority. Kids who come out of those kinds of situations either survive or go under. I chose to survive."

"It looks like we both took the same path."

Confusion clouded his thoughts. He couldn't figure out what she meant.

Without waiting for him to respond, she seemed to fill in the blanks. "We both chose to overcome our beginnings by never depending on those who let us down. I know I buried myself in raising my daughter and pushing myself to succeed at work. There wasn't much time for anything else. I think you probably did the same thing."

Once again his belief system was challenged, and he wasn't sure if he was comfortable with that. Didn't he like what he did? Didn't he get satisfaction from his success? But when was the last time he had enjoyed the fruits of his labor? It had been almost a year since he'd been to the vineyard. "Maybe you're right," he offered cautiously. "I hadn't thought of it that way before. I knew I had to get out of that concrete war zone, and education seemed to be the best escape. I was lucky. With hard work, I got some scholarships and met the right people. People who pushed me. I knew what I was doing was right, and I kept succeeding, which proved it for me. Actually, Julia, you're the first person who's challenged me. Suddenly you come into my office and I become the bad guy. You made me think."

He watched her gaze become distant. It was almost as if his words had started a flurry of her own thoughts. He knew, from years of being a manager, to let someone in that state finish their process, for sometimes the most brilliant idea will come forth.

Her voice was quiet and introspective. "Isn't it strange that we both had our fundamental belief systems challenged by an unexpected outside source? Val came into my life at the same time I came into your office. She made me face tough questions about the way I was living and, as much as I hate to admit it, I guess that's what I was doing to you."

He smiled. "Yeah, but I'm glad you weren't a ghost."

She laughed and looked away while asking, "Do you want more coffee?"

"No, I'd better get going. It's late and you've got to be tired." He took a deep breath, nervous about the next question he wanted to ask. He couldn't believe how insecure he felt around this woman. For some reason, above all the others, her opinion of him mattered. "You know, Julia, you never got back to me about dinner tomorrow night."

Obviously embarrassed, she got up and cleared the table. "Oh, I'm sorry. I got so busy at work that I forgot."

"Well?" When she didn't answer, he pressed on, "After the night we had tonight, we both deserve something normal. Without Val."

Turning from the sink, Julia said, "Without Val? Just the two of us?"

He couldn't help chuckling. "That *is* what I had in mind when I first asked you. What do you say,

Julia? I really enjoyed this," he said, gesturing to the table. "Why don't we find a nice quiet restaurant and continue?"

He could see her inner struggle, and a part of him wondered if she still thought of him as the ogre. "Hey, am I that bad?" he asked.

"Of course not. It's just . . . I don't know, I haven't had a real date in twenty years." She looked horrified. "Not that I meant we—we would have a *date*. I don't know what I mean."

Flattered and relieved, Steve stood and walked toward her. He could sense her state of near panic. Knowing she was scared and embarrassed, he realized he needed to quell her fears before he left.

"To be honest, when I'd asked, I had hoped it would turn into a date. If it makes you feel any better, it's been a long time since I went out with anyone genuine." He grinned, while searching in his pocket for the car keys. "Pick you up at seven?"

She reminded him of a deer caught in the headlights, but she managed to nod.

"Great. I'll see you tomorrow night then."

As he walked toward the door he heard her say, "Thanks for all your help tonight."

"Say goodbye to Val for me. It was an experience, to be sure."

She gently shut the door and locked it. Standing in the dark foyer, she took a little time for herself. Had she completely misjudged him? For a moment tonight at the table there was something vulnerable about him. He wasn't perfect. Just human, like all the rest of us. He had his baggage; he just hid it better than most. She felt flattered that he had opened up to her. She was sure he didn't do it often. It made her feel special. And he said she was genuine. Of all the things he said tonight, that meant the most to her.

A date. A real date. Could it be that he was interested in her, without Val? Although the idea of a date was exciting, it was also terrifying. She had spent twenty years building a protective barrier between herself and the outside world. It was what kept her safe. What would her life be like living beyond the wall? Maybe she didn't even have that choice any longer, for already she could feel that he had chipped away at the cornerstone.

# Chapter 10

"I knew it when I saw him! I *told* you he was the one! When are you going to start listening to me?" Nursing a hangover, Val had remained in a robe all day. She hadn't even bothered with makeup, and Julia could see that the daily aging was even more obvious.

"Will you please stop? The only reason Steve asked me to dinner was to discuss the people affected by the takeover."

Val sat in the overstuffed chair in Julia's bedroom, sipping a ginger ale and watching her dress.

"Oh, knock it off, Julia. You know the guy likes you. And damn it, you like him. I sensed how you felt when you were dancing with him last night. It wasn't business on your mind."

Dressed in a slip, Julia threw a discarded suit onto her bed. "I hate this! It's not fair. I have no privacy. Not a second to myself. It's worse than having a two-year-old in the house. At least with a kid you can hear them barging into the room, but you—you just barged into my mind without my permission!" She looked at Val and added in a heated voice, "That is unacceptable. From this point on I forbid you to invade my private thoughts. Do you understand? It's just not fair!"

Without giving Val a chance to answer, Julia stormed out of the bedroom, walked into the bathroom and slammed the door behind her. Leaning up against the frame, she held her arms around herself to steady her nerves and distance herself from Val. A barrage of questions entered her mind. What else had Val sensed? All her personal thoughts were now violated. Did Val know how aroused she was last night? Could she enter her dreams? It was all too terrible to consider. But if she had this power, would she also be brass enough to invade Steve's thoughts? Could she have planted the idea of a real date in his head?

The possibility that he had not asked her out of his own desire, but because some ghost was on a mission, made her want to cringe with disappointment.

A soft tapping began and Julia pushed away from the door. "Go away. Just go away and leave me alone."

"Look, I'm sorry. I want you to have a good time. You deserve it. You're right. I went too far, but I'd had a little too much to drink last night."

Julia opened the door with swift irritation. "A *little* too much?" She swept past Val and reentered her bedroom.

Val followed her and sat on the edge of the bed. "I'm sorry, Julia. I won't do it again. I promise."

Julia was searching her closet for the best outfit for a date. Nothing seemed right. She had business suits and casual clothes and a host of scruffy outfits to clean the house, but nothing for a date.

"Did you hear me? I promise I won't do it again."

Abandoning her search for the moment, Julia spun on Val. "Oh? Just like you promised last night to stay at the table? I don't think I'll bet the house on any of your promises."

"That one doesn't count," Val countered. "It was the first time, outside of shopping, that I've been out of this house. Maybe martinis and promises don't mix well."

"Obviously with you they don't."

"I know how important this night is to you. I swear I won't do anything to mess it up, cause you to be embarrassed, or invade your thoughts again. It's like Oscar night, and I'm not about to trip you while you go up the aisle. Tonight is your debut, and I wouldn't do anything to ruin the moment for you. You're my friend."

Julia stopped thinking and stared at the woman seated on her bed. There was sincerity and almost wistfulness in Val's voice. Maybe after everything that had happened in the last month they actually had become friends.

Julia's tone softened and she turned back to face the closet. "Well, then, since you're better at this than I am, would you help me find something to wear?"

Val walked up and put her arm around Julia's shoulder. "All right. Let's look. We'll come up with something."

When Steve arrived an hour later, Julia was as nervous as a teenager. She felt as though she were going to a prom and not just a simple date. But there was nothing simple about this date. Jesus! A date! Her! She hoped what she was wearing was okay. Val had taken her plain black suit, and added Paige's colorful blue and green silk paisley vest to wear alone under the jacket. She had even rooted through Paige's old jewelry box and found long dangling earrings and a bracelet. The look was definitely different and, to Val's credit, Julia knew she wouldn't have been able to envision such a fashionable creation alone.

Approaching the door, Julia took a deep breath. At least she didn't have to worry about Val tonight. She'd been on her best behavior and had even asked permission to see them off.

When she opened the door, she smiled at her date.

"Hi."

He looked handsome in the charcoal suit. To her amazement, he was carrying a small nosegay of steffanotis, the tiny white flowers nestled prettily in the dark green leaves.

"I can't believe you did this," she murmured, stunned by his gesture as he handed them to her and she held them to her nose. "They're my favorite flower. How did you know?"

"I didn't," he said, obviously pleased by her reaction. "They grow at the vineyard and I asked the florist if he had them."

"They're beautiful. Come in while I put these in water. It'll only take a minute."

He hesitated and extended his other hand. It was holding a small plastic box containing a delicate orchid. "This is for Val. I wanted to thank her for helping us to know each other better." He grinned. "It was an extraordinary night."

Julia returned his smile and motioned for him to come in. "Why don't you give it to her. I'm sure she'd appreciate it coming from you."

Steve entered her home and looked around him with a nervous expression.

"Val?" Julia called out. "Would you come down for a moment?"

To Julia's surprise, Val swept down the stairs dressed and in full makeup. When would she realize no one could see her? She supposed with Val it was her ritual to greet a man at her best. Invisible or not, it was the principle.

Smiling, Julia said, "Look what Steve brought you."

Val's face lit up as she approached and saw the exotic flower Steve held out in his hand.

"For me?" she asked, surprised by the gesture.

Julia turned to Steve. "She's here. You can give it to her."

Steve's expression was incredulous as the box floated out of his hand. "I still can't get used to this."

They both watched as the plastic lid opened and the flower rose in the air.

"I hope she likes it."

Val inhaled the light fragrance as she held the orchid to her face. "Thank you so much. This was so sweet of you."

Looking at Steve, Julia said, "She thanks you and says it was a sweet gesture."

He offered a shy smile in response.

Julia glanced down to her own bouquet. "Let me put these in water and then we can go."

Delighted, Val offered, "No, let me do that for you. You two run along and have a good time."

Julia handed the flowers to Val and, to Steve's amazement, he watched as his gifts floated down the hallway to the kitchen.

"Good night, Val," Julia called out.

"Yes," Steve added a little awkwardly, "Good night."

He had surprised her by picking a Philadelphia restaurant. San Marcos was an old landmark on the Main Line, renowned for its homemade Italian food.

"How did you know about this place?" Julia asked when they were seated at the table enjoying a glass of cabernet.

"I was looking for a restaurant that would allow us to have dinner and talk quietly over good food in a comfortable atmosphere. When I read that it was a restored mansion, I thought we should try it."

Julia looked around at the hardwood floors, the beautiful old rich woods that had been restored, and the quiet elegance of the furnishings. "It's perfect. I've heard of San Marco's, but I've never been here."

Steve smiled. "Great. We can discover it together."

The waiter came and handed them menus, then left them to consider their choices.

"Everything looks so good," Julia murmured. "I don't know where to begin."

"Would you care for an appetizer?"

Julia shook her head. "I think I'll just order an entree. Italian food is so filling." God, was she rambling? She had always hated this small talk, never knowing what to say.

After deliberating for what seemed like an eternity, Julia closed the menu and sipped her wine.

"Have you decided?" Steve asked, looking up.

"I think I'll have the angel hair pasta with the basil wine sauce."

Steve glanced down to the menu. "That sounds terrific. I think I'll have the same." He closed the menu and placed it on the table as he signaled the waiter.

When they were once again alone, he said, "I'm glad that you agreed to join me tonight. This is the first time since I've arrived at Coolback that I've had someone to share a real dinner with me."

Julia was surprised. "Where do you eat? In your apartment?"

He shook his head slightly and laughed. "I'm not a bad cook, but it feels like too much trouble to go through when you're alone."

"I know what you mean. When Paige first left, I lived on Campbell Soup and salad. But you have Mike Kerlocki and Garrett Morgenstern with you. Surely the three of you went out to dinner."

Shrugging, he answered, "For the first two weeks but that got tiring. It's so loud and frantic in those places. Lately I've been eating alone at a diner close to the corporate apartment."

The mother in Julia rose to the surface. "That's terrible. You shouldn't eat every night in diners." Catching herself, she whispered, "I'm sorry. I shouldn't have said that."

"Hey, it's okay. It's nice to know somebody cares."

She was embarrassed by her outburst, and tried to cover it with her next question. "How long will you be here? The transition is just about complete, isn't it?"

He nodded. "There are a few loose ends and I want to see how the new people I've brought in will work out. But, yes. It's almost finished. I guess I'll go back in about a month."

"Where is home? I've never asked."

"New York City. I have an apartment in the East Sixties. It's in a historical district on the east side, right off Madison Avenue. La Cirque is on the street behind me and The Hotel Plaza Anthée is right next door. It's nice, if you have to live in the city."

He must be completely bored in rural New Jersey, she thought. To have come from Madison Avenue to Podunk, Suburbia must be the worst assignment he'd ever had. "Well, that's one thing both you and

Val have in common," she said in a thoughtful voice.

"What?"

Julia caught herself. She'd been thinking aloud. "Both of you came from exciting places. Val left Hollywood and was forced to come here, and Amalgamated ordered you to Nowhere, New Jersey. It's kind of funny," she said, pausing to sip her wine. "You both got your orders from a higher authority, and weren't given much choice in the matter."

He placed his wine glass down on the crisp white linen tablecloth. "It might surprise you, but I actually prefer a rural environment. I grew up in concrete, and one summer I got involved with a program to take inner city youths into the Catskills. Ever since then, I've always dreamed of what it must be like to wake up in the morning and see hills instead of buildings, and hear birds instead of car horns blaring. That's why, when I made some real money, my first present to myself was the vineyard in France."

He looked away toward the large bay window. His voice sounded remote as he added, "But some present that turned out to be. I'm lucky if I get there once a year."

Julia remembered their first meeting in her office and regretted her earlier snipe about his vineyard. Never in her wildest dreams had she guessed that it was his escape from the ugliness of his childhood. And that made it all the more unfortunate, since the lifestyle he had created for himself rarely gave him the chance to enjoy it.

The words slipped out before she could stop them. "If you could do anything other than what you're doing now for a living, what would it be?"

Steve kind of frowned, tilted his head, and sat back in his chair as he thought about it. "What else could I do, at this point in my life, to make the same money I'm making now?"

"I didn't ask you about the money. Let's say, for the sake of argument, that there wouldn't be any financial impact if you made the change. What would you do?"

"Well . . . since I'm a lawyer, maybe I could consult on a freelance basis. Or I could teach the senior level management of takeover firms how to conduct a successful acquisition, but I guess that's the same as consulting. Or—"

"No, that isn't what I'm talking about. You're still trying to keep the money the same by using skills you've already acquired. What I'm asking is what's your secret passion? Do you like art? Music? If you could make the same money at your passion, what would it be?"

Running his hand through his hair, Steve squinted off into the distance. "I don't know how to answer. I've never considered it before."

Julia kept her silence and let him think. Maybe it was presumptuous to delve into his mind, but she really wanted to know. She was seeing so much more to him than she had once thought. He wasn't the snake or a vampire. He seemed like a man that was trapped by golden handcuffs.

"My passion . . . No, you can't make any money at that . . ."

He was about to dismiss the subject, but Julia couldn't let it go. "Look, you're well read, and I'm sure you've heard of a million harebrained ideas that turned into profitable ventures, from baby food to pet rocks. From hackers in a garage to MTV. Each one was a long shot, but it was somebody's passion. What's yours?"

He appeared embarrassed and took a moment before speaking. "I guess it would be to live at the farm in France and turn it into a profitable vineyard."

Excited, Julia grinned. "There. Was that so hard? You could think about it like a turn-around company. What would it take to make it work?"

As he pondered the question, he stared at her and she could see the concept taking root. "Well, I do employ a couple who live on a neighboring farm. They keep the vines healthy. Maurice and Odeale harvest the grapes once a year, and we sell them to local wine makers. But still . . . it would take so much to get the operation off the ground. I'd have to sell off almost everything to do it. Nice dream, but . . ." He again shook his head, as if trying to shake the thought out of his mind.

Steve's comments confirmed Julia's hunch. There was more to the man than met the eye. "You know you're more fortunate than most. If you wanted to change, at least you have an option."

The waiter arrived with their food, and both of them concentrated on the meal for a few moments.

Spearing a shrimp, Steve said. "Okay, now what about you? What's your passion?"

She looked up. "I thought we had gotten off that subject."

"Absolutely not," he teased. "Did you think you were going to get off that easy? 'Fess up. What's your secret passion?"

Although she knew his words only referred to their conversation, they still caused a blush to creep up from her throat. She knew she couldn't let him see it, or she'd give her thoughts away. And the very last thing she wanted him to know was how much he was affecting her.

"I guess my passion was my daughter," she said, while concentrating on swirling the pasta around her fork. "I couldn't say work was my passion. I care about it, but only because it enabled me to take care of my child the way I wanted."

His laugh was triumphant. "Hah . . . we seem to have the same problem while defining passion. I'm not talking about your daughter, or about money. What would you do for pleasure?"

She glanced up at him. "I really don't know. I've spent so many years devoted to Paige and working that I never discovered my own pleasure."

He seemed to ignore the implication in her words and tried to steer her back to the subject. "What do you enjoy doing in your spare time? There must be something. Movies? Theater? Art? Music?"

She thought about it for a few moments. "I never really had spare time. The only thing I can truly say I derive any pleasure from is gardening."

"Really?"

"I find it very relaxing. When Paige was home I used to have to wait until early evening before finding the time. But now on the weekends, I like to get up early and get my hands into the dirt before it becomes too warm. There's something about smelling the good, clean earth, and the quiet . . . after years of kids running in and out of my house it seemed like a refuge." She stopped and stared across the table. "But now, since Paige has gone, the quiet has been unbearable."

He looked at her with understanding and nodded. "Yeah, I know what you mean. But sometimes, even if you surround yourself with noise and lots of people, you can still feel the same way. I have for years. Maybe it isn't the noise you miss so much as not feeling connected any more."

Afraid of where the conversation was leading, she looked down at her plate and whispered, "Maybe."

Changing the subject, he offered in a cheerful voice, "Tell you what—how would you like to go hear some music after this?" He glanced at his watch and said, "It's still early, and I read about this jazz club right in Center City called Zanzibar Blue. Do you like jazz?"

She didn't answer immediately. "Well, to be honest, I haven't really heard a lot of it. Can I be truthful?"

He grinned and nodded.

"The jazz I was exposed to sounded more like musicians that kept tuning their instruments, and I wanted to clap my hands and say, 'Hey, guys, now let's get it all together and start a real song.' "

Steve sat back and laughed. "Okay, so you don't care for traditional jazz. Well, you're in for a treat. This place features contemporary jazz artists. It's a combination of jazz and blues, sort of like Billie Holliday music."

She perked up. "I love Billie Holliday."

Steve seemed pleased. "Then you should love this place. I was going to suggest you try the cannolis, but why don't we skip it and have coffee and dessert at the club?"

"Sure." Julia felt wonderful. Steve wanted to extend the evening. And so did she. This was turning into a real date. It was certainly turning out better that she had hoped. For some odd reason, she wanted to call Val and thank her, to tell her every detail of how perfect it was.

She didn't know what to expect when she walked into Zanzibar Blue. It was crowded, yet intimate. They were ushered to a table on the second floor and the artists were no more than twenty feet from them. It was an old-fashioned club where couples could talk and enjoy live music at the same time, very different from the large and impersonal singles scene they had experienced last night.

The quartet began with a sultry version of the song, "Fever," but the way the jazz vocalist sang it was a far cry from Peggy Lee. If Peggy Lee's version was considered hot, then this was positively scorching. The tempo was very slow and very seductive. Raw sexuality hung in the air as the woman huskily delivered each phrase. Julia felt the music pull at her. It was as if each sensuous note reverberated within her body and had its own special meaning. The same heat spread up from her thighs, causing her to shift in the chair. She was aware of a dull ache, a yearning inside of her, that hadn't been satisfied in a very long time.

God Almighty, what was she going to do? Steve was sitting close to her in the crowded, tight room. His arm was across the back of her chair, so he could see around the man in front of him. Resting her arms on the edge of the table, she was afraid to lean back and make contact. Last night when they were dancing, she had felt the same heat. Only tonight it was much stronger.

"Isn't she terrific?" Steve asked, leaning closer to her face to be heard over the music.

Julia merely smiled and nodded. She could smell that same dark and mysterious scent of his cologne and it instantly entered her nostrils and shot to her brain. It sent crazy thoughts . . . those male-female primal thoughts, and they scared the heck out of her. How would she ever get through this evening without giving herself away? Think, she told herself. Think rationally. She worked with this man. Not just worked with him, he was her boss. And he was leaving in a month to go back to his exciting life in New York. She was just a diversion. That had to be it. That and Val. How many people run up against the ghost of a glamorous movie star? Val said he'd have to come to her for answers. He was fascinated by what was happening in her life. It shook him up, made him think about possibilities.

She sneaked a look from the corner of her eye. But he seemed to really be enjoying himself. And at dinner, there were several times when they were talking about passion that he had stared at her with an intense look. Had she imagined that?

Self-doubt and inexperience flooded in on her. What did she know about any of this? The last man she had seriously dated she had married, and God alone knew what a disaster that had turned into. Every man that she had dated after her marriage, and there weren't many, had turned in to another disappointment. They didn't want to explore a relationship, only sex, and they definitely didn't want to be bothered with a child. Years ago, she had told herself this sort of thing wasn't going to be a part of her life any longer. She had even believed it. She had come to dread the constant state of indecision that comes with dating. Does he like me? Does he like my daughter? Will I see him again? Will he call? It was a torture that she had vowed never to repeat. Never again would she allow a male to be her mirror of self esteem. She had told herself that many people remained single and lived full, productive lives, and she would be one of them. She had been one of them! But now? All the walls of her barriers were shaky. It wasn't fair for this to happen. Not after so many years.

The song ended and everyone in the room applauded or shouted their praise. The singer acknowledged their reaction and signaled the band to begin the next number. After a waitress brought coffee and dessert to their table, Steve grinned as he picked up his fork.

"I can't remember when I've had such a good time. Thanks for coming with me, Julia."

*Oh, God . . . please don't let me think about the future. Not about tomorrow, or even later tonight. Let me enjoy the moment. Let me be more like a man.*

"Thank you for asking," she managed to say. "I'm having a wonderful time."

He caught her gaze and held it with his own. "Good. Then we'll have to come here again. See, I knew you'd like jazz if you gave it a chance."

She chuckled and attacked her dessert. What did that mean? *We'll have to come here again?* Were they going to have another date? Did he want to see her again after tonight? Damn. Those defeating questions slammed into her brain and she fought to banish them. Determined, she looked up to the quartet and paid attention. After a few minutes, she could actually hear how each note had a purpose, like musicians having fun with each other, giving each a solo, a time to shine on their own before returning and playing together. It actually did make sense.

They stayed for almost two hours, listening to another set. During the intermission, they talked about music and the night life in the city. He told her he had bought a magazine, and that's where he had read about the restaurant and Zanzibar Blue. Even though she lived only twenty minutes across the bridge, she hadn't known about all the small music and comedy clubs that flourished throughout the city. Their conversation was light. They talked and laughed easily together, and Julia was once more reminded of how different he was from her first impression. A totally different personality emerged. It reminded her of disliking a teacher and then meeting him outside of school.

When he drove onto her street, Julia's earlier nervousness returned. The drive from Philadelphia was enjoyable, interspersed with good conversation, classical music and laughter. She marveled that her first date in almost twenty years had gone so well. But now, with her house in sight, her body tensed with apprehension. What would happen when they said good night? Would he want to come in? Would he ask to see her again? If he wanted to come in and she said yes, would he take that as an invitation for more? And if she said no, would he think she really didn't have a good time? This was the part of dating that she hated. The terrible indecision.

He pulled the car into her driveway and shifted into park. Turning to her, he smiled and said, "So what do you think, Julia? Would you like to do this again?" His expression seemed hopeful and almost a little nervous.

Sensing he shared her apprehension, she smiled shyly. "This was really nice. I'm glad I gave the jazz club a try. I didn't know what I was missing all these years."

He seemed pleased by her comment. "It's always more fun to explore something different if you're in good company." Realizing what he'd said, he quickly corrected himself. "What I mean is that, for me, tonight was more fun because I was in good company."

She laughed, trying to ease his embarrassment. "I knew what you meant, and you're right. Ahh . . . no . . . I mean, I didn't think *I* was good company. I meant—"

"Julia," he interrupted and then laughed. "I think we both agree. Do you find this part of the evening a little awkward?"

"God, yes," she admitted and sighed with relief.

"So let's just say tonight was fun and we'd like to do this again?"

Julia nodded and smiled.

"Okay, why don't we take turns at finding new or different things to do?"

Julia thought for a moment, racking her brain for something he would enjoy. Then it came to her. "I've already had my turn," she said with a laugh. "I introduced you to Val. Now you have to admit, that was different."

He joined her laughter. "That's a hard one to top, but we did get you into a jazz club tonight, so it's back to you. It's your turn."

She peered at him with feigned patience. "Always the negotiator, aren't you?"

"Oh, c'mon. Don't look at me like that. For real, it's your turn."

"Seriously, Steve, what could I show you that you haven't already seen?"

"That's the fun of it all. You can do it."

Julia sat in the car and stared at her house. "I

could show you farm markets and how to shop for a balanced meal. And even how to cook it at home. And for my grand finale, I'll show you how to freeze half of it and have it again next week."

He laughed. "You can't use that one. I do know how to shop and cook a meal. I just don't feel like it when I'm away on business."

Julia racked her brain for a creative suggestion. What in the world could she show him, the man who had been everywhere but Disney World? Suddenly, it came to her. "I've got it," she exclaimed with triumph.

"What?"

"I'm not going to tell you. It's a surprise. The only thing I can say is that it has to be done during the day, and you have to wear jeans."

"Oh, God, what is it?"

"I'm not telling."

He was silent for a moment. "If this mysterious adventure has to be in the day, and we both work, then it must be on the weekend. That leaves tomorrow, or next weekend. Are you busy tomorrow?"

"Tomorrow is fine. Pick me up around ten o'-clock."

She couldn't believe that he wanted to go out again so soon. She was flattered and all of her earlier doubts vanished.

"It's a date."

Julia reached for the door handle and Steve shut off the motor. She knew he would walk her up to her house, but didn't want to deal with the awkwardness of saying good night on the steps. Hesitating, she turned back to face him.

"That's okay, you don't have to walk me up. We'll both have an early day tomorrow."

"I'm not going to come in, but I do want to see you to your door."

Even though it made her nervous, his request was reasonable. What could she say? He followed her up the steps and waited as she unlocked the door. Turning back to him she smiled anxiously.

"I had a good time."

"So did I. I can't wait to see what's in store for me tomorrow."

Panic seized her. It was the moment of truth. Would he kiss her or not? The seconds seemed to drag into minutes as he stared at her. Steve was probably trying to figure out what to do next. Ending the indecision, Julia murmured, "Well, good night."

To her surprise Steve reached for her, holding her shoulders and gently placing a kiss on her forehead. He whispered, "Good night. I'll see you tomorrow morning."

When Julia shut the door behind her, she leaned against it for support and grinned. She felt like Eliza Doolittle, as if she could burst into song. It had been an enchanted evening, better than she had ever expected.

If they had been dancing, she could have danced all night . . .

# Chapter 11

"Here's the report from the arbitration meeting with the union. Do you want to see it, or would you like me to file it?"

Julia looked up from the paperwork on her desk and smiled at her assistant. "Thanks, Meg. Why don't you leave it here? I guess I should read it first."

"You look chipper this morning. What's your secret?"

Julia tried not to blush. "There's no secret. It's just a beautiful day."

"Yeah, and we're stuck in here. I always get like this in the spring. At least we had good weather this weekend. Did you do anything special?"

For three years Meg had asked her that question every Monday morning. And for three years she had nothing exciting to report. Now that she did, she couldn't talk about it, at least not with co-workers. A slight tremor of disappointment ran through her. She wanted to share her happiness with everyone, but that wouldn't be appropriate. "No, nothing special. Did you get those health benefit printouts yet?"

Meg held a stack of folders in her arms. "No, not yet. I'll get on the phone after I file these."

Once more alone in her office, Julia sat back in her chair and let the pleasant memories return. Steve had really been surprised by her choice for their outing. She kept him in suspense, only offering directions as they drove north on the Jersey Turnpike. He still hadn't figured it out, even as they passed the signs for Great Adventure.

She chuckled to herself while remembering Steve's expression when they pulled into the huge parking lot. To his credit, he quickly got into the spirit of the moment and turned from a high-powered sophisticate into a fun-loving kid. They had a ball. Steve had insisted on going on the most treacherous rides, on filling them with food from every stand they passed. Although the mother in her had been appalled, she'd relented and had found herself joining him in a junk food orgy. By the time they left they were both exhausted, queasy, and laughing hysterically. Even that awkward moment when they'd arrived at her house had passed without incident. He had merely given her a quick hug and an even quicker peck on the forehead before leaving.

Now, thinking back, she had to admit that she was a little disappointed. Didn't he want to kiss her? Immediately she thought of Val, who had asked that question when she'd come home early Sunday evening. It was strange, for Val hadn't seemed like herself. If she didn't know better she would think that Val was still hung over. She hadn't even come down when Steve picked her up. And she'd still been in that robe when they had returned. She seemed more quiet and subdued than normal, but then, what *was* normal with Val? Something about her house guest bothered her. For the first time Val wasn't using any makeup. It was as if she were depressed. Val's only request had been a pack of cigarettes. Julia didn't think she had even bothered with eating.

Interrupting her thoughts, Steve popped in her office and shut the door behind him. Grinning like a mischievous little boy, he sat down in the chair that faced her desk.

"And how are you this fine morning, Ms. Edwards?"

She couldn't help grinning back at him. "Very well, thank you, Mr. McMillan."

"I have a suggestion," he said.

Julia looked up to the drop ceiling. "Oh, no. I'm afraid to ask."

"Don't worry, the big surprises are for the weekend. This is easy."

"Are you sure?"

He chuckled. "Since you've made several references to my poor eating habits, would you like to go with me to lunch today and make sure I get a balanced meal?"

"Today?" she asked with concern. "I couldn't leave here with you. It wouldn't look right, not with all that's going on in the office."

Steve's expression became serious. "I hadn't thought of that."

"It's not that I wouldn't love to, but you have to understand the sensitive nature of the office politics. You're the boss, and I'm the personnel manager. If people got wind of us seeing each other outside of work, the gossip would be horrendous."

He was nodding his head, silently agreeing with her.

"You'll be leaving in a month, Steve. But I have to work with these people. I wouldn't want anyone to think that the only reason my job wasn't affected was because I had a relationship with the boss."

"I'm sorry, Julia. I didn't mean to put you in a tenuous position. I just thought it would be fun."

"It would be, but . . ."

He sat up straight and thought for a moment. "I've got it. Who has to know? I could meet you at the diner by the corporate apartment. It's only seven minutes from here and no one from Coolback ever goes there."

She considered it. She wanted to see him, but not at the expense of her career. This was like recess for Steve, a time to play. For her, it was different. The consequences after he was gone would be real. Shaking her head, she murmured, "I don't know. It could be risky."

"Oh, c'mon, Julia. Think of it as another adventure. We'll discover meat loaf, mashed potatoes and peas."

She had to laugh, seeing that same glint in his eyes as when he'd first realized he was at an amusement park. "All right. Just this once. But we have to be very careful."

Steve stood and backed up toward the door while looking at his wrist. "Okay, since we're on a secret mission, let's synchronize our watches. ETA at the diner is twelve-thirty."

Julia sank back in her chair and grinned. "Get out of here," she said. "I have work to finish. God knows, I don't want to be fired."

He opened the door and paused to tap his watch again. "Twelve-thirty."

She turned the band around on her wrist and tapped the face of her watch. "Right, Chief. I just hope nobody gets wind of this."

He smiled. "Trust me."

She stared at the closed door and heard his words replay in her mind. What worried her was that she was beginning to do just that.


Perhaps it was because it was spring and the earth seemed to be coming back to life that she felt so in tune with it. Riding high from the lunch with Steve, Julia opened the door to her home and called out to Val.

Not hearing a reply, she followed the sound of the television and entered the living room. The sight of Val stopped her abruptly. Val didn't even look up to acknowledge her presence, but continued to stare through the haze of smoke at the television screen. She still hadn't gotten dressed and it looked like she hadn't even combed her hair. She was smoking a cigarette and a half-empty mug of coffee sat on the end table next to an overflowing ashtray.

Julia was about to scold Val for smoking in the house when she saw the expression of melancholy on Val's face, a face that looked much older than it did this morning.

"Hey, how can you see in here?" Julia asked in a light tone as she moved toward the window.

"Don't do that," Val muttered.

"I'm only going to open the window and let this smoke out." Julia pulled back the drape.

"It only looks worse in the daylight. I'd rather be blind than see this every day."

In the brief moments when Julia had pulled back the drape, she had glimpsed Val in the sunlight. Forcing her face to remain expressionless, she let the drape drop back into place. In the short time since she had left this morning, Val had aged considerably. Deep lines etched the once perfect skin and her hair seemed dry and brittle, as if robbed of all its youthful luster. Her once voluptuous mouth appeared tight with anguish and tears filled her dull eyes.

Feeling Val's pain, Julia sat down next to her. How could she tell Val about her great day when her friend was in so much despair?

Val's voice sounded gravelly, like that of an old woman who had been smoking all her life. "I saw a talk show today and there was Anne Jefferies who used to star on the Topper series. She was with Francis Bergen, Anne Blyth and Dina Merrill. They used to be so vital, so beautiful. Now they're reduced to selling jewelry on the Home Shopping Network. You should have seen them, Julia. It was so sad . . ."

Not knowing how to answer, Julia reached over and touched Val's hand. The skin felt thin and crepey, reminding her of her mother's before she'd died. Scared, Julia realized Val was more than depressed.

"You look like you haven't eaten all day. Let me fix you something."

"I'm not hungry," Val said, withdrawing her hand and reaching for another cigarette. "Why should I eat? To keep up my strength?" The laugh that followed was hard and bitter. "You know, Julia, I'm honestly glad I died young, if this is what it would have been like to get old and have people see me this way. At least the last time anyone saw me I was still beautiful." She exhaled a thick stream of smoke and turned to Julia. "I've done my part. You're happy. When in hell are they going to take me back and stop this nightmare?"

A rush of sympathy went through her. "I thought you said you would leave if I went out on a date? I went on two, and I had lunch with him today. I don't understand this anymore than you do."

Bitterness was still in Val's voice. "It shouldn't surprise me. I've always had to work hard for everything I wanted. Why should this be any different?"

Wanting to help, she searched her mind for anything to make it better. "Can you remember what you were told before you came here?"

Val waved the cigarette, expelling an impatient

breath. "They didn't tell me anything. It was just a feeling . . . a sense of being needed that drew me to you. What do I know? I should have remembered what my agent said—always get it in writing."

"Well, if it was just a sense of being needed that drew you here, maybe I'm not the only one that needed you."

There were a few moments of silence between them. It was obvious that neither considered that possibility.

"Who else was important in your life, Val? Someone who's still alive and might need you?"

"How would I know that?" Val demanded in an angry voice. "I've told you, there was no one in my life of importance."

Needing to comfort her, Julia overlooked the anger and said, "Val, you've helped me. Now let me help you. We'll get through this together."

Val crunched out her cigarette and pulled closed the edges of her robe with anger. As she slowly stood up, she said, "I've never needed help in my life. Even as a kid I was able to hold my own against all odds. You go fix yourself something for dinner, Julia. I'm going to bed."

She watched Val leave the room and mount the stairs, taking each step one at a time. The transformation was pitiful. At a loss, Julia called out, "Maybe you'll be hungry later?"

Val didn't answer.

* * *

All week long Julia enjoyed her secret lunches with Steve. It had gotten to the point where he didn't even call or discuss it with her. Passing in the hallway, or in a meeting, he would catch her eye and tap his watch. She knew what he meant and a silent communication would take place. The feeling was exhilarating. The only thing marring her happiness was Val's depression. It seemed to be getting worse with each day.

And how was she supposed to handle all of this with Paige coming home at the end of the week? On one hand she couldn't wait to see her daughter, but on the other was a feeling of apprehension about Val and Steve. So much had changed since Paige had left after Christmas. How could she ever explain a man in her mother's life—and a ghost!

Discussing Steve might prove difficult. She remembered talking to Paige about dating and giving her lots of advice, but to actually tell her daughter that she was now kind of involved was another matter entirely. She had no idea how Paige would react. It had been just the two of them for so long.

She had tried to talk to Val about Paige's homecoming, but Val was sinking further into depression. After their discussion, she had moved out of Paige's room and into the attic.

Julia had been appalled and they had argued about it. She had suggested the guest room. She would never have banished Val that way, but Val had moved her things up while Julia was at work. Each day it got worse. She never knew what she would find when she came home. Although Val rarely came downstairs anymore, Julia was almost fearful of going to the attic and seeing Val's worsening condition.

Val gave up television and seemed obsessed with the stacks of old *Life* magazines that she had found in the corner of the attic. Maybe she wouldn't have to discuss Val at all, since Paige would only be home for four days before leaving for Europe. But the thought of leaving her friend in an attic for four days frightened her. What would happen to Val?

The only person she could turn to was Steve. They would discuss it at lunch.

She arrived before he did and sat in their usual booth. She ordered a cup of tea and was staring into it, deep in thought, when she heard his voice.

"Just try and look natural," he said sliding into the seat across from her. "I think that guy behind you is a secret operative from Almalgamated. Do you think they're on to us?"

She smiled. "That's the least of my worries today."

His expression immediately sobered. "What's wrong? Don't tell me you're canceling our date for this weekend. I've got a big surprise lined up."

She stared at him. "I can't. Paige is coming home this weekend."

"Great. I can't wait to meet her."

Shaking her head, she played with the spoon. Why would she even think about introducing him to her daughter when he was merely a good friend?

It was true they had enjoyed each other's company, but they hadn't even held hands! "That's not all. I'm worried about Val. Do you remember me telling you how depressed she was becoming? Well, when I told her about Paige, she moved into the attic instead of the guest room. We had a terrible fight over it, but she says she just wants to be left alone until she's taken back."

"I thought your happiness was her mission. Aren't you happy?"

Julia looked up. "Of course I am. But since she didn't leave, there must be something else that's holding her here."

"What else could it be?"

"She said she was drawn here by a sense of need. I have the strangest feeling that there's something, or someone else, but she won't talk to me. If she were alive, she'd be diagnosed as clinically depressed. She doesn't get dressed; she rarely eats, and she sleeps a lot."

"Well, what can we do? What happened to make her so depressed?"

Julia thought about his questions. "The only thing I can think of is that she's aging so rapidly."

"Was it always like that?"

She shook her head. "It was gradual in the beginning. It seemed to pick up after the night we all went out."

"That was when you and I got together. I thought you had said her mission was your happiness. Maybe now that you're happy, she isn't needed.

Perhaps that's the way they're gradually taking her back."

"But I don't get it. She's already died once. She can't die again." A shudder ran through her. "I don't think I could take seeing that."

"Julia, we're not talking about our reality here. If we were, we wouldn't be having this conversation. What do we really know about any of this?"

Staring down at the formica table, Julia said, "I just wish I knew what to do to help her."

"What did you say earlier? You had a feeling that something, or someone, might be holding her here? Maybe if we could find out what that was, it would release her."

They ordered lunch, yet she was immersed in thought as they ate. What was he talking about? *We* could help Val? He was going to New York in a couple of weeks. It was nice that he had offered, but it was something she'd have to handle on her own. Why should this be any different than the other things she had managed to cope with all alone? She would find a way.

As usual, he walked her to her car. A light breeze blew the hair back off her face and she deeply inhaled the fragrance of spring. Steve was walking close to her and he reached out, putting his arm around her shoulders for comfort.

"I wish there was something I could do to make you feel better. Isn't there an authority on this? A priest, or something?"

In spite of everything, Julia grinned. He really seemed like he wanted to help. "I don't want an exorcism. I want to help her, not chase her away. And, anyway, who would believe this?"

"I guess you're right. I wouldn't want to do anything to hurt Val. After all, she was the one that brought us together."

They were standing at her car, and a moment of silence passed between them. Steve stepped in closer, resting both hands at her shoulders. She didn't move, closing her eyes in expectation of his usual kiss on the forehead. When she felt his mouth lightly touch hers, she was startled and opened her eyes.

Looking at her, he smiled. "I've wanted to do this since the first night, but I didn't want to offend you. This may not be the right place, or the way I had it planned, but I couldn't help it."

She was floored. Her heart was beating so fast she could hear it pulsing in her ears. At a loss for words, she continued to stare at him. All sorts of emotions swept through her. Dear God, he really did want her. Her!

Without waiting for a reply, Steve leaned into her again and brought his mouth down on hers. His lips were warm and tender, as if testing her reaction. She had waited so long for this, had fantasized so often about it, that she melted into his embrace. His arms tightened around her and she automatically slid her hands up his back as she returned his kiss. In that instant she knew that she wanted him. It was a primal urge, frightening her so much that she broke the embrace and rested her forehead on his chest.

"We are in a parking lot," she whispered.

Steve chuckled and gave her a quick hug before parting. "Then I'll have to choose a better place next time."

Julia smiled nervously and turned to unlock her car door. He opened it for her and she quickly slid behind the wheel to avoid embarrassment.

With his hand on the door, he leaned in and said in a low voice, "I'll call you later about the weekend."

Not wanting to discuss that issue again, she nodded and started her car. He stood watching her back up and she waved as she drove away.

He had kissed her. Actually kissed her. A real kiss this time, not just a peck on the forehead. And she had felt his body respond when they had embraced. It may have been decades since she was with a man, but she certainly remembered that blatant indicator. The years hadn't erased that from her memory. Nor had the years kept her body from responding in kind. God, what was happening? To feel this desire after all these years was bewildering. She wasn't a young girl. She was almost forty, and had given up ever feeling like this again. She had to keep telling herself that he was leaving. Years of being responsible had taught her to always look at the consequences. She didn't want to become some pathetic woman who fell in love and was left again.

She had to protect herself.

Determined to guard against potential hurt, she kept to her office and tried desperately to regain her concentration. Nothing worked. If she wasn't thinking about Steve, then she was worrying about

Val and Paige's homecoming. She kept looking at her watch. The hours seemed to drag. For the first time in years she actually wanted to bolt. Once the office had been her sanctuary. It was here that she'd felt in control. Now everything was in a state of upheaval. Being at the office made her crazy. Going home was depressing. There was nowhere to hide. And her daughter was arriving tomorrow morning right in the middle of all this chaos.

Needing a break, she forced herself to go to the employees' lounge for a cup of coffee and was grateful that no one else was in the room. She entered quickly and poured the last thick remnants from the bottom of the pot. Looking into the cup with distaste, she tried to doctor it up with powdered creamer and sugar. The creamer created dense white lumps that wouldn't dissolve and she stabbed at them with the stirrer.

"So you got the last cup, huh?"

Startled by the male voice, she turned quickly and saw Vince Demicci standing at the entrance to the lounge. She groaned inwardly and extended the cup. "You can have this, if you want it. Do so at your own risk, though. I think it's hi-test by now."

Vince shook his head. "No, thanks. You go for it. You probably need it more than I do."

Trying to hide her confusion, Julia asked, "I do?"

He leaned against the door frame. "Sure. It's hard work buttering up to the new boss."

He had a smug smirk on his face and she wanted to slap it off. She slowly curled her fingers inward to stop the urge. In the most controlled voice she could muster, she said, "I'm sorry? I don't know what you're talking about."

"Come on, Julia. Desperate times call for desperate measures. I'd use your advantage if I could."

Julia blanched at his appalling reference. How dare he make such an assumption? "Vince, that's always been your problem where I'm concerned. You've always felt it was an *advantage,* not hard work. I don't have to deal with this," she said, pouring the coffee down the drain and throwing the cup away. Giving him a pointed look when she left, she added, "Nor do I have to deal with you."

Thoroughly rattled, Julia reentered her office and closed the door behind her. They had only been going to lunch together for a week and already the office gossip mongers had started. She looked around the room and remembered being so proud of her accomplishments. What had once been her refuge now felt like a prison.

She had to get her life back on track.

Paige was coming home tomorrow.

# Chapter 12

Standing at the gate, she watched the plane make the connection to the jetway. Nothing was going to ruin Paige's homecoming. She had spent last night cleaning the entire house and adding loving touches to Paige's room. Fresh flowers and potpourri scented the bedroom with her daughter's favorite fragrance. A small bottle of the perfume was gift-wrapped and waiting on her dresser. Val was ensconced in the attic, and she hadn't even replied when Julia told her she was going to the airport. But none of that mattered now.

Her daughter was finally home.

First class passengers began filing into the airport and a knot of nervous anticipation formed in Julia's belly. She couldn't wait to see Paige and hold her again. That instinctive need for her child surged through her arms, making them ache with a sweetness only a mother could understand. Searching the faces of the crowd patiently, she hovered about the entrance waiting to see her beloved face. She spied

# We've got your authors!

If you seek out the latest historical romances by today's bestselling authors, our new reader's service, KENSINGTON CHOICE, is the club for you.

KENSINGTON CHOICE is the only club where you can find authors like Janelle Taylor, Shannon Drake, Rosanne Bittner, Sylvie Sommerfield, Penelope Neri and Phoebe Conn all in one place...

...and the only service that will deliver their romances direct to your home as soon as they are published—even before they reach the bookstores.

KENSINGTON CHOICE is also the only service that will give you a substantial guaranteed discount off the publisher's price on every one of those romances.

That's right: Every month, the Editors at Zebra and Pinnacle select four of the newest novels by our bestselling authors and rush them straight to you, even *before they reach the bookstores*. The publisher's prices for these romances range from $4.99 to $5.99—but they are always yours for the guaranteed low price of just *$3.95!*

That means you'll always save over $1.00...often as much as $2.00...off the publisher's prices on every new novel you get from KENSINGTON CHOICE!

All books are sent on a 10-day free examination basis, and there is no minimum number of books to buy. (A postage and handling charge of $1.50 is added to each shipment.)

As your introduction to the convenience and value of this new service, we invite you to accept

# 4 BOOKS FREE

The 4 books, worth up to $23.96, are our welcoming gift. You pay only $1 to help cover postage and handling.

To start your subscription to KENSINGTON CHOICE and receive your introductory package of 4 FREE romances, detach and mail the postpaid card at right *today*.

# We have 4 FREE BOOKS for you as your introduction to KENSINGTON CHOICE

To get your FREE BOOKS, worth up to $23.96, mail card below.

As my introduction to your new KENSINGTON CHOICE reader's service, please send me 4 FREE historical romances (worth up to $23.96), billing me just $1 to help cover postage and handling. As a KENSINGTON CHOICE subscriber, I will then receive 4 brand-new romances to preview each month for 10 days FREE. I can return any books I decide not to keep and owe nothing. The publisher's prices for the KENSINGTON CHOICE romances range from $4.99 to $5.99, but as a subscriber I will be entitled to get them for just $3.95 per book. There is no minimum number of books to buy, and I can cancel my subscription at any time. A $1.50 postage and handling charge is added to each shipment.

Name _____

Address _____ Apt. # _____

City _____ State _____ Zip _____

Telephone ( ) _____

Signature _____

(If under 18, parent or guardian must sign)

Subscription subject to acceptance

KC 0894

We have
4
**FREE**
Historical
Romances
for you!

*Details inside!*

a long fall of blond hair and stood on tiptoe while waving with excitement.

Paige spotted her immediately and let out a squeal of recognition, hurrying past the people in front of her. "Mom!" she yelled with a wide grin.

Julia's arms opened wide, waiting to be filled with that familiar body, to smell that familiar scent. Her baby was home.

The two women hugged and rocked, laughing and crying. Julia buried her face in Paige's silky hair and stroked her back. "I'm so glad you're home," she whispered, sniffling away her tears.

"You look great, Mom," Paige said when they finally parted. "Just look at you! Your hair is different. You have on makeup. What'd you do, get a boyfriend while I've been gone?"

Startled, Julia muttered with embarrassment, "Oh, Paige . . . please."

"I'm just kidding. But you do look wonderful— younger, or something."

Not wanting to explain, Julia threw her arm across her daughter's shoulders and gave her a light squeeze. "C'mon, let's go get your luggage. Speaking of boyfriends, any new developments in that area?"

"Oh, Mom . . . please." Paige mimicked.

They both giggled, joining the crowd of passengers and allowing themselves to be carried along with the sea of people hurrying to the baggage claim. The ride home was filled with Paige's chatter about parties, friends, dances, school and the pending trip to Europe.

Julia tried to listen to all of Paige's exciting news with interest, but her mind wandered back to her own problems and the apprehension she had about entering her own home. How would Val react to someone else living in the house, especially a beautiful young girl who had her whole life ahead of her?

The house was quiet as they carried the heavy bags into Paige's bedroom. Once inside, she fell back on the bed and sighed. "It's good to be home again." Pulling herself into a sitting position, she added, "But there's something different."

Julia immediately stiffened and looked about the room. What had Val done?

"It seems smaller. Weird, huh?"

Julia let out her breath. "Places always appear like that when you've been gone for any length of time."

"I guess . . . Oh, Mom, they're beautiful." Paige said, jumping up and going to the vase filled with irises.

Julia smiled. "That shade of blue-purple always reminds me of your eyes." How wonderful to have her daughter back in her room. She lovingly watched as Paige smiled, lowered her face and inhaled.

Julia pushed herself away from the doorway and walked into the room. She picked up the small present from the dresser and handed it to Paige.

"You shouldn't have, Mom."

"It's only little. Open it."

Taking off the white wrapping paper, Paige shrieked with delight. "Dune! How did you know?"

"You told me Maria had worn that fragrance and how much you liked it."

Her daughter came over and gave her a tight hug. "You're the best." She walked toward the bed while opening the box. "Sometimes at school I hear girls complaining about their mothers. I mean, they really don't like them," she said, sitting back on the bed and crossing her legs under her body. "And I feel sorry for them. When I tell them about us, they don't believe me."

Touched by her daughter's words, Julia could feel a lump forming in her throat. Not wanting to get too emotional, she said, "Enough about us. What about you?"

Paige laughed. "I told you everything in the car. I didn't give you a chance to say a word. Tell me about you. What's new? What's exciting? Has Mrs. Habard had her hysterectomy yet?"

"I don't think so," Julia said with a smile, envisioning their seventy-year-old neighbor who managed to include her "woman problems" into every conversation. What was odd was that she hadn't even spoken to the old woman all spring. Her usual gardening time had been taken up with more important matters.

As if reading her thoughts, Paige asked, "So, you never answered. What's new?"

Recovering quickly, Julia said, "Oh, you know me—Work and house. It never ends. Are you hungry? Did you eat on the plane?"

Paige nodded. "Some awful ham and cheese sandwich."

"You shouldn't eat on planes. Only if you fly first class or business."

"Well then, I guess it's going to be years before I can eat and fly." Her daughter laughed. "I'm going to be mighty hungry when I go coach to Europe."

The thought of Paige leaving made Julia say, "I'll make you something to eat. What would you like?"

"Nothing. I'm really not hungry," she answered, picking up the phone and punching in numbers. "I'm going to call Bridget and Jen. I know they're home from school already. Maybe we can go out tonight. Bridge? That you? Yeah . . ." she added with a wide grin when her best friend recognized her voice. "I know. I know! God, what if we flunked our exams?"

Winking at Julia to show she was kidding, she cupped the phone and mouthed *Thanks, Mom.*

Dismissed, Julia forced a smile and nodded as she backed out of the room and closed the door.

It really was her fault. She had been dreading the conversation when Paige asked her what was new. Lying would only make her feel guilty, she reasoned as she walked down the stairs and headed into the kitchen. She couldn't tell her about Val and she wasn't ready to tell her about Steve, so she had put her off with the remark about work and house. Then went right to the old standby of food—the sure sign to a mother that the conversation was winding down.

Entering the kitchen, she skidded to a halt and grabbed her chest as if to contain her heart inside her body. "Val! What are you doing down here?" she demanded in a raspy voice.

"I thought I wasn't banished to the attic," Val threw over her shoulder as she stood at the stove. "I'm waiting for the water to boil. I wanted a cup of tea. Besides, I also wanted to see what that daughter of yours was like. I feel as if I know her, what with sleeping in her room and listening to you go on endlessly . . ."

"Please, Val. Please go back to the attic. Don't do this to Paige."

Val turned and crossed her arms over her chest. She looked like a woman in her mid sixties. "To Paige? Always the daughter, right? I thought you had learned that lesson."

Not wanting to argue, Julia said, "Okay, then do it for me. You promised. Please . . ."

Val gave her a look of disgust and turned around to shut the stove off. "I can remember, Julia. I haven't lost my memory. Don't worry. I'll keep my promise. All I want is my tea."

The doorbell rang and Julia let out a yelp as she raced for it. Pulling open the door she saw Bridget Comway, Paige's closest friend since middle school.

"Hey, Mom," she called and wrapped Julia in a tight hug. "Did you miss me?"

"Yes . . . yes, I did," she muttered in a surprised voice. Since Bridget had spent almost as much time at their house as she did at her own, the girl had started calling her "Mom" several years ago. "I would have sworn you were just on the phone with Paige."

Bridget laughed. "I couldn't wait to see her. She's probably talking to Jen right now. We're going to make plans for tonight."

Julia let her in and waved toward the stairs. "Go on up," she said, and looked in the direction of the kitchen. Val was standing in the doorway, observing them while holding her tea cup with both hands. Desperately hoping to block Bridget's line of vision to the kitchen, Julia positioned her body in front of the hovering cup.

Bridget raced toward the stairway while shouting back, "The Fearsome Threesome are together again."

Julia ran her fingers through her hair and tried to smile while waiting until Bridget was out of sight. She then looked at Val.

Val merely raised her eyebrows once before walking away.

Shaking her head and letting out her breath in an aggravated rush, Julia walked into the kitchen and pulled out a mug from the cabinet. She didn't know if she could take four days of this. It would be torture waiting for Val to slip up again. Even though she was disappointed to hear that Paige was going out with her friends, maybe it would be better that way. She couldn't be with her daughter twenty-four hours every day to make sure Val behaved.

Picking out an herbal tea to soothe her nerves, Julia wondered just how much time she would spend with her daughter before she left. The thought of Paige going to Europe, traveling to foreign countries, not speaking the language, filled her with dread. There were wars and terrorists and spies . . .

God, she sounded so provincial.

The ringing of her line startled her and she quickly picked up the phone. "Hello?"

"Hey, lady. How are you?"

For a moment she couldn't speak. Just when she thought things couldn't be worse—

"It's Steve. Are you there?"

"Yes. I know it's you," she said, her vision darting to the entrance of her kitchen. She felt like a twelve-year-old sneaking a call from her boyfriend.

"Well, how are you? Did you get your daughter settled?"

"Yes. She has a friend over."

"Great. I guess you're happy."

"Yes . . . yes, I am."

"I can't wait to meet her. Maybe I could take you two out to dinner this weekend." It was a half question, half statement.

Julia turned back to the stove and cupped her hand around the receiver to muffle her voice. "I don't think that's such a good idea."

"You don't? Why? I thought we had talked about it."

"No, you talked about it. I never agreed." Sensing his withdrawal, she added, "Look, with Val and everything, I just think it's better to keep this as uncomplicated as possible."

"Are you saying I'm a complication?"

"No. I mean, yes. Right now, I'm attempting to

keep Val and Paige apart. I haven't even told my daughter about you."

"Really?" His tone had definitely taken a turn toward the cool, and she was immediately reminded of the first time she had seen him. The snake. The image was intensified as the awkward silence continued.

It's a negotiating tool, she reminded herself. Let your words hang out there and wait for your opponent to crack and speak first.

A sudden anger surged through her and she didn't give a damn about losing face. "Look, I'm sorry about this, but I can't see you this weekend. There just isn't any way I can do it."

Another prolonged, painful silence followed.

Finally, she heard him swiftly inhale and say, "Fine. Enjoy your weekend."

She said goodbye and hung up the phone. A knot slowly formed in her stomach, as she realized what she might have just done. It was the first time he had been angry with her and his clipped, chilly tone was a good clue to how annoyed he actually was. What was she supposed to do? What did he expect?

*Oh, Paige . . . I want to introduce you to Steve McMillan. He's my boss and we're dating. But don't worry, he's leaving in less than two weeks so he'll be out of our lives. My only problem is that I think I might be falling in love with him and making a supreme fool out of myself. Oh, and did I mention we have a ghost?*

"Mom?"

Julia spun around before her daughter entered the ktichen.

"Can I borrow the car? We're going to pick up Jen and then maybe go to Mario's for pizza. Is it okay?"

"Sure. I guess."

"We'll spend the whole day together tomorrow. Maybe tonight, if I don't get in late."

"Okay."

"Are you all right, Mom?" Paige asked with concern as she came closer. "If you want I can get Jen, bring her back here, and we'll just order out."

Thinking three girls laughing and shouting might prove to be too much for Val, Julia said, "No. Don't be silly. The keys are in my purse. Just be careful."

Paige kissed her cheek. "Okay, then. If you're sure?"

"Go."

"Thanks, Mom," both girls called, laughing as they departed.

Alone, the silence of the house sounded deafening. This is what it's going to be like, she thought, spooning raw sugar into her tea. Get used to it. No Paige. No Steve. No one. Not even a pet.

The thought suddenly terrified her and filled her with panic. It was okay all those years, she had told herself. She didn't need a man. She was self-sufficient. She earned her own way in this world and wasn't beholden to anyone. She ate when and what she wanted. She dressed for herself, and didn't give a fig for anyone's else opinion. She cleaned the house, or didn't, depending on her mood. If she wanted to paint or redecorate, she didn't have to consider another's taste. She had a good life. Better than most.

But I don't want to be alone forever, she mentally cried out. I don't want to grow old alone, without ever feeling loved again.

Lifting her chin, she looked toward the ceiling.

I don't want to be Val.

She brought her tea with her as she entered the attic. Val was sitting on the old sofa that doubled as her bed. Once, not too many years ago, Paige and her friends would sit up here in their makeshift clubhouse for hours as they gossipped, did homework, discussed boys, experimented with makeup and, finally, tried smoking. It was the last discovery that had closed the clubhouse for good.

Running a finger over the old piece of furniture that held so many memories, Julia sniffled back her tears and said in a hoarse voice, "Val, I need you. Would you talk to me?"

"Well, well, well . . ." Val muttered, looking up from her magazine. "You need *me*?"

She watched as Julia crossed over and took a seat at the end of the couch. Julia didn't answer immediately. When she finally spoke it was in a subdued voice.

"I don't want to fight, Val. This is really important."

She studied Julia for a moment and then curiosity got the best of her. "Well, then, spit it out."

Julia continued to stare into her cup. "I'm scared. I don't know what's happening any more. I keep losing people."

"What do you mean? Who have you lost?"

Sighing, Julia said, "My daughter, for one. And probably Steve."

"Your daughter? She looked pretty happy to be home. All that squealing and hollering, it sounded like a pig auction to me. It's no wonder why you haven't had a man in here for twenty years. Could you just imagine a romantic, candle-lit dinner with that noise over your head? How did you stand it?"

Julia smiled knowingly, and the sight annoyed Val. "You can't appreciate that precious noise until it's gone."

"It must be a mother thing. Something I, fortunately, don't understand."

"It isn't that, Val. It's losing my daughter. I can feel it. She doesn't seem to need me anymore."

"Oh, she needs you all right," Val said, feeling a rush of resentment. "Who pays the tuition to that fancy school? Who puts the roof over her head and the clothes on her back? Who bought the ticket and picked her up at the airport? Carried her luggage and took it up to a clean room? Oh, and let's not forget who bought her a little gift? And then offered to cook her something to eat and was dismissed only to find out she's going to eat at some crummy pizza joint? This is the girl who doesn't need you anymore?"

"You don't understand, Val. It's all part of parenting. It's hard for me to even explain. The best way I can put it is unconditional love. I would give my life for Paige without hesitation. I don't know anyone else I could say that about."

Val let out a breath of annoyance. "Unconditional love? Give me a break. Let me tell you about my mother's unconditional love. I was pushed out on a stage when I was nine. Singing and tapping my feet and holding that goddamned smile so long I felt my cheeks would crack and bleed. And all the while, Nora Kobilick was standing in the wings smoking a cigarette with the stage manager and trying to set up a date. My mother only unconditionally loved herself. That's the only kind of real love there is. You look out for Number One."

"I'm sorry you had such an unhappy childhood, but it wasn't like that between us. We were friends. Actually, best friends. I don't know why you're so angry with me, Val, but you don't understand. You'd have to have had a relationship like that to grasp what it's like to lose it."

Val hated the expression of pity on Julia's face. She may not have grown up in a house like this with a mother who doted on her every need, but her mother had taught her about the real world. The one where you do whatever it takes to survive until the next morning. "Well, face it, honey. Your precious Paige is on her way to being history. And why shouldn't she be? What do you expect her to do? Stay here in this house and grow old with you?"

Julia appeared horrified. "Of course not!"

Val could feel her lips turning into a tight smile. "If that's unconditional love, you can have it. That must be why I never loved anybody. Let her go, Julia. I'm stuck in this house with you. Look at me. I'm an old woman. You can grow old along with me."

Julia started to get up. "I'm sorry I disturbed you, but I came up here to talk. Not to be any more upset."

Reluctant to let Julia go, Val immediately went into character and assumed the role of peacemaker. Julia's comment about Steve intrigued her, since she had been feeling better today. It had been with a sense of gratitude that she hadn't seen any marked signs of increased aging.

She held out her arm. "No, don't leave. I'm sorry. I just can't deal with what's happening to me. Maybe seeing your daughter and her friends kick up their heels only added insult to injury. What were you going to say about Steve? What did you want to talk about?"

It was with a sense of triumph that she watched Julia slowly sit down. She really should have played that dramatic role..

"He called. He wanted to meet Paige, and I put him off."

"Why?

"I just couldn't handle it. I haven't even told Paige about him. I didn't see a reason, since he's leaving in two weeks."

"A lot can happen in two weeks." Julia appeared to be really upset. Maybe that was a good sign. She must falling for this guy. If that were the case, then she'd be able to leave and stop this horror.

"I'm so confused. I pushed Steve away so I could spend time with Paige, and now Paige has pushed me away to spend time with her friends. I don't know if I made the right decision."

It was odd. The more Julia anguished over Steve the better Val was beginning to physically feel. Her breathing seemed easier. The aches had lessened. And, looking down to the magazine in her lap, she was amazed to find that her vision had even improved. James Dean's face came into sharper focus.

Not sure how to proceed, she said, "Why don't you call him back? Your daughter is out for the night. It's never too late."

Julia perked up. "Do you think so? I don't know if I should call him. You don't think it would be pushy?"

Val shook her head. "If you want to see him, call him and tell him that. No man worth his salt would turn down that offer."

Julia's mood seemed elevated. "He did say he had plans for us this weekend . . ."

Val looked down to the picture in the magazine and blinked a few times to clear her vision. Again, it appeared fuzzy and she strained to read the photo credit beneath it. Was it possible? All of the rapid aging had started when Julia met Steve? But it made no sense. She had been sent here to help Julia find happiness, so why should she be punished for doing just that?

A terrible thought leaped into her mind. *What if*

*they sent me here to learn about this unconditional
love crap? To do all this to keep Julia happy? And for
what? To help some woman I didn't even know before
I got here? To live in an attic and age like a shrunken
old witch until I evaporate? What are they gonna do?
I'm already dead. And if there is a hell, I'm already
living it.*

A feeling of being back in control came over Val.
She didn't understand before. She didn't even know
she had an option. But now that she did, she was
directing this script.

Julia's voice interrupted her thoughts. "I'm
sorry," she whispered, coming back into character.
"Sometimes I don't hear everything."

"Steve mentioned that he had plans for us this
weekend."

"We'll that was pretty presumptuous of him,
wasn't it? He knew Paige was coming home this
weekend and how much you missed her. Men are
always so self-indulgent." Looking down, she saw
the letters in the feature story become clearer. "Especially rich, successful ones. I should know about
that. I can't tell you how many producers I had to
fend off on my way up the ladder. If you want this
man's respect, don't let him think you're an easy
conquest. If I had learned that lesson when I was
twenty-three, who knows where my career would
have gone."

Julia seemed to sink further into the sofa. "I tried
to explain to him at lunch that I didn't want him to
meet Paige, but he pressed the issue anyway. He
couldn't understand that this was our time—mine

and my daughter's. She's only going to be here for four days before she leaves again."

"Like I said, they're always thinking about themselves."

"It was like he was trying to change my mind when we were on the phone. As if he can walk right in and change my life. This might be a control issue, Val. I felt it on the phone. It was like he was negotiating with me."

Val sighed loudly. "Well, what do you expect? Men are in control. I used the one thing they couldn't control against them, but when all else is said and done, it is a man's world."

Anger flashed in Julia's eyes. "That may have been the case in your time, Val, but women don't have to accept that anymore. I, for one, never did. And don't intend to start accepting it now. I did pretty good on my own, and I haven't had to answer to a man in twenty years."

"Oh, yeah? Well, who's your boss? Is it a man or a woman?"

She watched as Julia stared out at a row of dusty boxes. "A man," she muttered.

"My point exactly."

"That's in my professional life. I don't have to accept anything in my personal life that I don't want."

Feeling unusually energetic, Val said, "Well, let the guy cool his heels then. I may not have your daughter's education, but I do know men. If he's interested, he'll wait."

Julia stood to leave and nodded in agreement.

"This time with Paige is too special. Maybe you're right. I don't know if I feel any better, but I'm not as confused. I don't know why I doubted my instincts. Thanks. Do you want more tea?"

Val looked down to her cup. "No, thanks. I still have some. I think I'll get back to this story about Jimmy Dean. Remind me sometime to tell you about the Human Ashtray."

Julia stared down at her and Val smiled at her confusion.

"What? A human ashtray? What does that mean?"

"Well, you know that he liked men."

"I thought you said you had gone out with him."

"I did. It was set up by the studio publicity department to keep his image intact and the studio's bank accounts rolling. It also kept his boyfriends screaming with jealousy. Maybe that's why he got into pain and bondage. There was a club in East Hollywood where he would beg people to put their cigarettes out on his body."

Julia was obviously shocked. "I don't believe that! James Dean?"

Shrugging, Val said, "It was the talk of Hollywood after he died. If you don't believe me, read the coroner's report. He noted the presence of small, thick, raised scars over his body. And they were old scars."

Walking toward the stairs, Julia threw over her shoulder, "I don't want to hear any more about this. I think I'll go do some gardening. It'll feel refreshing to get my hands in some real dirt instead of listening to someone else's."

Val laughed, her humor becoming perverse. "Okay, how 'bout Errol Flynn and his penchant for young girls?"

"Heard it," Julia yelled back, escaping down the stairs.

"Joan Crawford and—"

"Saw it," Julia interrupted. Her voice was getting further and further away. "Goodbye, Val. I need some clean air."

Feeling victorious, Val admired her own performance. It was great to work again, immersing herself in another character and using the skills she had learned. But what was even better was being back in control.

Survival. Now *that* was unconditional love.

# Chapter 13

"I'm only allowed two bags, Mom. And a carry-on for the plane."

Julia watched as Paige looked over the piles of clothes on her bed.

"How am I ever going to fit all this in them?"

She brought her arm up and rested her elbow on her daughter's shoulder. "I don't know. You're going to have to cut back. I guess . . ." She had put off thinking about her daughter's trip. She hadn't even wanted to discuss it, until Paige pushed the issue. But now it was upon her. Tomorrow, Paige was leaving.

"But I can't cut back," Paige protested. "I need everything."

Julia sighed, "Maybe ten pairs of shorts are five pair too many. And what about all those shoes?"

"Mom, I'm going to Europe for six weeks!"

"Yes, I know. Believe me, I know. But surely you'll encounter a washing machine in your travels? And if you bring sneakers, a couple of pair of shoes and sandals, you've got it covered. You can't expect to pack all this. The shoes alone would fill a small suitcase."

Shaking her head, Paige said, "I'm going to have to call Maria and find out what she's bringing. Maybe we could share stuff."

"That's a great idea. Don't worry. It'll all work out."

Paige sat down on the bed in the only clear spot. "I don't know what's wrong with me. I feel so nervous."

"About what?" Julia asked, moving a pile of tee shirts and blouses to sit next to her.

Paige frowned, while shrugging. "I guess it's the trip. I don't know. I have this weird feeling. Sounds dumb, right?" Her daughter looked to her for a reaction.

"It's understandable to be nervous about going somewhere totally different. It doesn't sound dumb at all."

"I know, but . . . it's not just going somewhere foreign that's bothering me. It's kind of a sense that nothing is ever going to be the same after this. *I'll* never be the same. It's like . . . growing up, or something. I can't explain it."

Paige's words frightened Julia. She didn't know how to respond. Was her daughter sensing Val in the house? Was that what was making her so uneasy? Or was she realizing that she couldn't remain a child forever?

"Are you afraid of that? Of growing up?"

"I'm not afraid of it, but I have to say I'm nervous." Issuing an uncertain chuckle, she laid back on a higher pile of clothes. "Being with the DeMarcos will help, but I'm really going to be on my own in Europe. I mean, I was on my own in school, but you were still a part of it. You paid the tuition; you were a phone call away. If anything happened, I knew you would be there. And I kept my butt in gear because I knew you would eventually find out if I didn't. Now I'm really going to be on my own, without answering to you, and the decisions I make will be without those influences. It's scary. What if I screw up?"

Julia smiled and ran her hand over Paige's hair. "Sounds like pretty grownup reasoning to me. If you're already thinking about yourself and possible consequences then I would say you're on the right path. I'm not sure what I believe in anymore. I've had reasons to question what I've been taught as right or wrong, or good and bad. I guess I see life as walking down a long road, and every so often we come to a fork in that road and are asked to make a choice that can alter our lives. Turn right, and it will bring you to this place in your life. Left, and it's totally different."

"But how do you know if it's the right choice?" Paige whispered. "Sometimes we make choices on the spur of the moment, on emotions. I know three girls who got pregnant last semester at school. None of them planned it."

Thank God they'd had this discussion last year before Paige had left for college. Julia listened with relief when Paige told her she was protecting herself from raising a child alone. Paige'd seen how hard it was.

"First of all, you are already thinking about consequences. Those girls weren't. And second, even if you do make a wrong choice initially, once you think it through, and see where it's leading you, you can always turn around and alter the path. You're an intelligent young woman, Paige. You have to learn to trust yourself."

"Thanks, Mom. I'm glad you have confidence in me, but I'm still a little nervous. It's just that everything is changing so fast around me. You're different, the house seems different . . . I don't know what it is about it, but I just have this weird feeling like everything's changing, and I can't stop it."

Julia wanted to hug her close. She understood how frightening change could be. Her own life had been stable and predictable for nearly twenty years, and now everything familiar was in upheaval. Once again, running her fingers through Paige's long blond hair, Julia said, "You're going to be fine, Paige. What you're going through is normal. Home will always be here, and good friends never go away."

Looking up to the ceiling Paige answered, "I know, and I appreciate that, but even when I went out with Bridget and Jen it just wasn't the same." Sighing, Paige added, "It's not like we didn't have fun, because we did. It was just that when we all started talking about school, and our new friends, I felt disconnected from them somehow."

Julia tried to comfort her. "You girls have just

had different experiences and met different people this past year. It's probably only an adjustment period until you catch up with each other."

"I guess you're right. I just wish I didn't feel this way about this house. It's bad enough feeling like this about your friends, but when it's home . . ."

Julia felt the muscles in her stomach tighten with apprehension. "Why don't you feel comfortable? What's the problem with the house?"

Paige hesitated before responding. "Mom, it isn't you. I just know I'll never be the same after this trip. I don't know, I just have this feeling. I don't know how to put it into words."

Julia chuckled, "I think you're doing a pretty good job. I understand. But what you need to understand is that everyone goes through this. Part of it is homesickness, the other part is meeting new people and making new friends."

Shaking her head, Paige said, "But I'm going away, and that will probably only make it worse. We used to sit up until four in the morning and tell each other everything. We were all so close that we could almost finish each other's sentences. I knew what they were thinking and feeling before they even said anything. Now, I share all of that with Maria, and she's the first person I think of when something special happens. I don't want to leave them behind, Mom, but I feel like its happening."

Julia smiled sadly. "You're going on with your own life."

"Yeah, I guess you're right. But it's still sad."

Hugging her daughter, she kissed her temple and whispered, "It's tough growing up, isn't it?"

Paige smiled. "Yeah. Everything used to be so simple."

"Okay, now what time does your plane take off tomorrow? Eight-thirty?"

"Eight twenty-five."

"That means were going to have to leave here around five-thirty to get to the airport an hour before your flight. We'll be meeting the DeMarcos at the gate, right?"

Nodding, Paige said, "Maria told me their flight from Ohio will get them there around six, so they will be there."

Her daughter still in her arms, Julia breathed in the scent of her child and whispered, "I'm going to miss you."

"I know. Me, too."

"You're growing up so fast and everything is changing for you, but I want you to know that the one thing that will never change is that I love you. And if you need me I'm only a phone call away."

Their embrace became tighter and Julia felt Paige's tears mingle with her own.


Val looked down to the sleeping girl and sighed. Once she had been that young, that vital. But she never had the advantages of a real home and family. She'd never gone to college, never even gone to a high school prom. And she'd certainly never had the opportunity of going to Europe. This kid didn't even know how lucky she was to go to sleep with a full belly and a roof over her head. She didn't have to push her bed against the wall and never sleep soundly because her mother's boyfriends might sneak in and take away her innocence. This kid had it all going for her and she didn't even appreciate it. Annoyance rushed through her.

Val turned to the desk and picked up an old teddy bear that Paige must have brought home from college. A teddy bear. Why, at her age she was Miss Swanson Frozen Chicken of 1944. Not that it was such a big deal, outside of the fact that she and her mother had food for the next month. But it was one more step toward her goal of becoming an actress, one more small push toward Hollywood. When she thought of everything she had done, every lousy job she had taken, every man she had pacified along the way, Val's hands tightened on the plush toy.

It wasn't fair. She had paid her dues. It shouldn't have been taken away from her when everything had been finally coming together. She should have had her chance.

It was better that Paige was going away for the summer. She didn't want to be around the girl, and Paige might interfere with her plans. Throwing the teddy bear back onto the desk, she knew she'd do whatever it took to stop aging.

Now that she understood the rules, she knew how to play.

\* \* \*

The New Jersey Turnpike could be the loneliest place in the world, with its endless streams of traffic and monotonous scenery. It was especially lonely since she had just seen her daughter off to Europe. The DeMarcos were lovely people and promised to look out for Paige. When they started to board the plane, Julia had to bite the inside of her cheek not to cry out with heartache. She'd felt completely alone in the world when she walked back through the terminal to her car. It was only when she was sitting behind the wheel that she let go of her emotion and sobbed.

Now, as she travelled closer to home, she realized how starkly this silent ride contrasted to the happy chatter on the ride to the airport.

It was so damned quiet, and there was too much time to think about the changes in her own life. What did she have, really? After all was said and done, not much. She worked for a company that was in upheaval. She had a house that was once her sanctuary, but now harbored a ghost. Although she still had a daughter, Paige was now a young woman with a life of her own. And, as foolish as it might have been, she had entertained the possibility of a relationship with a man, a relationship that couldn't go anywhere.

Paige was right. Everything was changing, and much too fast. At nineteen change can be scary, but also exciting and adventurous. At thirty-nine, change was terrifying, and disappointment was the most likely outcome. Why did she ever allow herself to hope again? She had done such a good job accepting the path she had chosen until Steve McMillan came into her life. He rekindled old hopes which brought back old desires and dreams, something she was better off without.

Val had been right. He had taken too much for granted. He was handling her like a well-thought out business deal. Of course she had fallen for it. It had been years since anyone had paid her any attention.

After all, his career was built on recognizing weaknesses and moving in for the kill. He was like a high-priced hit man. Cool. Professional. Get in, do the job, and then get out while leaving others to make sense of his havoc. The thought galled her. Did he actually think she was ripe for the takeover? What did he expect out of her? Why in the world would she want to introduce him to her daughter? It wasn't like he intended to get serious.

Taking a deep, settling breath, she passed a truck and looked for her exit. Thank God she hadn't gone to bed with him. She didn't think she would have been able to handle that one—to have been used and discarded before he moved on to his next hit might have destroyed her.

Life was confusing enough on its own without the complication of Steve McMillan. She had barely escaped with her self esteem intact.

Maybe Val really was her guardian angel.


She was not going. She was simply not going. How dare he tap his watch in full view of everyone? He had barely spoken to her all morning at the department head meeting, and when he did his tone was clipped and chilly. Did he actually think all he had to do was signal her and she would jump? What arrogance! Steve's attitude only confirmed her suspicions. She had been a marked target, and when he realized she wasn't an easy kill he had dismissed her.

Searching through the employee files for those that were discussed in the meeting, she slammed the cabinet drawer and flipped on her computer with disgust. She couldn't help glancing at her watch. Twelve-ten. All she had to do was wait out the next forty-five minutes. She pictured Steve sitting in that booth alone, waiting for her, and a satisfied smile came to her lips. It would serve him right.

Pulling up the pension benefits files on her screen, she tried to concentrate on the data needed for the follow-up meeting. Normally she would have been able to retain the information mentally, but with her concentration ruined, she pulled a yellow legal pad out and began to take copious notes.

A knock on the door interrupted her and for a fleeting moment she thought it might be Steve. It wasn't. It was someone worse than Steve McMillan.

Vince DeMicci swaggered into her office and took possession of the chair facing her desk. "Some meeting, huh? These guys are still at it. Cutting up the company and staking their claims on each division."

Julia took a deep breath and tried to remain calm. "There may be restructuring, but at least there won't be any new layoffs."

Vince scoffed at her comment. "Yeah, I've heard that one before. That's the party line Amalgamated gave at this meeting, but the real decisions take place in New York and we don't even have a representative up there."

"Well, all we can do is make our decisions on the information that we have. Right now, there won't be any new layoffs. I think they're trying to stabilize the work force at this point and get back to the business of manufacturing. To have people constantly worrying about their jobs is nonproductive."

Vince rested his arm over the back of the chair. "For all we know, Amalgamated may have bought us to take a loss. They now own the Bradford filament, so in two years we could merely be a tax write-off. McMillan's a cold son of a bitch. He just follows orders. He doesn't give a damn about us."

In spite of her anger toward Steve, she couldn't stand to hear Vince DeMicci attack him that way. "Steve McMillan is a professional. He's been forthcoming with all the information regarding the takeover and Amalgamated's plans. I don't think there's a hidden agenda, and that type of conjecture is just as nonproductive as the rumor mill."

"Well, well—that kind of defense surprises me, especially after the way you were treated at the meeting. I figured you two had a lover's spat, or something."

Every muscle in Julia's body stiffened in anger. "I'm going to have to ask you to leave. I won't even dignify that comment with an answer."

Standing up, Vince shrugged and said, "Hey, if I'm wrong, I apologize. I thought you'd like to know that I wasn't the only one to notice."

Once alone, Julia stared at the computer for several seconds. She then jumped up, picked up her purse and walked out of the office. Now she didn't have a choice. She had to see him.

Her anger was intensified as she marched up to the booth and saw him eating. Sliding into the seat, she said, "I want you to know I never intended to come here again."

He looked at her with an even gaze and slowly sipped his coffee. "Then why are you here?"

It infuriated her to see him so detached and reserved, treating her as if she were a hysterical client he was forced to endure. "I'll tell you why," she said, trying to steady her voice. "This is becoming too public. It's threatening my job. Because no matter what has happened between us, I expect to be treated with at least the same level of courtesy as other department heads. That means you don't single me out at meetings to vent your frustration, and you don't tap your damn watch to order me to lunch."

"I never ordered you to do anything."

"This may be just another job to you, Steve, before you move on to your next assignment, but I have to work here, with these people, and everyone noticed your behavior. I won't have you jeopardize my job or undermine my authority. Not after I worked so hard for both."

He sat back in the booth and said, "Your job isn't

in jeopardy, and you seem to be able to wield authority without any problem."

"What's that supposed to mean? Are you talking about this weekend?"

He didn't answer her and she didn't wait for him to respond. She addressed the issue that had been bothering her for days.

"What right do you have to insist on meeting my daughter? This is my life we're talking about here. Just like I have to deal with the people at Coolback after you've gone, I'd have to deal with a confused nineteen-year-old. Look, Paige is scared about all the changes going on in her life now. She didn't grow up with me running men in and out of the house, and I wasn't about to send her off to Europe wondering about her mother's boyfriend—because that's what she would have thought had all three of us gone out to dinner."

She looked out the window to the street outside. "You know, Steve, you don't have any ties that bind. You can breeze in and breeze out without consequences. It must be nice. For the last twenty years I've always had to think of the consequences."

Steve appeared unruffled by her outburst. "Are you through?"

She hated it when men said that. It made her grind her teeth together in annoyance. "Yes, but let me add that I think this whole thing was pretty presumptuous of you."

He leaned his elbows on the table. Looking directly into her eyes, he said, "No, Julia. I think it was pretty presumptuous of you."

She was ready to leave. "I have to get back to work."

"Not yet. I heard you out. Now hear me out."

She sat back in the booth and crossed her arms over her chest.

"It appears that you have the gift of mental telepathy to know what I've been thinking. Maybe Val's powers are rubbing off on you."

"Leave Val out of this," she muttered.

"You're right. This isn't about her. It's about us and what you assume my intentions were. I want you to know that while on assignment I don't make it a habit to conduct temporary liaisons. It isn't my style. Before meeting you I never mixed business with pleasure. Even though I don't have children, I do have decency. I never would have thought to insinuate myself into your daughter's life if this were a fling."

It was her turn to be silent. For some reason she didn't want to trust him. She had seen him work people before. As long as she went along with his program, there was no problem. But when she had challenged him on Saturday he had turned cool and distant. She couldn't tell if the man sitting before her now was telling the truth, or was trying to renegotiate lost ground. The risk was simply too great.

"I've got to go," she said getting out of the booth.

"It's your choice," he answered quietly.

His words haunted her on the drive back. Wasn't that what she had told Paige? Was she now at a fork in the road? And why did she feel like she had just taken the wrong path?

"Welcome home," Val said as she stood by the kitchen table and proudly waved toward it.

Julia saw the table was set with her good china and something smelled delicious. She looked toward the stove. "You cooked dinner?"

"Fried chicken. Waitressed in a greasy spoon for eight months in Beaumont, Texas, and when things got busy I helped the cook—a big buck that liked to wear silver tips on his boots, but never mind. What do you think, huh?"

"I think it's great," Julia said, placing her briefcase on the floor and slipping out of her heels. She didn't want to tell Val that she rarely ate fried foods, for it was such a pleasant surprise to find her active again. "You didn't have to do this. I could have made dinner."

"I wanted to." Val took the baked potatoes out of the oven. "Sit down and relax."

Julia did as she was asked and observed Val. "You're feeling better then?"

"I feel pretty good, and I was bored stiff in that attic. I'm sorry we had that fight. I guess I was a little shaken by . . . by what was happening to me."

"It's understandable," Julia murmured, thinking Val seemed almost perky. She still looked like she was in her mid-sixties, but she acted and sounded much younger. "Then you've accepted this . . . situation?"

Val was piling chicken onto a platter. "I don't know if I've accepted it or not. I just know that sitting up in that attic didn't make me feel any better, so I came down. I moved into the third bedroom like you wanted me to do last weekend. Is that okay?"

"Of course. With Paige gone it doesn't matter any longer. You know I never wanted you to stay in the attic."

"Yes. Yes, I know," Val said as she brought the food to the table. "Would you like iced tea with dinner?"

"I'll get it," Julia offered.

"No, you sit. You've been working all day. It feels good to keep busy." Val brought the filled glasses, handed one to Julia, and sat down. "Now, tell me about your day. Did you see Steve?"

Julia could feel herself tensing again. "I saw him," she said tightly before taking a sip of tea. "We argued."

"About Paige?"

"About Paige, about everything. I don't want to talk about it." She placed a napkin on her lap and served herself, even though her appetite had vanished.

"Okay. Forget Steve. We made a mistake with him. He wasn't right for you. That's the trouble with men, Julia. They always want to control you."

"Let's change the subject," Julia said as she cut into the chicken. The last thing she wanted to discuss with Val was whether Steve McMillan was right for her.

"Well, then let me tell you about my day. You'll never guess who was on 'Donahue' today. House-wives who moonlight as prostitutes! Have you ever heard of such a thing? There was this one wo-man . . ."

Julia wasn't listening. She was thinking about her argument with Steve. She could picture his face when he was telling her that, until her, he had never mixed business with pleasure, that he never consid-ered it a fling. God, she wanted to believe him, but even Val, the supreme authority on men, thought he was a mistake.

"You haven't heard a word I've said."

Julia looked up from her plate. "I'm sorry. What were you saying about housewives?"

Val seemed annoyed. "Never mind. I thought we could have a nice dinner and get things back the way they were. But you're sitting there moping about a man that was going to use you and then throw you away. Have you no pride, Julia?"

Stung by Val's words, Julia straightened her shoulders and said, "Sometimes I think I have too much pride, that I've worked so hard to get to where I am that I've lost the ability to trust any-one."

Val swallowed her chicken and dug into her baked potato. "You haven't eaten anything yet. Try the chicken. It's delicious, if I have to say so myself. Oh, and forget trusting anyone. Trust yourself." She smiled. "And you know you can trust me."

*  *  *

He didn't know why he was even bothering to work it out in his head. Never before had he stayed awake at night, wondering where he went wrong with a woman. With three hours sleep, he had arrived at the office feeling like he had a hangover. He couldn't concentrate on the paperwork in front of him, nor could he stop looking at the door to his office. He kept thinking, hoping maybe, that she would reconsider.

What was it about her? Why didn't he just shrug it off and move on? Was it because that's what she expected? That she had somehow known he was intrigued by her resistance to him in the beginning? He had to admit to himself that her dislike of him had initially been a challenge. Even when she questioned his value system, he wanted to show her she was wrong. Maybe in the beginning, when they first met, he had thought that having her would be a conquest. But it wasn't why he had shown up at her house that first night. He could admit it now, especially since he had admitted it last night—around two A.M. He was beginning to care about Julia in a way that he had never before felt with another woman. She was interfering with his work, making him think about other possibilities in his life. And he liked the feeling. The realization was shocking.

He wanted to be in her company as often as possible. He wanted to see her smile and hear her laugh. He wanted to show her things, see her react like she did in the jazz club to new experiences. He had even called his travel agent and booked his ticket for France. It had been too long since he was at the farm and he'd requested three weeks off after he'd checked and saw Julia hadn't used any vacation time yet. He knew she would love it there . . .

Now that was presumptuous.

He hated to admit how hurt he had been at the diner when she'd walked away from him. It had been a very long time since he had allowed that emotion, probably since he was eleven years old and his mother had told him he'd been a mistake, that she had never wanted children. He could still picture her waving her glass of scotch toward the door and yelling at him to get out of the apartment because he'd made too much noise. He had turned off the radio and left, vowing never to let anyone make him feel like that again. As he became older, he realized that love was power, and he isolated himself even more.

He didn't know what to do about Julia. His head told him to let it go; his heart said something very different. Of course she was scared. She'd been living in a protective bubble until Valentina Manchester arrived and burst it wide open. He couldn't imagine what it must be like for her to go home every night and deal with a ghost. How could he have expected a normal reaction? Especially with her daughter coming home. His life was built on change. Hers wasn't, and every reassuring constant in her life was now in chaos. He mentally ticked off the list. Coolback was in the throes of reorganization. Her house was infested with a ghost. Her daughter has just left for Europe with another family. And now he enters her life . . .

The picture became clearer. Julia had to have been traumatized. He had only been thinking about himself, and quickly realized it was his pride standing in the way. He was not used to losing, especially because of something so trivial as pride.

Suddenly, he knew what he had to do. Getting up, he walked down the hallway to her office.

# Chapter 14

His stomach twisted into a knot when he raised his hand to knock on her office door. He hesitated, not having felt this insecure in years. Pride. Taking a deep breath, he squared his shoulders, knocked twice, and opened the door.

Julia looked up when he entered, and he could see signs of annoyance on her face. Holding up his hand to stem any possible objections, he hurried to say, "This will only take a few minutes."

"Look, if this is about work, then fine, but if it isn't, then I thought I had made it clear Coolback wasn't the place to discuss anything personal."

He walked over to the chair in front of her desk and slowly sat down. "I've tried to call you at home, but you let the machine pick up."

"No, you didn't. And I never got any messages."

He was surprised. "Julia, I called you twice last night."

"I was home all night. The phone never rang."

"Well, I did call. Maybe your phone's out of order. We have to talk sometime."

He watched as she sat back in her chair and folded her arms over her chest. "This isn't the place."

She had obviously retrenched, and he mentally shrugged. He knew it would be a demanding exchange at best.

"I've been doing a lot of thinking. As a matter of fact, I couldn't fall asleep last night going over our argument in the diner." She appeared unmoved, and he hurried to continue.

"This isn't easy for me. I have a lot of pride, Julia. I'm not sure of where to begin." He always knew how to negotiate and, for the first time in years, he was at a loss. Having no frame of reference on how to continue with something this personal, he felt like he was flying by the seat of his pants.

"It's important for me that you understand. I want to try and fix this, if I can."

Steve looked down to his tightly clasped hands. This was so painful. Could he continue when this took more courage than facing an entire boardroom during a hostile takeover? He wasn't used to being vulnerable.

"From the time I was a kid, I've spent most of my life protecting myself," he began slowly. "When you realize that your own mother doesn't want you, you learn not to place yourself in emotional jeopardy." He looked up and tried to smile. "But recently, and for the first time in my life, the strangest thing happened. I started to let you in. I guess that's why I was so hurt when you didn't want me to meet Paige."

Julia unfolded her arms and leaned forward on her desk. "But, Steve," she said carefully, "you have to understand, I was scared. More than that, I was terrified."

He nodded and interrupted, "I know that now, and that's why I had to talk to you. Even though we have so much fun together, and have discussed a few really important issues, I realized this is one area of communication where we have trouble. I think it all boils down to the fact that we're both really afraid. We've both had experiences that have made it necessary to protect ourselves. So dropping our guard isn't going to be easy."

For the first time since their argument, he noticed a hint of a smile. "I guess you're right. I was just trying to protect myself from having to answer to my daughter about a situation that was too personal and confusing."

"Confusing? I thought the confusion ended with that kiss at the diner. It made it all clear for me."

"See, that's just it. The kiss may have made it clearer for you, but for me it just compounded the confusion. You're leaving next week, Steve, and I had to keep that in front of me at all times. I've never had a casual affair, and I didn't want to parade one in front of my daughter."

At least she was talking. Encouraged, he leaned his elbows onto her desk and smiled hesitantly. "I don't know, Julia, I feel weird about this, almost old-fashioned . . . like I'm courting you. Perhaps it's something I haven't done in a very long time, but I want you to understand that I never considered this casual. I had every intention of figuring out a way to make this work, even if it meant driving down from New York on a regular basis."

She shook her head. "But how could something like that work? Even Val now thinks that we're a mistake, and this was supposed to be her mission."

"This is between me and you. Consider the source. I don't give a damn about her mission. Sure, it'll take some work, but don't you think we have a right to happiness?" He smiled, realizing what he'd said. "Or is that being presumptuous?"

Julia laughed. "Maybe you're right. I don't know. I'm so confused. I don't want to pick up any more pieces of my life and try to patch them together. I'm too old for this. And I don't seem to have any luck with men."

The reference annoyed him. He figured that he'd been discussed at length. It was obvious that Val wasn't in his corner any longer, and she was affecting Julia's perception of him.

"Who's that talking, you or Val? Who are you going to trust? Someone who's alive, who cares about you, who wants to show you the world, and see you laugh, and then kiss those freckles right off your face? Or are you going to trust someone who's fading so fast that she may not even be there when you get in from work? I know what's happening in your house is extraordinary, but you and I live in reality. And the reality is that I care about you, and would never intentionally hurt you."

Tears appeared at her eyes. "Please, Steve, don't say those things here at work. If you walk out of here and I'm crying, everybody will know."

"I don't care if they know. My intentions are honorable."

Wiping back the tears, Julia giggled at his obvious declaration of courtship. "You're quite a negotiator, Steve McMillan. Do you ever give up?"

"Not on something that's this important to me."

Their gazes caught and held for a few intense moments. It was as if she were talking to him, telling him things that she wasn't ready to say aloud.

She broke the contact, and picked up her pen. "Thank you for saying that." Playing with the pen in her hands, she twisted the stylus in and out, and changed the subject. "But you're wrong about Val. If anything, she seems to be improving."

"She's reversed the aging? She isn't depressed anymore?"

"She hasn't reversed it, but it appears to have stopped. And no, she's not depressed anymore. She even seems happy. She made me dinner last night."

He sat back in his chair. "When did this happen?"

He could see Julia working out the question in her head. "I think it was Saturday. Yes, it was, after I got off of the phone with you. I went up into the attic to talk to her, and that was the first time I noticed."

He had made a small fortune for himself, and an even larger one for Amalgamated, by trusting his instincts. Something about this situation made him uneasy. It wasn't just having a ghost in the house, it was the influence of a manipulative entity on an innocent that bothered him. "Don't you find it ironic that when we first met, Val began to deteriorate?" he asked. "At least that's what you told me. Now, interestingly enough, when we have our first fight, or miscommunication, the lovely Miss Manchester seems to have revived, and is not in favor of completing her mission. Is it any wonder that she thinks we were a mistake?"

Julia's body became rigid, as if she were rejecting the concept. "Oh, Steve . . . I think you're way off base. Maybe your view of the world has left you a little bit skeptical, but I don't think Val would do that to me. Look, just like you, she's been through a rocky time as a kid and she has trouble trusting people, especially men. Val's view of the world is a bit jaded, and I think she was only trying to protect me from being hurt."

"Okay, maybe I'm wrong. It just seems like too much of a coincidence to ignore. And, to be honest, it's a little hard knowing that when you go home, Val won't be in favor of this relationship. Julia, I just wish we had a little time to discuss this outside of the office, though not in your home with Val hovering about. I can't even see her." He groaned. "She could be standing in back of me, giving you the thumbs up or thumbs down, and I wouldn't even know it. It's hard enough to convince you that I'm serious without an invisible critic."

Julia laughed. "You're right. That is something Val would do."

Pleased by her response, he pressed on. "Okay, I have a suggestion, and it's only a suggestion. What if I make dinner for us at the apartment? Would you be comfortable with that, if I promised to be a gentleman?"

Julia hesitated and smiled. "We're just going to have dinner and talk?"

"Dinner and conversation, I promise. We've done this before and you were safe. Tonight won't be any different."

"What time?"

"How's seven o'clock? Apartment 5B," he said standing up. "And I'm leaving before you change your mind."

He had learned something new today. Swallowing his pride wasn't as painful as he had thought.


"I hope you like it—I tried a new recipe. I found it in your cookbook."

Julia looked at the simmering pots and gasped. Holding her hand to her chest in apology, she tried to explain. "I'm so sorry, Val. I'm having dinner with Steve, and there was no way to let you know."

She watched as Val slowly took the ladle from the pot of spaghetti sauce and set it down. "Have you lost your mind?"

For the first time, the tone in Val's voice frightened her. She told herself that it was natural for Val to be indignant after having gone to all of this trouble. She would have felt the same way had the tables been turned. "Val, I know you're upset. I also know how disappointing it is to eat alone. We can have it tomorrow, and I'll even stop and get some Italian bread and Chianti."

"I didn't have to do this. I made it for tonight. How can you go out with that pompous ass after the way he treated you last weekend? It's pathetic. After twenty years a man pays you a little attention, and you lap it up like a starving dog."

"You are way out of line. Steve is not a pompous ass, and frankly, I'm hurt by your last remark. I think you owe me an apology."

"Apologize to you? I'm the one who made the dinner, the one you're walking out on."

"Val, you said you were my friend and only wanted my happiness. You know how insecure I am about this, and a real friend wouldn't go after my Achilles heel."

"You don't have my experience in dealing with men. I'm only trying to protect you from making a fool of yourself."

"Then be friend enough to let me make my own decisions. I've decided to have dinner with Steve." As she walked out of the kitchen, she stopped by the phone and picked it up to check for a dial tone. Shrugging when she heard one, she replaced it and said, "I'm going upstairs to change."

"Don't do this, Julia," Val warned. "You'll be sorry."

"I hope not," Julia answered as she left the room.

After taking a quick shower, she dressed in tan linen slacks and a cream silk shell. A touch of gold at her ears and neck completed the outfit. As she slipped her foot into her shoe, she looked at the phone on her night table. If Steve had called, why didn't she hear the phone ring? He wasn't lying. His surprise had been genuine. Picking up the receiver, she heard the dial tone. She placed it back down and shook her head. It didn't make sense. Something must be wrong with one of the phones. This time she picked it up and checked the back.

The ringer had been turned off. Flipping it back on, she put it down and went into the bathroom. Maybe she had done it by accident. But she hadn't touched any of the phones since she'd spoken to Steve on Saturday. Had Paige done it? Did one of the girls call her so late that Paige didn't want to disturb anyone? Julia brushed out her hair and applied a light application of makeup. Too late to ask Paige . . .

Then Steve's words about Val came back to her. It wasn't possible. Val wouldn't do that. But why was she so hostile about Steve? It had started on Saturday. When she passed Paige's room, she went in to check her daughter's extension.

The ringer had been turned off.

A chill ran down her back and she slowly placed the phone down on the table. This wasn't happening. Val wasn't turning on her. There must be an explanation. All she had to do was ask. A sudden rush of fear entered her body and she had to force her legs to carry her from the room.

Val was eating when she came into the kitchen. Without saying anything, Julia flipped the ringer back on the wall phone. The fear was quickly replaced with anger. "Why did you do it?" she demanded. "Why did you turn off all the phones?"

Val twirled her fork around the spaghetti. "I wanted you to get some peace. You were pretty upset by his phone call, or don't you remember, now that you worship the ground he walks on?"

"Don't be smug with me, Val. How could you do that? My daughter is in Europe. How would she reach me in an emergency?"

"You spoke to her when she landed. She's fine."

"You don't know that! And now neither do I, thanks to you!"

"Calm down. She didn't call."

Furious, Julia punched the rewind button on her answering machine, even though the light wasn't blinking. Steve's voice filled the silence in the room, telling her that he needed to speak with her. Not once, but twice.

She stood staring down at the machine. Her breathing was heavy and her heart was pounding behind her rib cage. "What are you doing, Val? And why . . . why are you doing it to me?"

"Survival, sweetie. It's a lesson you haven't yet learned. That man is going to eat you up alive and then spit you out when he leaves. And who's going to have to put you together again? Me. I was just trying to make it easy for everybody."

Julia spun around. "Why are you so against him? Why now? I thought he was the answer to your mission. If I found happiness, you would leave. You wanted to leave, Val. Don't you want that anymore?"

Val threw her fork onto her plate. "Of course I want to leave here! This," and she ran her hand down the front of her body, "this is my personal hell for every wrong thing I've done. Well, I've paid enough. When he leaves you, and he will—they all leave eventually—you're going to be in worse shape than when I arrived. So then, how do I get back?"

Anger took hold of her. "On Saturday you said that Steve was presumptuous. Now you're being presumptuous. I've gone through a lot in my life and I've put myself back together just fine without the help of a—a ghost. Trouble with a man might be disappointing, but not devastating. I'll handle my own consequences, just as I've always done."

Val ran her hand over her brow, as if she were tiring. "You don't know what a man can do to your life."

"Oh, I don't? What was Paige? What was that? The immaculate conception? The difference between you and me, Val, is that I've taken responsibility for my misfortunes. You've tried to manipulate or blame others for yours."

"You've had all the advantages, Julia. You don't know what it was like."

Julia's jaw dropped in disbelief. "I don't? Excuse me, who was left with a baby daughter and no support? Who worked her way up into management from secretary without a college degree? And, yes, Val, I did it before it was fashionable to promote women in the work force. You may have had to worry about yourself. I had a child. I had to make a choice. And it took me years . . . years! I could have gotten to this point a lot faster by sleeping my way here. I did it through hard work. I chose to work harder and longer to prove my worth. And I've had to prove it to every male boss I've ever had. That's the difference between us."

She took a deep breath to steady her voice. Now that she had begun to vent her anger, she couldn't seem to stop. "Don't you dare be condescending to me, or begrudge me the life I've built. I've worked too damn hard to have you minimize it like this. So, don't tell me your sad story. We've all got them. You made your choices. This is it, Val. Right here. Right now. For both of us. We are where we are in this moment, because of decisions we have made in our lives. And I'm going to tell you this one time only. Don't you dare touch my telephones again, or make decisions for me. This is *my* home!"

Val slowly rose from the table, leaning on the chair for support. "I may have made my choices, but thank God I was never as desperate for a man as you are now."

Julia turned away from her. "I'm leaving."

"You'll be sorry. Don't do it."

She picked up her purse from the floor and walked to the door. Opening it about six inches, Julia was shocked to have it yanked out of her hand and slammed shut.

"I can't let you do it," Val said from behind her in a tired voice.

Julia looked back over her shoulder and saw Val leaning against the archway of the kitchen. She was taking deep breaths, as though winded.

"I know what you're doing, Val. And it won't work. It's obvious that you're only trying to keep me here so you won't age. How is this different from what you accused me of doing to Paige? You can't keep me trapped in this house to grow old with you. You were right—I *am* alive, and I do have a right to live. So open the door, now!"

Julia tried the knob again. This time there was no resistance.

He ran his fingers through his hair and reached for the doorknob. Seeing a piece of lint on the arm of his sweater, he quickly flicked it off and smiled before opening the door.

"Hi, you're early. I was just preparing—what's wrong?" He opened the door wider and waved toward the living room. She looked worried, as if she'd just had terrible news. "Is it Paige? Is she all right?"

She shook her head and he crossed the space between them. Holding her shoulders, he said, "Tell me."

"It's Val." Her voice was low and emotional. "You were right."

He stared at her for moment, trying to reason out what she was talking about. What had Val done to her? "Here, come and sit down. Let me take your jacket." He led her into the room and placed her blazer on the back of the chair. "Sit down and tell me."

He watched as she slowly sank into the chair and

then stared at the stack of magazines on the coffee table. "Val turned off all the phones off after Paige left. And she tried to keep me from coming here."

He sat on the sofa and took her hand. "Are you all right? Are you hurt? You can't go back there."

Shaking her head, Julia smiled sadly. "No, I'm not hurt. I'll be okay. You see, we had it out. It was a terrible fight, and I said some terrible things. But I . . . I was scared. I couldn't believe what she'd done. Everything you said was true. When I told her about having dinner with you, she seemed angry, and we argued. I went upstairs and found that the ringers on all the extensions had been shut off, and when I confronted her, things got really ugly. I tried to leave, but she slammed the door on me just like she did to you the first night you came over."

Frightened for her, he asked in a hushed voice, "What did you do?"

"I told her to let me out, but I noticed that she was also becoming weaker as I was getting more firm in my decision. Slamming that door had taken a lot out of her, and I knew she wasn't strong enough to hurt me. I opened the door and I left."

"My God, Julia, you can't go back there."

Her head snapped up. "That's my house, and I won't let anyone force me out. She can't hurt me. The aging has started again."

"I don't care . . ." He was shocked that she would even consider it.

"I'm safe, Steve. Now that she realizes I know what she's doing, she's powerless. All she can do is get older and weaker."

"You can't live like that." His brain searched for something to make her reconsider. "We have to get some help."

"Where?"

"I don't know," he muttered. "A priest. A channeler . . . something."

From out of nowhere, she suddenly burst into laughter.

He thought she was becoming hysterical, and it frightened him even more.

As if reading his thoughts, she waved her hand in front of him and said, "No . . . I'm sorry. I couldn't stop it. I just had a mental image of you, Mr. Perfect Businessman, trying to find a channeler. How would you go about that? Through the yellow pages?"

Relieved, he sat back and couldn't help smiling. "You must be feeling better. You never miss a chance to tell me how stuffy I am."

She sobered immediately. "I never said you were stuffy. Serious and a little narrow-minded, but never stuffy."

He stood up. "Would you like a drink? A glass of wine? I know I want one."

Again, she smiled. This time it seemed genuine. "Thanks. I'll join you. I believe I could use a drink."

When he returned, he handed her a glass and waited for her to taste the wine.

"It's delicious," she said. "I usually don't drink wine."

"Chateau Minuty, from the Côtes de Provence."

In answer to her blank expression, he added, "I'm

sorry. It's from Provence, where I have my farm."

"This is made from your grapes?"

"I don't think so, but it's from the area." He held his glass up in a toast. "I can't think of anything appropriate to say in this circumstance."

He could see her thinking. "Why don't we drink to answers?"

Touching her glass, he nodded. "To answers, then."

They both took a sip and she said, "Do you think there are any?"

"Of course. There's always a solution to a problem, if you keep your head and stay calm. The answer is in your brain. It may just take a bit of time before you retrieve it."

Smiling, she said, "Okay, then let's let it simmer a bit. And speaking of simmering, what is that wonderful aroma? What did you cook?"

He looked toward the kitchen. *"Paupiettes* of sole . . . stuffed with salmon."

"You're kidding? You can cook like a gourmet, but you eat at a diner?"

He chuckled, and then said, "It's no fun to cook for one. Why don't you bring your wine and join me? I have to check on dinner."

"Can I help?"

"Sure. I didn't start the salad yet, and I'd like some company in the kitchen."

They chatted easily while preparing the meal. He noticed how well they worked together, and it amazed him how much he enjoyed sharing his personal space with Julia. It was comfortable, if not almost comforting, to have someone there to talk and laugh with.

He couldn't help being flattered by her genuine appreciation of his efforts. All during dinner, she praised everything, from the light seasonings on the sole, to his choice of dessert. He had to admit that he had a hidden agenda in choosing everything French. But he hadn't found the right moment to bring it up.

Loading the dishwasher together, they talked about Paige's trip to Europe, and he tried to steer the conversation back to his objective.

"Have you ever thought of going to Europe, Julia?"

"Of course I have. Who hasn't? But I never thought about it seriously."

The kitchen clean, Steve poured the coffee. Handing her a cup, he said, "Why don't you think about it? Seriously."

She stared at him, and he could see the confusion in her expression. "Why? I could never afford to do that, especially with tuition to pay."

"Come sit down with me. I want to talk to you." He led her back into the living room and they sat on the sofa. She appeared nervous, but he knew he had to press on. It was now or never. If he could only find the right words . . .

"A lot has happened to you this year, Julia. When's the last time you took a vacation?"

Julia looked down at the coffee cup that she was holding on her lap. "This year has been stressful, I'll grant you that. But, even if I wanted to, I don't have the money to take such an extravagant trip. For the last seven years, I used my vacation days to catch up on things I let go around the house. Or Paige and I would take day trips to the shore." She smiled. "The last real vacation I took was to Disney World."

"You owe this to yourself."

"Steve, what are you talking about? A trip to Europe?"

He hesitated, feeling nervous about her reaction. This was harder than closing the Coolback deal. "Before you say no, hear me out completely. I have time off before my next assignment, and I want to go to my farm in France. That conversation that we had on our first date got me thinking about it. I really need to go and check the vineyard, and I'd like you to come with me. You've got three weeks of vacation due you from Coolback."

"You can't be serious."

"I'm very serious. It's the ideal solution to the situation in your home. It would be the perfect way to spend some stress-free time together without worrying about Val's manipulations or the gossip at Coolback. Who knows, we might even be able to meet up with Paige."

She looked up at him and shook her head slightly. "This is unbelievable. It sounds too good to be true. But I can't go to Europe. I don't have a passport, the money—"

"You can get a passport, and I've accumulated enough frequent flyer miles over the last year to get you to China and back. But we'll settle for a first class seat to Nice."

"I don't know what to say. And seeing Paige . . ."

"And yes, meeting Paige. I know I've pressed this issue before, but I don't think you understood my motivations. You've made it very clear how important your daughter is to you. She's a vital part of your life. I can't help it, I want to know everything about you."

She placed her coffee cup on the table and leaned back on the couch. Sighing she said, "Steve, this is really hard for me. I feel like a novice, and I haven't done anything like this in a long time." With a startled expression, she quickly corrected herself. "No, that's not what I meant. That didn't come out right. What I mean to say is, I've never been to Europe, or away with a man. What if it becomes awkward? It could ruin everything."

"If we stay here, Val could ruin everything. We need a chance to get to know each other, Julia. We're both free of obligations right now. If you want, we can do this. I want to show you the vineyard. It's beautiful this time of year."

"It sounds like it could be wonderful." Julia looked down as though embarrassed. "I know you're trying so hard with me. I know you're not used to this long . . . courtship, as you call it, and I appreciate your patience. I want to go, Steve. I'd love to see your home. I'm just scared."

Pleased by her admission, he asked, "Scared of what?"

"We would be together for three weeks, and—I don't know how to put this—it's been so long, and this is so sudden."

"I would never ask you to do anything that you're not comfortable with. But I hope you feel comfortable with me."

With tears in her eyes, she looked up and said, "I am, and that's what's scaring me."

He reached out and dried her moist cheek with his thumb. "That's a beginning," he whispered, still touching her face. She brought her hand up and gently held his wrist.

In a tiny voice, she whispered, "Would you just hold me? I know I have to go home soon, but I need to feel secure, somewhere."

If this was as much as she could give right now, he'd gladly accept it. Pulling her into his arms, he held her close, while resting his chin on the top of her head. He ran his fingers up and down her back, hoping to soothe her. She'd been through a lot tonight. He had forced himself into her office. She had confronted Val and tried to reclaim her home. And tonight, he'd sprung the trip to France on her. Yet, for all of his honorable intentions, she felt so good in his arms.

"I can't wait to show you the south of France. We can spend a few days in Monaco before going to the farm. The bougainvillea is in bloom, and the mountains look so green this time of year, before the summer sets in. The farm is twenty minutes from San Tropez, and every Monday morning there's an open air market on the square. During the rest of the week, you can sit at a sidewalk cafe, and watch the old men play bocce ball. But on Monday, that three block square is filled with vendors. At one place you can buy beautiful flowers for six francs, move a few paces down to buy shoes, or jeans, and next to that will be a butcher's stand with meats from the butcher's own farm. Then there are pastries like you've never seen in your life. Antique furniture, paintings, t-shirts. You have to see it to believe it."

"It sounds magical . . ."

He felt her breath through the material of his shirt, and questioned his gentlemanly resolve. Stroking her hair, he murmured, "You can help me decorate the farmhouse. I haven't had the time since it's been renovated."

He couldn't believe he was talking about going to the market, or decorating, when what he really wanted to show her was in the bedroom. Before, he would have followed through with that thought. But now, he was surprised to find himself more concerned with Julia's needs than with his own. And right now she needed comfort and support.

She lifted her head from his chest, and looked at him. "I can't believe that I'm about to say this, but I want to go."

Exhilaration rushed through him, and he tried to keep his expression calm.

He whispered, "I'm glad. You won't be sorry, Julia."

Their eyes met in a powerful gaze, and his restraint weakened. He stared at her mouth, drawn to it, wanting to taste it. Gently pulling her to him, he lowered his lips to hers. His kiss was light and questioning, and she seemed to yield to him. No longer afraid of her reaction, he deepened the kiss. She opened her mouth in response, allowing his tongue to enter. This time he felt her full participation, and gave himself over to it. He felt his own breathing deepen with desire. Never in his life had he waited this long for a woman. He wanted her.

Knowing he had to end this torture, he brought his hands up to cup her face, and pulled back. "Julia, if you want me to keep my promise, we'll have to stop this."

After a stunned moment of recollection, she lowered her head and giggled. "I guess you're right. This was only supposed to be a night of dinner and conversation."

He couldn't believe he had shut the window of opportunity, especially since she hadn't voiced any objections. As he watched her sit up, he mentally cursed this self-imposed chivalry.

"You don't have to leave yet, do you?" he asked as he watched her stand. "It's not that late."

She smiled and straightened her blouse. "I think I'd better go home. It's been a long day," she said, picking up her blazer.

He followed her to the door and fought against the need to pull her back into his arms. "Are you sure you're all right to go home?"

Turning back around, Julia said, "I'll be fine, and when I get home Val should be asleep."

"Why don't you let me go with you? I don't feel

comfortable about letting you go back there alone."

"No, I'll be fine. Really. Quite frankly, Steve, if Val saw you it would only be worse."

"All right, then call me when you get home. Promise."

"I promise."

Wanting to protect her, he dismissed any apprehension from his mind, and gathered her into his arms. "You be careful, lady. We have a trip planned," he said with a smile. "I can't wait till Friday."

"Friday? So soon? How can I arrange to take a three week vacation on such short notice?"

"Your department wasn't affected by the take-over, and everything's calmed down in the company. Your assistant can handle it for three weeks. Don't worry. Just go home and pack. The sooner you're out of that house, the better."

Julia rested her head on his chest, and murmured, "Everything's happening so fast."

"I'll arrange the tickets. You just bring your birth certificate to work tomorrow, and we can get your passport during lunch."

Bringing her head up quickly, she said, "But I'm paying my own way."

"Julia . . ."

"No. I'm serious. I can afford airfare and everything else. And I accept your offer of a room."

"But we're flying first class," he objected.

She smiled up at him. "What's wrong with coach?"

"What's wrong with first class?"

"You need to get in touch with the common folk."

"I object to your insinuation, but we shall discuss this at length tomorrow. What I want to know is if your statement was also a way of telling me you would like your own room."

She stared into his eyes and he thought she was about to kiss him. Instead, she smiled very seductively and said, "We'll discuss this at length another time. Good night."

Slowly turning away from him, she opened the door and left before he could recover. He let out his breath and blinked a few times. Julia Edwards had just flirted with him! And there was nothing coy about it.

# Chapter 15

How in the world was she going to fit everything into two bags? She realized exactly how Paige had felt. It wasn't as if she knew what to pack for Europe. And being on a three-week-long date only made it worse. She had shopped till she dropped, trying to find attractive ensembles to bring. She had even spent a small fortune on lingerie. Julia stared down at the pretty silk gowns. Dear God, had she already bought into the concept of sleeping with the man? Panicked, she realized in one horrifying moment that she hadn't even considered contraceptives. The last time she had even thought about it, she'd needed a prescription. Now there was a cadre of choices openly displayed on the grocery shelf. When she had done three weeks worth of food shopping for Val, she hadn't even gone down that aisle. And she couldn't picture herself asking Steve McMillan if he had packed condoms. She knew it was the adult thing to do. She had watched Oprah, and even lectured her daughter about safe sex, but now confronted with the reality for herself after twenty years, she knew she had to make an adult decision. And it made a heck of a lot more sense to do it here in the States, rather than to stand in the middle of a pharmacy in a foreign country with a French-English dictionary trying to negotiate some form of birth control.

She looked at her watch. Steve would be here in an hour to pick her up. Shop Rite opened at seven. She crammed everything into her bags and left them on her bed as she decided Shop Rite was her only choice. She paled at the thought of standing in a check out line at seven-thirty in the morning with only items of birth control in her hands.

How was she ever going to get through this day?

When she returned home, she heard Val stirring about and she clutched her plastic bag of contraband close to her side as she passed the guest bedroom. After three days of constant turmoil, the last thing she needed was Val's running commentary about her lack of experience with men.

Walking into her bedroom, she stopped and stared at the jumble of clothes that were strewn over the bed and onto the rug.

From behind her, she heard Val's voice.

"You can't leave me, Julia."

She spun around and saw Val clinging to the doorway for support. "How could you do that?" Julia demanded, as an adrenalin rush of anger swept through her body. She raced into the room and started picking up clothes and flinging them into the suitcases. "How dare you ruin this for me? Steve's going to be here in ten minutes!"

Tears gathered at her eyes. She swiped at them with the back of her hand as she grabbed a sun dress off the floor. Jamming shoes back into a bag, she glared across the room. "You are so damned selfish, aren't you? It doesn't matter how old you've become, you still think that everyone and everything revolves around you."

Val slowly walked over to the overstuffed wing chair by the window and sat down. "It's called survival, sweetie. I can't let you go."

Julia rounded on her, clutching a shoe in her hand. "But whose survival? Mine or yours? 'Cause I'm not going to survive around you. You tried anger. Guilt. The silent treatment. Now you're resorting to tantrums, and I won't have it. Get it through that inconsiderate blond head of yours— I'm going, and there isn't a damned thing you can do about it."

She noticed that tears were slowly falling down Val's cheeks. Her eyes narrowed and she took a deep breath. "And I thought you had already pulled out all the stops. What role are you playing now, Val? Baby Jane? The abandoned, aging invalid? It is a shame you didn't get to play that dramatic role. You would have been terrific."

"You're damn right I would have." The tears immediately stopped. Val's expression became hostile.

"Hey, tears on an aging actress aren't becoming. So knock it off and listen to me. I'm leaving here in less than ten minutes and I've had it with your fits of temper." She resumed stuffing her clothes back into the suitcases. "I've tried during the last three days to reason with you, hoping that you could somehow be happy for me. But it's obvious that your only concern is yourself, so now I'm going to take a page out of your book, Val. I'm only going to be concerned about myself at the moment. I've done everything I can for you. There's enough food for three weeks. All the bills are paid, and there's even a carton of cigarettes under the sink."

Zipping the first bag closed, she started on the second. "This isn't working the way it is. We need some time apart. Since you can't leave, I will. I suggest you make good use of this time to figure out what your mission is, because it obviously isn't me. There's something else that's keeping you here and my happiness isn't it. If you hate this situation as much as I do, then you should think hard about your past. Something else is anchoring you here. You have to be truthful with yourself. No more lies, Val. No more manipulations, roles or fantasies. Take a long hard look in the mirror and figure out who you are. I can't help you anymore."

Julia zipped the second suitcase closed and sat on the edge of the bed. Sighing with emotional and physical exhaustion, she said in a tired voice, "If I didn't go on this trip, then I'd be giving up on life."

Both women stared at each other for a silent moment before the doorbell broke through the eerie quiet in the room. Julia got up and stood before Val.

"Be well, Val," she whispered, fighting back her own tears. "I don't want to leave like this, and I don't want anything bad to happen to you while I'm gone, but neither one of us can make rational decisions right now. And I have to go. I know I've said it before: I can't stay here and grow old with you. I need to find out what's out there." She smiled hesitantly. "I have you to thank for that gift. You pushed me when I was too afraid to even try. Can't we part friends?"

Val's hard expression didn't change. "Friends?" she scoffed. "You seem to be the only one who benefited from this deal. Mark my words. You'll regret the day you left me. I curse this trip, and you along with it."

Picking up her bags, Julia walked toward the bedroom door as the bell again sounded. Sorrow was mixed with anger. "Always the actress, Val—right to the end. Goodbye."

He shifted his weight again and turned a little to ease the ache that was crawling up his body. He knew it was hopeless, that aching desire to move, to appease the pain. It was her fault. She was so close that her perfume elevated his senses to new heights. Her body was touching his and he thought he might scream. He couldn't take it. This was unfair. And what made it worse was that he had brought this upon himself. Courtship . . . it had its price, he thought. He let out his breath with frustration.

"How long are you going to continue to do that?"

"Do what?" he asked with mock surprise.

"That sighing. You could have sat in first class."

He stared at the unappealing tweed covering the seat in front of him. "So you've said, at least eight times since we left New York." She had insisted on paying for her own ticket, and had informed him that she couldn't afford to fly first class. Not even business class. Although she'd said it would be perfectly fine if they sat apart, he had felt like Sir Walter Raleigh when he'd bought his coach ticket. He'd obviously forgotten just how bad an overnight flight across the Atlantic could be.

"Why don't you get up and stretch your legs? It might help."

He noticed that she was still reading the magazine she had bought at the airport. She hadn't even looked up when she'd spoken. The trip had started out so great this morning. They had left South Jersey and were at his apartment in New York by ten. He had been pleased by Julia's compliments when she saw his place. They'd eaten lunch and then he packed. By six-thirty they were at the airport. Everything had been easy and smooth, until they were about thirty thousand feet in the air—and then he knew he was in trouble.

The seats were so narrow. There was no leg room, especially since Julia had insisted that they bring their own food. Her two large plastic bags were obstacles to his finding any degree of comfort. Every time he got up and walked back to the head, the woman on the other side of Julia showed her annoyance. It had gotten to the point he dreaded coming back to his seat and resuming the tortured position.

"I'm not getting up," he said, while looking at his watch. "Wonderful. Only four more hours to go."

"Please, Steve. Stop complaining. There's nothing wrong with your seat. Everyone else is managing just fine."

He looked around the cabin and then rested his head and closed his eyes. "Everyone else doesn't have eighty dollars worth of food from Sid's Deli under their feet."

"It's not under your feet. It's on the side. I have it, too. How many times do I have to tell you about my friend, Sheila—"

"Oh, please," he interrupted. "I've heard all about Sheila who contracted food poisoning while flying to California. This isn't even the same airline. Do you know how foolish we're going to look when they serve dinner, and we pull out chicken sandwiches and potato salad?"

"At least we won't get sick. I did the same thing for Paige, only I made the food. Now stop acting like an adolescent and resign yourself. There's really nothing else you can do."

She was right. He had already checked with the flight attendant. There were no empty seats in business or first class, but the fact that she was right didn't make him feel any better. She was so stubborn and independent. Even when he offered to lend her the money, for he knew she wouldn't let him pay, she had refused. What did she think it would do to her? Did she think that if he paid for the airline tickets she would be indebted to him, and he would take his due one way or the other? She really was paranoid if she believed that of him.

"Let's drop the subject, all right?"

"Fine." She went back to reading her article.

He knew he was being a pain in the ass, and couldn't stop himself. It was this damned courtship. Over a month! Never in his life had he waited this long for a woman. He kept reminding himself that Julia wasn't just a woman. She was special. She was worth it. She was also the most stubborn woman he had ever met. First the food, which seemed a bit eccentric to him. And then these damnable seats. He couldn't see how upgrading her ticket with his frequent flyer mileage compromised her feminist sensibilities. Thank God he had made the reservations in Monaco and they were staying at a decent hotel. If it were up to her, she'd have them holed up at a pensione.

The flight attendants rolled the dinner cart up the aisle and he whispered, "Oh, goody. Chow time."

"Let's wait until everyone else is served," she said, placing her magazine in the pocket of the seat in front of her. "That way we won't be conspicuous."

When the attendant asked about drinks, he ordered wine and gladly accepted the small bottle. About five more of these ought to do it, he thought. One way or another, he was going to get some sleep this night. And he was also going to eat every bit of food that was blocking room for his legs. He wondered if she thought him irritable or just plain spoiled. Suppressing a sigh, he reached down for the largest bag from Sid's Deli. This ought to be a memorable meal.

She heard it. It was another sigh of annoyance, she thought as she pulled down the tray table. She refused to get into an argument with him and treated him the way he was acting—like a spoiled teenager. Hadn't she done everything his way? From getting the passport in Philadelphia while being caught in a spring shower, to leaving this morning at eight o'clock even though she only had four hours sleep followed by a horrendous argument with Val.

She didn't want to think of Val now, but her thoughts kept coming back to this morning. She had told Steve everything in the car on their way to New York City and honestly believed that she and Val needed some time apart. She really couldn't take much more. The fights. The threats. The constant apprehension, not knowing what the next day would bring. Never in her life had she been at such a loss. It had been a relief to leave, for her home had become a prison. Ever since she had announced her independence she had felt the tension, and it was unbearable. The night she had returned after dinner at Steve's apartment, she'd walked into the kitchen and had stared at the mess Val had left. It had taken her almost two hours to clean up and, when she'd passed the guest bedroom on her way to her own, she had been so tired that she hadn't even bothered to say good night. The next day when she told Val about the trip, Val had threatened her, vowing to keep her home.

She had tried to leave on friendly terms, hoping that when Val saw she was determined to go they could at least part pleasantly. She would never forget the look on Val's face, an old face lined with wrinkles of anger. Nor could she forget Val's parting words.

*I curse this trip, and you with it.*

Was that why her patience was running thin with Steve? Was that why he acted so annoyed with her? If this was how the trip was starting then perhaps they were doomed to three weeks of suffering each other's company. How could everything have been so wonderful for them on the ground and so miserable once in the air? Okay—so he was used to better seating and better service. That's why bringing their own food had made sense to her. He was almost embarrassed when they went through security and she had to tell them the contents of the plastic bags. Did he think he'd made a mistake by inviting her, that she wasn't sophisticated enough for him? She had appreciated his gesture of sitting with her in coach even after she had insisted he fly first class. Really, what difference would six hours apart make? Opening the plastic wrap around her chicken sandwich, she dearly wished that he had listened to her.

"Potato salad?" he asked, sounding like a waiter.

Julia accepted the small container and placed it on her table. "Thanks."

"Knife and fork? Sid thinks of everything," he said, handing her the small packet. "There's even salt and pepper."

"Thank you," she murmured, tearing open the plastic. "It smells good."

He didn't say anything and she thought it was probably better if they just ate in peace.

"Ahh . . . Julia?"

The chicken sandwich was delicious, with fresh tomatoes and lettuce on a huge croissant. Unable to answer while chewing, she turned her head to him.

He looked beyond her to the table next to hers. Leaning in, he whispered, "I'm sorry for being cranky about bringing our own food. What is *that* she's got in front of her?"

Julia looked to her left and saw a small mound of something brown in the airline dinner that was hard to define. Swallowing, she leaned closer to Steve and whispered back, "I don't know if it's beef or chicken or pork. I don't even know if it's meat."

Steve grinned and suppressed a chuckle. "I don't either, but it must be the entree if it's surrounded by vegetables. I take back everything I said. Thank God you brought food, or I'd be mighty hungry by the time we landed in Nice."

"Are you apologizing for being insufferable for the last three hours?"

To his credit, he looked over at the woman's dinner and nodded. "I am. I'm sorry for acting like a—what did you say? An adolescent? Now that we're eating the contents of this bag, there's actually room for me to stretch out my legs. I'm a bit taller than you, Julia, and my legs were cramping from the tight space."

Digging into her salad, she hesitated and turned her face toward his. She smiled into his eyes and said, "I accept your apology. I hope this means that we can forget the first three hours of this trip and can begin enjoying it."

He stared back at her. "This is your first trip abroad and I've begun it so poorly. I really am sorry."

"You're forgiven. I guess I should apologize to you for not accepting your offer to upgrade my ticket. I wasn't being stubborn, but I also didn't think about your comfort. It's just that I don't want to feel . . ." She struggled to find the right word.

"Obligated?" He supplied it.

She nodded. "This is so scary for me. The last time I went away with a man it was twenty years ago on my honeymoon."

"Where did you go?" he asked and then took a bite of his sandwich.

"Promise you won't laugh?"

He nodded.

"Niagara Falls."

He almost choked as he tried not to laugh. When he finally swallowed, he gasped for breath. "Don't do that. Don't make someone laugh when they're eating. I could have died!"

She giggled as she handed him his glass of wine. "You asked me. I was just answering your question."

"You went to Niagara Falls? Really?"

"Really. We didn't have the money for plane fare, so we decided to drive. It was a little hokey, but the falls were spectacular." She took a bite of her sandwich and was pleased that they seemed at ease with each other again. There was no curse. Everything would be fine.

After dinner they watched the movie and Steve held her hand, running the tips of his fingers ever so gently over it . . . feeling her nails and knuckles and every line on her palm, as if wanting to familiarize himself with each detail. It was so gentle, so tender, so damn sexy, that she thought she would scream. At one point, she slipped her hand from his and looked at him in the darkened cabin.

"I can't," she whispered, hoping he would understand.

He only smiled and nodded.

It was late. The movie was long over and almost everyone else around them was asleep. They had blankets and pillows and Steve had pushed up the armrest that separated them. She was cuddled under his arm and they were both under the blanket.

It had started out as just her hand resting on his chest, feeling the way it expanded with each breath. She had no idea when she started to caress him. She only knew that her hand moved of its own accord, as if seeking to memorize him the way he had done with her fingers. She wanted to feel him, to feel the heat of his body next to hers. It was as if her skin was more sensitive around him. She could feel the muscles of his stomach under palm, hard and contracting with her touch. The beating of his heart felt stronger and faster. And his breathing had become slow and deep, as if he too felt the intensity of each caress. Never had she thought to feel this way again. The wanting, the craving . . . It started at her knees and spread feverishly up her thighs. The sensation made her draw shallow, quick breaths as she traced a button on his shirt, toying with the dangerous idea of going lower. How could this be happening to her? This longing had been buried inside of her for two decades and she felt its powerful force.

"Julia?" His voice was so quiet that she almost didn't hear it.

"Hmm?" She was relaxed and happy. It had been so long since she felt like this. There was no one to worry about. No job. No child. No ghost. She felt free to be herself for the first time since she was young.

His hand slipped under the blanket and captured hers. Holding it close to his chest, he whispered, "I've finally found something I like about coach."

"Yes?"

"In first class the seats are separated. I wouldn't be able to hold you like this."

She smiled lazily. "Then I'm glad we're back here."

"Me, too. But I'm going to have to ask you to keep your hand still, or I'm going to embarrass you right in front that woman on your left. Have you ever heard of the Mile High Club?"

She muffled her laugh against his chest. "I'll behave."

He kissed the top of her head and sighed. "Just until we land. I think this might be the longest night of my life."

She lifted her head and kissed the bottom of his chin, feeling the beginnings of stubble. His beard barely touched her, a caress soft and quick, yet it sent a wave of desire straight from her mouth, down her body, right to where the fever focused. Not willing to let him go, she shifted in her seat to ease the ache.

Groaning, she whispered against his chest. "I think I owe you an apology. There really doesn't seem to be enough room back here."

She could hear his chuckle rumbling in his chest.

"Good night, Julia."

"Good night, Steve." If she had trouble getting through this night, and they were in public, how in the hell was she supposed to pull off a night in a hotel room? Suddenly she was filled with self doubt. She hadn't had sex in twenty years. How would she measure up to the women he had known? He wasn't the one who had practiced abstinence for two decades. What if it wasn't like riding a bicycle? What if she did forget?

What if she wasn't any good?

Sitting at the small table in front of the long French window of their hotel room, Julia breathed in the sea air and gazed out to the view displayed before her. If she had had the energy, she would get up to find her camera to capture the postcard-perfect scene. After an initial burst of excitement, she could feel jet lag settling in and energy seeping out of every pore. She needed rest. "It's so beautiful," she breathed in awe, taking in the turquoise harbor that was host to hundreds of pristine yachts.

"There's the palace up on the old rock," Steve said, pointing to the right. "The concierge said Rainier is in residence."

Julia held up her hand in the manner she had seen on television. "If he's looking," she said with a grin, "I'm giving him the royal wave."

Steve grinned back. "I wouldn't be surprised if he saw you. People who live in Monaco have told me that Rainier takes his rule seriously. If you notice how the palace is situated, his view is of his entire kingdom. All two square miles. See the way the apartments and hotels are built into the side of the mountain? I've been told that if you put up an awning that Rainier thinks will break the uniformity of his view, the authorities will insist that you remove it."

"Really?" She looked around her to the crowded dwellings. "All these people crammed into two square miles. It's like a glamorous ghetto."

Steve pulled apart one of the croissants they had ordered with café au lait to keep them awake. "Actually, Monaco is smaller than London's Hyde Park, but it's believed to be the safest place in the world. I think I read somewhere that there's one policeman to every eighty people. It's pretty amazing."

She turned toward the view from the opened French window. "Good Lord, will you look at all these boats? And the one out beyond the entrance to the harbor—is it a cruise ship?"

"Just a minute." He got up and went to one of his leather bags. Pulling out binoculars, he came back to the table and sat down. As he held them up to his eyes, he smiled.

"Here. Take a look." He handed the binoculars to her and waited until she had focused on the huge ship. "That's the Atlantis II. She's owned by a Greek named Niarchos and she's kept here in Monaco nine to ten months out of the year. He's in his seventies or early eighties, and spends most of the year in Switzerland. He comes here in the summer. From what I've heard when he arrives by helicopter to—see the landing pad on her top deck? When he arrives, all the boats in the harbor blow their horns to welcome the old man back to Monaco."

"I can't believe I'm here," she whispered, using the binoculars to span her line of vision. "It's so . . . breathtaking is the only word to describe it."

"I think it must have been even more so when the hills were dotted with lovely old villas. They were torn down to make room for all these apartments. If you look at the mountain, you can still see the terracing from the Roman occupation."

She brought the binoculars down to her lap. "How do you know all this?"

"I read quite a bit, and I ask questions. Especially about an area where I've purchased property."

"But your vineyard, isn't it an hour away?"

"Forty-five minutes if traffic isn't too bad. Now tell me, Julia, look out there. What impresses you the most?"

She turned back and took in the spectacular view. "I'm not sure," she murmured. After a few minutes, she said in a hushed voice, "I think it's the light. I don't know how to put it. There's almost a magical glow to the pastel colors of the homes and apartments. Everything seems warm and soft. I guess it sounds silly."

"It's the perfect answer," he said in a serious voice.

She looked back to him and he seemed to be studying her face.

"That's why the Impressionists came here to paint. Perhaps it's because this tiny kingdom is wedged between the southern Alps and the Mediterranean that it captures the sun's rays in such a way. I'm so pleased you noticed it."

She smiled and slid her hand across the table. Placing her palm in his, she gently squeezed it and said, "I'm so pleased you brought me here. Thank you, Steve."

They didn't say anything for a few moments until Steve cleared his throat. "Well, why don't we unpack what we'll need for today and tomorrow? Based on the way you packed after Val got into your bags, I'm sure you'll want to have something pressed for dinner tonight."

She slowly brought her hand back and put the

binoculars on the table. "You're right. My bags are a mess." She pushed the chair out and stood.

He rose with her and nodded. "Just call the valet and have what you need pressed. I thought we'd have an early dinner at the hotel and then go for a walk afterwards."

"Does this mean I can take a nap?"

Grinning, he said, "You shouldn't. You should try to stay awake until at least nine o'clock tonight."

She ran her fingers through her hair. "My body is telling me to take a shower and get some sleep."

"If you do, you'll regret it. You might get some sleep now, but you might also wake up at four in the morning. Take my word for it. I've done it, and it's not fun."

She nodded in agreement. "I'll try."

He kissed her forehead and gave her a quick hug. "I'll come next door at quarter to six. That'll give you time to take a nice long bath and get situated."

"Okay. And, thanks . . . I know I'm tired, but I want you to know that it was really nice to have had someone else handle all the arrangements. It's been a long time. I've been so used to having to do everything myself, and this was a welcomed change."

She handed the valet a sapphire raw silk sheath and the clothes she would need tomorrow. Coming back into the room, she sat between the two suitcases on the bed and looked at the disarray with disgust. She really should dump everything out and start again. The mere thought of what Val had done infuriated her, and she wondered if she even had matching pairs of shoes. Pulling out a pair of jeans, she neatly folded them and reached into the bag to grab a handful of underwear.

In the midst of her task, her arms felt weighted and her lids became heavy. She looked at the pillows behind her with longing. If she could just lie down and rest she would get her energy back. She promised herself she wouldn't fall asleep. A nap. That's all she needed.

Lowering her head to the pillow, she moaned in relief. It felt so heavenly. Her legs curled up and she wrapped her arms around the other pillow.

Behind closed lids, she thought back to the morning. Arrival in Nice had been exciting and confusing. Everyone spoke French, so she had to look to Steve to translate through customs. He had rented a car and took her for a long drive through Nice, Monaco and Monte Carlo. She felt like a typical tourist, gaping at the magnificent architecture, the beautiful gardens and palm trees lining streets. And the cars. She had never seen so many Porches, Jaguars, Lamberghinis and Rolls Royces in one small area in her entire life. Hell, she'd never seen that many even in the movies. And the streets, narrow and winding. Everything was so clean, so pretty . . .

Five minutes . . .

That's all she needed.

She wouldn't sleep.

Just rest her eyes . . .

\* \* \*

They walked hand in hand down the Rue Princess Caroline, a pedestrian-only street mall of tiny boutiques and sidewalk cafes. Those they passed as they made their way to the harbor, nodded and offered a friendly, "Bon nuit." Julia noticed the pretty melody to their speech and tried to mimick it in return.

Everything was so romantic and she momentarily leaned her head against Steve's shoulder. "I love it here," she murmured, as they entered the Boulevard Albert, a large street in front of the harbor. All the boats were lit with tiny white lights, making it appear magical.

He squeezed her hand. "I'm glad. Wait until tomorrow. We're too tired tonight but tomorrow we'll see the Oceanographic Museum. Jacques Cousteau's submarine is on display in the entry hall. There's an exotic garden in the Aquarium that I think you'd enjoy. When they excavated, they discovered an immense cavern 300 feet below the surface. Would you believe that they even found a prehistoric cave dwelling? It's something to see."

She shook her head in wonder. "Can you imagine that a place like this is built on the same rock where simple cave men lived? It makes me think about history, civilizations. In America, we're impressed with buildings that are two hundred and fifty years old. We seem so young compared to all this."

Stifling a yawn, Steve nodded.

"You're tired," she said as they walked past a bench. "Why don't we sit down?"

"Okay. I think I'm finally having to give into

fatigue here." He sat down heavily and waited for her to join him. When she did, he put his arm around her shoulders as they looked out to the sea. "You seem to be dealing well with jet lag."

She rested her head on his shoulder. "I have a confession. I only laid down for five minutes. I promised myself—"

Turning abruptly, he gave her a sly look. "Five minutes? That's why you're so perky at three a.m. New Jersey time."

She giggled and brought his arm back around her shoulder. "I couldn't help it."

"Well, tomorrow I'm not going to have any mercy on you. We're doing every exhibit. Every museum. Every cave. Every shop . . ."

"Okay. I feel fine. You're on. If this is a challenge, I accept."

He nodded while staring glassy-eyed toward the water. "Just you wait, Ms. Edwards. Let's see how well you get through the night."

Rested, she snuggled against him while wondering exactly what he meant by that statement. Ever since she had joined him for dinner, she had asked herself that same question. Would they pick up at the hotel what had started on the plane? For someone who hadn't had sex in almost twenty years, she was amazed to find the need for it was constantly interrupting her normal thoughts. When she sat across from Steve during dinner, she started off admiring the way he was dressed, how handsome he was. Then, as the evening progressed, her admiration became more basic. She began to stare at his mouth, noticing the way he tasted his wine. Remembering the way his kiss felt on her lips. His hands drew her attention, recalling how they felt on her skin. And his eyes . . . the way they had looked when he told her how beautiful she was in the sapphire dress. It had become ridiculous. She couldn't seem to concentrate on conversation or dessert. Instead, she had been fantasizing about how they would spend the night. He had gotten two rooms, as promised. The Hermitage Hotel was exquisite and romantic, and she found herself wondering whether she had put up too much of a barrier, one that Steve would be too much of a gentleman to cross.

They sat in silence, feeling the warm breeze play over their skin. Steve rested his head on hers and she snuggled in closer to him, enjoying the warmth of his chest. Everything was so perfect, so romantic. They were able to sit and enjoy the enchanted night in comfortable silence.

It was like living out a fairy tale, she thought. There was the palace up on the hill. The royal barge was moored on the moonlit sea. Her patient prince held her in his arms and she even had a fairy godmother, albeit one with misguided intentions, but who had been instrumental in getting her here. The scene was set. The mood was right. This evening was ripe for a happy ending.

Julia tentatively rested her hand on his stomach and once again felt his steady, even breath. This was the night, she thought and a shiver of excitement raced through her veins. She wanted to be with him. She wanted to lie next to him, to feel the length of his body against hers. They had waited so long and he had been so accepting of her need to go slowly. But now her needs had definitely changed. That slow, lazy heat had begun at dinner, infusing her body with desire. She didn't care that she was almost forty years old. She didn't feel like a mother or a responsible professional. She felt like a woman on fire.

"I hope this night never ends," she whispered and then sighed with anticipation.

She felt his body jerk upright.

"Huh? I'm sorry . . . ? I must have dozed off."

She turned her head to look at him. His eyes were heavy, in need of sleep. "You fell asleep?" she asked in disbelief.

He yawned and tried to shake himself awake. "No, I'm all right." His bloodshot eyes told a different story.

She choked back a protest, stood up, and held out her hand. "No, you're not. You need to get some rest. You've tortured yourself long enough. Let's go back."

He let her pull him up from the bench, reluctantly admitting defeat. "You're right. I'll be in much better condition tomorrow."

They were not going to make love tonight. That was obvious. Feeling a little let down, she led him across the wide street and thought of something light to say so he wouldn't sense her disappointment. "Well, I would hope so, Mr. McMillan. Because tomorrow we're seeing every exhibit, every museum, every cave, every shop . . ."

He laughed and slid his arm around her waist. "All I need is a good night's sleep."

She tried to ignore the sensations that his touch was sending through her. Seeing the hotel in the distance, she breathed in a sigh of frustration.

A good night's sleep? Not likely for her!

# Chapter 16

He knew she was exhausted. She had been a trooper of a tourist, wanting to cram as much as possible into one day. The two square miles they'd covered had felt like twenty. Yet the amazement on her face, and the way she took in each new sight with a sense of awe made him see Monaco through her eyes. Everything seemed more wondrous, more spectacular than he remembered. She had even won five hundred francs at the casino in Monte Carlo, and acted as if she'd hit the lottery. Her excitement was contagious.

It had been his intention that they have a leisurely dinner in her room and then he would leave and let her get to sleep. Her eyes were heavy-lidded, and it gave her a sexy, lazy look that evaporated his good intentions. Her voice had even become husky and low from lack of sleep, but the effect it had on him was to awaken his desire. He really should leave.

Pushing back his chair, he stood up. "I'm going

to let you get some rest. We have an early drive tomorrow to the farm."

Slowly rising, she gave him a sleepy smile. "You don't have to leave. I'm not . . ." She tried to stifle a yawn. "I'm not that tired."

He smiled and gathered her into his arms. "That's why you can't keep your eyes open."

Like a kid fighting sleep, she widened her eyes and said, "I'm okay."

He couldn't resist her any longer. "You're more than okay," he whispered into her mouth, just before his lips captured hers.

When the kiss ended, she sighed and rested her head against his chest. "It feels so good here in your arms," she whispered.

Deeply inhaling, he fought his impulses and said, "You have to get to bed. You can barely stand on your feet."

"My feet do hurt," she admitted. "But you could still hold me."

"In bed?" Maybe she wasn't as tired as he thought?

"I'd like to cuddle for a little while."

He groaned inwardly. Cuddling? His memory flashed back to their plane trip. It was a torture he didn't want to repeat. How could he remain unmoved when this warm, soft, sensuous woman would be lying next to him in bed? "I could massage your feet," he offered, hoping that the distance would put out the fire in his groin.

"That's really nice," she breathed against his

chest. "But I just want to be held. Would you mind?"

He took a deep breath to anchor his resolve. He could do this. Hadn't he been able to let her leave his apartment? Hadn't he endured the slow, sweet agony on the plane? Hell, he had even survived months of being celibate. One more night to make it perfect for her. Tomorrow they would be at the farm, well-rested and settled in one place. He could do this.

"All right, then," he said, putting her from him. "Off to bed, young lady."

He watched as Julia slipped off her sandals and slid onto the bedspread. She pulled the pillows out from under it and put one under her head. Patting the other, as if beckoning him, she smiled while looking perfectly innocent. He hesitated for a moment, fighting the urge to make love to her.

He could do this.

Ten minutes later, he felt her steady breathing against his chest and knew she was asleep. She felt so right in his arms that it was with reluctance that he slowly eased her away from him. He sat for a moment and studied her face. Who would believe this, he silently wondered. He was falling in love with a woman he hadn't even been to bed with. The thought made him smile. He had been to bed with Julia, just not in the conventional way. Nothing with Julia Edwards was conventional.

\* \* \*

She had left an enchanted land, full of castles and fairy tales, to cross a chain of formidable mountains that slammed her back into reality. Steve drove the Mercedes on a four-lane Autoroute that cut through the steep terrain with a maddening, furious, pace. The way cars jockeyed for position turned her knuckles white. "How fast are we going now?"

"Around ninety."

"Is that kilometers, or miles per hour?"

"Relax, Julia. You have to keep up, or it'll be more dangerous. I've done this before. I'll get you there safely. I promise."

She tried to distract herself by studying the scenery. The landscape was varied as they traveled the serpentine road. One minute they'd pass a dry, weathered area, then they were hit with lush greenery. And then it would change again as they drove around a sharp turn.

"Dear God, look at that!" she whispered in awe. A chain of brilliant red mountains rose up in front of her.

"La rocher de Roquebrune sur Mer," Steve said, and quickly translated. "Roquebrune by the sea. It's at the end of the Esteraells mountain chain."

"It's breathtaking," Julia said, staring up as they neared the magnificent product of nature. "Look, there's a little house, or something, up there."

"It's a medieval chapel nestled in the rock," Steve said and breathed a deep, contented sigh. "Now, I feel like I've come back to Provence. Every year I pass that mountain and start to get excited. I can't wait to see the farm and what improvements have been made. It's hard when everything is done by phone or fax. I miss so much."

"Well, we'll be there soon, right?"

"Pretty soon."

"What are these trees called? They remind me of large *bonsai,* but not exactly. The bare trunks sort of rise up to meet a canopy of greenery. They almost look like a woman's parasol."

"That's very good, Julia. They're called parapluie, umbrella pines."

She took in everything, wanting to memorize each detail so she could pull it from her mind when she was home. This was the vacation of a lifetime and she knew if it weren't for Steve, she never would have experienced this magic.

They passed the time reminiscing about Monaco, the sidewalk cafes, the discos where they had danced. They'd even seen Prince Albert and his entourage at one. No wonder she had nearly collapsed with fatigue.

She couldn't believe she had fallen asleep last night. It was as if something were working against them, keeping them from becoming too intimate. She immediately thought of Val, and her curse. The first night Steve had been exhausted. And last night she had dozed off. The man had been in her bed, and she'd fallen asleep. She shook off the uneasy thought, determined not to let anything ruin this trip. The fact that Steve had covered her with the bedspread showed that he wasn't angry, and he'd seemed excited and upbeat this morning when they'd met for breakfast. He couldn't wait to show her his farm. She had to keep telling herself that all would be well. Her mother had always said that everything happened for a reason. They hadn't yet made love because it wasn't the right time, not because he didn't want her—and not because of any silly curse of Val's.

Perking up when they left the major highway at Le Muy, Julia vowed that if Val were keeping them apart it wasn't going to work. They traveled for some time until they turned off to a smaller road that took them to a hill village.

"This is so pretty," she said as they drove through the quaint little street.

"Welcome to Grimaud, and the French countryside," he said. "We're about five minutes away from the vineyard."

"So soon?"

"We made good time."

"Oh, look, a post office. I really should send postcards. I can't believe I forgot in Monaco."

"We had so much to see," he said with a grin as he drove through the narrow cobblestone street. "We really didn't have much time for anything else."

She smiled, knowing what he meant. "Well, once we get to your farm it won't be as hectic. Oh, look. . . ." As they left the village, she pointed to a high stone wall that was dotted with deep violet bougainvillea.

"Here we come to the roundabout, the small circle where we turn off toward the farm. See where it

says Collobrières? Now pay attention, so you'll
know how to come back into town."

She gave him a sideways glance. "I'll be driving?"

"Absolutely. We're going to be here for over two
weeks. The farm produces vegetables, but we'll have
to go to the butcher and the patissiére. And you
want postcards."

"But why would I have to drive?" she asked nervously. "From what I've seen they drive like New
Yorkers—and when I go to New York I take the
train."

He laughed. "You're not paying attention. We're
on my road. Right after this small bridge we make
a right."

"You own the road?"

"No, not the road, but both sides of it. This
mountain over here is mine. I bought it so no one
could build in back of me."

As they crossed the small one-car bridge, she
gaped at the beautiful wooded area behind the high
stone walls.

"I hope Odeale remembered to unlock the gates.
I called her when we arrived in Monaco."

Julia knew from past conversations that Steve
had hired neighboring farmers to look after the
vineyard while he was gone.

They soon pulled up to large wooden gates, remi-
niscent of the turn of the century. "Here we are," he
said, opening the car door to get out. "Mas des
Muriers. It loosely means farmhouse of the mulber-
ries."

Julia heard the anticipation in his voice and

gasped with wonder. She watched him walk up to the massive gates and heave them open. When he turned back to the car, he smiled proudly. After he slid behind the wheel, she touched his arm. "Thank you for including me in this. I can't wait to see your home."

He slowly drove through the gates and she watched his face come alive with child-like expectation. She could almost feel the current of excitement bubbling through him. It was contagious.

"Oh, Steve, this is beautiful!" she exclaimed. The house was situated above the vineyard, against the woods that bordered the road. She could see that the original three-story farmhouse had been expanded by additions on both sides. The entire structure was painted in soft yellow pastel, nestled underneath a terra cotta tile roof. Geraniums, impatiens, and bougainvillea were scattered about profusely, in flower beds, clay pots and hanging baskets. Even the two huge urns on either side of the front door dripped with sprays of colorful summer flowers.

He turned to the left, using the service road in front of the vineyard, and stopped the car by the wide stone steps which led up to the garden and then to the house.

"I don't know how you could ever leave this place," she said as she opened the car door and stepped out. Leaning against the car, as if for support, she repeated, "I love it."

Steve came up to her and took her in his arms. "I'm so glad you like it."

Ascending the stairs together, they crossed the small expanse of lawn and were almost at the front door when it was flung open. A small, robust woman in her early sixties beamed with pleasure as she opened her arms wide and greeted them.

"*Ah, bonjour, Monsieur* Steven! Welcome home. *Comment allez-vous?*"

"*Trés bien, Madame* Odeale, *et vous?*" he answered as he joined her in a warm embrace.

Julia watched the friendly scene and listened as the older woman answered in mixture of French and heavily-accented English. "*Pas trop mal, merci* . . . I am but an old woman who is happy to see the sun rise each morning. Enough of me, please. Let me greet your lovely mademoiselle."

Still holding Odeale's shoulder, Steve beamed and turned her toward Julia. "Please let me present someone very special. Madame Odeale, meet Julia Edwards."

Julia smiled and extended her hand, but was immediately swept into a continental embrace by Odeale. The old woman kissed both her cheeks, and then came back to plant a third.

"Welcome, *Mademoiselle.* I have prepared everything for you, just so. *Monsieur* Steven said to make your stay perfect. I think even he will be pleased."

"Thank you so much. Everything here is so lovely." Julia looked out to the vineyard again. Acres and acres of precise rows of fruit-laden plants flanked a windmill off in the distance. The entire spectacle was framed by chains of mountains that seemed to reach to the sky. It was prettier than she could have ever imagined.

"The vineyard looks good, Odeale," Steve said as he joined Julia's gaze.

Odeale's voice was filled with pride. "The boys, they have worked hard to keep the vines healthy. The color is just now coming into the grape."

Steve turned to Julia with a smile. "The boys are Odeale's sons. They're in their thirties."

Julia smiled at the older woman. "For a mother, age has little to do with it. They're always our children, aren't they?"

Odeale's face, wrinkled from years of living in the sun, took on a beautiful expression of understanding. "Ah, oui, *Madame*. You have children?"

"A daughter. She's nineteen."

"But, non! You are much too young for a daughter this age." Odeale look at Steve as if searching for confirmation.

"It's true, although I've yet to meet her. She's in Italy, and we're going to see if we can bring her here for a visit."

Odeale looked at Julia with a puzzled expression. "She's *Italien*, not *Americaine?* I thought *la Madame* was from *États-Unis?*"

Steve laughed. "No, you misunderstand. *Madame*'s daughter is visiting friends in Italy."

Odeale nodded, as though pleased that her first assessment was correct. "Come out of the hot sun and let me show *Madame* how I have prepared for your arrival."

She led them into a grand foyer that had a domed

glass ceiling. The walls were feathered with a pastel marbling effect, and the floor was of smooth quarry stone. Even though there was no furniture, Julia was speechless. They both were waiting for her reaction, and she knew she had to stop gaping. She turned around in a full circle. The living room was to her right with floor-to-ceiling windows overlooking the vineyard and a marble fireplace with vases of fresh flowers on the mantel. To her left was an immense dining room that was bare, but its stone flooring was edged in a frieze, an exquisite pattern of French mosaic tile. Looking at Steve, she whispered, "I don't know what to say. I'm speechless. *This* is a *farm* house?"

Odeale glanced up at Steve with a worried expression. "Is *Madame* not pleased?"

Julia rushed in wanting to correct the impression. "Oh, no, no." Struggling, she added, "I can't find the words to say how beautiful it is."

Odeale smiled broadly. "It is a beautiful house, but it is not yet a home." She looked to her employer. "It needs a woman's hand, *non?* There is but little furniture."

Steve grinned back, looking to Julia like a man catching a reprimand from an elderly aunt. "Julia has agreed to help me with that."

Odeale rubbed her palms together. *"Trés bien.* About time. Too many years of hammering and plaster. The house is ready for people to love it again."

Steve appeared embarrassed by the woman's

words and cleared his throat. "I'll go get our bags and Odeale can show you the rest of the house."

"No, no. Give me your keys and Maurice will bring the bags to your bedroom. You will show *Madame* your house. It is only right, *non?*"

As though realizing that Odeale would only put up more of an argument, Steve reached into his pocket and handed over the car keys.

"You have done a good job, *Madame*," he said in a sincere voice to the woman. "The house looks well cared for."

"*Merci*," Odeale answered, highly pleased by his praise. "I will find Maurice." Before leaving, she smiled at Julia and added, "*Au revoir, Madame.*"

Knowing she was going to like this small, feisty woman who wasn't afraid to speak her mind, Julia smiled warmly and said, "*Au revoir, Madame* Odeale. It was a pleasure to meet you."

When they were alone, Julia walked up to Steve and wrapped her arms around his waist. "A *farm house?* No one could ever accuse you of exaggeration. This place is magnificent!"

"You like it?"

"Like it? I love it. Now show me," she said, taking his hand and pulling him into the living room.

"As you can see, there really isn't much here," Steve said when they were standing in the middle of the room.

"Nothing here?" Julia answered, sweeping her gaze about the huge room. An off-white damask-covered sofa sat in front of the fireplace next to a small glass and wrought iron coffee table. An arc lamp stood next to the sofa. It looked to Julia like the lonely arrangement had been pulled together by one person to read by the fire. She smiled as her vision captured a high-tech stereo system on the floor in the corner. It seemed totally out of place in the charming room. Empty wooden shelves flanked the fireplace.

She walked over and ran her hand over the exquisite molding that encased the shelves. "Look at this," she whispered. "Look at the detail. Such craftsmanship went into this. Don't you have books that you want to put here? You could store the stereo in the cabinet underneath."

Steve expelled a little chuckle. "I was hoping that you'd be interested in helping me decorate. I can tell that my earlier worries that you might not be so inclined were wrong." Moving beside her, Steve threaded his arm through hers and gently tugged her forward. "Come—let's go exploring, *madame.*"

Julia followed his lead with excitement. They walked through the empty dining room, which was big enough for a banquet table. As they crossed the threshold to the kitchen, she stopped and gasped. The floor was tiled with old terra cotta, and the room was warm with light that shone on the marble counter tops and island. The marble was almost the same color as the floor. A wrought iron rack hung over the island, just waiting for copper pots to fill it. Two restaurant-size ovens were built into the wall, and she wondered at the size of everything. The house seemed constructed for large gatherings and entertaining.

Walking up to the counter with its vibrant yellow and blue pottery filled with fruits and vegetables, she said, "This is really a big house. What did you plan to do with it?"

Steve looked embarrassed, as he picked a grape and popped it into his mouth. Shrugging, he answered, "I don't know. I fell in love with the place, and for the last couple of years I've been working with architects to complete it."

"But the way they designed it—it's as if you had a large family in mind, or you expected to entertain a great deal. How many bedrooms are there?"

"Four."

"Four? As large as the rooms down here?"

"Just the master bedroom. Come on, I'll show you."

Julia hesitated, feeling a little nervous about moving upstairs just yet. "But I haven't seen everything down here."

"Oh, it's not that interesting," Steve said taking her hand. "Just past the archway to your left is the pantry, and there's an outer flower garden that sits off of it. Then there's the laundry room next to the pantry," he waved with his free hand. "That other doorway leads to a little room that I've claimed for an office. Now, unless Odeale was really diligent, that place stays in a constant state of disarray."

Steve led her up a sweeping stone staircase to the second floor. She passed unfurnished bedrooms and baths until they reached the end of the hallway. Julia stopped and stared at their combined luggage on the highly polished floor.

"It's the only bedroom that's furnished."

Recovering quickly, she said, "Oh, no. That's fine," and turned to look at the huge bedroom. The king-sized bed was dwarfed in the immense room. There was an antique carved armoire that reached the ten foot ceiling. Floor to ceiling shutters were opened, revealing a magnificent view of the vineyard beyond. A small terrace overlooked a beautiful flower garden and a pond with benches. Again, Julia saw Odeale's touch as she turned back to the room. Fresh flowers were in vases that stood on tables at either side of the bed.

Julia turned her gaze to Steve. "How can you stand to leave this and live in apartments?"

Steve shrugged. "I need to work to keep it all going."

She knew he was successful, but he must be *really* wealthy to afford this. Suddenly Julia felt intimidated. Was she out of her league? Here she was, a woman from suburban New Jersey, playing in the south of France. She had to remember it was just a vacation.

"And here's the bathroom," Steve said, interrupting her thoughts. She turned around and her breath caught in the back of her throat. The scene looked like it was from a movie set.

She slowly walked down two steps and stood in the middle of a room that was the size of a normal bedroom. Green marble covered the floor and walls, even the tub and shower. Brass fixtures and sinks contrasted sharply with the surrounding ivory marble cabinetry. The shower was the size of a large walk-in closet, with brass jets at different levels to hit every angle of the body, and a built-in marble seat within the glass enclosure. Odeale had even put fresh flowers in tall vases around the marble tub.

Julia walked back to the steps leading into the bedroom and sat down. Overwhelmed by the magnificent bathroom, she sighed. "I don't know what to say, Steve." She felt him move closer as he sat down next to her on the polished wooden steps.

"Is everything all right?" he asked with concern. "Is something wrong?"

Shaking her head, Julia said, "I guess I'm shocked. All this time I had pictured an actual farmhouse—not this," she waved her hand toward the bathroom. "I keep expecting someone to yell 'cut', then stage hands to take all of it away."

Steve reached out and gently pushed her hair behind her ear. "What's really bothering you, Julia? Tell me."

Suddenly her eyes filled with tears, and she looked down. "I don't know how to put this. I'm embarrassed and I don't want to offend you."

In a hushed tone, Steve asked again, "Tell me."

She sighed and wiped a fat tear from her cheek. "I'm just a regular person, Steve. It wasn't until I walked into this house that I realized the difference between us."

"What difference? What are you talking about?"

She waved her hand out before her. *"This!"*

Steve looked into the bathroom and back toward her. "I don't get it."

Julia let out an exasperated sigh. "You're accustomed to the best, and I'm accustomed to getting by."

"What are you talking about? Your home is beautiful."

"It's not like this . . . You're rich, and I'm not."

She heard him slowly let out his breath. "Now you are coming close to offending me. I've never judged people by the size of their bank accounts. And I'm not rich; I've just invested wisely. Didn't you listen when I told you where I came from? Don't you think that I appreciate all of this? Once a year I come into this house and see the progress, and I wanted to share my excitement with you. How could you think that I was that shallow?"

The tears just wouldn't stop, and she sniffled them back in order to answer him. "It's not you. It's me. God bless you that you've been able to do this for yourself. It's just that . . . I don't want what we've had to end, and I know that eventually the differences will get in the way."

He took hold of her shoulders and turned her to him. "Do you realize what you've just said, Julia?"

She stared at him blankly, trying to remember her words.

The corner of his mouth lifted in a hint of a smile. "You said that you didn't want what we've had to end. Take it from someone who's courted you for months—from you, that's almost a commitment." His smile deepened and he tilted his head toward the bathroom. "Couldn't you be comfortable here?"

Julia's mind raced with a dozen thoughts at once.

What was he trying to say? What in the name of God had *she* said? Commitment? He seemed pleased, yet . . . "Of course I could be comfortable here, who wouldn't be? But—"

"No buts," he interrupted. "We're here. We're comfortable. And, quite frankly, Julia, I've waited long enough."

Julia's eyes widened with the implication of his words. "What about Odeale?" she asked frantically, hedging for time.

He kissed her gently on the forehead. "Odeale has gone home."

"What about the man who brought our luggage?"

He lightly kissed her lips and breathed into her mouth, "Everyone has gone home, Julia. Any more questions?"

She nervously looked down to the buttons on his shirt. "I guess not," she stammered. "I'm just nervous."

"Then we'll start slowly." Steve pulled her into his arms and began to run his fingers up and down her back while placing soft kisses along her neck.

"You have nothing to be afraid of," he whispered, and each breath on her skin sent shivers through her body. She could feel her heart racing with a mixture of excitement and fear. She wanted to do this as much as he did, yet a part of her still felt insecure.

She felt him unbutton her sundress at the shoulder and he brushed the exposed skin with his lips. Julia heard herself moaning in reaction, as he moved to her other shoulder and performed the same ritual.

"I have waited so long for you," he murmured in a husky voice, as he ran the tips of his fingers over her shoulders, down her arms and back again.

She looked into his eyes and saw the depth of emotion that accompanied his words. "I know you have, and I for you," she whispered. Her skin shivered in response to his touch. He stood up and reached for her hand. Placing her palm in his, she allowed him to help her rise. When she stood, the cotton sundress slid down to her waist. Suddenly shy, she crossed her hands to cover her breasts.

"No, don't," he said in a voice that sounded raw with emotion. "You're so beautiful." He reached for her hands and placed them at his neck.

Julia forgot all her doubts, all her fears, as he lowered his head to hers. The kiss started out as gentle and searching, a mere grazing of lips, but soon became fired by a need kept too long under control. His tongue entered her mouth as if claiming it for his own and she gladly surrendered. The kiss was hot and feverish. He broke away and gasped, desperate for control. Julia unbuttoned his shirt, needing to feel his skin against hers. When she had finally freed the last button, and pulled the edges of his shirt apart, Steve clasped her in a tight embrace and she gasped at the searing naked contact, flesh to flesh.

It was fast and furious . . . hands roaming over skin and through each other's hair, as though wanting to burn the memory of their bodies into each other's touch. His mouth left hers to trail kisses down her neck until he finally reached the sensitive tip of her breast. Ribbons of pleasure radiated through her body, and she weaved her fingers through his silky hair, hoping the moment would never end. All too soon she moaned with disappointment as his mouth left her breast and descended down her body. Kneeling before her, he tugged away her dress and panties, leaving them to gather at her feet.

She tensed with apprehension, knowing his intent. Wanting it, but fearing it. Running his hands ever so gently up her thighs to cup her bottom, he buried his face in her and breathed against her tender flesh. "Trust me," he whispered.

The hot exhale of words made her moan in delicious pleasure as her body yielded to his mouth. She grabbed the wall for support and closed her eyes as he continued to taste her. When she thought such exquisite pleasure would surely drive her mad, he took her to a new height as he lifted her leg over his shoulder and kissed her more deeply.

"Steve . . . please . . ." She had no idea what she was asking for. It was a dazed, mindless plea. Bursts of intense pleasure came hard and fast, shocking her with their intensity. She felt herself crumbling, weak and pliant in his arms as he caught her and carried her to the bed. She was almost crying with her need for him. Their eyes locked as he threw his shirt to the floor and ripped all clothing from his body. Julia lay back on the bed, watching him, memorizing every inch of him, needing to feel him inside her.

Never before could she remember experiencing such a primal urge. Nothing else mattered. The craving and yearning was as essential as breathing. Instinct overcame restraint, as her hand reached out and she pulled him to her.

"My God, Julia. I want you."

He entered her quickly, filling her, and easing the ache. Her back automatically arched and her legs wrapped around him, bringing him in closer, deeper. She wanted to make him a part of her, to feel as if they were one.

They moved in an ancient dance, as old as time itself. She felt his body tense and shudder as he threw back his head and called out her name. Knowing she had brought him such pleasure only increased her own. Holding him even tighter, she buried her face in his shoulder, cried out, and followed him over the edge.

The room was quiet, save for their ragged breathing. She could feel his heart pounding against her own, and she ran her fingers over his back, calming and soothing them both. Steve raised his head and looked down at her. A tender smile was at his lips as his eyes lovingly caressed her face.

"Are you all right?"

Her smile was lazy and happy. She gently pushed his hair back off his forehead. "I'm better than all right," she said. "I'm ecstatic. I just want to lie here for a moment and experience it."

He kissed the tip of her nose. "Julia, I have never been with a woman that reacted—that—like that."

She started to giggle. "Well, it has been twenty years."

His laughter resounded in his chest and he slid off her, turned her around, and held her against his chest. His arms wrapped about her, his knees were against the back of her own. They fit so well together, she thought with contentment. She could imagine falling asleep like this. Surely she'd never want to wake up.

"Well, be forewarned, Madame Edwards," he chuckled against her neck. "Now that you've ended your celibacy, I don't intend to let you fall back into it."

She laughed, loving the feel of him, the way his hands followed the curve of her thigh and waist, making her want him again. "I think you've unleashed a wanton creature," she gasped as she arched her bottom against him. "I also think I should get up and take a shower while I still can."

He brought her more tightly into his embrace and Julia could feel his desire for her return as he ran the tip of his tongue down the center of her back.

"You can do whatever you want," he whispered, and his breath sent shivers of longing over her sensitive skin. "What do you want, Julia?"

She slowly turned around and faced him. Looking deep into his brown eyes, she ran her finger over his bottom lip and answered, "I want you."

It was bold, practically brazen, for someone like her, yet his answering smile told her all she needed to know.

# Chapter 17

She was wearing white shorts, a shirt, and sandals. Her hair was pulled back into a pony tail, and she hadn't worn makeup in two days. Pulling a loose bunch of carrots from the earth, she couldn't ever remember being this happy, not even after Paige was born. By the time she'd brought her daughter home from the hospital her marriage had been over, save for the legalities. She knocked the dirt from the carrots and placed them in the basket beside potatoes, string beans, and cherry tomatoes. It seemed like a lifetime had passed since she was alone with an infant to support. Here in the south of France, it was hard for her to relate to that frightened lonely woman of twenty years ago. Then she had worried about keeping the electricity and the telephone from being disconnected, about having enough money to feed and clothe her child. Now she was in the most beautiful place she'd ever seen, feeling as though God had given her this gift of paradise after years of struggle. Even if it only lasted two weeks, she would be grateful for every day. She'd never felt more alive, and she realized how insular her life had been. It amazed her that she could travel across the world and feel so at home in a country where she didn't even speak the language.

It was this place. It was magical.

When Steve had shown her the garden yesterday, she had been positively floored. As usual, he had been modest in his description. She stood in the center of a sixty foot rectangle of ground that had been neatly sectioned off to produce every vegetable and fruit imaginable. She could walk down a pebbled row and pull potatoes from the rich, dark earth. Corn that wasn't yet ready to pick grew high. She marveled at how Odeale had planted the garden to make use of every available space. There were even fresh herbs. Basil, coriander, dill, marjoram, lemon sage, and mint thrived next to lush ripe strawberries and raspberries.

Picking a fat strawberry, she popped it into her mouth and walked into the greenhouse. A profusion of green table grapes hung from the vine-covered ceiling. She picked a bunch and added them to her bounty. Toward the back of the greenhouse were several lemon trees, and she decided to make lemonade for lunch. She began picking the ripe fruit, bringing them first to her nose to smell the fresh citrus scent, and she reminded herself to gather mint for the lemonade before she left. Her basket became heavy with her harvest, and she switched hands as she walked out into the sunshine.

It seemed like heaven on earth. Not for the first

time, she wondered how Steve could leave it. For the last two days she had been walking on air, not wanting to think about the day when she'd have to relinquish Eden. She loved the farm. She loved the pond down the path where she fed hunks of day-old French bread to the huge carp and frogs. She loved the house that, even half-empty exuded warmth. And, God help her, she had fallen in love with the man. Everything was so perfect. Maybe too perfect. She'd been conditioned all of her life to wait for the other shoe to drop. Was she afraid of happiness, knowing nothing lasts forever? She mentally shook herself to banish the negative thoughts. If this heaven only lasted two weeks, she was going to enjoy every day.

"You are not at this again."

Startled from daydreaming, she looked up and saw Steve grinning at her.

"I'm harvesting lunch," she said in her own defense. Was she spending too much time here in the garden? "The dinner you made last night was wonderful, but it's my turn to cook."

"I thought we were going to drive into St. Tropez this afternoon," he answered, taking the heavy basket from her. "Julia, you've turned into Farmer Gray."

She laughed. "I can't help it. I love it here."

"You and Odeale spent three hours in this garden yesterday. What more can you see?"

Julia looked around in awe. "You have no idea what she's done here. All of this is grown without any chemicals, and from home-culled seed." She reached in and drew a bunch of carrots from the basket. "Do you realize how rare it is for me to see carrots outside of cellophane?"

Taking one from her hand, he took a bite and grinned. "You really are happy here, aren't you, Julia?"

Their gaze caught and held for a few questioning moments. She answered honestly. "I don't think I've ever been happier in my life. Maybe that's what scares me. I wish we could freeze this moment in time and stay here in paradise."

Steve switched the basket to his other hand and threw his arm over her shoulder as he led her out of the garden. "Well, this paradise needs some furniture. That's why we're meeting the decorator in St. Tropez. Come on, let's take the short cut back to the house. Lord, this is heavy," he said, as they crossed the drive in front of the gates. "What do you have in here?"

Julia reached down and picked a couple of grapes. "Lunch."

Steve started laughing as he lifted the basket as though weighing it. "Who do you expect to feed? There's enough food in here for a small army."

"Oh no, there is not. *Now* you exaggerate! This is the only part of the estate that even resembles a farm. Whatever's left, I'll give to Odeale. Nothing will go to waste."

They entered the house through the patio, and she took her shoes off at the entrance. The cool stone felt good on her bare feet, and she again realized the foresight that went into the planning of this house. Although the temperature outside was in the high eighties, the interior, even without air conditioning, was cool.

He followed her into the kitchen, and she walked over to the sink to wash her hands. When she turned around he had placed the basket on the island and was grinning at her. "What's so funny?" she asked as she brought the basket to the sink.

Steve shook his head as if highly amused. "Look at you, Julia," he said, running his gaze up and down her body. "You're barefoot, sunburned, wearing no make up, and you still look beautiful."

"I'm happy," she answered simply.

"I think you're in love."

Startled, she stared back at him.

His grin widened. "At least with the farm."

She turned around to the sink. "You may be right." Emptying the basket, she began to spray the vegetables with water. Suddenly, she stopped and turned back to him. "Sometimes, when you're on vacation, even though you're having a great time, you know that you have to go home and get back to the nine-to-five routine. Your mind has no trouble accepting that you can't go on sipping pina coladas by the Paradise Beach Club pool forever. You know it's just a vacation, not a lifestyle. But this, Steve, this is a lifestyle, not a vacation. You should see your face when you come in from talking with Maurice and his sons about the vineyard." Julia shook her head. "There's a glow in your eyes that I don't think Amalgamated ever generated. You're happy here. And I guess I just don't know how you could go back to New York City after being down on the farm."

He smiled. "You've actually bonded with this place."

"So have you, but you haven't admitted it yet."

Steve leaned forward and rested his elbows on the counter. "Haven't bonded to it? I'd call it more like bondage. Although, I'm not complaining . . ." He waved a hand toward the vineyard outside. "All of this didn't happen by magic."

"I didn't mean to imply that you haven't put in a lot of hard work and a great deal of money. But you only enjoy it once a year."

"Well, that's what I meant about bondage. The old golden handcuffs."

"That must be so stressful, worrying about expenses and mortgages and payrolls. I don't know, as lovely as it is, I don't know if I could live with that kind of pressure."

Steve walked around the island and took her hand. "Come here. Sit down for a few minutes. I want to talk to you."

Julia wondered whether she had crossed the line with her direct questions. He seemed so serious all of a sudden. When she was seated at the kitchen table, Steve held her hand and looked deeply into her eyes.

"When I was growing up, my parents lived from paycheck to paycheck. And sometimes, when they were into the bottle, there was no paycheck. We got thrown out of more apartments than I can remember. I never knew when there would be electricity.

Or water to flush the toilets. So I decided if I ever came into any money, I would create a place where that couldn't happen to me ever again."

God, his childhood had been worse than she had thought. "But, Steve, to kill yourself to maintain something like this . . . You say you want security. Why didn't you buy something where you could pay off the note in fifteen years? Something low maintenance that you could hold onto when you retire?"

Steve smiled gently. "That's what I did, Julia."

Her eyes widened. "What?"

"Let me tell you how I paid for this."

She shook her head. "That's not my business. You don't have to tell me."

"Yes, I do. This has been an issue between us since you've walked into this house. That's why I have to tell you. Because I don't want anything like this to come between us."

Julia looked down to her lap, feeling as if she had already invaded his privacy and had overstepped her bounds.

"No," he said, squeezing her hand. "Please look at me. I want to tell you how I paid for this place."

She returned her gaze to Steve's and held on. She wondered if this new level of intimacy might destroy the one they had just built.

"When I was first starting out in business, a mentor told me that it was far easier to work with a lump sum of cash than to pay for things on time. He told me never to let a lump sum of money get away from me by chipping away at it for foolish things.

Money can dwindle down to a pittance with nothing to show for it. He said that to go into debt for things I wanted was just as foolish. Things that once brought happiness would become a noose around my neck if I had to struggle to maintain the payments. Those beautiful things soon start to own me he said, instead of me owning them."

Julia withdrew her hand and ran her palm over her forehead. "But I thought you said that you were in bondage. You talked about golden handcuffs."

Steve smiled. "Perhaps I was being a little melodramatic. I go before the parole board in six weeks when I close my next deal."

"I'm not following you. What are you talking about?"

"Okay, let me explain how I'm paid."

Again she shook her head. "This is far too personal."

"Hey, it's not as personal as a shared shower."

She actually blushed, remembering what he'd done to her that morning. She knew that for the rest of her life, every time she walked into a shower, she would remember his lips on her wet skin. Lord, have mercy . . . The memory was too intense for the serious moment and she said, "I don't want you to feel that you have to explain anything."

"Here, give me back your hand." He held it firmly within his. He said, "Well, if you're considering a joint venture, full disclosure is essential."

Julia's body tensed with an odd mixture of joy and confusion. What was he saying? She didn't even want to guess, or misinterpret his meaning. Better to just let him talk and think about it later.

"Now," he continued. "As I was saying . . . I make a substantial salary, but I didn't use that to buy the farm. Sure, the money keeps my apartment in Manhattan going, and it pays for my car, my living expenses. But this place was built with the bonuses I receive every time I close a deal for Amalgamated. And the quarterly dividends from my investment portfolio pay for maintenance and upkeep here in France."

Trying to take everything in, Julia's jaw dropped in astonishment. "Bonuses?" This wonderful place was paid for out of *bonuses?* To be able to buy something like this . . . without touching his salary?

"Over several years," Steve said. "I put this property together gradually. Every year I tried to make significant improvements. I can get pictures from the architects to show you just what was here before I started. It really was a farm house, Julia, when I bought it."

"Wait, let me get this straight," Julia said with disbelief. "There's no mortgage on this place?"

His smile was filled with pride as he shook his head. "No. None. I pay the taxes and maintenance. This year my improvement is furnishings. And speaking of that, if we don't get a rush on, we're going to be late for Madame Duchatel at *Intérieur Sud.*"

She sat back in her chair and stared at him, struck speechless by his latest revelation. This man . . . He looked so handsome. He had a light sunburn that contrasted with his dark hair and the pale yellow shirt he was wearing. Once again she found it difficult to reconcile her first impression of the hard-edged, steely businessman with the man before her. This version was so open, so sweet, so sexy. She found it hard to keep her hands off of him. And best of all, she respected him. In that moment, she realized that for her, love and respect were intertwined. The one couldn't survive without the other. She wanted to blurt out her love to him, to tell him that she hoped a joint venture was possible. Even the business-oriented way he talked didn't bother her anymore. But what did that mean? Joint venture? Was he talking about marriage? Living together? Or was he merely referring to that fact that they were lovers, and she was about to help him spend his money? She wasn't secure enough to tell him about her love, but she would tell him of her respect.

Her eyes began to fill with tears of raw emotion. "Do you realize what you've done, Steve? What you've accomplished in your life? Where you've taken yourself from an ugly childhood? How many people could have done this? You're a remarkable man, Steve McMillan. And I want you to know that I respect you."

She watched as his eyes, too, became moist. Bringing her hand up to his lips, he placed a kiss on her fingers. "Thank you, Julia. I've been working at gaining your respect ever since I met you."

"Well, I'm sorry it's taken me this long to tell you that you've had it." Getting up, she moved closer to him. He pulled her onto his lap. She wrapped an arm around his shoulders and kissed his forehead. "I was pretty tough on you in the beginning. I'm sorry for that."

"Don't be sorry," he said, running his hand down her thigh. "You taught me a few lessons I needed to learn."

She tried to concentrate on his words, not on the shivers of delight that came from his touch. "What lessons?"

"About life. About . . . never mind," he said, and abruptly stopped his seductive caress. "We'll talk about this later. Right now I want to know if we're going to have lunch here, or if we should wait until we finish in St. Tropez. But I must admit that I'd appreciate having something in my stomach before we start shopping."

She stood up and grinned down at him. "Excuse me, but I didn't *climb* onto your lap. I was pulled there. And, if you'll recall, I was about to prepare lunch when you stopped me."

The look in his eyes was sexy and mischievous. "Julia, if I hadn't made you get up, we would not only have missed lunch, but also Madame Duchatel."

Catching his meaning, she laughed and backed up around the island. "Oh, no, Steve. I wouldn't let you miss this appointment. I *know* how much you want to go shopping for furniture. I wouldn't want to keep you from going over yards and yards of drapery cloth, and—"

"Please, enough! There was a reason why this phase has been put off till last. You're going to have to be patient with me, Julia. Furniture shopping is at the bottom of my list of fun things to do, right down there with elective surgery. It's something that has to be done, but any sensible person postpones it for as long as possible."

Turning on the water, she laughed as she rinsed off the fruit and the remaining vegetables. "Oh, but you've never gone shopping with me. I promise you, it'll be fun."

"Ah huh, but I don't think I'll bet the farm on it."

Looking out the window over the sink to the vineyard, Julia's mood immediately changed, and she sighed. "No, Steve," she whispered. "Don't ever lose this farm."

The fleet of delivery men had finally gone for the day. They had brought the last of the paintings to be hung, and had left the medieval chess set to be unpacked. Julia stood back and admired her work, glad that she had talked Steve out of giving Madame Duchatel free rein with his money. When they had arrived at the ritzy shop in St. Tropez last week, Julia had been initially intimidated by the beautiful French woman. It'd taken less than a half hour before she'd realized that, even for France, the woman's prices were exorbitant. During a few minutes when they had been alone, Julia had whispered to Steve that they would only be selecting material for drapes and would look elsewhere for the rest. Steve had seemed skeptical at first, thinking she was merely pinching pennies. But that hadn't been her

objective at all. She'd wanted to create an environment that was more than just sterile catalog perfection. Back at the farm, Odeale had pointed her in
the right direction. Using a young decorator in
Cogolin, she'd worked with her to find eclectic
pieces that mixed a combination of periods to
achieve comfort, beauty and warmth.

It had been hard work searching through tiny
boutiques, antique shops, art galleries and haunting
open-air markets for just the right pieces, but the
whole process had been exhilarating. Even Steve
had joined in. He had been a good sport when he'd
been swept up with the adventure. Best of all, she
had overcome her fear of driving in France. After
the decorator had called to say that she had found
the refectory table for the dining room, Julia had
taken the car to meet the woman as though on a
mission. Now, every morning she started the day by
driving to the patisserie in Grimaud for fresh bread
and pastries. She was even learning a little bit of
French along the way.

"Does this look right?"

Julia turned and watched as Steve painstakingly
measured the wall. She shook her head, smiling at
his elaborate analysis of where the exact spot was to
nail a picture hook. Her process was much simpler.
Look at the wall. Look at the bordering windows.
Hold it up until it looked right. Watching him now,
she could thoroughly understand why Steve had
such trouble envisioning the finished result. They
really did make a good pair. One was right-brained,
the other was left.

"I can't really tell from just looking at a hook in the middle of the wall," she said, coming closer to him. "You'll have to hold it up."

He glanced over his shoulder. "You're kidding, right? This thing must weigh over a hundred pounds."

"Okay, I'll help you lift it and we'll get Odeale." She called for the woman who had become her friend. Julia knew that she and Odeale shared the same vision for the house.

Odeale appeared at the entrance to the living room, unwrapping heavy brown paper from an Etrusco-Roman vase. "Julia, these are *magnifique!* They go on the fireplace mantel in the dining room . . . yes?"

Seeing one of the pair of vases that she had found in a tiny shop in St. Paul de Vence, Julia drew a breath of delight and left Steve. "They came!" she exclaimed and took the delicate vase from Odeale's hands. "Won't they be perfect over the fireplace?" she asked, and walked into the dining room to see for herself.

"We can cut roses from the garden," Odeale chimed in, as she reached into the box on the old, highly polished refectory table and pulled out its mate.

Julia placed the vase on the mantel and stood back in awe. "Yes. Red and white roses to go with the Cluny tapestry."

Both women's gaze locked for a moment on the lavish woven and embroidered textile. The beautiful colors depicted a medieval lady playing a harp and

surrounded by a forest of animals. A small unicorn
lay at her feet. As soon as Julia had seen it in Mou-
gins, she knew it should hang in the dining room. It
seemed to capture the perfect essence of Eden.
There was splendor. There was nature. There was
magic. It was how she felt about the farm.

"Ah, Julia . . . ?" Steve called out to her from the
doorway.

She blinked a few times and said, "Oh, I'm sorry.
We forgot about you."

Steve chuckled. "I'm glad I wasn't holding that
painting while I was waiting."

"Odeale, you stand back across the room. Would
you tell us when it's centered between the two windows? Steve and I will hold it up against the wall."

All three came back into the living room and
completed their task. When the artwork was hung,
they stood back in admiration. It was a huge Im-
pressionist oil, portraying a busy, turn-of-the-cen-
tury Parisian street. The colors were a warm blend
of ivory, apricot, pale lemon and soft green. Ivory
sofas faced each other in front of the fireplace.

An entire wall of glass doors led out to the flower
garden. There Julia had arranged two pale lemon
moiré chairs by a wrought-iron table. Its thick, pale
green glass held the marble base for the chess set. A
second grouping of sofas and chairs by the windows
that overlooked the vineyard were of soft green
watermarked silk. It was a room that spoke of elegance and simplicity.

"It's beautiful, Julia," Steve said, praising her.
"You did it. It's finally a home."

"And you did it in time for your daughter's visit tomorrow," Odeale added triumphantly.

Julia took a deep breath and ran her fingers through her hair. "But there's still so much left to do. I still have to unpack and hang the copper pots in the kitchen . . . And, Odeale, did they deliver the faience plates?"

"Madame?" Odeale said with a look of confusion.

"The square yellow and blue plates for everyday use—the cups and saucers, the tableware—you know . . ." She looked at Steve for help. "How do you say dishes in French?"

*"Vaissele."*

Odeale brightened with understanding. "Ah, *oui,* they came this morning."

"What about the formal ones? We have to find them, especially since the DeMarcos will be here tomorrow. It took me forever to find them," she said. "Odeale, did you see them? They have about an inch of hammered gold around the rim." Panic started to set in and her vision began to blur with tears. There had been so many boxes, so many deliveries, so many strangers walking in and out of the house, and she had spent so much of Steve's money on them. They couldn't be missing.

"But, Julia," Odeale soothed, "we unpacked them three days ago and placed them in the buffet."

"That's it," Steve announced, as he pulled her into his arms. "You've been running around like a madwoman for a week and a half. You've done a phenomenal job, performed miracles, but even God had to take a rest. We'll unpack the kitchen, you're going upstairs to have a bath. I don't want any arguments. Odeale and I will finish this, and I'll call you down when dinner's ready."

She pulled back and looked up at him. "I'm okay. Really."

He kissed a tear from her cheek and said, "No, you're not. You're exhausted, you're starting to get circles under your eyes, one minute you're laughing and now you're crying. I appreciate everything you've done, darling, but now I want you to listen to me. I'm going to pour you a glass of wine, and you're going to take it upstairs. Paige is coming tomorrow, and I insist that you enjoy her visit."

Julia's lips trembled, trying to hold back a fresh onslaught of tears. Saying good night to Odeale, she didn't resist Steve as he led her from the room.

The water was warm and soothing. A glass of chilled wine sat on the marble edge of the tub. Scented bubbles clung to her shoulders as she rested her head back against a thick, fluffy, towel. She could hear strains of classical music drifting up from the living room. Through the open window, she could hear the night music of the insects and bullfrogs.

It was totally relaxing, totally wonderful—so why was she crying?

It had to be because Paige was coming tomorrow. Having Paige's itinerary, she had contacted her daughter at the hotel in Milan. Paige had been surprised and happy to hear from her, but floored to find out that her mother was three hours away in France. After hastily explaining her relationship with Steve, she had extended the invitation for an overnight visit. Avoiding more intimate questions, she'd quickly asked to speak to Mrs. DeMarco. She'd been able to avoid the inquisition on the phone, but she knew it was coming tomorrow. That had to be the reason why she was so edgy.

All the bedrooms were now furnished, and it was quite obvious that she and Steve were sharing the master bedroom. What was she going to say to her daughter? She briefly thought about using the fourth bedroom herself during the visit, but quickly banished the idea. Steve would never understand, and she couldn't hurt him that way. It frightened her that he was becoming as important to her as her child. After twenty years of celibacy, she now had to address her own sexuality. It would've been so much easier had Steve met Paige in Jersey. Why hadn't she listened to him?

Julia closed her eyes, letting the tears fall into the water. She was tired. As she rubbed the sponge over her body, trying to wash away her weariness, she felt the signs of her period coming on. Her breasts were tender, and she'd felt bloated and achy for two days. At least that explained her weepiness. It also gave her a reason not to make love with Steve tomorrow night with her daughter sleeping down the hall.

She was too damn old for this.

# Chapter 18

Julia stood in the kitchen arranging fruit and an assortment of cheese on a silver platter before bringing it to the coffee table in the living room. She wanted everything to be right, and had spent the morning meticulously going through each room. Everything was in order, from fresh flowers in each bedroom to scented soaps and hand towels in the guest bathrooms. More than once she had to stop and remind herself that she was a guest in this house as well. This was Steve's home, not hers. Maybe because she had felt such an attachment to the farm, it had been easy to invest so much love into decorating it. It was hard to explain her affection. Never before, not even in her home in New Jersey, had she felt such a strong sense of belonging. Though she was nervously awaiting her daughter's arrival, she still experienced a creeping dread of having to leave all of this in four days.

"Julia, they're here."

She felt the bottom drop out of her stomach as

her head jerked up with Steve's announcement. He stood at the entrance to the kitchen, looking casually handsome in khaki pants, and a pale blue oxford button-down shirt. His finely tailored navy blue linen blazer emphasized his broad shoulders. The highly polished loafers he wore without socks completed the picture. If she wasn't so scared, she would have smiled. He was adorable.

"Well, come on. Paige is here," Steve urged. "Don't you want to go out to greet her?"

Julia nodded. She wiped her hands on a towel and straightened the wide Battenberg lace collar of her white cotton dress. "Of course, I want to greet her. I'm just nervous."

He walked up to her and held her. "It's going to be fine." He placed a kiss on her forehead. "Let's go. Your daughter's here."

Holding her hand he led her outside.

Julia stood next to Steve in front of the door. She unconsciously removed her hand from his and clenched them. What if Paige was angry? What if she didn't like Steve? The same questions that had tormented her last night came back with a vengeance.

"Relax," Steve whispered from the corner of his mouth as the dark sedan came to a halt before them. "This is your daughter. She loves you."

Julia took a deep breath and smiled as she watched Paige emerge from the car. Long blond hair framed that precious face, now a little sunburned, and all fear in Julia vanished. Waving crazily, she left Steve and hurried down the walk to the stairs.

"Paige! You're here!"

The DeMarcos waved as Paige hurried up the steps to meet her.

"Mom, I can't believe you're here! This place . . ." She looked around the vineyard and to the house. "It's fabulous!"

Julia grabbed her daughter and hugged her tightly. "I missed you," she murmured, burying her face in her daughter's hair. "I guess I had to follow you over here."

Paige pulled back and looked over Julia's shoulder.

Julia immediately felt the tension in her daughter's body and turned to look at Steve. "Paige, I'd like to introduce Steve McMillan." She looked about anxiously for an appropriate identification. Unsure, she blurted out, "This is his farm."

Smiling, Steve came forward and held out his hand. "Paige . . . it's a real pleasure to finally meet you. Welcome to France."

Julia watched the exchange, seeing how Steve held Paige's hand between both of his, how Paige seemed to size him up. Although Paige was polite, she withheld real warmth. Julia couldn't blame her daughter. Certainly Paige was confused by her mother's recent behavior.

The DeMarcos came up the stairs and Julia greeted them and introduced them to Steve. The DeMarcos were good people, easy to talk to and immediately friendly. Paige and Maria stood next to each other looking at the house and chattering.

She caught Steve's eye and, as if reading her mind, he announced, "Let's go inside. Julia's prepared a wonderful lunch."

Once in the foyer, Julia had to smile at the women's reaction to the place. It reminded her of how she'd felt when she'd first entered the house. There was a collective gasp as Steve led them into the living room. After a few minutes of pleasantries, the group scattered. Steve went into the kitchen to get the chilled wine. Mr. Demarco visited the downstairs bathroom, while Julia took the women upstairs to freshen up.

With the two guest bathrooms occupied, Julia led Paige down the hallway to the master bath.

"This is absolutely incredible," Paige gawked at the elegant room. She spun around in disbelief. "Who is this guy?"

Julia smiled, and said, "Use the bathroom first, Paige. We'll talk for a minute before we go back down." Turning from her daughter, Julia walked up the steps and sat down on the bed. She knew this discussion was inevitable, but had hoped to postpone it until they had more time. Almost too soon, Paige walked into the bedroom and sat down beside her.

"Okay, so who is he? You met at work? So what does he do? Why didn't you tell me about him when I came home from school?"

Julia reached for Paige's hand to stop the barrage of questions. "Steve is very special to me. As I told you on the phone, we met at work. He's a negotiator for Amalgamated Energy, and has been investing in this farm for years."

Paige got up quickly and walked over to the open glass doors that led to the terrace. "This isn't a farm, Mom."

"I know. That was my initial reaction too."

"Well, why didn't you tell me about him?"

Julia could hear the mixture of anger and hurt in her daughter's voice. Steadying her own emotions, she took a deep breath and answered. "Paige, you have to understand, when you came home I wasn't sure where this was leading. I had never introduced you to a man, and I thought it would be less confusing to wait until I felt more sure about the relationship before I told you about him. He's really wonderful. In fact, we argued because he wanted to meet you before you left for Europe and I was against it."

"So how long have you known this guy? And why would you treat me like I was a little kid that couldn't handle the fact that my mother had a boyfriend?"

Julia dropped her gaze to the polished wooden floor. She'd known that this was coming, and she had obviously handled everything badly. Her eyes filled with tears and she silently cursed her inability to control her emotions. "Paige, I'm sorry if I hurt you. I should have told you about Steve, but I was only trying to protect you. How could I send you halfway across the world if you were worrying about me?"

Paige waved her hand toward the bed impatiently. "Oh, like I'm not worried about you now? You're halfway across the world with a strange man. A man I've never even met. This isn't like you, Mom."

Julia stood up and faced her child. "No, Paige, you're wrong. This *is* like me, and I didn't even know it till I got here." She walked over to her daughter who was standing by the terrace with her arms tightly wrapped around her waist. Gently, Julia pushed Paige's long blond hair behind her ear.

"Look, honey, I'm not trying to dump this on you, but you have to realize that it's been a long time since anyone paid attention to me as a woman. After your father left us twenty years ago, there was no one in my life but you. There's more to me than the parenting, housekeeping, and work, but I buried it for twenty years by trying to do the right thing. And then you left. You were gone. You were the center of my life, and I suddenly realized how empty my life had become." Julia wiped the tears from her eyes and, looking out to the sky, smiled. "And then from nowhere, God sends me this gift, this man. This patient, kind, loving man . . . how can I explain it any better than that?"

Paige's eyes brimmed with tears. "Mom, I always wanted you to be happy, but I can't help it if I'm worried about you. I don't want you to be lonely for the rest of your life, but I also don't want you to get hurt." Paige cast a sweeping gaze around the room.

"I don't want this to come out wrong, but the man seems pretty wealthy and—"

Julia placed her hand on Paige's shoulder, interrupting the flow of her daughter's concerned words. "I know that you probably think Steve is just some rich playboy, that he isn't serious about me. That's what I thought too when I first met him, and it took him an awfully long time to convince me otherwise. Perhaps that's why I couldn't bring myself to allow him to meet you. I had to be sure first. But, Paige, he's the most honest person I've ever met, and he has bone-deep integrity. I really trust him, and I wish you two could like each other. He's really important to me. Both of you are."

Paige looked at her directly. There was no confusion or tension in her expression now. Her gaze had become open and serene. "Mom, do you love him?" Paige asked quietly.

Leave it to the most cherished person in her life to ask the most difficult question in her life. Julia had avoided her own feelings for so long on this issue she wasn't sure of how to respond.

Nervously, she took Paige's hand, and gave it a light squeeze. "We'd better get downstairs. We've left the DeMarcos and Steve alone for far too long, and the lunch that I've worked so hard to prepare will be ruined if we don't." Catching the new intensity in her daughter's look, she added softly, "I promise that we'll talk about this later. I'll answer all of your questions, and we can stay up tonight as long as you'd like. But please, Paige, just let me get through this visit. I can't even think now."

"Okay, but I have to ask you just one more question."

Julia braced herself.

"Where did you get that dress? I love it. You look so different, almost glowing."

Julia's body relaxed and she laughed. "I found it in a little shop in St. Tropez."

"You guys went to St. Tropez?" Paige exclaimed with excitement. "Where all those great sidewalk artists are and everything? Maria told me all about it. I'm just dying to go there! Mom, this really has been wonderful. Do you believe we're in Europe?"

Julia threaded her arm through Paige's. "Well it ain't Jersey, is it?" They both laughed as they walked down the hall. "We'll go there tomorrow. It's only fifteen minutes away. And, Paige, wait till you see—everyone is so beautiful. The men, the women—I felt like a troll."

Paige shook her head. "Well, you don't look like one. You look like a woman in love." Paige squeezed her mother's arm. "As long as you're happy, Mom, I'm happy."

Julia kissed her daughter's cheek, then hugged her. Her baby was growing up. Paige had accepted her as a woman. Life was truly full of surprises here in Eden. Perhaps this magical place held the real treasure that had been given to her—acceptance.

They had finished lunch—lemon sage chicken, tomato basil zucchini and shallots over fresh pasta. The meal was going well. She had overcome her initial hesitation when Steve poured the chilled wine for Paige and Maria. As she served dessert—a fresh fruit torte, the conversation took an unexpected turn.

"Mom, when we were in Milan, we met Antonio, Maria's cousin. He's going to school for fashion design. The more he talked, the more Maria and I thought it sounded wonderful. You should see Milan. And the school. I think Milan's replaced Paris as the world's leading fashion center."

She watched her daughter look across the table to the DeMarcos before continuing.

"Maria and I thought that it would be great to spend a semester or two going to school with Antonio. We've checked, and the credits are even transferable. You know I've always been interested in design, and this could be a fantastic opportunity. Mr. and Mrs. DeMarco have checked out the school, and are even considering letting Maria come back to study abroad for the fall semester. What'd you think, Mom?"

Julia merely stared at her daughter, trying to measure her words before she spoke. Taking a deep breath, she exhaled long and evenly. "Paige, you're doing so well in Ohio. Why would you consider something so risky?"

"That's just it," Paige said in an impassioned voice. "We're talking about Ohio versus Milan, in a field I've always wanted to get into."

Julia's throat felt tight. "There are fashion schools in New York. Why do you have to go half-way across the world to study in this field?"

"Didn't we have a talk upstairs about the differences," Paige challenged, looking at her mother meaningfully.

Julia was horrified at her child's implication. She gave Paige a threatening mother's glare to let her daughter know that she was close to the edge. "I'll need more information. Why don't we discuss this later?" she intoned.

Paige shook her head, and picked up her glass of wine. "That seems to be your answer to everything lately," she muttered into the glass.

"Why don't we all go outside?" Steve interrupted diplomatically. He stood, putting his hand on Maria's father's shoulder. "Joe wants to take a tour of the vineyard."

"What a wonderful idea," Mrs. DeMarco said, trying to restore the earlier peace. "It looked so lovely as we drove in."

Maria and Paige pushed their chairs out and stood up. Maria started to clear her place setting. "Lunch was delicious, Mrs. Edwards. Thank you."

Clutching her wine glass to her chest, Julia forced a pleasant smile. "You're welcome, Maria. Don't bother with the dishes, we'll do them later. I think we could all use some fresh air."

He first led them to the pond, trying to reestablish a happier mood. He talked to Joe about the size of the goldfish and carp, and almost laughed when the girls screeched at the leaping fish that jumped from the water each time a tiny crumb of bread was thrown. While all peered into the water, he looked over at Julia and blew a secret kiss in her direction.

It was funny how close he had become to this woman in such a short time, he thought. He knew without words how nervous she was about Paige's visit. He knew that when she was upstairs she had talked to Paige about him. He also knew how upset and embarrassed she was by her daughter's announcement, and the way Paige dangled the new information she had about them at the table. Julia was such a private person, and this public challenge had to have been difficult for her.

Julia chatted on with Sophia DeMarco and took the lead as she escorted them to the vegetable garden. Paige hung back from the small group, as though wanting to avoid her mother's company. Steve decided that now was the best time to talk to this young woman about her mother, the woman he loved.

Holding out a large chunk of hard bread to her, he looked at the water and said, "If you throw a piece as far as you can to the other side, bullfrogs as large as land turtles will hop out."

Paige ripped off a hunk and flung it across the murky water. As one fat frog did an Air Jordan before disappearing into the pond, Paige was enchanted. "Look at that! This place is great. Was this pond here, or did you put it in? My mom said you'd been renovating for years."

Steve put his hands into his pant pockets, and studied the water. "The pond was here. Most of the renovations were done to expand the farmhouse." He sensed Paige nodding, and they stood for a few moments in silence. "So, you like Europe?" he asked in a low thoughtful voice.

"I love it. I don't even want to go home. And now the DeMarco's have this trip all planned out and everything, but I'd prefer to just go back to Milan and start school now if I could."

"You know Julia's just worried about you. She's had a lot of changes recently in her life. This last one kind of threw her."

"I just wish she could understand. This is the chance of a lifetime, and I don't want to end up like all the rest of my friends. It's hard to explain . . . I see people taking liberal arts classes that will get them nowhere when they graduate, or taking up majors that they hate just because their parents want them to." Paige turned to him and said passionately, "This is *my* life we're talking about. I can't help it if I didn't know this was what I wanted to do until I saw it in Milan. I don't want to be like everybody else. I don't want to do what I'm told is right instead of what I feel is right."

Tears brimmed in her eyes and he saw the deep resemblance to Julia shimmering in them. "Your mother just wants you to have a marketable skill when you get out of school. Life doesn't change. It's tough. You still need to earn enough to put a roof over your head and food in your stomach, and the fashion design industry is hard to break into and risky if you do."

"I don't know if you can picture this," Paige replied, "but I have a belief called the rocking chair theory. Here's what it's about. After twenty five years of doing what you hate, just because it makes you money, or because it's considered the responsible thing to do and it fits in with the status quo, you'll be sitting in a rocking chair one day, looking back on your life. I can't bear the thought of looking back at mine, wondering what it would have been like had I just tried to do what I loved, and followed my heart, instead of doing what everyone expected. I don't think there's anything sadder than being old and discontented, knowing that there's no more time in my life to change it. I'll tell you something. The money doesn't mean that much to me if I have to go through the rest of my life doing something that I hate, even if I'm good at it."

Steve stared at this woman-child. The sounds of the insects receded as he made eye contact with her. "Where did you learn this?"

"I watched my mother do it for twenty years. And at college, the more friends I talked to, everybody's parents fell into the same sad mold. What happened to their dreams? When did everybody get so afraid to take a chance? I'd rather fail at something I loved then never to have tried at all."

Truth from the mouths of babes. He knew she was talking about herself, yet she seemed to bring his entire life into focus. He'd been in the rat race for two decades, and had given Amalgamated seventeen years. Julia said everything happens for a reason. Standing here at this pond with this fair-haired replica of Julia, he made a momentous decision. In that moment, he knew he was going to give the vineyard a go, and he also knew he was going to ask Julia to be his wife. She belonged here even more than he did.

"I'll tell you what, Paige—if you want, I'll talk to your mother for you. I don't think you're going to have as much trouble as you'd suspect. If things work out the way I hope they will, your mother will only be three hours away from your new school."

She looked up at him, and he could see the full implication of his statement becoming clear to her.

"I love your mother, Paige, and I believe she loves me. She's been trying to convince me to follow my dream of living here and making a go of this place. You can see how she's fallen in love with the farm, and I want to keep her happy. She should be able to stay here as long as she wants. She's breathed life into what I originally thought of as an investment. And seeing your mother's vision for the vineyard, now I don't think I can part with it, or her."

Paige's smile was a little embarrassed. "Does this mean you two are going to get married?"

"If she'll have me. I haven't even asked her yet, but first . . . I need your blessing."

"I don't want my Mom to be hurt." Paige's voice filled with emotion. "She's had a rough time. She works so hard, and I know most of it was for me."

Steve slipped his arm around her shoulder and lowered his head to hers. "Paige, I want you to believe me when I tell you that I'd never do anything to intentionally hurt your mother. She's made me revisit my own past and re-evaluate my own life," he chuckled lightly, "although we're not yet in rocking chairs." Making her look at him directly, his voice became serious. "She's loving, intelligent, beautiful, and funny. She's a good person, Paige, and I would never do anything that would make her change. I'll take care of her. She won't have to work at a job she hates, and can stay at a place she loves. I know this is sudden for you, and although we don't really know each other yet, I hope you can believe that."

Paige was openly crying. "I love her, too. I just want her to be happy."

"There's an awful lot of that going on around here," he said, wiping away a tear. She really was a good kid, and he was going to see to it that she got every opportunity to follow her dream. He knew what it was like to have a fire in the belly. All this kid needed was someone to believe in her and a few good breaks. He handed her his handkerchief. "Let's go find your mother."

They entered the vegetable garden, and Steve smiled as he saw Julia acting as tour guide while she excitedly pointed out every vegetable she passed. When the small group walked by the strawberries, Julia insisted that they each try one, beaming with pride. He felt Paige tug on his arm as they joined the group. Handing him back his handkerchief, she glanced at her mother and then back at him.

Her lips were trembling with repressed emotion as she whispered, "You're right, I've never seen her this happy. For what it's worth, I guess you have my blessing."

Steve gathered her into his arms and kissed her

forehead. Relief swept through him. "Thank you, Paige," he whispered back. "It's worth a great deal to me, and I won't let you down."

He suddenly felt like he was part of a family. It was something he had never before felt in his life.

Later that night, in bed, he held Julia in his arms as she cried against his shoulder.

"But fashion design! Every teenage girl thinks she can become a fashion designer. And who's this Antonio?" she lamented, as another wave of muffled sobs overcame her. Steve rubbed her back, trying to soothe her.

"But Paige isn't every teenager. That child of yours is far older than her years. She's got a good head on her shoulders, and a lot of common sense, thanks to you. She made me realize something today, and it was almost spiritual. Your daughter talked about being old and looking back on wasted years. And the more I thought about it, the more I couldn't deny that truth." Steve brushed the hair back from Julia's wet cheek. "I think life is just a long road we travel, and every once in a while, there's a fork in it."

Julia gasped. "Wait a second. That's exactly what I told Paige before she left for Europe." She sniffled and said, "Do you think we've been together too long? We're actually starting to think alike."

Steve smiled and held her closer. "That's a good sign, not a bad one." He felt her body begin to relax in his arms.

"I've certainly been going down a lot of new paths lately," she whispered.

"Well, depending on which choice we make, which path we take, we'll end up somewhere different. One will be hard and rocky, with stumbling blocks along the way to caution us to turn around and go back. Most people don't even pay attention, Julia. If they make the right choice, and take the right path, everything starts to fall into place. I'm not saying you don't have to work hard, or that there won't be obstacles, but you'll find solutions and overcome them if you're following your destiny."

"Are you saying that Paige is at a crossroads?"

"Julia, all three of us are at a crossroads right now."

"What do you mean?"

His heart slammed against his rib cage. He tried to think of the best way to lay out his offer. He could use the farm as an inducement, since he'd already talked about a joint venture. But as soon as the analytical thoughts began, he stopped.

This had to come from the heart.

Pulling her up to him so he could look into her eyes, he took a deep breath and started down his own new path. "Julia, I think you know how I feel about you, but I need to say the words. You are the best thing that has ever happened to me. You came into my life, shook it up, and showed me what a good life can be. And the funny thing is, your daughter and I had a conversation today, and she did the exact same thing. She's so much like you that I'm beginning to love her already. And, using your words, I respect her, and the difficult choices she's about to make. I'm telling you all of this because I'm scared. I'm about to make two important decisions that will alter my life. One is about the farm. I'm going to try to make the vineyard profitable."

"Steve, I'm so happy for you."

"This is going to be a big step, because it'll mean having to give up a full-time position with Amalgamated."

Julia lifted her head further back and even in the moonlight, her expression appeared shocked. "But what will you do?"

"When we go back to the States, I'm going to talk to them about part-time consulting. The more I think about it, the more I suspect that I might be able to come out even. It may sound crazy, Julia, but the going rate for a consultant is higher than for a paid employee. If this works out, I might have to go to the States every other month for a few weeks. It will be a lot better than this insane grind of constant travel."

"I'm so glad you found a way to work it out. You belong here."

"So do you." He took another deep breath. "Now, for the other . . . I've never done this in my entire life, so I don't know if I'm doing it right." He reached up and held her beautiful face between his palms, gently running his thumbs over her cheekbones. "Julia Edwards, I love you, and I'm asking you to be my wife."

She stared at him in the moonlight for a few seconds before letting her head drop to his chest amid a new flood of tears. He wrapped his arms around her tightly, and held the back of her head as fear rushed through him.

"Jesus, what did I do? Did I do it wrong? I don't have any experience in this."

He felt her shoulders shake and she raised her face to his. Relief immediately washed through him as he saw her brilliant smile.

"Steve McMillan," she whispered through her sniffles. "I've been waiting twenty years for someone to love me like this. You came into my life and swept me off of my feet. You made me believe in possibilities again, and in love. I do love you, and I'll follow you to the ends of the earth," she said, her voice quavering with emotion as she nuzzled her face back into the crook of his shoulder. "But, please, can we just stay right here at the farm?"

He looked up to the stream of moonlight reflected on the ceiling. "Is this a yes? Does this mean you'll marry me?"

She giggled and brushed his neck with a kiss. "Yes." Another kiss was placed higher. "I'll marry you," she whispered, her breath hot and electrifying against his skin. "I'll marry you, I'll marry you, I'll marry you . . ." Each kiss came closer to his lips until she captured his mouth with her own.

The next morning as they sat around the dining room table finishing breakfast, Julia looked across the long expanse of wood and smiled at Steve. She watched as he cleared his throat, stood up, and tapped his knife against his glass of orange juice.

"I have an announcement and I can't think of a better time to make it, or better company to be in."

His gaze never left hers as he raised his glass in the air.

"I am honored to announce that this wonderful woman sitting across from me agreed last night to be my wife."

Guests at the table broke out in cheers and Paige jumped up to embrace her.

"Oh, Mom, I'm so happy for you! You deserve this."

Julia's throat constricted with fresh emotion. She never thought anything like this was possible for her. She had her daughter's approval and love, a wonderful man, and a new life ahead of her. She felt truly blessed. As she took in the joyous scene, she couldn't find the words to describe her happiness. Mr. and Mrs. DeMarco offered individual toasts. Maria came over and hugged her. Paige ran to Steve's side and was immediately swept into an affectionate embrace. Accepting a kiss of congratulations from Joe DeMarco, she watched the warm exchange between Paige and Steve, and mentally offered an sincere prayer of thanks.

Paige hopped around with excitement and, grabbing Maria, the two girls spun around with laughter. Suddenly Paige stopped, and asked, "So when are you two guys going to do this thing?" Her hand raised in declaration before they could answer. "And I'm putting in for maid of honor."

Julia laughed as she and Steve came around the table to meet each other. They slipped into a familiar embrace and faced the others. "We're planning on being married here at the farm," Julia said. "We're leaving in a few days to go back to the States to tie up loose ends and work out the legalities of being married in a foreign country. But we hope to be back within a month and, since you'll all be in Europe, we'd like to invite you to the wedding." Julia held her hand out to her daughter and Paige joined her and Steve.

She looked at her grown child and saw all of the years of hard work, struggle, and love that had brought them to this moment. "Of course you're going to be a part of all of this. Who else but you would stand up for me at my wedding? You're my daughter and my best friend. Since we plan to live here at the farm, we'll be close enough to see each other. If you get all of the information, we'll sit down and talk, and see if we can give Milan a go."

Paige's eyes filled with new tears and she hugged Julia. "Oh, Mom, thank you so much. You won't be sorry. I'll prove it to you. I'll work really hard. You'll see." Paige looked at Steve and gave him a tight hug. "Thanks for believing in me. Take care of my mom."

Steve stood in between them with an arm around each. He looked down at Paige and said, "I plan to do just that. Since we're going into St. Tropez this morning, how would you like to help your mother pick out her engagement ring?" While raising his head, he smiled to the DeMarcos. "In fact, you're all a part of this. Joe and Sophia, if you hadn't brought Paige to Europe, I couldn't have convinced her mother to follow. So why don't we all make this a day of celebration."

Joe reached over and picked up his glass of orange juice and raised it. "Salute! Congratulations again. What are we waiting for? *Destinazione* . . . St. Tropez!"


It had been two wonderful days with her daughter, but now Paige and the DeMarcos were continuing their trip. Standing on the wide stone steps in front of the house with Steve, she watched as the car drove through the gates. A thoughtful sigh escaped from her lips as she leaned her head against Steve's shoulder. "I hope we're making the right decision with Paige. Did I agree to let her go to school in Milan just so she'll be close to me here in France? Fashion designing is like being an actor. Only the top three percent ever make it." She turned to Steve and looked at him directly. "I don't want her to regret her career choice for the rest of her life."

Steve shook his head. "If she doesn't do this, Julia, that's what she'll regret. You've got to let her follow her own path."

"But she's so young."

"That's why she's got time. Look, let the kid go to school for a year. See if she has talent. Three years ago, Jean Paul Bernard was having financial difficulties and Amalgamated white-knighted his design house. That merger gave him the cash flow to save his floundering *haute couture* line. Jean Paul and I have a good working relationship. If Paige has talent, she won't be out on the street."

Reaching up, she touched his face and whispered, "You are such a good man. I can't believe how lucky I am to have found you. I hope you're in this for the long haul, because I never intend to let anything come between us."

At that moment, the sun's rays sparkled off the cluster of diamonds that surrounded the large aquamarine stone on her finger. When the jeweler said that the aquamarine represented peace, calmness, and devotion, she had known it was the perfect ring for the perfect love.

# Chapter 19

The sun was beginning to set behind the mountain range, casting a rosy orange blush over the vineyard. It was her favorite time of day. Picking up a fallen dried stick of bamboo, Julia tore the dead leaves from it and took it as a walking cane while she said goodbye to the farm.

"I think we'll use *Patisserie du Chateau* in Grimaud. Monsieur Baudelaire said they would only need four days notice."

Odeale nodded as she accompanied her around the perimeter of the vineyard. "He will make a beautiful wedding cake. He is a fine *patissier.*"

Julia looked across the vast rows of vines to her future husband. He was engaged in a lengthy discussion with Maurice and his sons. She smiled, secure in the knowledge that they belonged to each other now. It was a rare feeling of contentment. She wanted to hold on to it forever.

"How many should I prepare for, for the wedding?"

Julia looked back to the dirt service road. "I'm not sure, Odeale. It will be a very small, intimate affair. Probably around ten, but no more than fifteen. You and Maurice are invited, also your sons and their families. It will be wonderful to have your grandchildren at the wedding."

"You like babies . . . yes?"

"Absolutely, but it's been a long time since I had one of my own."

They walked for a few minutes in comfortable silence. Since they were leaving tomorrow morning for the airport in Nice, this would be the last time she would be able to walk the property until she came back for her wedding.

"You have become the chatelaine of *Mas des Muriers,* with your walking stick, and straw hat, and love for the land."

Julia thanked her for the compliment. As they neared the windmill, she added, "Hopefully Steve and I will grow old here together."

"Ah, but children . . . they keep you young."

"Yes, I suppose so, but my daughter is grown now. She'll be going to school in Milan. I hope she visits here as often as possible, but I'm afraid I'll have to wait for grandchildren of my own to keep me young."

Odeale stopped walking. "But, *non.* Surely, Madame, you won't do that?"

Julia turned around and looked at the older woman. Her eyes were wide with shock. "Odeale, what are you talking about? Do what?"

"You are not too old for this child."

Julia merely stared at the woman. What in hell was she talking about? "What child? I don't understand." Had she said something that Odeale mistranslated?

Odeale put her hand to her chest in relief. *"Mon Dieu.* Oh, Julia, you gave me such a scare." Her face broke into a smile and she kissed each cheek, again coming back for a third.

Julia merely blinked, holding onto her hat. What in the world had brought about this sudden outburst from Odeale?

Holding Julia's hands Odeale smiled kindly, and said, "We speak of your child. Did you not yet know?"

It took a full thirty seconds before Julia comprehended Odeale's words. Throwing back her head, she laughed. "Oh, no, Odeale. You misunderstand. We're not getting married this quickly because I'm having a baby."

Odeale shook her head avidly. "Oh, Julia, that is not what I say. I know Monsieur Steve loves you, and would marry you." Clasping her hands together under her chin, she literally beamed. "But the baby, this is yet another gift . . . yes?"

Julia kept shaking her head. "Odeale, I'm not getting through to you. There is no baby."

Undaunted, Odeale clucked her tongue while placing her hand on Julia's cheek. "You're not too old. It's in your face."

Stunned, Julia stepped backwards as a feeling of dread washed over her. "Odeale, you're wrong." Immediately her mind thought back to every night she had been with Steve. They had used birth control every single time. It was impossible.

"Perhaps I am wrong, maybe it is just the happiness of your wedding that I see in your eyes. But Odeale is rarely wrong about such things. I have told my own daughters, and the wives of my sons. Some even before they knew."

This was her last dinner tonight at the farm, and she wanted it to be special. "Odeale, this is one time where your predictions are wrong, I assure you. We'll have to play with your grandchildren until we get some of our own. Considering my daughter's age, I hope that's not for many years to come."

Odeale gave her a knowing smile. "As you say, Madame," then placed a single kiss on her cheek. "But this is for *bon chance*, for good luck."

Julia shrugged and shook her head. "Come, let's walk back to the house now. I want to take a shower before dinner."

Odeale's words haunted her as she threw her clothes on the bed. Good luck? Is that what happens when you get old? You start making crazy predictions? Even if she were, how could Odeale think being nearly forty and pregnant would be a happy thing?

Leaving the bedroom, she walked down the stairs into the bathroom and turned on the jets in the shower. Even though her period was four days late, she'd certainly had enough excitement and turmoil to have delayed it. And they had used birth control every single time, even in the shower. That had been hilarious. She turned around to grab a towel when

her vision fixed on the two wooden stairs leading
back into the bedroom.

*Every single time, except the first . . .*

Frozen with sudden fear, she remembered the
crying, the tenderness of her breasts, the cramping,
the mood swings, the fatigue. Dear God in heaven,
this couldn't be happening. Not here. Not now.

Julia shut the shower off and ran back into the
bedroom. Grabbing up her clothes, she threw them
back on, and raced downstairs for her purse and the
car keys.

"Julia, where are you taking the car?" She spun
around at the car door like a surprised thief. Steve
was walking toward her from the vineyard.

"I have to go into town before it closes. I'll explain later," she yelled back, and slid behind the
wheel.

Fifteen minutes later, she stood in a *pharmacie*
and stared at the shelves trying to find the correct
product. She had an instant flashback to when she
had started this trip. Hadn't she brought all of that
damned birth control to avoid standing here feeling
this helpless?

*"Avez-vous besoin le medicament?"*

Startled, Julia turned to the clerk at her side. "I
need a pregnancy test."

*"Pardon? Je ne comprend pas Anglaise. A Gri-
maud on parle francaise."*

Julia looked at the man as tears of frustration
filled her eyes. *"Je nais parle pas francaise.* Please, I
do not speak French."

The man let out a sound of annoyance and began

speaking so rapidly that she hadn't the slightest idea of what he was saying. Knowing it was almost closing time, she searched for a way to make him understand.

"Ah, a baby test." Seeing even more confusion on his face, she began to mime a pregnant woman. Her hands made a wide circle out from her belly, then she shrugged her shoulders and pointed to herself.

*"Ah, oui, oui, enceinte épreuvé?"* He pulled a long rectangular box from the shelf and handed it to her. She almost wept with relief as she thanked him and walked to the counter to pay for it.

Back at the farm, she closed herself into one of the guest bathrooms and tore open the box. To her horror, the instructions were in French. She turned the paper over and over, looking for the dual language companion that she would have found if she were in the States. Sitting on the toilet seat, she told herself to calm down and tried to figure out how the thing worked. She made out *blanc* and *rouge* to denote white and red. Obviously white would be not pregnant, red would mean a disaster. All she needed was five minutes to find out if her dreams were coming to an end.

Huddled on the bathroom floor, she held the stick up in front of her in disbelief. The tiny dot was red. Not white. Not pink. Flaming red. God could not have done this to her.

Val had. It was the curse.

\* \* \*

"I know something's bothering you. Why won't you tell me what it is?"

She sat on the bed in her robe, her wet hair leaving droplets on the bedspread. She kept looking at the long planks of wood on the floor, slowly shaking her head in shock. Steve stopped dressing for dinner and sat down next to her. She couldn't even look at him.

"Are you upset because we're leaving tomorrow morning?"

She shook her head.

"Is it Paige?"

She shook her head.

"What is it? If you don't tell me I can't help you?"

"You can't help me," she muttered.

"Is this like PMS or something? Are you getting your period? Do you have the blues?"

Julia jumped up from the bed and glared down at him. "If I had PMS, I wouldn't have a problem, now would I?"

Steve stared back at her with confusion. "What does that mean?"

Julia flung her hand up in exasperation as the damn tears started again. "Of course *you* wouldn't know! And then again, why would you? You're just like every other man," she began as she started pacing the room. "How I would love to go through life, blithely unaware of the consequences of taking my pleasure whenever, and with whomever, I wanted!"

Steve stared back at her. "Have you lost your mind? What the hell are you talking about?"

"I'm talking about you," she answered, hearing the anger in her voice and not caring. "I'm talking about men."

Steve stood up and crossed his arms in front of his chest. "As long as we're sniping about the sexes, if the PMS remark offended you, I apologize. Let's call it a hormonal imbalance. I've heard of women not making any sense when they begin the change of life."

It was as if she stood outside her body and watched it move toward Steve. When she reached him she shoved him back onto the bed in anger. "How dare you! I do not have PMS. I wish I did. Nor am I going through the change of life," she yelled down in his startled face. "I'm not that lucky."

She stepped back from him and folded her arms in fury and protection. "So we might as well just call all this off. I'm not going to get married again for appearances just to be left! I'm not going through that hell again."

Hot tears coursed down her face and she didn't bother to wipe them away. She had spent two weeks in paradise, only to be cast out at the end. She should have known nothing good lasts forever.

Sitting up, Steve said, "Julia, calm down. What are you talking about?"

Jamming her hand in her pocket, she ripped out the pregnancy test stick. "I'm talking about this," she proclaimed, holding it up as if it were a sword in front of her. "I'm pregnant!"

Silence filled the room. Steve blinked several

times incredulously. Finally he collected himself. He whispered in a shocked voice, "You're pregnant?"

"Great detective work, Sherlock. You finally got it."

He stood up and gathered her resisting body into his arms. "Julia, this is wonderful. You're not happy?"

How she would have loved to place her head on his shoulder and cry out her fears. But she had been down this road before. Pulling away from him, she walked through the glass doors and out onto the terrace. As she gazed at the vineyard below her, she ran her fingers through her wet hair to stop the raging headache and said, "I'm too old to start over alone with a young baby. And I'm too tired. I believe you love me, Steve, but children change everything. What we had was so perfect, and now it can never be the same. My first husband resented having to marry me, and hated the way I looked when I was pregnant. Then when Paige arrived, he hated the attention I gave her. Perhaps that's why he felt the need to go to other women. And this time I don't even have my mother here for support. So let's not pretend."

Steve came up behind her and turned her around to face him. "Don't compare me to that man. He was a fool. I know the value of a family, since I never had one. I've lived the horrors that unloved and unwanted children go through, and I vowed that if I ever had kids of my own, I wouldn't let a day go by where they'd wonder whether or not they were loved. I will never leave you, Julia," he said, drawing her into his arms. "You're scared by your past, and you have every right to be. But I asked you to marry me before I even knew, and this just makes it perfect."

"But children change everything, Steve," she whispered against his chest. "You just don't know."

Stroking her back he murmured into her hair, "Don't you think I've spent years knowing that my own time was running out to have children? I put off a wife and family, not because I'm a confirmed bachelor, but because I know what a hell it is for kids to grow up between warring parents. I wanted to be sure that I had a lifelong partner beside me before I proposed to anyone. I never felt that way until meeting you. I also wanted to make sure that any child of mine wouldn't want for anything."

Turning her around to the vineyard, he held her back against his chest. "Look out there, Julia. Wouldn't this be the perfect place to raise a child? What more do you need except trust? I love you and I'll never leave you."

"But I'll be forty years old when this baby's born."

"Twenty years wiser this time," he murmured into her damp hair.

She leaned back against him and he encircled her with his arms. His hand reached down her body to caress her belly. In that moment she knew she could trust this man. He wouldn't leave. Placing her hand on top of his, she whispered, "We're having a baby."

He quickly spun her around and hugged her

tightly while letting out a shout of joy. "We're having a baby!" he repeated, and then yelled out over the vineyard.

*"We're having a baby!* Hey, Odeale, Maurice! We're going to have a baby!"

Julia laughed and waved to their neighbors as they left for their own farm.

Odeale waved and shouted back, *"Felicitations!"*

Eden had not cast her out after all.

# Chapter 20

"It is completely out of the question. You are not going into that house without me." Steve turned into her driveway and stopped the car. He fixed her with an authoritative stare. "This is not a debate, this is not up for a vote, this is not an option. The situation in there is far too dangerous, and you are carrying my child. Case closed. End of discussion."

Julia tore her gaze away from his and looked at her house. Her geraniums and impatiens had withered and died from lack of water. It was almost surreal. The house that was once so important to her now appeared empty and distant. For a brief moment, she wondered if someone weren't paving the way for her to leave everything behind.

"Are you listening to me?"

Julia whispered, "Val won't hurt me," and opened the car door.

Rushing to her side, Steve took her keys, then bounded up the steps before her. "I'm going in first," he commanded.

At the front door, just as Steve was about to insert the key, Julia held his arm. "What if something's happened to her? I don't even know if she's even there. What if she's died?"

"Julia, she's a ghost."

"I know, but I'm afraid of what we'll find."

"Stay behind me," he ordered and stuck the key into the lock.

Julia held her breath as the door opened. Immediately, she heard Frank Sinatra blaring from the stereo. They walked into the foyer, and Julia could see the kitchen was neat, and the living room was clean. Walking into it, she shut off the music.

"Val?" Even to her own ears her voice sounded uncertain.

Julia cast her gaze toward the stairwell, and she gasped as she saw the woman before her. Leaning against Steve, she muttered, "Oh, my God!"

Steve grabbed her and began ushering her toward the door. "We're outta here!"

"No, wait," she said, pulling herself away from him as she walked toward the stairs. "Val, what happened?" she asked in amazement.

"Hey, toots, you're *back!* It's been as lonely as hell around here since you left."

"But you—you're young again!"

Val sashayed down the stairs, swinging her hips with casual seduction. "Yeah, I know. Is this not a kick? Here, come give me a big hug. I can't tell you how much I've missed you."

She heard Steve's voice behind her. "What's going on? She's young again?"

"Yes . . ." Julia stammered, "It's positively unbelievable."

Val walked up to Julia and hugged her. "Tell Steve not to be afraid. I'm gonna give him a kiss."

"Steve, it's okay. Val wants to give you a kiss." She watched as Steve stiffened with apprehension.

"I wasn't gonna bite him," Val said with a little laugh.

Steve put his hand to his face and muttered, "She smells good."

"Shalimar," Julia and Val said together.

"I always knew I liked this guy," Val purred, coming back to stand by Julia. "So, kiddo, tell me about your trip."

Julia waved her hand in front of her. "In a minute. First tell me when did this happen, and how?"

Julia couldn't stop staring at Val. She looked exactly the way she did when she first appeared in her bedroom. Beautiful, sexy, and sassy. The original Valentina Manchester had returned.

"It was the strangest thing. Let me tell you, Julia, when you walked out of here three weeks ago, I was really pissed off. But after I knocked around here for almost two weeks by myself, I sat down one day and had a good cry. I really missed my one and only friend, and realized how right you were. I was trying to keep you and Steve apart because I just couldn't stand what was happening to me. But I suddenly realized that I loved you, kiddo. And losing you was worse than getting old. So I started cleaning up the house, wanting to make it nice for your return. Every day that I did something for you, I started feeling better. I had given up looking in a mirror, since it was so damn depressing. But then one day last week, when I was cleaning the bathroom, I took a good look. I was also getting younger."

Julia just shook her head in disbelief. "You're kidding?"

"What's going on?" Steve asked.

"I'll explain it later," she said, cutting him off.

Val giggled. "Julia, from that point on I've been working like Hazel the maid. I cleaned out your closets and drawers, and even your attic. I started wearing make-up again, and look—I even fit into my old dress. Thank you, Julia."

"I didn't do anything," she protested.

Val crossed the short distance between them and weaved her arm through Julia's. "Oh, yes you did, kid. I kept thinking about our conversation in the attic, when you talked about Paige and unconditional love. When I realized that I loved you more than I hated getting old, I finally understood."

Julia embraced Val, and whispered, "I love you, too. I was so scared to come back here . . . I couldn't stand it if anything had happened to you . . . Even if you weren't here, I hated the way we parted."

"Okay, don't get weepy on me now. Tell me about you. Have you hooked this guy yet?"

Julia laughed and, leaving Val, walked over to Steve. Lacing her fingers through his, she raised her left hand to show Val her engagement ring. "Does this qualify as hooking him?"

Steve muttered, "I don't get it," as Val squealed with delight.

"I'm proud of you, honey," Val said as she came closer to inspect the ring.

"We're getting married in a month, and we're going to live in France." Julia watched as honest tears welled in Val's eyes.

"In France?" Val asked.

Steve blurted out, "Tell her you're pregnant, so no funny business."

"You're pregnant?" Val said just above a whisper. The tears overflowed and ran down her cheeks. "I'll be right back. I have to get a tissue." Val ran up the stairs, and Julia heard the bathroom door close.

"What's going on? Something's happened. Everything's changed, I can tell."

Julia saw the tension in his face and immediately said, "It's all right. Go into the kitchen and make a pot of coffee or something," she said as she took off her coat.

"What do you think you're doing? I'm not leaving you alone with her."

She walked over and gave him a kiss on the cheek. "Relax. I'll be fine. I'm going upstairs to talk to her. She's upset."

"You think I'm gonna let you go up there while she's upset?"

Julia smiled and gently pushed him toward the kitchen. "She's not angry. You wouldn't understand. This is a woman thing."

"I still don't feel right about this," he said, walking further into the kitchen.

"I promise you. I'll be fine," she answered, already turning toward the stairs.

She knocked once and asked, "Can I come in?" There was no answer, and she slowly opened the door.

Sitting on the edge of the tub, Val was covering her face with a tissue as she sobbed uncontrollably into it. Coming in, Julia put down the toilet seat and sat on it.

"Tell me what's wrong, Val," she asked, running her hand down Val's arm.

"I'm sorry," Val mumbled into her hands, and then crumbled the tissue to wipe the running mascara from her face. "Oh, Julia, I've made such a mess of my life."

"But that's not fair. You weren't given enough time."

Val wiped her nose and looked over at her. "Oh, yes I was. I had enough time. I just didn't use it right. There was enough time to marry a man who loved me, and to have a child. I just thought I had forever. I lived my life not caring about other people or how I made them feel. Just because I was trying succeed didn't mean I had to wipe my feet on every man that tried to get too close. I did some ugly things, Julia, that I'm not proud of. And you know what? That man still loved me, no matter what."

"What man?" Julia whispered.

"Johnny Cochrane," Val sniffled. "One of the sweetest, kindest men in the world, who was always there to pick me up. And what did I do to him? I dumped him because he didn't have enough money or power. Because he couldn't get me where I thought I wanted to go fast enough." Val's voice broke with emotion. "Julia, I even made that man leave by the service entrance so people wouldn't see him go. God, if I could only go back and make it up to him . . ."

"Johnny Cochrane?" Steve placed a cup of herbal tea in front of her. "No coffee for you—you're pregnant."

Julia accepted the tea and nodded. "Yes, he was the only man she ever loved, and our happiness brought it all to the surface. I had to calm her down."

"John Cochrane, the director?" Steve asked again, sounding confused.

"No, no, Val said he was a photographer."

"That's right, John Cochrane. He started out that way, but he's well known in the movie industry. Kind of a recluse now, since he had a stroke a couple of years ago."

Julia stared at him. "Is he still alive?"

Steve shrugged, "I think so."

"How can we find out?" Julia asked, excited by the possibility.

"I could make a couple of calls?"

"Do it."

"Now?"

"Right now."

Twenty minutes later, Steve returned to the table. "This is really weird. John Cochrane is living with his niece right outside of Greenwich, Connecticut. He sold his Hollywood home and she's been taking care of him since the stroke."

The idea that had started twenty minutes ago, now became a quest. "Do you have his niece's number?"

He pushed the piece of paper across the table to her. She looked down and said a quiet prayer before standing and picking up the phone.


He was sitting in an Adirondack chair, facing a lake. Although the weather was warm, he had a hand-crocheted afghan around his bent shoulders and a wheelchair sat empty at his side. As they approached, Julia could see him staring blankly out to the water. Val almost rushed past her, but she held her hand firmly. Letting her voice drop to a mere whisper, Julia said, "Remember what we agreed to in the car. He's an old man, and has had a stroke. You have to let me do all the talking. We can't do anything that will scare or upset him."

She could see Steve sitting down at Leslie Cochrane's kitchen table, as planned, and Julia breathed a sigh of relief when she observed the niece pouring two cups of coffee. They would have a few minutes alone with Johnny, and she hoped that would be enough time for Val.

"Mr. Cochrane," Julia said as she knelt down by his side and touched his arm. He turned his face toward her by just a fraction, and Julia could see the damage from the stroke. Yet she could also see that he had once been a handsome man, and she looked up at Val standing behind his chair.

"Mr. Cochrane, I'm Julia Edwards. I came to speak with you for a few minutes. I wanted to talk to you about Valentina Manchester."

"I don't give interviews," he said in a slow, labored voice, and looked back to the lake.

"I'm not a reporter, and I'm not here to interview you. I'm here to tell you how much she loved you."

She could see how much it cost him to turn his head back toward her. "What do you want?" he said in a ragged voice. "She never loved me."

"Oh, but you're wrong. She loved you very much. She was just too afraid to show you."

"Go. Please . . . go," he said with a gasp. "You couldn't have known her. You're too young."

Clutching the back of the chair with one hand, Val ran her fingers through the old man's hair. Johnny closed his eyes, leaned his head back against the wood, and sighed. Julia could swear he felt the touch.

"Tell him, Julia, how sorry I am that I asked him to leave by the back door. And tell him I never slept with Barney Milken. I should have never let him leave thinking that."

Julia gently placed her hand on the man's knee, and said, "I know this may sound strange to you, but I have to give you this message. Val says she's sorry that she made you leave by the back door that last day, and she wants you to know that she never slept with Barney Milken. Please believe me, Mr.

Cochrane, I would never make up something like this to hurt you."

The old man had opened his eyes with her words, but now closed them as tears streamed down his sallow face. "How do you know this? I loved her so much, and she never believed me. After she died, a part of me died with her, and I never could replace her. Every woman paled in comparison to Valentina. If only she could have lived, I could have directed her in the dramatic parts she craved. She needed them almost like a narcotic. I would have helped her see that she was so much more than just a pretty face."

Julia heard Val sobbing behind him.

"Why are you crying, Miss Edwards?" he whispered, as his face contorted with raw emotion. "It's my sorrow, not yours."

Julia watched as Val slowly came around the chair to stand in front of him. "She's not sobbing, my love. I am."

The old man opened his eyes and clutched his chest.

*"Mi tresora."*

Frightened, Julia stood up as Val extended her hand to him.

"I have loved you since the moment we met, Johnny. You were the only man that loved me for myself. Despite everything I did, you still saw the good in me. Even when I couldn't see it in myself. Let it go now, darling. Let go of the pain and come with me."

Julia backed away as the old man reached for

Val's hand. A younger man left his body and slowly rose from the chair. She watched in awe as the two lovers embraced.

Looking over Johnny's shoulder, Val smiled at her and said, "Thank you for this gift. Unconditional love . . ."

Julia brought her hands up to her face to wipe away the tears. They were together again, for eternity, and when she opened her eyes the two were no longer there.

She stood for a few moments, looking out to the lake as she tried to control her emotions. Val had come back looking for love. That's all. Surely, it was the strongest force in the universe.

Turning away from the lifeless form in the chair, Julia walked toward the house and toward her new life.

# *Afterword*

When you are old and gray and full of sleep,
And nodding by the fire, take down this book
And slowly read, and dream of the soft look
Your eyes had once, and of their shadows deep;

How many loved your moments of glad grace,
And loved your beauty with love false or true;
But one man loved the pilgrim soul in you,
And loved the sorrows of your changing face.

And bending down beside the glowing bars
Murmur, a little sadly, how love fled
And paced upon the mountains overhead
And hid his face amid a crowd of stars.

William Butler Yeats
1865–1939

## YOU WON'T WANT TO READ
## JUST ONE — KATHERINE STONE

**ROOMMATES**                (3355-9, $4.95)
No one could have prepared Carrie for the monumental
changes she would face when she met her new circle of
friends at Stanford University. Once their lives intertwined
and became woven into the tapestry of the times, they would
never be the same.

**TWINS**                    (3492-X, $4.95)
Brook and Melanie Chandler were so different, it was hard
to believe they were sisters. One was a dark, serious, ambitious New York attorney; the other, a golden, glamourous,
sophisticated supermodel. But they were more than sisters — they were twins and more alike than even they knew
. . .

**THE CARLTON CLUB**        (3614-0, $4.95)
It was the place to see and be seen, the only place to be. And
for those who frequented the playground of the very rich, it
was a way of life. Mark, Kathleen, Leslie and Janet — they
worked together, played together, and loved together, all behind exclusive gates of the *Carlton Club*.

*Available wherever paperbacks are sold, or order direct from the
Publisher. Send cover price plus 50¢ per copy for mailing and handling to Penguin USA, P.O. Box 999, c/o Dept. 17109, Bergenfield, NJ 07621. Residents of New York and Tennessee must
include sales tax. DO NOT SEND CASH.*

# CATCH A RISING STAR!

## *ROBIN ST. THOMAS*

**FORTUNE'S SISTERS**                                    (2616, $3.95)
It was Pia's destiny to be a Hollywood star. She had complete self-confidence, breathtaking beauty, and the help of her domineering mother. But her younger sister Jeanne began to steal the spotlight meant for Pia, diverting attention away from the ruthlessly ambitious star. When her mother Mathilde started to return the advances of dashing director Wes Guest, Pia's jealousy surfaced. Her passion for Guest and desire to be the brightest star in Hollywood pitted Pia against her own family—sister against sister, mother against daughter. Pia was determined to be the only survivor in the arenas of love and fame. But neither Mathilde nor Jeanne would surrender without a fight. . . .

**LOVER'S MASQUERADE**                                    (2886, $4.50)
New Orleans. A city of secrets, shrouded in mystery and magic. A city where dreams become obsessions and memories once again become reality. A city where even one trip, like a stop on Claudia Gage's book promotion tour, can lead to a perilous fall. For New Orleans is also the home of Armand Dantine, who knows the secrets that Claudia would conceal and the past she cannot remember. And he will stop at nothing to make her love him, and will not let her go again . . .

**SENSATION**                                            (3228, $4.95)
They'd dreamed of stardom, and their dreams came true. Now they had fame and the power that comes with it. In Hollywood, in New York, and around the world, the names of Aurora Styles, Rachel Allenby, and Pia Decameron commanded immediate attention—and lust and envy as well. They were stars, idols on pedestals. And there was always someone waiting in the wings to bring them crashing down . . .

*Available wherever paperbacks are sold, or order direct from the Publisher. Send cover price plus 50¢ per copy for mailing and handling to Penguin USA, P.O. Box 999, c/o Dept. 17109, Bergenfield, NJ 07621. Residents of New York and Tennessee must include sales tax. DO NOT SEND CASH.*